TELL IT

In his debut novel, John Pruitt takes us back to a time where black lives truly didn't matter in the South, but it was a time black votes began to matter. The characters in this novel tell the story of the media's role in changing race relations in the South, and the behind-the-scenes political alliances that helped to bring change. Pruitt's meticulous character development and scenery depiction put me right there in the story. Gripping from beginning to end and hard to put down.

MONICA KAUFMAN PEARSON
journalist and former WSB-TV news anchor

Tell It True is the rare work of fiction that does justice to an important historical event. In a narrative inspired by the brutal 1964 murder of Colonel Lemuel Penn, a black Army reservist, in rural Georgia, veteran Atlanta TV newsman John Pruitt brilliantly brings to life a cast of activists, politicians, clergy, and law enforcement officers caught up in the case. At the heart of the novel are two brave, young journalists who at great risk tell the story true. This is a book that will keep you up nights.

STEVE ONEY
author of *And the Dead Shall Rise* and *A Man's World*

It's not surprising that John Pruitt's debut novel, *Tell It True*, draws upon his real-world experiences covering Georgia in the 1960s. He has done a remarkable job capturing the tensions that existed among those who wanted immediate change and those who welcomed a more gradual approach. This is a captivating book that will take you back in time—through the words of one of our state's most-trusted journalists.

MARIA SAPORTA
founder of SaportaReport and a Georgia journalist since 1980

This is an important book, beautifully written, and more necessary now than ever. John Pruitt has written a novel that shows us how we really are, not how we wish to be. And from that dark and lost place, he has given us a map away from ruin, if only we have the courage to take the right path.

PHILIP LEE WILLIAMS
author of *The Heart of a Distant Forest*

MERCER UNIVERSITY PRESS

Endowed by

TOM WATSON BROWN
and
THE WATSON-BROWN FOUNDATION, INC.

TELL IT TRUE

A Novel

JOHN PRUITT

MERCER UNIVERSITY PRESS
Macon, Georgia

MUP/ P656

© 2022 by Mercer University Press
Published by Mercer University Press
1501 Mercer University Drive
Macon, Georgia 31207
All rights reserved

26 25 24 23 22   5 4 3 2 1

Books published by Mercer University Press are printed on acid-free
paper that meets the requirements of the American National Standard
for Information Sciences—Permanence of Paper for Printed Library Materials.

Printed and bound in the United States.

This book is set in Adobe Caslon Pro and American Typewriter (display).

Cover/jacket design by Burt&Burt.

ISBN   978-0-88146-847-2 (hardback)
ISBN   978-0-88146-867-0 (paperback)
ISBN   978-0-88146-866-3 (eBook)

Cataloging-in-Publication Data is available from the Library of Congress

For Andrea

and

Our family

ONE

THE BRIDGE

TOO LATE, JARVIS PENDRY realized that the two pinpoints of light directly ahead were the frightened eyes of a raccoon. His instincts told him to brake, but his mind overruled his gut. Hitting the brakes on this narrow country road could send him skidding into a ditch or a tree. He lifted his foot from the gas pedal and braced for impact. The raccoon never moved, frozen in place by the onrushing headlights. Pendry felt the thump and the shudder of his tires rolling over the carcass. He then returned his foot to the accelerator and resumed his speed, leaving one more piece of roadkill to rot on the highway until the buzzards cleaned it up.

Pendry was on his way home to Maryland after Army Reserve training at Fort Benning. As a lieutenant colonel in the reserve, he drove south every summer to spend two weeks in the stifling heat of the Georgia base to fulfill his commitment. He was more than ready to celebrate the Fourth of July with his family in Baltimore after another unpleasant experience in the Deep South.

On the base he was treated as a peer by the other officers and saluted with respect by soldiers he encountered. Some of them knew of his heroism in the Battle of the Bulge, when his contingent of black replacement troops wiped out a German machine gun nest. The unit's white commanding officer commended Pendry for his heroism, but the young lieutenant received no medal. Pendry viewed it as another slight from an Army that treated Negro soldiers as inferior and unworthy of equal status with white troops.

As he lay shivering in the frigid misery of his foxhole, Pendry had bitterly questioned his decision to enter the ROTC program at his college. Upon graduation in 1944, Second Lieutenant Pendry was quickly called into service and, after training, shipped off to Europe where his all-black company performed menial support jobs for the white troops on the front lines. The Army then considered all Negro troops unsuitable for combat, but that changed when the Germans launched their counteroffensive in the Ardennes Forest. Black units were needed to hold the line, and their performance there and elsewhere began to change attitudes and policies. After the German surrender, Pendry decided to stay in uniform and remained on active duty in a fully integrated Army through the Korean War.

Pendry now found the military to be relatively colorblind, and he was proud to be a part of it as a reservist. But when he left the confines of Fort Benning, he faced a much different and more difficult reality. On the streets of the town near the base, Pendry, wearing civilian clothes, felt ill at ease. He carried his six-foot frame with the confidence of a man of accomplishment, an educated professional, an officer in the US Armed Forces, but as far as most of the whites he encountered off-post were concerned, he was just another black man same as all the rest. His outward confidence only made it worse. It made him appear "uppity."

Because of this, Pendry preferred to remain on-post, shopping at the PX, going to the base movie theater in the evenings, or stopping by the officers' club for a few beers with fellow reservists. He couldn't wait to get back to Maryland, where his community treated him with respect and the racism he occasionally encountered was more subtle. But homecoming required a drive across Dixie, a long road trip that could be difficult for a black person.

It was July 2, 1964, and he'd heard on his car radio that President Lyndon Johnson had just signed the new civil rights law. He was thrilled to hear about this historic milestone, but a pang of guilt tempered his happiness. Unlike the heroic civil rights leaders and their followers who had forced this outcome by risking and sometimes sacrificing their lives, Pendry had done nothing other than write an occasional check to the NAACP. He believed fervently in the movement but had never taken part in a protest and seldom made his feelings known to his friends, white or black. He and his wife Evelyn were living a comfortable life in the Baltimore suburbs. He had a rewarding job with a local corporation. Their two boys went to integrated private schools. Now in his mid-forties, he feared putting it all at risk. He chose to passively watch the civil rights revolution on the nightly newscasts and suppress the occasional twinge that he was AWOL from the front lines in this conflict.

His annual trips to Fort Benning were sharp reminders of how far the South had yet to go. The new law was a huge step, but old ways died hard. If he stopped at a motel or restaurant, he knew he'd still be refused service. No new law could change that overnight. He allowed himself to look forward to the day when he could drive his family to vacation in Florida without fear of being denied service because of their race. But tonight, it was good to know that he had an uncle who lived near his route who had happily agreed to put him up for the night.

The only problem was that Uncle Willie lived in a rural area thirty miles off the main highway, and Pendry wasn't sure he was on the right road. He'd driven for miles on the dark two-lane and hadn't seen any sign of civilization except for porch lights on scattered houses sitting far back from the road. He realized he needed some help, and as much as he hated to, he would have to try to find someone and ask for directions. He also hoped for a vending machine to purchase a snack, since he'd eaten the spam sandwich from the officers' mess hall hours ago. A young Puerto Rican private in the kitchen had offered it to Pendry, reminding him he'd find few if any places along his route that would serve food to a black man.

Pendry saw a faint green glow up ahead and, drawing closer, realized it came from the lights of a gas station. He slowed and pulled into the pale aura created by the florescent lights inside. Pendry eased his car past the two vintage gasoline pumps and parked in front of the small cinder-block building. He rose from the car seat stiffly, stretched to limber up a bit, and then stepped through the screen door below a sign that said "Soseby's."

A heavyset man sat on a stool behind the counter, his arm resting on a cash register. He was in the process of extracting a potato chip from a crumpled bag next to a can of beer. He paused as he saw Pendry enter, then put the chip into his mouth and began to chew slowly. His jowly face had no expression. Above the counter was a crude hand-lettered sign: "We reserve the right to refuse service to anyone."

Pendry saw two other men sitting at a small table by a vending machine across the room. They watched him as he stepped inside and released the screen door to snap shut behind him. One was about forty, wearing a faded plaid short-sleeve shirt that was too small for him. The shirt fabric constricted his beefy upper arms and strained to cover his bulging belly. The other, who appeared to be in his twenties, was skinny and wore a dark T-shirt with a faded image of Elvis Presley. His head was narrow, made even more so by the short crew cut that gave his ears and thin neck more prominence. Both men fondled their beer cans and stared at Pendry as if he were interrupting something, but they said nothing. On the wall behind them, a large rebel flag was nailed to the wall.

Pendry chose to remain just inside the screen door. He spoke to the man at the counter.

"Excuse me, sir. I'm trying to find Shiloh Crossroads. It's not on the map, and I think I got bad directions. Can you help me?"

Pendry tried to make his voice sound respectful without seeming obsequious, but he couldn't quite pull it off. While he was used to giving orders with an authoritative voice, the unfriendly atmosphere in this place led him to soften his tone almost to the point of servility. He was disgusted with himself, but in this case he felt discretion was the better part of valor.

The man at the counter swallowed his potato chip and took a swig of beer.

"Shiloh Crossroads? You boys ever hear of Shiloh Crossroads?"

The older man at the table looked at his companion with a drunken gap-toothed smile but said nothing. The young one curled his upper lip in a sneer, lifted his beer can, and drank deeply.

"Guess we can't help you, boy," snarled the man at the counter. "By the way—where're you from? Don't sound like you're from around here."

"Maryland. Just trying to get home and needing to find my uncle's house so I can spend the night."

The young man at the table spoke up with anger in his voice.

"Who the hell is your uncle?"

"His name is Willie Brooks. Do you know him? Can you direct me to his house?"

"You ain't one of them agitators, are you? Comin' down here to stir up trouble?" His speech was slurred. He turned to the man next to him.

"Shee-it. I bet he's one of those agitators. I bet LBJ sent him down here to test that damn new law. Maybe we ought to whip his black ass."

Pendry felt his heart pounding with both anger and concern, but he was too controlled to react to his emotions. He realized any response would reduce him to their level and only incite them further. And he was badly outnumbered in the middle of hostile territory. Better to stage a strategic withdrawal—a military euphemism for cut and run.

"I can see I'm not welcome here. I'll be going now."

He backed toward the door, opened it with his eyes still on the men, and walked briskly toward his car. As he pulled away, he noticed the younger man watching from behind the screen door. Pendry's tires chewed and scattered the gravel of the pullout as he gunned the engine and moved onto the blacktop. He wasn't sure where he was going, but he wanted to put the experience he'd just had as far behind him as possible.

His chest heaved, his hands shook, and the sweat coating his face dripped down his neck, making him feel clammy. The blast of warm, humid air coming through his window actually chilled him, and he rolled the window up as he drove with one moist hand gripping the steering wheel.

He reluctantly acknowledged to himself that his initial apprehension when he entered the gas station had turned to fear. What must it be like, he thought, for a black person to live in a place like this and have to constantly deal with the indignity and threats of violence he had just endured? He knew Evelyn would be upset when she heard the story. He considered not sharing his experience with her, but he knew she'd eventually find out. They kept nothing from each other. But tonight, Evelyn was far away, and Jarvis Pendry was alone on a dark Georgia road searching for a safe haven for the night.

He was pretty sure he wasn't going to find Shiloh Crossroads until well after Uncle Willie's bedtime. The rural community wasn't on his road map, and it was clear he wouldn't find anyone who could help him in this godforsaken backwater. He had little choice but to find a town where he might be able to call Uncle Willie from a pay phone or at least find a place to get a little sleep in his car.

He slowed and looked for a spot to pull off the road so he could check his map. The road was descending into a valley, and through the light cast by his headlights Pendry saw he was entering thick fog rising from the stream at the bottom of the hill. Hunched over the steering wheel, peering into the mist, he saw a bridge just ahead and noticed a pullout on his right, probably a parking spot for people who fished the stream.

Pendry slowly eased off the road and onto the deeply rutted red clay of the pullout. He put the car in park, flipped on his interior light, and unfolded his map. He left the engine running and his headlights on. He was so focused on trying to find his place on the map that he failed to notice the headlights of a vehicle coming down the hill behind him at high speed.

Suddenly he saw the reflection of the headlights in his rearview mirror and heard the car's noisy engine as it rapidly approached. He could tell the vehicle was slowing as it neared him. Perhaps the driver had noticed his idling car just off the roadway and was being cautious.

Pendry turned his head as the sedan pulled alongside his car and stopped. A bright light blinded him—a strong flashlight beam directed right at his face. Pendry raised his arm to shade his eyes as the first blast from a shotgun shattered his car window. His raised forearm was shredded by the tiny missiles of buckshot and glass, some of which also found his chest and neck. He screamed in pain and surprise an instant before the second blast took away his face and penetrated his brain.

The tires of the gunman's car squealed as the driver floored the accelerator and sped across the bridge, disappearing into the moonless night.

The mangled body of Jarvis Pendry lay slumped across the front seat of the blood-spattered car. The cacophony of crickets and tree frogs coming from the stream bank had been silenced. The only sound was the low hum of the car's still-running engine, its headlights trying to pierce the fog's enveloping shroud.

TWO

INDEPENDENCE DAY

AS GIL MATTHEWS panned over the angry crowd, his camera lens steadied on the man whose image forever came to mind whenever he thought back on this day, the man he called Mr. Peepers. He looked just like the TV character, thin, short, and ordinary—the bespectacled personification of meekness. Gil always imagined him droning through some menial job, going about routine tasks in a reasonably competent but lackluster way, accepting what life dealt him. He no doubt did what his wife told him, never complained to a waiter, and rarely pressed an argument. But resentments festered, waiting for their moment to erupt.

The moment for Mr. Peepers came on this sweltering July Fourth at Southside Stadium. He was standing, like all those packing the stadium, jabbing his thin, hairless arms toward the musky southern sky. Sweat boiled from his forehead, streaking his reddening face and soaking his T-shirt into a clammy, torso-hugging mat. He was like a born-again at a tent revival, jumping, flailing, and screaming at the top of his lungs, though his message was anything but Christian.

"Kill 'em," he bellowed. "Kill those black sons o' bitches."

Even in the chaotic confusion of the moment, Gil knew he was recording the face of the South in 1964. Not the jowly red face of the potbellied blustering lout so often put on display on television newscasts. No, Mr. Peepers was the guy next door, the neighbor who might give you a wave as he mowed his lawn, an ordinary Joe in a free fall of hatred.

Gil aimed his camera for shots of this face and all the others that would tell the story. The noontime sun was in perfect position, directly overhead and casting no shadows. Everything in camera range was clear. His wide shots revealed the frenzied crowd sprawling across the concrete stadium seats. Beyond the other side of the brown, withered grass of the football field, Atlanta's skyline shimmered through the summer haze like an unfinished mosaic. A former mayor had once declared it the city too busy to hate, but that euphoric proclamation belied the reality of the times. There was more than enough hate to go around. As a newsman Gil saw it every day, but never like this.

Four black college students had marched into the rally of segregationists just as the day's speakers were whipping the crowd into a lather over the landmark Civil Rights Act signed into law just two days earlier. The young protesters wore black T-shirts with a red lightning bolt stitched on the back. They carried signs crudely printed with the words "Freedom Now."

When the crowd realized the intrusion, it stirred, rumbled, then ignited like a giant beast rising to defend the fetid carcass of a recent kill. They ripped the cardboard signs from the demonstrators' hands and tore them to shreds. White toughs surrounded the students, engulfing them, pushing them up against a chain-link fence that separated the football field from the spectator area.

Several in the crowd grabbed some of the metal folding chairs stacked by the fence. They began slamming them down on the heads and bodies of the four young men. Blood and sweat mingled and glistened on the black bodies. One of the protesters screamed in pain as the edge of a chair slammed into his head, opening a crimson gash.

Those who couldn't reach the human targets screamed obscenities at them. One obese woman jumped up and down, stringy strands of hair matted against her wrathful face, the dimpled fat of her upper arms jiggling as she bellowed unintelligibly.

Gil, his arm still cocked, cradled the silent camera between his cheek and shoulder as he methodically worked his way toward the melee, horrified yet strangely exhilarated by the scenes he was capturing. Growing up in an Atlanta suburb, Gil had been taught that Robert E. Lee was a saint, the *Gone with the Wind* movie was an honest portrayal of slavery, and modern-day Negroes didn't have it all that bad. He had long ago discarded those notions, and now his job as a newsman required him to expose the Southern myth to the world. But as a native Southerner, he had a personal price to pay. His father once called him a turncoat for stirring up trouble with his civil rights coverage and making the South look bad. But for Gil it was simply a matter of capturing whatever happened on film and letting the pictures tell the story. He'd tried to explain, but his dad refused to try to understand his prodigal son of the South and the job he had to do.

Suddenly someone was singing over the public address system.

God bless America
Land that I love...

The rally leaders were trying to control the crowd by having the scheduled country singer belt out a patriotic song, but it wasn't working. They had been far too effective in bringing their audience to the point of no return with their violent invective. There was no stopping the momentum they'd created. Gil wished he had a sound camera to capture the music on his film. It would be just the ironic touch he needed.

From the mountains, to the prairies
To the oceans white with foam...

One of the leaders, a local state representative named Riley Swint, was at the microphone now, seizing it from the country singer who had failed so miserably at his assignment.

"Ladies and gen'lemen," he yelled, competing with the over-modulated squeal of the microphone. "Please calm down. Let these poor boys go. They ain't got the sense God gave 'em. They ain't worth it. Let 'em go."

Swint and the other speakers stood on a bunting-draped flatbed truck parked on the football field, separated from the crowd and the violence by the chain-link fence. Despite their inflammatory rhetoric, they recoiled at the thought of actual violence and disavowed the direct role they had played in causing it.

Gil felt a tinge of nausea as he held the camera high overhead in order to shoot over the crowd into the pocket of mayhem where the blacks were fending off the attack as best they could. Two had buckled and fallen, moaning as the blood gushed from their wounds. The other two, one with an Afro, sagged against the fence, arms folded over their heads and faces, taking the battering and struggling for survival.

Gil saw that only four or five white men were throwing punches. Most of the others stood around screaming encouragement. A few looked on with dazed expressions. Others turned away in stunned disbelief at what was happening.

"Please, ladies and gen'lemen. Calm down."

Swint's lazy drawl drained his pleas of urgency.

"We got to have aw-da here."

At that moment someone grabbed Gil from behind, pinning his arms to his body and then flinging him across the concrete tier where he'd been filming. As Gil staggered sideways, he felt a sharp blow on the back of his neck. That dropped him to his knees, and he struggled to rise. The camera, which he still clutched by its leather hand strap, dangled at his side. He glanced to his right as a tall, gaunt man came at him again. His face was red, and a large vein pulsated in his forehead just below the hairline of his crew cut. He spewed his words through gritted teeth.

"Goddam lying reporters. I'm gonna beat your ass."

He raised his clenched fist to strike again, but Gil ducked beneath him and swung the camera into the attacker's belly. The man was quick and agile and moved back to absorb the blow. Then, before Gil could come out of his crouch, the man clubbed him twice over the head with his forearm.

Gil crumpled, and the swirling confusion around him faded in and out of his consciousness. He had a dim awareness that the crowd was scattering, the shrieking slowly dwindling. He wanted to be left in peace, but someone was pulling him along the concrete, dragging him away from the crowd, his legs limp and his arms dangling.

The last thing he remembered before he blacked out was a scraping noise, metal on concrete. It was the camera, strap still in hand—the camera containing the film that would shock its viewers and make him a hero in his trade.

THREE

NEWSROOM

"HEY, TOMMY, WHADAYASAY?"

Tom Burke knew the Brooklyn accent well, though he'd never met its owner. It was Vince Perlman, one of the network's most obnoxious producers, and Burke had expected his call. Perlman only made contact when he wanted something, and on this day he wanted something very badly. He wanted Gil Matthews's exclusive film of the melee at Southside Stadium for tonight's national newscast.

"You guys get any of that shit at the stadium down there?"

Burke hated dealing with the network. The producers were usually abrupt, abrasive, and condescending. They treated the affiliate stations in the South like foreign bureaus, as if the people working there were stationed on some alien outpost and had acquired the grosser characteristics of the natives.

Burke, who had come south from Ohio in the fifties, resented the stereotyping. As a Midwestern transplant who once had the same misconceptions, he knew how little the network decision makers in Manhattan understood the region and its people. They saw the South in the same way they told the nation and the world about the South. To them it was a primitive land of simple, narrow, sometimes violent rustics. They felt it was their mission to expose this warped yet fascinating, culture to the "enlightened" world.

As news director of WDX-TV, it was Burke's job not only to run the newsroom but also to deal with the network's incessant demands for every sensational piece of film his photographers shot. There were plenty of network crews covering the race beat in the South, but they were spread thin, never knowing where the next regional flare-up would occur. Almost always, the local photographers were on the scene for the first pictures of breaking news. And when a local station had great pictures, the network producers expected the local news director to cooperate.

Perlman and his network colleagues felt comfortable dealing with Burke. After seven years covering the cauldron of the civil rights movement, Burke was seasoned, tough, and unflappable. Yet he sometimes wondered if his Midwestern accent gave them the extra assurance they needed that they were dealing with a competent professional instead of a Southern bumpkin.

"What stadium shit, Vince? Football season's two months away."

Burke knew Perlman assumed that WDX had the only pictures of the violence. An Associated Press reporter, Mindy Williams, had covered the seg rally at Southside Stadium, and when the violence erupted she had witnessed the assault on Gil. Her account went out to newsrooms around the country on AP's three o'clock national summary. Burke knew that when the network types read that report they would be salivating at the prospect of leading their nightly news with graphically violent images, pictures their competitors would not have, pictures that would invade living rooms and dens across America, stoking the audience's perceived lust for the sensational.

Perlman was under pressure and didn't have any more time to waste with coy banter.

"Hey, man, don't shit me. The stuff is all over the wires, and they're on my ass to get the pictures. How good's your stuff?"

"We'll know in about five minutes. Film's coming off the processor now. But my photog thinks it's good, and he's one of my best."

Perlman sounded relieved but far from relaxed.

"Let me know what you've got as soon as you can. Can you feed at four thirty?"

"Should be no problem."

"By the way. How's your guy? What's his name?"

Burke hesitated. The nets were always on the prowl for good

shooters, and he didn't want to put too much of a spotlight on Gil. There was little doubt in Burke's mind that Gil would eventually be picked up by a network, and today's story would only accelerate that process. He decided not to stand in Gil's way.

"He's Gil Matthews. He'll live. Actually, he's fine, and when he gets some of your network money for this feed he'll be even better."

GIL KNEW THAT he had seen and experienced something extraordinary, but he couldn't make it real for anyone else unless the mental images that still played in his mind were indeed captured on film. He was a confident photographer, but doubts always gnawed at him until the film emerged from the processor and he could verify for himself that the images were actually there. Nothing was as real to him as the grainy portrayal of reality on celluloid.

The anticipation put a slight tremble in his fingers as he threaded the film through the projector's maze of sprockets and grooves and then flipped the switch. With a metallic clattering sound, the film began making its torturous way through the old projector, which beamed a bright vacant square on the white wall serving as a screen. After several seconds that seemed like minutes to Gil, the blank square began to fill with the flickering images that until now had existed only in his mind's eye. The melee at Southside Stadium was just a memory for all who were there, a memory that would selectively interpret what really happened. But Gil's film was reality, the official record. The world would see it and remember it.

Co-workers, including Burke, crowded into the small projection room to witness the first unedited viewing. After about forty seconds of routine shots, wide-angle crowd views, a few close-ups of spectators and gesticulating speakers, the violent scenes began. For the next minute and fifteen seconds, no one spoke as the drama of Gil's filmed images danced on the wall. The only sound was the noisy whirring of the projector.

Some of those watching, cameramen and reporters, gave the film the full respect it was due, then turned to Gil with handshakes and slaps on the back. But there was no time for Gil to bask in the congratulatory glow.

Anchorman Grayson Kincaid, using the wire report and Gil's own description of the event, typed out forty-five seconds of copy, reading each sentence as he completed it, stopwatch in hand. The script was timed and marked, and Gil disappeared into a darkened room to edit the scenes to match Kincaid's words.

Reeling the film through a lighted editing viewer, Gil cut the key scenes as they appeared, physically tearing the film and hanging the separate strips from small sprocket-hole pegs next to him. Then he spliced the strips of film together, scraping emulsion, brushing on a small amount of glue, closing the hot splicer, waiting a few seconds, and then testing the splice by tugging gently at it.

Slowly he assembled the film portion of the story. Time was getting short. The feed was scheduled at four thirty, and it was approaching four fifteen. He had seen some editors buckle under the intense pressure of editing a network feed as the clock relentlessly ticked on. Gil, however, relished the challenge and thrived under the tyranny of news deadlines. He worked calmly, moving with a deliberate rhythm until he tested the last splice and wound the film tightly on a reel. He handed it to a waiting projectionist and walked to a viewing area to watch the film being fed to New York, where it would be taped for broadcast on the network nightly news at six thirty. At six o'clock, viewers of the local newscast would see his creation, his reality, which this time would forever and always be the only reality that mattered.

ABOUT A DOZEN people gathered below the raised television monitor in the newsroom and watched as the report on the stadium riot appeared on the air for the first time. The normal clamor of the newsroom quieted as everyone—reporters, editors, writers, and employees from other departments—stopped what they were doing to watch and listen as the voice of senior anchorman Grayson Kincaid told the story. "A

July 4th segregationist rally turned violent today as four black protesters tried to stage a civil rights demonstration…"

On the screen were scenes of the crowd, then a shot of Riley Swint regaling the audience, then a swirl of bodies with occasional glimpses of the black students being pummeled by angry whites.

"When the students appeared at Southside Stadium, the crowd went wild and attacked them. Some of the attackers used metal folding chairs to beat the demonstrators."

Metal folding chairs appeared over the heads of the crowd then disappeared as they were slammed into the victims.

"Rally leaders, led by State Representative Riley Swint, called for calm, but they failed to restore order."

The filmed scene shifted to an overhead shot, the shot Gil had tried in desperation, holding the camera as high as possible and pointing it down into the crowd, hoping for the best. He'd been lucky. Two of the blacks were in the picture, and it was obvious they were bleeding. The picture jumped several times as Gil was jostled, but the victims remained in frame, their attackers clearly visible swinging their fists and the metal chairs.

"Our cameraman, Gil Matthews, got these exclusive pictures of the attack. But he, too, was attacked by some in the crowd."

The pictures on the screen suddenly jerked and spun, showing the sky, the ground, a face, and the ground again. Then the composed, concerned face of Grayson Kincaid appeared on camera.

"Matthews was roughed up but not seriously injured. Fortunately, police were able to move in and restore order. Two of the black students were badly injured. They're in the intensive care unit at Grady Hospital tonight. The other two were treated for cuts and bruises and released. All four are charged with demonstrating without a permit. No other arrests were made."

GIL WATCHED THE fruits of his labor on the monitor in Tom Burke's office. Burke was ecstatic. The film was wonderful, the network was going to be happy, and the station general manager might forgive him for exceeding his overtime budget for the month. He slapped his chubby hands on his cluttered desk and looked at Gil with a cynical smile.

"You are one lucky SOB. You know that? We send you out to cover a routine seg rally on one of the slowest days of the year, and you bring back great stuff. Nice going."

"Thanks. Right place, right time. Or maybe wrong place, wrong time. Anyway, I'd rather be lucky than good."

"Today you were both."

Gil had a pounding headache, but he was exuberant. He stretched out in the chair, his lanky frame extended to its full length, legs straight out in front of him, his rear on the edge of the seat, his head resting on top of the chair back. He pinched the bridge of his nose between his thumb and index finger and closed his eyes.

"Where's it going to play in Nightly?" he asked.

"You're the lead. What else? They love your work. Your stock at net is going way up. Next thing you know they'll be sniffing around here and offering you a job."

GIL STROLLED THROUGH the newsroom accepting congratulations from his peers. He was tired, aching, and hungry. A pocket hung in shreds from his pants, ripped as a policeman dragged him away from his assailants. He could smell the pungent odor of dried sweat mingled with the dust of the day that coated his body and stained his shirt. But he wouldn't have given up this moment for the world. It was the moment of triumph, the moment that made up for all the frustrations and failures that were so much a part of the news business. It was his moment and he wanted to savor it, because he knew it couldn't last.

FOUR

THE REVEREND

Reverend Elijah Timmons looked at his watch and then at the rack of ribs sizzling on his backyard grill. The afternoon sun's westward descent had reached the leafy crown of the big white oak that stood in regal solitude at the rear edge of his yard. The shade he'd been craving throughout this sweltering Independence Day had finally reached him, and he was grateful. The air hadn't stirred since sunup, and the heat had built relentlessly, imprisoned within the perpetual hazy dome of mid-summer. At times the humidity made him feel as though he was suspended in a pond of molasses, moving in slow motion, struggling for just one breath of clean, clear air.

Timmons was sweating profusely as he prodded the layers of graying, smoking charcoal, and a rancid stain spread slowly through the underarms of his white short-sleeve dress shirt. He noticed disapprovingly that his neighbor two backyards away wasn't even wearing a shirt; it never occurred to Timmons to be seen in anything but his standard white broadcloth. As a minister and community leader, he felt an obligation to look the part, even while laboring over the rickety, rusting portable grill. He felt that keeping his collar open and tieless was concession enough to the informality of this summer holiday.

He puddled dollops of his special barbecue sauce on the smoking ribs, slathered it over the meat with his basting brush, then headed for the back door. It was time for the nightly TV newscasts. Timmons always tried to watch the news when he could, but tonight had a special urgency. He'd heard about the trouble at Southside Stadium earlier that day and wanted to see how TV, particularly the networks, handled it.

His wife Mattie was working on the potato salad in the kitchen as

Timmons passed through on his way to the small, windowless room in the center of the house that served as their den.

"Watch the ribs, hon. I'm gonna check out the news."

It was a routine Mattie Timmons had come to patiently accept. She understood that her husband's nightly appointment with the television set didn't have nearly as much to do with his desire to stay abreast of current events as with his need to know *how* the world was being told about the movement.

Reverend Timmons was a key local figure in the civil rights crusade. He had been using his pulpit at Mount Gilead African Methodist Episcopal Church to condemn the South's racial apartheid since he first began preaching fresh out of divinity school in the mid-fifties. His uncompromising sermons, delivered with the rolling cadences of one who was born to move and inspire, had attracted a huge following. He was in constant motion when he spoke, rocking back and forth, bouncing up and down on the balls of his feet, sweeping his trembling arms in a mighty arc over his audience, raising his hands to the heavens in supplication, then rigidly locking them to the ornate molding of his pulpit as if he were about to vault into his congregation below. His voice careened from a booming crescendo to a harsh whisper, each exclamation punctuated by vigorous nods and murmurs of "Amen" and "Uh-huh" from his spellbound flock. He often rapped the huge open Bible before him, undergirding every condemnation of racial injustice with bedrock Christian principles. He saw his people as the Children of Israel bound for the Promised Land, and himself as the Black Moses who would take them there.

Despite his dreams of prominence, Timmons was frustrated during the early years of his ministry by his lack of impact outside the sphere of his church and neighborhood. Even though he spoke with power and vision, his sermons were not unlike others delivered with equal fervor in other black churches. He had longed to expand his outreach, to begin putting his words to work, to effect the change he advocated.

In 1958, Timmons approached other young black ministers about forming a leadership committee to pool the resources of their congregations. Ten ministers had met at Mount Gilead AME on a rainy Saturday night to discuss the possibilities, and after sizing each other up and realizing the potential of a coalition, they agreed to set up the Christian Action Council, electing Timmons the chairman.

In that role, Timmons chose the strategy of demand and negotiation, trying to work with the city's white leadership for concessions rather than fighting it. Dealing with the hidebound power structure was frustrating and sometimes embittering, but Timmons felt more could be gained through moral persuasion than by confrontation. His statements for the cause were powerful and compelling but never frightening, and the responsible white community listened with guarded respect. This was a Negro they could deal with—a reasonable man who understood the difficulties of making too many changes too fast. All but the ignorant knew that cracks were spreading across the face of the South's segregationist regime. Timmons's mission was to convince those in power to let the old system crumble in an orderly fashion, helping to decide when and where each shard would fall so they could be around to retrieve the pieces when the time came.

Timmons turned on his television set and flicked the dial to WDX just as the drum-and-trumpet march theme of the local newscast was beginning. Normally he would expect a visual catalogue of the day's wrecks, homicides, and holdups, and, on the Fourth of July, a few parades. But he knew today would be different. The violence at Southside Stadium was bound to be the lead story.

Timmons understood that as television news chronicled the movement, it also propelled it. Televised scenes of gushing fire hoses and police dogs unleashed on black demonstrators in Birmingham were devastating. The moral impact of those scenes shown around the world spoke more than any volume of movement philosophy, more than any legislative action, more than the best sermon he could ever compose. He understood that scenes like those made the victory of his cause inevitable. But tonight, the nation would get its nightly civil rights dosage from his town, Atlanta.

He stepped back from the small set as the violent images appeared on the screen. He had seen just about every significant filmed news report on the civil rights crusade so far, but few approached the intensity of the life-and-death struggle of these young students attacked by a mob. He was filled with a curious mixture of exhilaration and revulsion. He knew these scenes would outrage people around the world and bring more support for the movement. But the unreasoning brutality of the attack left him queasy. How can people hate that much, he wondered, and how in God's name do you reach them?

While Mattie rushed through the back screen door to rescue the blackening ribs, Timmons placed a call to his aide Emanuel Slocum, who was catching up on some paperwork in the CAC office in the basement of Mount Gilead AME. He, too, had been stunned by the news footage.

Timmons needed information. "Any idea who these kids are?"

"I got no names. But the word is they're part of a new student group at Morehouse."

"Find out what this new group is all about. They were lucky not to be killed. This is the kind of stupid freelance thing that gets everybody all excited but doesn't change anything. It makes a big sensational splash on TV, everybody gets all worked up, then we have to come in and pick up the pieces."

Slocum sounded worried. "I've heard a few things about this group—Student Coordinating League. They think you preachers are dragging your heels. They want to be more confrontational."

Timmons wasn't surprised. "These campus groups spring up from time to time. But they are a rabble. And dangerous to the movement if they aren't properly channeled. I'm concerned they're getting so much coverage."

Timmons remembered his days at all-black Ogeechee College in South Georgia. He'd led a sit-in at a drug store soda fountain in the college town. Wearing dress shirts and slacks, he and five classmates occupied the stools at the soda fountain and refused to leave. Three cops arrived and forcibly removed them, dragging them from the store and flinging them into the back seats of waiting police cars. A small crowd of white teenagers stood nearby, taunting and jeering. Timmons and his friends were thrown in jail for three days and fined thirty dollars each. The local newspaper printed no story, the outside world never knew what happened, and the drug store's soda fountain remained a privileged sanctuary for whites only. It was Timmons's first and last sit-in.

"Emanuel, maybe there's a way to play a little piggyback here, seize the initiative, if you will."

"How's that?"

"Two of the kids are at Grady Hospital. Let's arrange a bedside meeting, followed by a CAC news conference. We'll demand that all charges be dropped. Set it up and call the TV stations. Let the networks know as well."

Slocum said he'd call back as soon as he arranged it.

Timmons returned to the kitchen where Mattie was patiently waiting at the table with their two young boys. The ribs lay on a platter in the center of the table, the potato salad was spooned onto the plates, and the iced tea was poured. Their youngest, Andy, gnawed on one of the ribs that his mother had broken off for him. His face was coated with barbecue sauce. When he saw his father, he put the rib back on his plate and sheepishly wiped his mouth with his tiny, bare arm.

Timmons scraped his chair back and sat down. He looked at his family and bowed his head. The shockingly violent pictures he'd just seen on the news continued to invade his thoughts as he tried to pray. He concentrated on pushing them aside to think of his beloved family now gathered around their table on this unique American holiday that he could only grudgingly acknowledge. He prayed that his children would always remember his sacrifices to gain a free and independent life for them.

"Our gracious Heavenly Father, bless this food to the use of our bodies and us to your service. And deliver us from the hands of our enemies who revile and persecute us. Forgive them for they know not what they do. And Lord, help us to understand that all good things come to him who waits. We've waited long enough, Lord, and we know our time is at hand. In the name of Jesus Christ our Lord, Amen."

FIVE

INSURRECTION

GIL DROVE HIS news cruiser slowly up North Avenue as he crossed Georgia Tech's urban campus. The white Chevy station wagon with the WDX-2 logo emblazoned on both front doors attracted glances from students on the sidewalks, but when they failed to see a recognizable TV personality, they put their heads back down and hurried on to class.

The groundbreaking ceremony for a new student center moments before had been routine and dull. Gil had shot thirty seconds of film as Tech and city officials posed with their silver shovels spading up chunks of red clay. Only two days earlier, he'd been basking in the praise for his filmed exclusive at Southside Stadium, a story that "shocked the nation," in the words of one newspaper columnist. Now he was back in the rut of filling the daily newscast with pictures of wrecks, fires, petty crimes, and, today, a groundbreaking. How the mighty have fallen, he thought as he left the campus for his next assignment.

He crossed the bridge over the expressway and turned left into the Varsity for a quick lunch. No sooner had he parked in a curb service slot than a black man appeared at his car window, smiling broadly and bouncing impatiently from foot to foot. He wore a red waiter's jacket and a cowboy hat adorned with bandanas, scarves, beads, and badges. Over the pocket was the embroidered name, "Willie Joe."

"What'll ya have, Mr. TV man? What'll ya have? Need me to sing the menu for you?"

Willie Joe, the Varsity's most colorful character, knew curb service customers were usually in a hurry, but he also knew they loved his act and would take the time to enjoy it. Gil was a regular and just wanted to eat.

"That's okay, Willie Joe. I already know it by heart. Let me have a couple of chili dogs and a frosted orange to go."

"You got it, Mr. TV man. Sit tight. I'll be right back."

Gil guessed Willie Joe was in his mid-fifties and probably struggled to make a living on a minimal salary and tips. He sometimes wondered what Willie Joe's life was like when he wasn't showboating for customers in the parking lot. Did he have a family? Children? Hopes for the future? These questions might never have occurred to Gil before he witnessed four young black men risking and almost losing their lives for a better future.

Gil was born in Atlanta, raised in a typical middle-class suburban neighborhood by parents who never questioned the way of life in the South. The system worked for them, and even though in unguarded moments they might acknowledge racial inequities, they were not about to suggest that they be corrected. They looked down on those who waved rebel flags and used racist slurs. Gil had once been chastised for using the "N" word when he was eight years old. His father said the term was not acceptable in their household, but Gil cynically assumed he never objected to it anywhere else.

Like most white Southerners in the fifties Gil, had virtually no relations with black people other than the domestic workers he occasionally encountered. His schools were white havens. He wasn't even sure where the black schools were, but he took comfort in the assurances from state leaders that they were "separate but equal." The small liberal arts college he attended had only one black student, a lonely Congolese exchange student whom Gil and most of his friends made no attempt to befriend. He had a nagging guilt about that.

"Here you go, Mr. TV man. Two chili dogs and a frosted orange. You enjoy that now. Yessir! You enjoy them dogs."

Willie Joe passed the takeout box and drink through the car window and took the bills Gil offered. Then he leaned closer and spoke in a low voice, without a hint of his usual theatrics.

"That was you who shot that story, the one about the boys who almost got beat to death. I saw it. The world needs to see it. Keep telling it true."

Then, suddenly back in character, Willie Joe smiled, jauntily touched his bony fingers to his forehead in a semi-salute, and backed away looking for the next drive-in customer.

The two-way car radio crackled.

"Gil? You need to get over to Grady right away. Timmons is holding a news conference at two. It's apparently about those kids roughed up at Southside on the Fourth."

Gil grabbed the hand unit from its holder and responded.

"Okay. I'm on the way."

He weaved his way through the tangled network of downtown streets, eventually guiding his station wagon onto the ramp leading to the hospital emergency room. He parked in the usual spot behind other media cars along a concrete wall on which "No Parking" was stenciled in large yellow letters.

He began pulling his gear from the wagon's tailgate. He yanked the sound camera from its padded case, attached it to his shoulder pod, and hefted it to his shoulder where it rested, freeing his hands to untangle and plug in microphone and amplifier cords. He clipped a small battery-powered light over the zoom lens of his camera, put earphones over his head, made sure his light meter was hanging around his neck, and headed for the hospital door. His body was festooned with gear, bulky and cumbersome, but necessary if he wanted sound with the pictures.

A perky young redhead, a new addition to the hospital's public relations staff, ushered Gil to the fourth floor. She was generally pleasant, although he could detect in her beaming, freckled face a slight air of suspicion. She was probably a recent college graduate, warned by her wizened PR colleagues to be wary of reporters. Too often they would challenge the corporate line that she was supposed to protect.

But on this day, Grady Hospital had little to fear from the news media. It was only serving as the backdrop. Still, the PR people had to be sure that the setup was flawless and that if something negative happened, the hospital would not be blamed. That's why a cadre of hospital administrative staff herded the news people to a holding room and kept them there until all the players were ready to raise the curtain.

Gil saw that, in addition to the two other television stations in town, a network crew was also there: a cameraman, light man, and sound man. Gil envied the network's ability to assign three people to do the job that the local stations handled with one. The union contracts with the New York-based networks mandated multiple technicians on each assignment, but there were no such benefits for local crews in the South where unions had little clout.

Someone tapped him on his arm, and Gil, still burdened by the camera on his right shoulder, swiveled his body to his left. It was Mindy Williams, the AP reporter who had broken the news of the Southside riot for the wire services.

"Gil, you did a great job at Southside. Incredible film. But I was afraid you were going to be badly hurt. I see you've recovered nicely."

"It must have looked worse than it was. I didn't see you there, but I'm glad you were."

"I was behind the third redneck on the right."

They both laughed. Gil was always happy to see her.

Mindy's appearance belied her reputation as a tough reporter. She looked almost frail, with a short, petite body and delicate hands. She had a slightly turned-up nose and lips that always seemed on the verge of an impudent smile. Her accent was soft, radiating Southern charm without a hint of the naïveté that so often goes with it. Her brown hair was bunched in a ponytail that dangled to barely touch the narrow valley between her shoulder blades. It seemed to be trying to counterbalance the Pentax camera that hung from her neck, resting on her chest.

Her fragile appearance and pleasant demeanor had lured many an unsuspecting quarry into her trap. She seemed so helpless and innocent that people she targeted for a news story would relax, even get overconfident. And then she pounced, often skewering public figures before they could realize what was happening.

"Any idea what Timmons is up to?" Mindy asked as she checked the lens of her camera for smudges.

"I was about to ask you the same thing. Looks like we'll find out soon."

The hospital's head of public relations walked in and announced, "All right. Let's move into the hall. Reverend Timmons is arriving."

There was a clattering of gear as crews hoisted cameras to shoulders, checked microphones, tested lights, and finally crowded toward the door and into the hospital hall. The clump of men, women, and machinery swept down the corridor, forcing doctors and nurses coming the other way to flatten themselves against the wall unless they were lucky enough to escape through a room's open door. The public relations director led the way past the nursing station and into one of the patient wards. He wheeled to face the oncoming mass and raised his arms signaling a halt.

"This is the room where the two victims are recovering." The PR man swiveled his upper body and pointed dramatically toward an elevator about fifty feet away. "Reverend Timmons and Reverend Harris will come up on that elevator, walk into this room, visit with the patients, and then will answer any questions you have right here once they come out of the room. You cannot go inside the room to film, but we will leave the door open so you can shoot from the hallway. You'll have to take turns. And please remember, this is an active hospital ward. Minimize the commotion. We must think of the patients."

Gil glanced at Mindy, arched his eyebrows, and muttered under his breath, "An aspiring Cecil B. DeMille."

Mindy whispered, "Here they come."

Gil spun around as his right eye hugged the rubber padding of the camera's viewfinder. Through his lens he saw a stocky, middle-aged Negro in a brown suit step out of the elevator and head toward them. It was Timmons. A younger, slimmer black man followed him, also wearing a suit and carrying a briefcase.

Timmons squinted as he walked toward the glare of portable lights that made his caramel skin look waxy white. He nodded and smiled at the milling media cluster, although he could make out no faces, only a silhouette of the crowd bristling with shadowy alien appendages—cameras, microphones, and light stands.

"I'll have a press release and a few comments in a moment—but first we want to visit these heroic young men and give them our thanks."

Timmons turned and walked into the hospital room, followed closely by his companion. The three-man network camera crew used numerical superiority to block everyone else from getting a view of what was going on inside. Their cameraman, Ned Brockett, stood with his feet planted widely directly in front of the door, a sound man on one side and a light man on the other.

Gil was continually irritated by the way the network crews tried to run roughshod over the local news teams. He shouldered his way between Brockett and the sound man.

"Hey. Move over. Give us a shot."

Brockett, a tall, wiry, white-haired veteran, glanced toward Gil, even though he kept his camera rolling. He decided to give the kid a break.

"Okay, let him in."

A small gap opened for Gil and his camera. He could barely see into the hospital room, but he had a usable shot. He saw Timmons sitting on the edge of one student's bed. Timmons appeared to be talking, but the student, whose head was bandaged, said nothing. He barely seemed to be listening. Then the student turned his head away from Timmons, and Timmons got up and moved out of sight, presumably to the other student's bed. At that point everyone stopped filming and waited for the two ministers to emerge and hold their news conference.

Timmons stepped out of the room and back into the media's converging incandescent beams, which struggled to override the sickly florescence bathing the hospital corridor. The cameras crowded close, their protruding lenses and the outstretched microphones almost seeming to pin Timmons against the wall.

"Gentlemen of the media," Timmons began, pausing as he noticed Mindy. "And lady." He nodded at her and smiled. "We are here at Grady today to call attention to a very sad turn of events in our city. Two days ago, the Fourth of July, a day set aside to celebrate the freedoms that we as Americans are guaranteed under our Constitution, four young Negro men were brutally attacked and beaten by a white mob. Who were these young men? Were they troublemakers, as some have implied? Agitators? Communists? No, my friends, they were none of these. They are simply idealistic young Morehouse students standing up for their God-given rights as Americans on our unique national holiday—rights that so many Negro Americans continue to be denied to this day."

The tempo of Timmons's cadences quickened as he leveled his most self-righteous stare into the semicircle of glassy lenses. In each of them he could see his own tiny reflection.

"And here in our city, which some say is too busy to hate, these young men were beaten to within an inch of their lives by white people driven into a hate-filled frenzy by some of those who claim to be leaders in our society. The CAC hereby condemns those who disgraced our nation and our city by their actions. We applaud the courage of these young heroes of our Negro community. To charge them with any crime is callous, but the charge of demonstrating without a permit is a mockery. We hereby demand that all charges against them be dropped. CAC is also demanding an immediate meeting with the mayor and other city leaders to find ways to assure the safety of our people in this lawless environment."

Timmons had carefully prepared his remarks to be brief and pointed. He knew that the cameras would get his entire statement and probably run most of it on the nightly news. If he strayed from his text and rambled, he knew the cameramen would stop rolling to save film, increasing the chances that some of his choicest remarks wouldn't be recorded. But now that he knew the TV crews had what he wanted them to have, he asked, "Any questions?"

A voice came from behind the crush of cameras and reporters. The tone was insolent, sarcastic.

"Yeah, man. I got a question for you."

Timmons craned his neck and shaded his eyes from the glare with both hands to see the questioner. Reporters and cameramen turned to see where the question came from.

A young black man began pushing through the media, heading for Timmons.

"That was very impressive, Reverend Timmons. Very impressive. But my question for you is this, man. Where the hell do you get off speaking for us?"

The young man was dressed in dungarees and a black T-shirt with a red lightning bolt on the back. A scraggly beard framed his surly face, and the corona of his Afro glistened with particles of sweat.

The lights had swung around to illuminate the youth as he made his way toward Timmons, who now stood in darkness, his mind racing to understand what was happening.

The flare of light swept back to Timmons as the angry young student stepped in front of his face and leveled a slender finger at his chest.

"The Student Coordinating Council does not need your help," he said, emphasizing each word with repeated jabs of his finger against the fabric of Timmons's crimson tie. "Take your Uncle Tom ass and get back to your churches. Your time is over. Our time is now."

Stunned and confused, Timmons felt at a loss for words, but he knew he had to think of something. The camera teams banged into each other, maneuvering to get better shots of the surprise confrontation and the reverend's gaping, bewildered face.

The words came slowly, his confident baritone now a throaty rasp. "Brother, what do you mean? We're together. We're on the same side. The movement needs you. We need you. And you need us."

But the young man had turned his back on Timmons and now

faced the cameras, taking command.

"Know now that the Student Coordinating League is standing up, black and proud, and demanding what is our due in this sick society you call America. We are tired of waiting for Uncle Tom Timmons to produce results. He and his cronies are far too comfortable hobnobbing with whitey while our people suffer. We disavow the tired and weak policies of the CAC and the sheep who espouse them. We will not stand by and see our brothers cut down by ignorant peckerwood red-neck trash or by the white-collar racists who call shots in the establishment power structure. I say to you the Student Coordinating League will be reckoned with. I say to you we will be heard."

And with that the young man raised a clenched fist, turned, and disappeared around a corner.

Quickly the cameras were back on Timmons. He was bathed in sweat and unsuccessfully trying to hide his humiliation.

Mindy fired a question.

"Reverend Timmons, it appears the CAC is going to have some serious competition from this student group, the Student Coordinating League. What's your reaction?"

Timmons forced a smile. "Youth must be served, and sometimes that youth is quite impetuous. I'm sure that when this young man cools down we'll be able to reason together and find a common ground. In the meantime, we won't let this distract us from the job at hand. Lady and gentlemen—good day."

Timmons and his colleague hurried down the hallway. Rather than wait for the elevator, they took the stairs. By the time they reached the ground floor they were almost running. There was insurrection in the ranks and no time to waste.

SIX

MARCUS

MARCUS TURNER WAS careful to observe the speed limit as he drove through town toward the Morehouse College campus, even though he felt like gunning the grumbling engine of his ramshackle '57 Chevy for all it was worth. He was so exhilarated he didn't want to stop at the red lights that dangled overhead at almost every intersection. At this moment they were just another impediment placed in his path by White America, but this was no time for a confrontation with a cop. In his agitated state he might smart off and be thrown in jail. The confrontation would have to come later, at a time of his choosing. Now he had to get back to campus to tell his comrades of his triumph at Grady Hospital.

Last night they had planned the humiliation of Reverend Elijah Timmons, and today the scenario played out perfectly. All that remained now was to see how the evening news would handle it. He wondered if the networks would think it significant enough to give national coverage. At the very least it would give them one more opportunity to run the sensational film of the violence at Southside Stadium.

Marcus was outraged that Timmons tried to use the beating of him and his three companions for his own selfish ends. They intended for their protest demonstration to serve notice of a new activist group on the scene—a coalition of students who were not afraid of confrontation. Marcus thought their protest would be sure to get news coverage, but he had not calculated the potential for violence. The worst the students imagined was a rough police escort out of the stadium or perhaps a brief trip to the city jail. They never anticipated being almost beaten to death. Marcus knew he was lucky to be alive. He had escaped with only bloody abrasions on his arms and neck and badly bruised ribs that were causing intense pain.

Marcus realized they had botched things by failing to clarify whom they represented. The Student Coordinating League was not mentioned in any news report. The four young blacks were identified only as college students, leaving the audience to assume that they were publicity-seeking freelancers and not part of a carefully laid-out plan. That failure was painful enough, but Timmons trying to capitalize on SCL's failure was simply too much. When Marcus got word of the reverend's planned news conference, he realized that SCL would have a second chance to dramatically announce itself to the world.

Marcus's car, once bright red but now faded to a dingy rust-dappled brown, rumbled through the central business district with its sleek commercial monuments rising serenely from the careless jumble of street-level clutter. Lunch hour had just ended for most downtown workers, and the streets were relatively free of pedestrian traffic, save for a few women scurrying in pairs from one air-conditioned department store to another. In several hours, the white shoppers would be gone and belching buses would begin lumbering in from the city's north side. They would disgorge their cargo of black women who'd put in a long day keeping house and tending babies in the shaded domains of the city's affluent whites. Their long journey only half finished, they would gather at their bus stops, waiting for the next bus to their own neighborhoods of teeming tenements or clapboard shacks on the downtown area's southern fringe. The younger ones would laugh, joke, and horse around, but the older women would just gaze glumly into the middle distance as heat waves from the pavement shimmered around them, patiently awaiting the next step in the endless cycle of buses.

Now Marcus was driving into a light industrial area of the city, just west of downtown, approaching "catch on corner." A cluster of black men in filthy, tattered work clothes stood on the sidewalk half-watching each passing car. Some of them crouched against the side of a store front, rolling dice and sipping from bottles of cheap wine. They were always here, hoping someone would drive by and offer them a job. Those jobs were always backbreaking with paltry pay, but it would be enough for some wine and perhaps a quick bet on the underground lottery, "the bug" as it was called. The ones still waiting were a sorry-looking lot. The young, stronger workers were always picked up shortly after sunrise. Now these few were left, and it was increasingly obvious they would find no work today.

A twinge of depression began to tug at Marcus as he thought of these brothers and sisters who seemed doomed to lives of desperation. And yet they probably never viewed their lives as desperate. They were numbed by generations of poverty and ignorance and simply accepted their station in life without questioning. All around them a mighty tide was changing history, but would they feel that impact? Did they care? Had the movement done anything for them? Had it stirred the dormant vestiges of racial pride from past centuries? Or had it only made it more difficult for them to deal with the white world they depended on for a living?

Marcus couldn't shove these thoughts aside as he crossed the old steel-trussed bridge over the Southern Railway tracks, turned onto busy Northside Drive, and approached the sycamore-shaded campus of Morehouse College.

He pondered the notion that most black people were sheep. For a hundred years since the Civil War, they had acquiesced to the iron fist of Southern segregation. Martin Luther King, James Farmer, John Lewis, and other leaders of the movement had tried to rouse them from their subservience, but for the most part the movement was being carried out by a very small group of blacks. The masses might cheer silently from the sidelines, but they were nowhere to be found on the field.

The old guard leaders had made strides, but Marcus felt the time had come for new leadership to take the battle to a new level. College students of the fifties had started the sit-ins, and now it was time for students of the sixties to take control. It was time to put the preachers like Timmons and their talk of compromise and concession out to pasture. It was time for more activist, hard-edged leadership to put the white establishment on notice that their time was coming to an end.

He realized that his own parents, both devotees of King and Elijah Timmons, would condemn his actions. They were among that small group of black Americans who had made it to the middle class. His father was a high school principal, his mother a housewife. They had met while students at Tuskegee Institute in Alabama and married upon graduation. Andrew Turner had gotten a teaching job at a local high school and eventually worked his way up to principal. Luvetta Turner also taught for a while but left her job when Marcus was born.

The Turners lived in a small white frame house in a middle-class black neighborhood in the city's southwestern quadrant. Marcus grew up in what could only be considered a privileged environment for blacks in that time. He had a yard, a bike, a cocker spaniel, and even a neighborhood swimming pool. But most importantly he had two educated parents who placed the highest premium on his schooling.

They pushed him to go to Morehouse because it was close to home and enjoyed a reputation for turning out solid graduates who replenished and expanded the community of businessmen, professionals, and politicians composing Atlanta's black middle class. Marcus considered going north to school, but the thought of traveling to an alien culture worried him. He decided to stay in the South and delighted his parents by choosing Morehouse. He'd worked hard his first two years to excel academically, helping realize his parents' dreams for him. But in his junior year, the spirit of the movement captivated him and his studies began to suffer. Marcus didn't care. He saw the opportunity to be directly involved in the most historic revolution of his lifetime, and nothing could keep him from it.

His parents understood his idealistic zeal and even encouraged it to a point. But they were uncomfortable with his ideas of confrontation and often clashed with Marcus over philosophy and tactics. They had led reasonably comfortable lives for blacks in the South and were concerned about what would happen to them and their neighbors if events moved too fast. They had become adept at enduring the humiliations of a racist society and were willing to wait for ordered change. They didn't want Marcus to be a firebrand.

But, of course, Marcus was a firebrand and gloried in that role. If his parents suffered because of it, that was just one more price to pay for the cause.

Marcus lurched his car into an open parking spot along the curb outside his red brick four-story dorm and headed across the matted, colorless grass long ago killed by countless footfalls and the bleaching sun. He bounded up the first two steps in the stairwell, but the stabbing pain from his injured ribs reminded him to take the rest of the steps one at a time. Reaching the top, he paused to collect himself and then began striding down the long, stifling fourth floor hall to his room, where five of his classmates waited. He burst through the door and immediately began slapping their outstretched palms with both hands, saying with exaggerated dialect, "We done it. That's right, we done it."

"Whatchu done, man, whatchu done?" one of them laughingly asked, playing along.

"Old man Timmons done been tramplin' out the vintage where the grapes of wrath is stored." Marcus's voice rose and fell in trembling waves as he mimicked a fire-and-brimstone country preacher. "He done felt the fateful lightnin' of my terr'ble swift sword. His ass gonna be marchin' on."

After their laughter subsided, Marcus giddily explained how he had commandeered the news conference, how he had surprised and humiliated Timmons, how three TV stations and one of the networks were there recording it all.

Then they began to plan their next move, the move they hoped would make their Student Coordinating League a name to be reckoned with, a force that would stir the masses and shake the city's racist system to its core.

SEVEN

SUPER SEG

"LADIES AND GEN'LMEN, I give you a man who will fight to preserve our way of life."

Riley Swint's face could barely be seen over the microphone, even though he was on his toes, his hands gripping the sides of the lectern as if to hoist himself higher. The water glass beside him danced precariously.

From his position in the roped-off reporter area, Gil pulled out his meter to carefully measure the light falling on Swint's face. He then slightly opened the aperture setting on his camera lens, refocused, moved his thumb to the camera switch, and pressed it. Four other cameramen standing behind their tripoded cameras went through their variation on the same routine, rolling film for the grand finale of Swint's introduction of the man they all called "Super Seg."

"I give you a man who will not kowtow to the arrogant intellectuals in Washington who think they know what is best for us. He is one of us, and when we elect him, we can be sure our streets and families will be safe. We can be sure our children will go to schools where education is the priority, not social experimentation. We can be sure that the people of our great state will be represented by a man who is not afraid to stand up to the federal guv-ment and the agitators for what we believe. Please raise your hearts and voices to welcome a great American, the next guvna of Georgia, Roscoe Pike."

The crowd erupted as a tall, gaunt man rose from his chair on the stage, waving with his left hand and grabbing and pumping Swint's extended hand with his right. His brown polyester suit seemed much too small for his lanky body. As Pike waved to the crowd, the sleeves of his jacket slid almost to his elbow. His narrow head was crowned by a brushy crew cut that swept forward to culminate like the tip of an arrowhead just above the creases of his glistening forehead. The huge Confederate battle flag nailed to the wall behind him seemed to cast a reddish glow on his already flushed face. His lips curled into a half-smile as he scanned the adoring crowd. His squinting eyes suddenly shadowed as he raised a hand to shield them from the glare of television lights all around.

"My dear friends, it's so good to be in Alcovy County today. It's good to be in a place where the law is enforced and where agitators don't get away with nothin'."

The mostly male audience roared in approval, clapping, nodding, and shouting. "You tell 'em, Roscoe. You tell 'em."

"For all those blacks causin' so much trouble—we know where they belong. Behind bars! Why, I think they ought to put 'em so far back in jail they'll have to pump daylight to 'em. Let 'em rot."

Applause and laughter again shook the room as Gil swiveled his camera for a crowd reaction shot. A full complement of media had shown up for Pike's campaign appearance in a small barbecue restaurant on the far outskirts of the metro region. The area was still considered rural, although subdivisions, fast food franchises, and other traces of creeping suburbanization would no doubt soon begin filling the pastures and kudzu patches.

"Now, my friends, I see the TV networks are here with us today."

Pike gestured toward the media corral at the back of the room. Some in the audience looked toward the forest of tripods and the journalists standing around them. There were scattered boos. The crusty network veteran Ned Brockett, his glasses pushed up on his thatch of white hair, took his eyes away from his camera and glared back at the audience. Brockett had been on the race beat in the South since the late fifties and had absolutely no fear of the redneck element. He'd been cursed and even roughed up several times, but he'd learned that the ones who made the most noise were the least to be feared. His correspondent, who'd just arrived in the South from Chicago two months ago, wasn't so unruffled. He nervously stared down at his note-pad and pretended to take notes by scribbling.

Brockett and the other news veterans understood they were part of Pike's act. They were all handy foils, targets of opportunity, stand-ins for the civil rights leaders and federal judges who were far out of range. Gil viewed most of the Pike supporters as the dregs of humanity, just like those who'd beaten the demonstrators at Southside Stadium, the ones who could always be counted on to make the South appear to be a primitive land populated by illiterate bullyboys. They were the high school dropouts who lived in shacks and trailer parks, driving pickups with rifle racks, wearing T-shirts and tank tops, living for the weekend when they could drain sudsy six-packs into oblivion. Should equality ever be attained for the Negro, Gil thought, these whites would have no one else to look down on. That sense of innate racial superiority was all they had, and if they lost it, they would be nothing. And yet the people in this room, those who hung on Roscoe Pike's every phrase, this doomed segment of Southern society, composed the image of all white Southerners for most of the world. They were always willing to be used, both by politicians like Pike and by civil rights strategists look-ing for simple dupes to illustrate the righteousness of their cause. And with every loutish appearance on a television newscast, they unwittingly hastened their own demise. Gil felt a deep sense of shame that his her-itage was rooted in the same soil.

"These people come down here from New York and Washin'ton and think they can tell us how to live our lives. They go out and make heroes out of these Communist agitators, like Martin Luther King. I tell you they look down on us white people. Those network announcers sit up there in their studios with their prettyboy makeup on, and they look down their snobby noses at us. We know what they want. They want us to mix the races, and they won't be happy 'til they have our homes, our jobs, and our women. It's all part of the Communist plan to mongrelize the races and bring this great nation to its knees. And I tell you, I will not let that happen. Elect me as your guvna, and I will see to it that our way of life is preserved for you and your children."

Pike smiled and strutted around the podium as the crowd hooted and jeered at the group of reporters in the rear of the room. He raised his arms for quiet.

"Now the current guvna, Atlanta's mayor, and others who claim to be our leaders have tried to talk with the black folk, tried to keep 'em happy. They got their black policemen, they got their seat at the front of the bus, they got their law that says they can come into a restaurant and sit right down next to you and your family. You'd think they'd be happy with that. But no. No, they want more. They won't stop until they're runnin' the show—runnin' everything. And the day will come when it gets bloody. We got to stand up and say 'no more.' We got to draw the line and say 'Boy, don't you cross that line.' We got to stand up for the rights of red-blooded, God fearin', white Americans. We got to do it today. Are you with me? Are you with me? Let's hear it then."

Cheers, whistles, and rebel yells filled the stifling meeting room, and the building vibrated with stomping feet. Gil panned his camera over the crowd and then back to Pike on the stage. Someone approached the edge of the media pen and screamed, "God damn lying news people. Tell it true now, tell it true."

Pike was now wading into the milling crowd, pumping hands and slapping backs. Gil, Brockett, and the other cameramen had moved into the crowd to follow and film Pike's triumphal departure. Their microphones recorded the banter, Pike saying "Good to see you" or "I need your help, now, you hear?" to the response of "Give 'em hell, Roscoe" or "We're with you, Roscoe." Someone passed a straw hat that was rapidly filling with dollar bills.

Pike moved through the building with his adoring throng enfolding him, like the nucleus of a pulsating organism. He touched every outstretched hand until he got into a waiting car and was slowly driven away as the crowd cheered and waved.

As Gil disassembled his camera equipment, he noticed Mindy

approaching.

"I've got to find a phone to file my story, but after that can I bum a ride back to town with you? I came here in a cab."

"Sure," said Gil. "Take your time. It's early and I don't have another assignment."

Gil paused for a moment to watch Mindy as she walked away. He was looking forward to her company on the ride back.

GIL WAS LOADING his gear into the station wagon in the gravel lot when Mindy came out to join him. Dust swirled up from the tires of departing pickups and cars still eddied in the air, looking for a stable spot to settle. Some of the grainy particles discovered Gil's sweat-moistened skin and clung there. He felt disheveled and dirty and self-conscious as he climbed behind the wheel. Mindy opened the passenger door and waited as Gil cleared her seat of empty film reels, hamburger wrappers, and other debris that had been gathering there for days. Then she gracefully slipped into the car and angled her body toward Gil. He noticed her skirt ride up to about mid-thigh before she quickly pulled it back to just above her knees.

Feeling a bit awkward, Gil turned his head and began backing from his parking spot.

"Welcome to my humble chariot. Sorry for the mess."

Mindy snickered as she gingerly picked up a hardened French fry and tossed it into the back seat.

"This is what I'd imagined your bachelor pad to look like. Besides, there's nothing humble about it. You've actually got air conditioning!"

"Ah, yes," Gil replied. "The station put factory air in all its wagons. Just one of the perks of working in TV."

"Well, Gil, your lowly wire service scribe thanks you for your beneficence."

He pulled out of the parking area, accelerating as he arced onto the highway. The big station wagon shuddered as it gained speed, its air conditioner roaring as he flipped it to super cool. The rush of air set the ends of Mindy's shoulder-length brown hair dancing as she sat back and closed her eyes with an exaggerated "Ahhhh."

He turned to Mindy with a sarcastic smile.

"Was Super Seg worth the un-air-conditioned cab ride?"

Mindy glanced at him, returned the smile, then turned to look down the highway ahead.

"Full of sound and fury. Pike never disappoints," she said. "He is a quote machine. But it's you TV guys he lives and dies for. He's not going through this act for a rip and read radio newscast in the boondocks. He's never better than when he's got the cameras all around him. And the networks—when they're with him he's always in rare form."

Gil nodded but kept his eyes on the road. "Yeah. He feeds us and we spew it out to the public. What a beautiful relationship."

Mindy pulled out her notepad, looked at it briefly, then flipped it on the seat. "It's scary to think he could be our next governor."

Gil gave a humorless chuckle. "We'd be in high cotton. Great stories every day. Turmoil and confusion would reign. Maybe we ought to pull for the guy." He paused briefly then added, "Seriously, what are the odds of Pike winning?"

Mindy was silent for a moment and then spoke slowly with mock solemnity. "And what rough beast, its hour come round at last, slouches toward Bethlehem to be born?"

Gil turned his head to face her with a quizzical look. "Huh?"

"Yeats. 'The Second Coming.' It's the yin and yang of my complex personality. Writer of pedestrian wire service copy on the one hand, poetry-quoting dilettante on the other. Sometimes the twain do meet. They just did."

Gil turned his eyes back to the road. "Maybe you should have been a poet."

Mindy chuckled sarcastically. "And miss all the acclaim that comes with writing wire copy for AP customers who give me no credit? One of these days maybe I'll get a job in TV so I can be famous like you."

"Ha! I did have my moment in the sun, but I've learned that fame is fleeting."

"Well, Gil, at least you had a taste. I do like my job, but it's thankless. I am anonymous."

"Not to me," Gil replied. "And with apologies to Mr. Yeats, can we get back to the topic? Can Pike win?"

"Sure. He's got his hardcore support, but he turns off a lot of white voters, those who want a more genteel form of discrimination. They don't use the 'N' word, but they're scared to death that blacks are going to end up in their children's classrooms or living next door. They are really the key to this election. Will they go with an overt racist like Pike or a more conventional candidate like Harrison Parker?"

The traffic was building as they entered the northern fringe of the city. Strip malls and fast-food franchises had spread into the area as developers rushed to keep up with the subdivisions sprouting on almost every piece of vacant land. Main traffic arteries, once freely traveled, were now choked with commercial clutter and traffic lights. Gil was trying to get around a bus belching black exhaust fumes.

He glanced at his watch. It was two fifteen. Still early, but he shouldn't waste time getting his film into the processing lab at the station. With luck he'd have the developed film in hand by three fifteen, and if nothing else interrupted, he could have the story written and edited by five with an hour to spare before news time.

He spoke as he accelerated and pulled out to pass the lumbering bus. "Harrison Parker? Interesting."

Mindy nodded. "Parker knows how to make the segs feel he might be one of them without resorting to the crudeness of Pike. At the same time, he gives moderates hope that he has progressive instincts. It's hard for anyone to know exactly where he stands. Parker has to dodge and weave on the race issue and play to those put off by Pike's campaign style. But there are so many voters who just want to stick it to LBJ and the federal establishment. And what better way to do that than to put Pike in the governor's mansion?"

Gil gunned his engine, speeding up to clear the intersection as the yellow caution light turned red. "That's a very scary thought. Governor Roscoe Pike." His voice sank to a reflective whisper barely audible over the whoosh of the car's AC. "Governor Roscoe Pike."

They drove on in silence toward the city and the deadlines that awaited.

EIGHT

HEROES

THE GRAINY BLACK and white picture on the small television set quivered as it struggled to find some stability. Hiram Soseby slapped the side of the set as though a dose of discipline might correct things, but the blow resulted in a series of black bars floating on the screen from bottom to top. He could barely make out the gesticulating image of Roscoe Pike stoking up his crowd, but the audio came in clearly.

"We got to stand up for the rights of red-blooded, God-fearing, white Americans," Pike screamed as the crowd yelled its approval.

Soseby slapped his hand on the counter, and with a trace of a smile said, "Damn right! You tell it, Roscoe!"

Then, his face returning to its normal sullenness, he cursed the television set for failing to send him decent pictures of the event. He had tuned into the news just to see coverage of the Pike rally in neighboring Alcovy County.

Soseby's son Caleb, who'd been putting gas in a customer's pickup, walked back inside through the screen door.

"God damn it, boy," Soseby said in a low, menacing tone. "How many times have I told you to get up on the roof and fix that antenna? I can't get a damn picture on this TV. You need to angle it more to the south to pick up the signals. Pickett County's forty miles away from the nearest tower."

Then he condescendingly pointed toward the big rebel flag nailed to the wall. "South is that way."

"OK, Daddy. Cover the pumps for me, and I'll climb up and fix it." Caleb walked toward the storeroom to get a ladder. "We probably ought to think about a new TV. Maybe one of those new color sets."

Soseby muttered another curse, turned off the TV, and slouched on his stool behind the counter, which was littered with old receipts and other scraps of paper, several empty coffee cups, a mason jar sprouting pens and pencils, and an out-of-date Sears Roebuck catalog. On his right was the NCR register that had once been his pride and joy but now suffered from years of the accumulated grime of oil-stained fingers, rust, and a balky cash drawer. Under the register on a shelf beneath the counter was Soseby's revolver, a loaded .38 Smith and Wesson. The double-barreled shotgun that had once been within easy reach under the counter was no longer there. Soseby had hidden it after it served its grisly purpose on the Peavine Creek bridge.

On a small bookcase along the wall behind Soseby's stool were several issues of *The Thunderbolt*, a periodical published by the National States Rights Party. Soseby began leafing through the current issue, which included articles advocating the deportation of Negroes to Africa and castigating Jews for their role in the civil rights rebellion.

He could hear Caleb clattering about up on the roof as he glanced through the dust-caked window looking out on the pumps and the highway. He hoped no one would pull in for gas until Caleb was available. He'd reached the point in life where he didn't want to wait on people, even though he knew his business was dying.

A flash of reflected sunlight and rumbling gravel announced the arrival of a car pulling off the highway. The vehicle bypassed the gasoline pumps and parked behind the building. He knew the car and driver well, but he was not happy.

"What the hell are you doing here, Randall?" he said as a man with a slight limp entered the room. "Didn't I tell you to stay away?"

"I'm sorry, Hiram. I'm kinda a mess these days. I just thought it might help me to talk about it with you and Caleb."

Randall Scoggins stood in the middle of the room, swaying slightly and clutching the baseball cap he'd removed from his head when he came inside. His stubby legs seemed barely capable of supporting his ample torso. He looked to his right as Caleb appeared.

"Hi, Randall. I was up on the roof and saw you pull in. What's up?"

The elder Soseby didn't wait for Scoggins to respond. "Randall's having a hard time," he said, in a mockingly sympathetic tone. "He just wants to talk about things." He eased off his stool and crossed his arms. "We're not talking about anything," he said to Scoggins. "What's done is done. And we are in the clear if we just keep our mouths shut. Nobody knows what happened to that spook but us. Nobody knows where he was when he disappeared. It could have been anywhere between well south of here and Maryland. They'll never find the body or the car. It's all going to be fine. Don't worry."

Scoggins clutched his crumpled hat, looked at Caleb and then back at Hiram.

"Okay. It's just that…well, you know, it got out of control. It's hard to deal with."

Soseby walked around the counter and put his hand on Scoggins's back in a comforting way. "Randall, we did something we had to do. You need to go home and stay there as much as you can. Don't come around here for a while. Try not to get too drunk. Pretty soon the memory will fade, and everything will be back to normal."

Scoggins nodded and turned to leave. "Thanks, Hiram. I feel better." The voice was mechanical and unconvincing.

Caleb stepped aside as Scoggins shuffled toward the door.

"Oh, Randall, one last thing," Soseby said as Scoggins departed. "One day our people will consider us heroes for what we did."

Scoggins looked back briefly, his eyes sagging with fatigue and sadness.

"Heroes," he mumbled under his breath as he walked into the blinding light and suffocating heat. "Heroes, my ass."

NINE

PARKER

THE LATE MODEL dark blue sedan swerved along the two-lane blacktop, its young driver doing his best to avoid the potholes dimpling the road's surface. He found the challenge a daunting one, and every ten seconds or so the vehicle's tires hit a depression that jolted the car and the three people inside it.

In the back seat, gubernatorial candidate Harrison Parker was trying to scribble some notes for the speech he would soon make, but the sedan's swerving and shuddering made it almost impossible to write legibly.

As his pen careened over a page in his pocket notebook, Parker yelled, "Damn it, Billy. If you can't miss the holes at least slow down. This is like driving in a third world country."

"Can't help it, boss." Billy Watson, his young aide, was hunched over the steering wheel, staring intently at the roadway, jerking the wheel to the right, then to the left. "Got to get you there on time. We're way late."

Parker turned to the other passenger sitting behind the driver.

"Sorry. He's right. Guess we just have to deal with it."

Mindy Williams smiled and said, "No worries. I'm fine."

She had been riding with Parker all day from campaign stop to campaign stop, taking notes for a feature story to run for her wire service on the weekend. She had walked behind Parker as he shook hands along the main streets of several small towns, trying to get the flavor of the campaign, to gauge people's responses to the candidate, always listening for a comment that might make some news.

Parker was grateful for the attention and made every effort to accommodate Mindy. He would have preferred to be accompanied by a television crew, but he could hardly expect the stations to cover him in rural backwaters like Heflin County two hundred miles from Atlanta. He hoped a television camera or two from Savannah might cover the event he was heading to, but he couldn't count on it. No, he'd have to be content with a print reporter who would give her readers far more detail than a television reporter, though the impact would be minimal compared to exposure on the tube. But any coverage was better than no coverage at all.

Parker was Georgia's attorney general, but before that he had served in the legislature for a decade. He represented the city of Macon in the center of the state, the place he was born and raised and where he established a highly successful law practice. He was forty years old, but his ruddy complexion, slender build, and shock of light brown hair made him appear younger. His natural attractiveness, his carefully chosen wardrobe, his fluid, articulate speaking style, and his stunning wife Mary and their two children all added to the aura of a man destined for bigger things.

He had been elected attorney general four years ago, seizing the opportunity when the man who had served in that post for decades retired. During that campaign, he did what all successful politicians in the South felt they had to do to be elected. He hewed to the segregationist line, promising to fight the federal government's efforts to remove racial barriers. But once in office, he had tried to find legal compromises and avoid confrontations with civil rights attorneys and black leaders challenging Jim Crow laws. He knew that overt resistance would make him a hero to those fighting social change, but in the long run it would be a losing proposition and damaging to his state.

By avoiding the strident rhetoric of segregationist leaders and making accommodations when possible, Parker had been portrayed by journalists as a "New South" up-and-comer ripe with political possibilities. He was viewed as someone who could follow in the footsteps of the current governor, Carlton Sawyer, whose moderate racial stances surprised and pleased the urban business elite but alienated rural voters who felt betrayed. The state constitution forbade a second consecutive term, so voters would neither be able to endorse nor condemn Governor Sawyer at the ballot box.

So the question persisted. Would the voters cast their ballots for a man who was considered moderate and flexible, or would they give the governor's office to the candidate who promised resistance to the forces of inevitable change? The Democratic primary would answer that question. The winner of that primary would be the odds-on favorite in the general election where Republicans offered only token opposition.

Parker pondered the electability question as the car bounced down the pockmarked highway. He gazed out the window at the passing countryside. It was farm country, and the fields of corn, peanuts, and tobacco were browning and withering under the unrelenting southern sun. Along the roadside were small homes of farm workers—shacks really—with barefoot and shirtless children playing on the hard-packed dirt of their yards. Their fathers would be working as hired labor on the farms in the area if they were lucky enough to even have a job.

He considered how much these downtrodden whites had in common with black families whose rundown homes also clustered in separate neighborhoods along the highway. Poor whites and blacks struggled to find menial work to feed their families and survive. Their children for the most part dropped out of school, not understanding the value of education as a way to break out of the poverty cycle. They are all in the same boat, he thought, and they share common goals, but racial prejudice keeps them apart, keeps them suspicious, resentful, and full of fear—even hate.

The blacks were almost powerless because their votes had been suppressed by intimidation in the rural counties. Poor whites, on the other hand, could be counted on to vote, and political demagogues played to their fears and prejudices to bring them to the polls. These whites voted to keep blacks down because they were afraid of losing their spot in the Southern caste system, a spot just above blacks, the only ones they could claim were inferior to them.

Parker understood that the groundswell of impending change could not be stopped. It could be slowed, but the final result would be the same. His challenge was to find a way to lead his people through this societal revolution. But he had to get elected to do this, and that would require a certain amount of pragmatic pandering to a white audience not yet ready to accept the reality of changing times.

Billy slowly pulled the car off the road onto a gravel drive leading to a large field. A crowd of several hundred people had assembled there, and they milled around listening to a country-western band playing upbeat tunes from a flatbed truck on the edge of the field.

When the car stopped, Parker opened the door and was immediately hit by the furnace-like blast of heat still building under the cloudless sky. An obese man in a sweat-soaked sport shirt and khakis greeted him. It was State Representative Wilson Skaggs, his friend and political ally.

"Hi you, Mr. Attorney General. Good to have you here in Heflin County. We've all been waitin' for you. Need anything to drink? Sweet tea? Coke?"

Parker shook Skaggs's hand and gave him a pat on the back as both men headed for the drink stand. Mindy followed, jotting occasional notes as she walked.

"Who's that cute thing with you?" Skaggs said sotto voce.

"She's a reporter. Writing a profile for AP," Parker replied, then added with a smile, "Strictly professional."

Skaggs gave a cynical laugh. "Mary know?"

"She knows a reporter is traveling with me. She doesn't know it's Mindy. But it doesn't matter. She knows she can trust me."

Skaggs leaned his head closer to Parker. "Sounds like you've changed since our days in the legislature. Did Mary know about those parties at the Henry Grady Hotel?"

Parker snapped back. "That's ancient history. And yes, she does know. And yes, I have changed."

Parker tried to hide his resentment over Skaggs probing his

marriage. He and Mary had had their troubles, but that was all behind them.

Mary hated the rough and tumble of political campaigns. She was a very private person and much preferred to be home with the children. Parker fully understood, even though her charm and beauty were always assets when she was by his side. But when he needed strength, advice, or even a stinging critique, he could always depend on Mary for loving support. He was counting the hours until he could be home with her once again for a brief respite from the tawdriness of the campaign.

With Skaggs's help, Parker's advance team had done a good job raising a crowd. About three hundred people had gathered for the event, attracted by free barbecue, a local band, and the promise of some stem-winding political speeches from locals seeking office and, of course, the state attorney general who was running for governor. Parker was savvy enough to know that most of those in attendance came for the free barbecue.

As Parker sipped his iced tea, the band stopped playing, and a candidate for the county commission climbed onto the flatbed trailer and began to speak into a hand-held microphone. Immediately, there was an ear-piercing modulating squeal over the loudspeakers placed on either side of the trailer. The local candidate put more distance between his mouth and the microphone, quieting the feedback.

As the speaker droned on about protecting white school children from the dictatorial arm of the federal government, Parker dipped his head close to Skaggs and asked, almost in a whisper, "How're things looking here?" Mindy hovered nearby, but it was obvious Parker did not want her to overhear the conversation, and she discretely kept her distance.

Skaggs blotted his forehead with a sopping wet handkerchief. "I'm in some trouble, as you know. Twenty years of representing this county, and now I get opposition because I refuse to bow down to Roscoe Pike."

"I appreciate your support more than you know," Parker responded. "You'll be okay. Just keep telling them what you've done for them.

They'll be there for you when it counts."

Parker was aware that his tone was less than convincing, but Skaggs seemed to appreciate it nonetheless.

What Parker really wanted to know was how things were going for *him* in this part of the state and what Skaggs could do to help. He took another sip of tea, so sweet it was almost sickening. "How's it looking for me?"

"You've got your work cut out for you," Skaggs admitted, also speaking in low tones. "Lot of people here think you might cave in to the blacks. That's the word being spread by Pike's people. They say you love national attention and will do anything to get it, even if it means selling out the white people of this state like Governor Sawyer's done."

Parker nodded slowly. None of what Skaggs told him was a surprise, but the information still raised his anxiety level. He needed to win some of these counties in farm country, and he feared he couldn't do so without resorting to rhetoric tinged with racial code words that would imply where he stood without revealing his true feelings.

Parker put down his tea, placed his hand on Skaggs's sodden shoulder, and began moving toward the flatbed. "Well, time to make my case."

The country western band struck up a tune, and scattered applause and a few rebel yells accompanied Parker as he jogged up the steps of the flatbed and trotted over to grab the microphone.

"Good to be in Heflin County today. It's a special part of our state, and it's good to see so many good friends here." More scattered applause. By this time Parker was an expert in quickly sizing up crowds, and this one seemed courteous but skeptical. They weren't on his bandwagon, but perhaps he could sway them.

He looked over the crowd and spotted a television news car pulling onto the fringe of the field. The reporter and cameraman hustled to get their equipment out of the vehicle and into position to film his remarks. He'd have to buy some time for them to set up. Getting exposure on the evening news was a lot more important to him than wasting his message on a less than enthusiastic handful of locals.

Parker launched into some jokes he told at almost every speech and then said kind words about Skaggs and why he should be reelected. After five minutes of this banter, the local TV crew had their camera on a tripod and a microphone lying on the bed of the trailer where Parker stood, close enough to get decent sound.

Confident that the camera was ready to roll, Parker moved into his main message. "You know, our state has many challenges. We need to do a better job of educating our children, getting jobs for our people, keeping our streets safe for law-abiding citizens. What we don't need is the federal government coming in to tell us what we should do and how we should do it."

The crowd burst into applause punctuated by cries of "Damn right" and "Tell it like it is." The TV reporter tapped his cameraman on the shoulder to be sure he was still rolling. Mindy scribbled speech fragments in her notepad.

"Those faceless bureaucrats in Washington don't know what's best for our people. We know what's best, and if you elect me, I promise you we will make the lives of all our people better, and I'll keep the feds out of your lives. We have a proud heritage, and I want to make sure it continues. I have a strong record of standing up for you and our way of life. Elect me governor, and I promise great things are in store for Georgia. I need your vote to move our state forward, to keep our destiny in our hands, not the hands of bureaucrats in Washington. Vote Harrison Parker, and you'll be glad you did."

Scattered cheers and applause began before he finished, and Parker was pleased to see the cameraman swiveling to show the reaction of the audience. This was his standard stump speech, but he thought it had gone over better than usual. The band launched into its version of "Dixie" as he raised his arms overhead and clenched his fists. Surveying the crowd milling about below, he knew he was not one of them and never would be, but he needed them to believe he shared their values and would fight for them. If the end justified the means, he thought, so be it.

TEN

WELCOME TO DIXIE

REVEREND TIMMONS WAS bemused by the incongruity of a plantation house in the middle of a modern metropolis. "Old times there are not forgotten," he thought as he approached the neoclassical mansion that housed WDX-TV. Timmons was aware that the call letters reflected the station's original slogan: "Welcome to Dixie." The building perched atop an expansive, gently sloping lawn of lush, verdant zoysia. Huge magnolias framed the columned structure that was nestled in an understory of azalea, rhododendron, and dogwood.

As Timmons climbed the broad brick steps leading to the double-doored entrance, he almost expected to be greeted by a plantation master all decked out in white with a hoop-skirted belle on his arm. Instead, he saw an attractive young brunette with a beehive hairdo sitting behind a reception desk. She gave him a cool welcome as he stood beneath the huge crystal chandelier in the open foyer.

"Good afternoon. I'm Reverend Elijah Timmons here to see your general manager."

The receptionist looked down at some papers on the desk, and without looking up asked, "Do you have an appointment?" There was a hint of suspicion in her soft drawl.

Timmons was offended by her dismissive, skeptical attitude, but he stifled his immediate impulse to upbraid her for her lack of respect.

"Yes, I do. Two o'clock. With Mr. Hill and I believe your news director as well."

He used his minister's voice, deep and forceful, letting the receptionist know clearly that he was a man not to be taken lightly.

She offered a tight-lipped smile and reached for the phone on her desk. "Just a moment sir. I'll check with Mr. Hill's secretary. Would you like to have a seat?"

Timmons nodded slightly, moved to the lobby sofa, and sat down, wondering how she would welcome a white guest. He was well dressed in a blue suit and red-striped tie, his black dress shoes gleamed, he carried himself confidently, and he spoke with an educated minister's vocabulary, and yet he did not merit the same respect a more modestly dressed and inarticulate white person would have received in the same circumstances. The antebellum atmosphere of the WDX plantation made his experience with the receptionist all the more aggravating. He thought of complaining to General Manager Ronald Hill but decided to let it go and concentrate on the mission at hand.

Timmons rose as Hill's secretary approached from an office suite connected to the lobby. Her warm smile and cheerful greeting soothed his resentments.

"Welcome, Reverend Timmons. Please follow me. Mr. Hill is expecting you."

Timmons was ushered down a short hall with framed archival photographs lining the walls. They reached an alcove containing the secretary's desk, and then she ushered him into a spacious oak-paneled office. A large marble fireplace took up the wall to his right, tall windows to his left looked out onto the green sweep of the station's front lawn, and straight ahead behind a mahogany desk sat WDX Vice President and General Manager Ronald Hill.

Hill rose and walked around his desk to greet Timmons with a firm handshake. "Reverend Timmons, welcome. Good to see you again. I think you know our news director, Tom Burke."

A short man, balding at the temples and wearing khaki pants, a blue shirt with button-down collar, and a blue tie, stepped forward to offer his hand. His tie was blotched by small coffee stains and knotted so loosely that it didn't hide the collar button. Hill gestured to Timmons and Burke to take a seat around a coffee table in a corner of the office. Timmons sat on a small sofa, Hill and Burke in Queen Anne chairs across the table.

"Now, Reverend, what can we do for you?" Hill shifted in the chair that seemed too small for his lanky frame, crossing his legs and interlocking his fingers, his elbows settling on the chair's armrests.

Having met Hill on several occasions, Timmons felt comfortable with him. He was engaging, intelligent, and full of good humor. He was originally from New York and carried none of the racial baggage of executives raised in the South. He was a man who could deal with Timmons on a level of mutual respect.

Timmons also knew that the corporation that owned WDX and seven other stations around the country was run by pragmatic but progressive leaders who would use the power of media for positive change, particularly in their Southern markets. As the leader of WDX, Hill wanted to see a peaceful transition to a more equal society, and he knew his station could play a powerful role. But while his corporate bosses would commend him for editorially speaking out on local civil rights issues, they would not be so supportive if he alienated his core audience and saw profits and ratings begin to sag. Hill was always walking a tightrope, piloting a course that kept pressure on city and state leaders to accommodate change while also keeping his predominately white viewing audience happily watching his programs and buying their advertised products and services.

Timmons cleared his throat and began speaking in his most serious tone. "Gentlemen, as you no doubt know, we've got some upstarts in town who threaten to undermine all we've been able to achieve over the past decade. We think you're giving them coverage out of all proportion to what they deserve."

Hill slightly adjusted his position, lifting his chin from the cradle formed by his interlocked fingers. "Reverend, no one can question the leadership role you've had during some very troubled times in our city. You've gotten plenty of coverage, and it seems to me most of it has put you in a pretty positive light, even though you aren't exactly a beloved figure in the white community. Now some of your younger people are upsetting the apple cart. Part of this new black power thing. You may not like it, but it's news, and we're obliged to cover it."

Hill shifted in the chair again, recrossing his long, thin legs, his pants hiking up and exposing a hint of bare shin between the cuff and his dark socks. He never took his eyes off Timmons, waiting for his response.

"Mr. Hill, by giving undue coverage to these students, you undercut me and the responsible leaders of the Negro community. And you increase the chances that things will spin out of control. While I may not be popular with your white viewers, I guarantee my tactics are a much better option for them than these kids. They don't want to negotiate. They want to burn it all down."

Hill turned to Burke, who had been sitting quietly, listening. "Tom, it sounds like Reverend Timmons doesn't like our news judgment. What do you think?"

Burke paused briefly, tugging gently at his earlobe. "Reverend Timmons, when you have students challenging your leadership, when they disrupt news conferences, march in the streets, defy authority, go to jail, get beaten up—that's news. And we report it, like it or not."

Timmons frowned, then spoke in his deep baritone. "Mr. Burke, I certainly understand your need to find the sensational and the bizarre to spike your ratings. But a measure of responsibility is required to keep things in perspective. If you continue to sensationalize, we will all reap the whirlwind."

Burke was angry, and Hill knew it. He quickly stepped in before Burke could respond.

"Gentlemen, let's back off for a moment. Reverend, I can assure you we are always analyzing how we cover the news, and how that coverage affects our viewers' lives. And while we respect your opinion, we cannot and we will not ignore our responsibility to cover all the news. If you don't approve, I'm sorry, but that's the way it has to be."

Hill turned to Burke. "Tom, I know you've got a newscast to get on the air, so you'd better get back to the newsroom. Thanks for coming."

Burke rose and, giving an unsmiling nod to Timmons, turned and left the office.

Hill watched him go and then looked back at Timmons. "I probably shouldn't have involved Tom in this discussion. He's a serious newsman, maybe a little crusty around the edges, but as tough and good as they come. He doesn't like it when anyone questions his judgment or his fairness. Come to think of it…neither do I."

"I understand," Timmons responded, softening the tone of his voice. "I didn't mean to question the integrity of your operation."

"Reverend, covering racial issues is a huge challenge for us. While you march and hold news conferences demanding equality under the law, there are those who resist that change and will speak just as forcefully about their views. We have to cover both sides."

"Yes, I suppose that's so. But how can you give equal coverage to racists who would just as soon see us dead? How can you give legitimacy to that primitive point of view?"

Hill shifted in his chair and uncrossed his legs, planting both feet firmly on the Persian rug beneath them.

"Look, Reverend. Segregationists accuse us of being in bed with you civil rights leaders. You and your followers say we give far too much coverage to the outspoken opponents of integration. We can't ever completely satisfy either side—and we don't try to."

Timmons interrupted with fervency in his voice. "But surely you cannot deny the righteousness of our cause!"

Hill paused, then spoke quietly in measured, almost confidential tones. "No. Tom Burke wouldn't tell you this, but I can. Tom's a newsman. I'm a businessman. As a businessman I want to see my station prosper, and for that to happen, our city must prosper. Our city cannot prosper if racial conflict leads to violence by either side."

Timmons settled back and stroked his chin as Hill continued.

"So—and this has to be between you and me—it is in our station's interest and our city's interest to have black leaders who are responsible and reasonable. Of course, you have to posture with your demands for concessions, but you and your colleagues understand that you can't have it all now. We must move gradually. You are a leader our power structure can deal with. That's why you're here in my office right now."

Timmons was surprised by Hill's candor. He had expected the standard journalism 101 lecture but instead had received a look behind the curtain of the city's strategic plan to cope with the rapidly shifting tides of history.

"Thank you for being so candid, Mr. Hill. I do, indeed, have what I would call a constructive relationship with the mayor and the business community—the white power structure, if you will. They understand I must keep the pressure on, and I understand they cannot comply as quickly or as fully as I publicly demand. But if my leadership is jeopardized, things could spin out of control quickly. We don't want fire hoses in the streets any more than you do, but it could happen here if you don't help me in the face of this challenge."

Hill rose from his seat and offered his hand as Timmons rose to accept it. "Reverend Timmons, I think we understand each other. Let me see what I can do. We both want what is best for our city, I'm sure."

Hill walked with Timmons from his office into the lobby and to the double front door. "Goodbye, Reverend. Thanks for coming by."

As Timmons walked down the brick steps to his car, he realized his mission in coming to the station remained unaccomplished. If anything, he had worsened his problem by elevating Marcus Turner's profile even more. Marcus and his followers were news, and there was nothing he could do to change that.

ELEVEN

EVELYN

THE WORDS WOULDN'T come. Elijah Timmons had been sitting at his desk in the office of Mount Gilead AME Church for two hours and had yet to finish a paragraph of his Sunday sermon. The distractions all around him sorely tested his ability to concentrate. Children released from choir practice ran through the halls laughing and yelling, his secretary Myrtice debated on the phone with her husband about a new sofa they were considering, and the window air conditioner groaned as if on the verge of collapse.

Most distracting of all were the images of his humiliation at Grady Hospital that kept playing in his mind, images seen by thousands of news viewers, images that could never be erased. He had worked so hard to become a respected leader in his community, but now that role was threatened by rabble rousers with no respect for him or his nonviolent tactics. Uncle Tom Timmons, they had called him. He had to find a way to put them in their place. But how?

His reverie ended suddenly when Emanuel Slocum stuck his head through the doorway.

"Excuse me, Reverend, but there are some people here to see you."

Timmons wearily nodded, resigned to whatever ministerial duty might be required. A marriage counseling session or perhaps advice on a wayward teenager.

"Okay. I might as well see them. Can't get any work done in all this commotion."

Slocum ushered a middle-aged woman and an older man into Timmons's office. The woman was very attractive, slender, and refined, wearing a stylish brown skirt and white blouse. The man with her was anything but refined. He was tall, rail-thin, and wore denim coveralls over a faded blue T-shirt. Sparse gray fuzz covered his scalp, and the reflection of the ceiling light on his skull made him appear almost bald. He seemed hesitant and remained in the background as his companion stepped forward and extended her hand to Timmons.

"Reverend Timmons, my name is Evelyn Pendry, and this is Willie Brooks, my husband's uncle."

Timmons enfolded her delicate hand in his and gently held it as he studied her for a few seconds.

"Mrs. Pendry, Mr. Brooks, it's a pleasure to meet you. How might I help you?"

"My husband, Jarvis, is missing. He left Fort Benning late last week driving home to Baltimore. He was supposed to spend the night with his uncle Willie, but he never showed up. I'm afraid something has happened to my husband, and that's why I drove down here—to try to find him."

Evelyn's voice was soft but firm, and Timmons silently wondered if she sang in her church choir—or even attended church.

"Well, Mrs. Pendry. This is certainly disturbing. First I've heard of it. But why are you coming to me? Aren't the authorities investigating?"

Evelyn sighed deeply and shook her head. "I have talked to the state authorities, and they don't seem terribly interested in finding my husband. I get the distinct feeling they view him as just another black man on a lark who'll turn up one of these days. That's why I'm here. I'm hoping you can put some pressure on these…these people. I don't know where else to turn."

Her voice began to tremble. "My husband is a fine man, a self-reliant man, but he's also a black man traveling alone on the back roads in a state full of racist rednecks. My theory is he got lost trying to find Uncle Willie's house…and…well…." She trailed off into silence.

Timmons let the silence hang for a moment, not sure how to respond.

"I am so sorry, and I understand why you're here. Let me see what I can do. Perhaps I can bring some pressure to bear, and, of course, I do have media contacts who might be able to help."

Timmons looked past Evelyn and directed a question at Brooks, who was standing behind her, eyes focused on the floor. "Mr. Brooks, what part of the state do you live in?"

"I live in Shiloh Crossroads. That's in Pickett County not far from Armistead. Way out in the country. I was worried Jarvis might not find my house after dark. When he didn't show up, I called Evelyn. She hadn't heard from him neither."

Timmons had never heard of Shiloh Crossroads, but he was familiar with the reputation of Pickett County. He'd heard there once was a sign at the county line decades ago using a racist slur followed by the message: "Don't let the sun set on you in Pickett County." It was a memory he chose not to share with his guests.

"Reverend Timmons," Brooks continued, "I'm just worried he ran into some bad people. We do have some bad people in Pickett County—Klan people—and I'm worried that something bad happened to my nephew. We're afraid to know, but we have to find out. Can you help us? Help us find Jarvis?"

Timmons stroked his chin as his forehead crinkled into a deep frown. He had a sense of dread about what might have happened to Jarvis Pendry. He also couldn't help but wonder if this was the Lord's way of providing him an avenue toward redemption after what happened at the hospital.

"Yes," he responded. "Yes, I will help. It is unconscionable that state authorities have not aggressively pursued this case. But I must tell you it is not surprising. If they will not respond, we will. We will focus the public's attention on this outrage, and we will find your husband, Mrs. Pendry. God willing he'll be okay."

He asked his guests to take seats in his office as he walked back to his desk and picked up the phone.

He dialed the number of WDX General Manager Ronald Hill. Once Hill was on the line, Timmons said, "Mr. Hill, I have a story for you. And I think the network will be interested."

TWELVE

SHILOH CROSSROADS

GIL KEPT HIS eyes on the road as his index finger moved over the car radio buttons, punching each in succession until he found what he was looking for. He shifted his hand and dialed up the volume as the Beatles' latest hit "Hard Day's Night" blared from the speaker. His head moved back and forth with the beat, and he sang along, thankful he was able to shed his inhibitions in relative privacy as he drove north toward Pickett County.

He was also grateful for some time away from the city. Leaving the traffic and suburban sprawl was always a reminder that Atlanta was just a small part of a much larger and far different world.

The two-lane road he now traveled was typical of so much of the state. The view was mostly pastureland and pine forest, meandering cattle, ragged billboards, and the occasional small stream hidden by overhanging branches of hardwoods that had claimed their places along the moist and fertile creek banks. Kudzu was constantly on the march, sending its rapidly growing tendrils in all directions, covering open ground, abandoned farmhouses, rusting farm equipment, and every unfortunate tree that happened to be in its ravenous path.

The soon-to-be completed I-85 had made this backwater route obsolete. The small businesses that had so far managed to survive were now doomed. The few storefronts he passed were boarded up and covered by graffiti. The only signs of commerce were the occasional gas stations, small shabby structures with bare dirt driveways leading to outdated pumps.

Gil was heading to Shiloh Crossroads to see what he could find out about a missing man named Jarvis Pendry. His news director, Tom

Burke, told him Pendry disappeared on a trip home to Baltimore from Fort Benning, possibly in Pickett County where his uncle had expected him to spend the night. Gil's assignment was to see what he could find out, shoot some film of the area, interview Pendry's uncle, and do a story on the missing man. Word was Pendry's wife might be staying with the uncle.

As he crossed the line into Pickett County, Gil was reminded of the county's dark racial history. A couple of shacks along the highway had flagpoles with faded rebel flags hanging limply. It was discouraging to think that attitudes were much the same in rural counties all over Georgia. Generations have come and gone, he thought, but attitudes have remained pretty much constant. Gil wondered when or if change would ever come.

Shiloh Crossroads didn't appear on his state road map, but Gil had a pretty good idea of where it was. He found it logically enough just west of where the state highway crossed Shiloh Road. The community wasn't an official town, just a cluster of modest houses and a small convenience store. Other than three black children playing outside the store, there was no sign of activity.

Willie Brooks's home was a small frame house set back from the road, down a gravel driveway lined by rosebushes and perennials like the wild and delicate Queen Anne's lace. The home rose from a sea of cobalt blue hydrangea blooms that contrasted beautifully with the white paint that had yet to lose its sheen. Despite its hardscrabble surroundings, Gil knew this home showed the owner's pride.

As he pulled up in front of the house, an old yellow lab that had been asleep on the front porch struggled to a sitting position and let out a couple of muffled and very unthreatening ruff-ruffs.

A tall, thin man opened the screened front door and emerged from the house, followed by a younger woman. They appeared to be expecting him.

Gil got out of the car, mounted the porch steps, and introduced himself to Willie Brooks and Evelyn Pendry.

"We can't thank you enough for coming here to help us." Evelyn appeared to be on the verge of tears, and he could hear the strain in her voice.

"Well, I hope we can help you," Gil said. "Why don't you tell me your story?"

They motioned Gil to a cane chair on the porch while they both sat on a wide swing hanging from the slatted ceiling. The old lab limped over and settled himself beneath the swing, laid his head between his paws, and, with a deep sigh, drifted off to sleep.

For the next half hour Evelyn told Gil everything she knew about her husband's disappearance. She said the last conversation they'd had was his telephone call from Fort Benning just before he left on his homeward journey, and he'd told her of his plans to stay with Uncle Willie. Since then, there had been no word, and she was assuming the worst.

"I think we need to get the news out that something's happened to my husband. I tried to contact the sheriff of this county and others, but they wouldn't even listen. They say, 'Oh, he'll turn up,' like he's some kind of vagrant or ne'er-do-well. They just won't give me the time of day. That's why I went to Reverend Timmons. He's helping us in contacting state authorities and, of course, news reporters."

Gil, who'd been writing all this in his notepad, looked up and into Evelyn's eyes as he asked the next question as gently as he could. "What do you think happened to your husband?"

She stared at him for several seconds and looked down. The only sound was the creaking of the chains as the swing swayed slightly.

"I fear my husband has been harmed. A black man traveling at night through this godforsaken area—who knows what might have happened. My Jarvis is a strong man, a proud man, a man who knows how to handle any situation. But I feel something terrible has happened, and we have to find out. You need to focus attention on this. We need answers now!"

Before Gil could respond, he heard the sound of crunching gravel.

A black and tan police car turned into the driveway. The emblem of the Pickett County Sheriff was emblazoned on the front doors.

Gil glanced at Brooks. "Looks like we're about to get some attention."

Brooks kept his eyes on the approaching cruiser as it eased up the driveway. "Maybe. But I see that's Sheriff McSwain. So it may not be the kind of attention we're hoping for."

THIRTEEN

THE HIGH SHERIFF

LUCAS MCSWAIN WAS born in Pickett County, starred as a lineman for Pickett County High School's Ragin' Rebels, fought with Patton's Third Army in Europe, and mustered out of the service with a law enforcement career in mind.

McSwain returned from the war as a local hero and was quickly hired as a sheriff's deputy. The rookie lawman was adept at learning the ropes of law enforcement in the rural South. His professional development included the art of knowing which cars to stop for speeding—the ones with out-of-county license tags—and which offending drivers to let off the hook—county commissioners and their family members, for example. He understood there were times when it was in his best interests to look the other way, to be discrete and, on occasion, merciful. Those occasions seldom if ever pertained to black citizens who ran afoul of the law in Pickett County.

As a deputy, McSwain had hauled in hundreds of blacks on charges of illegal gambling, drunk and disorderly conduct, resisting arrest, speeding, driving with a broken taillight, and the catch-all charge of loitering. Often the charges were trumped up, but black residents of Pickett knew that resistance was futile or even dangerous. Beatings in the county jail were common and, at least once in deputy McSwain's career, fatal. The cursory investigation in that case determined the young black man died of a heart attack. The deep gashes in his skull were never explained.

McSwain distinguished himself to county leaders by the selective way he wielded his power, and when the former sheriff retired, the young deputy had been the obvious choice to succeed him.

After ten years in the top job, McSwain's stocky, muscular line-man's physique had morphed into a build more typical of a rural South-ern sheriff. His girth had increased substantially, and every morning he noticed in his shaving mirror the inexorable formation of jowls. He chalked it up to aging, beer, and too much time sitting at his desk or prowling around the county slouched behind the wheel of his cruiser.

As he parked in front of Willie Brooks's house, McSwain saw a black woman and a young white man sitting with Brooks on his front porch. All three stood to watch him as he sauntered to the foot of the porch steps and looked up at them, adjusting his Stetson to shade his eyes from the sun.

"Morning, Willie."

Brooks acknowledged him with an unsmiling nod. "Sheriff."

McSwain was used to a more obsequious greeting from his black constituents. He had seen Brooks around but didn't know him well and didn't think he had ever been in trouble with the law. Maybe he should keep a closer eye on him.

"Willie, I understand somebody who was coming to see you never showed up. Your nephew, right? We've had a few calls, so I thought I'd drive out here to see what I can find out. You the wife?"

Evelyn spoke firmly with a voice McSwain didn't often hear from local blacks, a voice without a hint of subservience.

"Good morning, Sheriff. I am Evelyn Pendry, and I'm glad you're here. My husband Jarvis is missing, and I think whatever happened to him happened here in your county. I've tried to get your department involved without success, so it's good to know you're on the case, so to speak."

McSwain slowly moved his gaze to Gil and then pointed to the clearly marked WDX-TV station wagon he'd just parked alongside.

"That your car? You a reporter?"

"Yes sir. I'm Gil Matthews from WDX-TV News. Just trying to find out what's being done to locate Mr. Pendry. Mr. Brooks and Mrs. Pendry have been filling me in, and I'd like to talk to you about how your department's handling this."

Gil used a respectful tone, aware of the risks of confronting the sheriff in his own domain.

"Well, well, well," McSwain said with a chuckle. "Big-city news boy comin' out here to make my county look bad without a lick of proof that anything happened here."

"Sheriff, we don't want to make you or anybody else look bad," Gil quickly replied, his tone becoming defensive. "We have a missing man, a war veteran, a prominent Baltimore businessman. He was coming here to spend the night and disappeared. Like it or not, that's a story, and it's potentially a big story. Pickett County will be in the spotlight no matter what, and I think it's in your best interests to help us get to the bottom of this."

McSwain scowled dismissively and turned his eyes back to Evelyn. The mid-morning sun was hitting him squarely in the face, making him squint as he looked up at the shaded trio on the porch. Perspiration drops dotted his forehead and trickled down his face as a feeling of unease stirred in his gut.

The sheriff sensed that Evelyn Pendry was a woman he could not easily ignore. There was a refined dignity about her. She stood there on the porch with her arms crossed, a diminutive figure exuding strength and quiet anger. The directness of her gaze and the firmness of her voice had an almost intimidating effect on McSwain. He was accustomed to seeing fear in the eyes of his black constituents and getting respectful though sometimes grudging compliance. There was no hint of that from this woman.

"Lady, I don't know what happened to your husband. At this point he is just a missing black man. He'll probably turn up fine. I resent you calling the TV news. That just makes my job tougher."

There was no hesitation in Pendry's reply. "Just a missing black man? Sheriff, we are talking about my husband. I'm not from here—not from the South. I don't know your ways. But I do know that where I'm from, law enforcement would take this very seriously—unlike you.

I will not let this rest. Nor will I refrain from trying to get this story out. If you won't help me find out what happened to Jarvis, well…there are other ways."

The realization hit McSwain that this woman could be a problem for him. Implied intimidation wasn't working on her. She already had a local newsman here who was going to do a story, and there was potential for more outsiders coming into Pickett County if the story got bigger. He'd seen what happened in other rural counties when locals stirred up trouble over racial discrimination concerns. News reporters came in and caused further agitation, and then national news people might enter the picture and really roil the pot. In those cases the local sheriff often became the villain, the face of Southern bully-boy racial prejudice and brutality.

"Tell you what," McSwain said, quickly altering course. "Suppose I put the word out to my deputies, and we'll do a little investigation, check out the roads, talk to some people—see what we can find out. I'm sure it's nothin', but you've come a long way, so I'll help you out. Might want to check with the other counties in the area too."

Evelyn was surprised by the sudden shift in tone but put little stock in his promises. She sensed McSwain was intelligent enough to realize the negative potential for him and his county if the story turned out to be what she feared most. She resolved not to take the pressure off.

"Thank you, Sheriff." Her tone was flat, devoid of any hint of gratitude. "We'll be waiting to hear what you find out."

"Okay, then," the sheriff said as he took two steps back from the porch. He looked at Gil. "So what kind of story are you doin'? We don't need you stirrin' things up."

"Not sure yet," Gil responded. "I'm still getting my facts together, but we would like to interview you at some point."

"Nope. No interviews. Don't expect any cooperation from me or my men. You reporters don't tell it true. But Willie, Evelyn, we'll see what we can do to help you. I'll be in touch."

McSwain turned and walked back to his still running cruiser. As he turned the vehicle around and headed down the driveway, a call from his dispatcher came on his radio.

"Base to Sheriff. Base to Sheriff."

"This is the sheriff. Go ahead, Bobby."

"Sheriff, you heading back this way? There's somebody here to see you."

"I'm twenty minutes away. Who is it?"

"Says he's a GBI agent. Wants to talk about that missing black fella. And oh yeah—you've had a couple of calls from Baltimore. Somebody from a newspaper and another from a TV reporter up there."

McSwain slumped in his seat as he guided his cruiser down the dirt road to the blacktop leading to Shiloh Crossroads. "Ten-four. Be there shortly. Out."

He tossed the radio hand unit onto the front seat. He gripped his steering wheel hard and stepped on the gas, silently cursing Evelyn Pendry for pushing him into currents he was far from sure he could control.

FOURTEEN

THE DEAL

EVERYTHING WAS BETTER in the city's sanctuary for the elite. The homes in Buckhead were lovelier, the lawns greener, the air cleaner. Even on the sultriest summer day, the canopy of towering oaks sheltered this enclave from the unrelenting sun, making it seem a few degrees cooler than the ordinary world outside.

Verdant expanses of fescue and Bermuda swept up from street level to gray stone and stucco mansions surrounded by flowering rosebushes, boxwood hollies, junipers, and other ornamental plantings. The rolling terrain gave virtually every home a hilltop or hillside setting. Their lawns sloped down to the narrow, winding streets from which passersby could lift their gazes to admire the sumptuous abodes of the wealthy on high.

Harrison Parker often drove through this neighborhood on the way to his state capitol office just to admire its lushness and exclusivity—and of course the new governor's mansion now under construction, which he one day hoped to occupy. But on this Saturday morning Parker had a different destination in mind—the home of Devereaux Inman.

Inman was Atlanta's foremost power broker, a businessman and philanthropist who worked behind the scenes to guide the actions of the politicians who were elected to run the city. Parker was intrigued by his invitation and cancelled two campaign events to accept it.

Inman's home was at the end of a serpentine driveway that weaved through oceans of hydrangeas, rhododendron, azaleas, and, near the summit, mountain laurel. Strategically located sprinklers fired their pulsating bursts in rotating 180-degree arcs, making the natural moisture of the morning dew an irrelevant afterthought.

Parker drove his sedan slowly up the hill, admiring the neoclassical two-story structure that loomed above him. The façade was a mix of stucco and brick painted a dazzling but tasteful white. As his car crested the hill, he pulled into a large cobblestone parking area to the side of the house. Stepping from his car, he got a glimpse of the acreage behind the house—a large pool and pool house, a putting green, and what appeared to be a vegetable garden. Beyond these sunny and open areas were dark phalanxes of oak, sweet gum, beech, and hickory.

A yardman was clipping the boxwood hedge along the stone walkway to the front door, and as Parker passed by he nodded to the stooped figure and began to extend his hand before he thought better of it. It was the reflexive action of a vote-seeking candidate, and even though Parker knew black voters might view him with suspicion, he needed their support. He could tell by the yardman's awkward reaction that he didn't know who Parker was, and that was probably a good thing. This meeting with Inman was supposed to be a secret.

Parker knocked on the huge wooden front door, and after a few seconds a uniformed maid appeared and ushered him into the spacious open foyer. Parker couldn't resist the temptation to look upward. Two stories above, leaded glass windows filtered shafts of tinted sunlight into the entry hall, softening the formality that seemed to prevail everywhere he looked.

"Harrison, how are you?"

Devereaux Inman entered the foyer with an extended hand. Parker, initially startled, raised his hand to grip Inman's. He hoped Inman hadn't noticed him gawking like some rustic, but he knew his host would have taken full note.

"Thanks for the invitation, Mr. Inman." Parker opted not to use Inman's first name because he didn't feel it would be appropriate. He also chose to overlook the fact that most people would call him "Mr. Attorney General." He didn't expect that courtesy from Inman.

Inman broke the grip and swept his arm in the direction of his library. "Let's go where we can talk."

Inman was one of the most powerful men in the South, but his appearance was not intimidating. He was just short of six feet tall and so slim he almost looked unhealthy. His pale complexion and thinning gray hair did nothing to change that impression.

He was sixty-three years old, a self-made man who had risen from a bank teller's job to president of Southland Capital Bank, the city's oldest and most prestigious financial institution. He had never married.

Parker followed Inman across the floor of white marble that had been mined from quarries in Georgia's northern foothills. They walked through an arched doorway into the library, a windowless room that was dim and intimate. Floor-to-ceiling bookcases adorned opposing walls, flanked by dark oak paneling. Two upholstered easy chairs sat facing a fireplace on the far wall. Inman gestured toward one of the chairs and invited Parker to take a seat.

Once they had settled, Inman called out to a waiting uniformed butler to bring two Bloody Marys.

"My favorite Saturday morning beverage." Inman nodded toward Parker with an almost imperceptible smile.

On the coffee table between them was a copy of the *Savannah Morning News* with Mindy Williams's profile of Parker prominently displayed. The article had appeared in several newspapers around the state under the headline "Harrison Parker: New South or Old?" Mindy had portrayed Parker as a man caught between the past and the future, a candidate who could not publicly reject his segregationist past any more than he could fully embrace a progressive tomorrow. He was trying to have it both ways, the article implied, subtly courting segregationist support while hoping more moderate voters would back him because they had no other choice.

The butler arrived with drinks on a tray and carefully handed each man the spicy red mixture.

"Thank you very much, Toby. That will be all."

As Toby slowly backed from the room with his empty tray, Inman raised his glass and took a sip. Parker did the same.

Inman settled back and gestured toward the newspaper. "What did you think of the article?"

"It's caused me a few problems. Makes me look a bit"—Parker paused, searching for the right word—"devious."

Inman chuckled. "In the world of politics, to be devious is not necessarily a vice. And it seems to me Miss Williams has you pegged pretty well." He shifted in his chair, crossed his legs, and took another sip of his Bloody Mary. "You are in a difficult place. You need the votes of white moderates—no idea how many of them are out there—and the blacks, but you can't openly ask for their help. If you run even slightly to the left, you play right into Roscoe Pike's hands. You can't win unless you cut into Pike's support. You've got to convince a lot of those lower-class whites that you'll be a better governor for them than Pike. But you and I know those folks are not going to vote for anyone who talks about civil rights or economic progress for the poor black people of our state."

Parker realized Inman had sized up his situation perfectly. He had indeed skirted the edges of segregationist support for months, but he hoped he'd been able to muddy the issue just enough to hold on to the middle—those voters he had to win.

Parker began to speak but Inman cut him off. Devereaux Inman had the floor, and he was far from finished. He uncrossed his legs, planted his feet on the Chinese carpet, and leaned forward toward Parker.

"Our city is at a great crossroads. We can go the way of Birmingham with its short-sighted leaders who unleashed police dogs and fire hoses and made that city an object of shame and ridicule before the world, or we can find a way to make accommodations to the blacks to keep the peace, to keep them in bounds while we still call the shots. The South is very fertile ground for great economic enterprise. We've been held back for so long by two great challenges—air conditioning and race. We've solved the AC part, but race is a much more complex challenge, and I don't expect we'll ever solve that one completely. But we can make progress, and if we show the world that our city is willing to try, willing to work with our black citizens, then there are an awful lot of companies who'd love to set up shop here and thrive on what we can offer—a progressive and peaceful setting, great climate, cheap labor. We are at the crossroads, and you, Harrison Parker, can be the instrument, the leader who takes us down the right road."

Inman slumped back in his seat, signed heavily, took another sip of his cocktail, and waited for Parker to respond.

"I like the sound of that, Mr. Inman. If I win, I assure you I can work with you to move our state forward. But I'll need your help."

Inman stroked his chin with his left hand as Parker spoke. Then he leaned forward in his chair again and set his drink on a side table.

"You will have our support. You will need it. It's going to be a high-wire balancing act. You need to win over segregationists who have misgivings about Pike while not scaring away Negro voters. You'll need to talk like a states' rights conservative but keep race out of it. That will be your signal to black voters that you might be worth taking a chance on. They won't love you, but they'll vote for you to keep Pike out. We just have to hope enough of them actually show up to put you over the top."

Inman picked up his drink, shook the glass briefly, then drained it before continuing. "Harrison, you've done a good job so far of blurring the issues. I don't know what's in your heart, but I'm hoping your pragmatic brain will guide you in this campaign. Once you're elected you'll be more free to speak your mind *and* your heart."

The two men rose and shook hands.

"Thank you, Mr. Inman. I understand and appreciate your support."

"For the record, this meeting never took place," Inman cautioned. "Nobody knows you're here except for my confidants. We will make things happen for you—money, advice, editorial support—but no one must know. It's the way I operate." Inman smiled and winked. "And I think we both know a public endorsement from big-city fat cats isn't going to help you much in rural Georgia."

Inman walked with Parker to the front door.

"Good luck. Remember to stay on message and call anytime you need advice."

As Parker walked to his car, he once again noticed the yardman, still trimming the endless hedge. The man looked up briefly, nodded, then continued clipping. Parker wondered if the hedge trimmer had any awareness of the campaign or the potential impact he and other black voters could have on the outcome.

Parker had just been given the blessing and support of Devereaux Inman and his shadowy cabal of rich and influential magnates. He welcomed this unexpected boost to his campaign, but he also worried about the cost of his cooperation. It was a double-edged sword to be sure, and the path to victory would be marked by compromises, but as Inman had said, Parker was a pragmatist. He would do what he had to do to win.

FIFTEEN

PEAVINE CREEK

THE SEDAN THAT had once belonged to Jarvis Pendry slowly emerged from the languid brown water of Peavine Creek, its turquoise color almost totally obscured by mud and debris. The vehicle moved jerkily as it was dragged up through the underbrush of the creek bank, the three taut cables attached to its undercarriage straining with each foot of progress. The whirring and grinding of the cable reels on the tow trucks forced the lawmen standing at the top of the decline to raise their voices.

Once the vehicle had cleared the water, they could see the shattered driver's side window. As creek water spilled from the chassis and cascaded back into the creek, they saw a leg partially emerge through the window.

Sheriff McSwain raised his arms into the air and yelled, "Stop!" The ruined car shuddered to a halt as the cable reels paused. McSwain and Agent Bill Conyers of the Georgia Bureau of Investigation slipped and slid down the steep incline to the car and looked inside.

Through the broken window they saw the bloated corpse covered by mud, twigs, and decaying leaves. The odors of decomposition mingled with the musky smell of the almost stagnant stream, causing the young agent to feel a hint of nausea. McSwain, hardened by combat in Europe, was unfazed. Though the body was unrecognizable in its current state, both men knew it was Jarvis Pendry. Conyers stifled his urge to vomit and motioned for a state photographer to come down and record the crime scene.

Two fishermen had discovered the partially submerged car earlier that day as they looked for an opening in the trees to drop their lines about a hundred yards upstream from the bridge. They had walked down an overgrown, rutted roadway that led from the bridge along the creek bank and then spotted the vehicle. Briars and other weeds had almost choked the road from view, but there was just enough room for a car to pass. The tire-matted vegetation made it obvious that Pendry's car was driven this way and then pushed down the bank through a gap in the trees and into the creek, where it remained submerged until discovery eight days later.

As the photographer moved around the vehicle snapping pictures, Sheriff McSwain and Agent Conyers scrambled back up the slippery bank. It seemed clear to both men that Pendry had been murdered at the bridge. Shotgun pellets had chipped the concrete at the end of the bridge, leaving scores of tiny white scars peppering the dingy surface. The killers had driven the car with the body still inside and dumped it in Peavine Creek.

Both men could feel tension building as they considered the impact of this murder and the challenge of solving it. They were still breathing hard from climbing the creek bank. Sweat droplets welled from their faces, trickling down to be absorbed by the dampening collars of their shirts.

Conyers turned to look at McSwain. "Well, Sheriff, looks like we've got a tiger by the tail. The media's gonna be all over this one. We're really going to need your help getting whoever did this."

McSwain kept his gaze fixed on the wrecked car as the photographer completed his work. "Well, Bill. I was just about to say you and your state buddies can stand ready to assist *me* in the unlikely event I need your help. From all I can see, this crime was committed in Pickett County—and that's my jurisdiction. Of course, you state boys have all the scientists and labs and all that stuff, and I may need some of your— *expertise*—don't you know. But otherwise, I think me and my folks can handle this just fine."

McSwain was slightly taller and much beefier than Conyers and had worn a lawman's badge much longer, but the young agent was not intimidated. Conyers was of average height and slim, but he had the rangy moves of an athlete, and his short-sleeve dress shirt revealed wiry and well-muscled arms. His crew cut made him appear even younger than he was, but the steady gaze of his cool gray eyes conveyed a sense of authority.

"Sheriff, I understand your concern. We don't want to intrude on a local matter. But the victim was traveling across county lines, he's from out of state, and—let's be honest here—he was a prominent black military officer. There's no way you can keep this a quiet little Pickett County matter. I think before this is over, you're going to want us to be involved."

McSwain turned his head toward Conyers. "Maybe so. But I doubt it. We handle things our own way in Pickett County. We don't need much outside help from the state or anyone else. We don't want feds in here. And we don't need no media watching our every move either."

At that moment, as if on cue, Mindy Williams emerged from the brush along the abandoned roadway, notebook in hand and Pentax camera hanging from her shoulder. Behind her was Gil Matthews with his camera mounted on his shoulder. They had walked in from the bridge.

The sheriff was angry. The veins in his broad, dimpled nose darkened. "What the hell are *you* doin' here?" McSwain recognized the cameraman from his earlier encounter, but he'd never seen Mindy. She stepped up to face the sheriff, pausing briefly to swat away a buzzing mosquito.

"I'm Mindy Williams from the AP. What can you tell us about the recovered car? Is Colonel Pendry's body inside? Are there any suspects?" She raised her notepad and prepared to write the sheriff's responses.

Gil aimed his camera and began filming the exchange. McSwain raised his hand and thrust his palm toward Gil's camera, blocking the lens.

"No pictures! Not until I say so," McSwain shouted. "This is an active crime scene, and you're not allowed to be here."

Gil lowered his camera lens slightly to stare at the sheriff, but he kept the camera running while Mindy pleaded their case.

"Sheriff, this is a major story. We have every right to be here to cover it. Please allow us to do our job."

Conyers moved closer to the sheriff and gripped his elbow. "Sheriff...a word?" He guided a reluctant McSwain several steps back, turned away from the reporters, and spoke softly. "I know you don't want my advice, but I'm giving it anyway. This is just the beginning. Reporters are going to be all over this story—and not just locals like these two. You're gonna have the networks here, the *New York Times*, all manner of obnoxious Yankees who will run right over you to get what they want. You'd better get used to it. You don't have to like them—hell, you don't even have to respect them, but you better learn how to handle them because if you don't, you'll be made to look like an authoritarian fool. You don't beat news people on something like this. The more cooperative you are, the better for you and your county. I know that's against everything you believe, but that's just the way it is."

Conyers had been a state investigator for six years and knew how reporters operated. He'd even taken a few journalism courses at the University of Georgia as he pursued his degree in criminology. When he entered law enforcement, he quickly allowed himself to be cultivated by enterprising reporters looking for reliable sources. They found him to be someone they could trust for inside information, and they protected him from exposure to his law enforcement colleagues. When he learned about the discovery of Jarvis Pendry's car, he had tipped off his closest contact—Mindy Williams.

McSwain seemed perplexed and a bit confused by what Conyers was telling him. Being a sheriff in a rural county was akin to being a potentate. The county was his fiefdom, and his subjects were loyal, respectful, and sometimes fearful. He dispensed his brand of justice without fear of being challenged. Now this young upstart raised the specter of his insular domain being invaded by forces he could not control.

He was beginning to feel overwhelmed. He knew the state could quickly take over his investigation. And what if the case went federal— some sort of civil rights violation claimed—bringing in the FBI?

McSwain was not used to this kind of pressure, but he was savvy enough to understand that he needed needed to consider the advice Conyers was giving him. There was no time to reflect on his options or ponder his next move. Reporters were here, and the time was now.

He moved back toward Mindy and Gil, who'd been watching their conversation, even though they couldn't hear it.

"Okay, let's see if we can find a way to coexist out here. I don't know who tipped you off, but I'm not happy about it." McSwain's voice dropped to a grudging mumble. "But here you are, and I understand you've got jobs to do—but so do I. Go ahead and take your pictures. I'll try to answer your questions, even though at this point we don't know much, and we've got a ton of work to do."

Gil focused his lens on the sheriff and started his camera as Mindy, poised with notepad and pen, began to fire questions. Conyers stayed in the background, making fleeting eye contact with Mindy. He knew she was subtly conveying her thanks for his help. He hoped her gratitude might one day lead to something more.

SIXTEEN

SOSEBY

IT WAS JUST after noon, and Mindy was feeling the pressure. She needed to file her story—a story she knew would be a national headline. Until today Jarvis Pendry had been a missing person, but now this Maryland war hero was apparently the latest victim of racist killers in the rural South.

Despite the sheriff's grudging responses to her questions, she had enough to quickly write her story and dictate it to the regional bureau. Right now it was an exclusive, but the clock was moving, and she desperately needed to find a telephone to break the story.

Although Gil had been on the scene thanks to Mindy sharing her information, he still had to drive his film to the station for it to be processed and edited before the six o'clock news. Her story reported to Associated Press would go around the world well before that.

She and Gil hiked back to the cars they'd parked along the highway near the bridge. Gil would drive directly to the TV station, and Mindy would try to find a business or home where she could borrow a phone to dictate her story. She thought of the gas station they'd passed a few miles back on their way to the bridge. Gil said he needed gas and would stop there as well.

They both pulled their cars onto the dirt and gravel driveway of the pale green cinder-block building, home of Soseby's Gas and Sundries according to the sign on the roof. Gil parked alongside one of the old pumps, Mindy right by the front screen door. Seeing no attendant, Gil began to gas up his vehicle while Mindy pulled open the screen door and entered.

She noticed a "Pike for Governor" sign taped to the wall to the left of the door. As her pupils adjusted to the dim interior, she saw a man behind the counter silently staring at her.

"Hello, I'm Mindy Williams of the Associated Press. Do you have a phone I could use?"

The man shifted his position slightly and, continuing his stare, answered with a contemptuous snarl.

"No. Not for you. Not for any goddamned news reporters. Get your ass out of my store and be on your way."

Mindy responded without hesitation. "Sir, I really need to use your phone. It's an emergency. A man has been murdered up the road, and I need to get my story out."

She thought she saw an almost imperceptible reaction by the man, not of surprise so much as acknowledgement.

"You see that sign?" He jerked his arm upward, pointing his thumb toward the crudely lettered sign on the wall behind him. "We reserve the right to refuse service. So request denied."

At that moment Gil came through the door and stood behind Mindy, quickly sensing the hostile confrontation. "I need to pay you for the ten dollars worth of regular I just put in my car."

The man behind the counter erupted in anger. "You one of those TV boys? Wish I'd seen your car before you pulled in. If I had, I wouldn't let you pump. Gimme that ten, and then you two get out of here."

They heard a pattering of gravel outside as a dark blue Ford Fairlane pulled off the highway and parked alongside Mindy's car. Agent Bill Conyers emerged from the car and stepped inside.

He nodded to Mindy and Gil, then looked at the proprietor who'd crossed his arms across his chest in a defensive stance behind the counter. No one had to tell Conyers he'd walked into the middle of trouble.

"I'm Bill Conyers. GBI. Is there a problem here?"

Thankful for Conyers's intervention, Mindy rushed to explain. "We just stopped here to get some gas and use his phone to file my story, but he's telling us to get out. He doesn't like news people, to put it mildly."

A slight frown crinkled Conyers's forehead as he slowly nodded. "I was on my way back to headquarters and saw your cars. Just thought I'd stop by to get some gas and be sure all was okay. Glad I did."

He then directed his attention to the man behind the counter. "Hello, sir. May I ask your name?" His tone was courteous but firm, the tone a lawman uses when quick compliance is not optional.

The man hesitated briefly before responding. "Hiram Soseby. I own this place, and, as my sign indicates, I reserve the right to refuse service to anybody I don't like. That might include coloreds, but it surely applies to news reporters too. I support law enforcement so I will serve you."

Conyers glanced at Mindy and Gil before fixing Soseby in his gaze once again. "That's very nice of you, Mr. Soseby, but I'd like to ask you kindly to allow Miss Williams to use your telephone. Something terrible has happened in your county, just up the road in fact, and people need to know about it. It won't take too long, and we'd all appreciate your cooperation."

Soseby realized that despite his polite tone, Agent Conyers was giving him no choice. After a slight pause he spoke grudgingly. "Phone's over there. Be quick about it."

Soseby slumped back against the wall behind the counter. Glancing at Gil he said, "I'll take that ten dollars too."

Mindy rushed to the phone, dialed the AP bureau, and began dictating the story she had composed on her notepad while Soseby watched sullenly from across the room.

"The body of a missing reserve Army officer has been discovered. Jarvis Pendry of Baltimore, Maryland, a Negro, was apparently ambushed by shotgun as he drove home from reserve training at Fort Benning. His car was pulled from a creek in rural Pickett County today, eight days after he was first reported missing."

Mindy dictated a few more paragraphs and hung up with a huge sigh of relief. As she passed Conyers she silently mouthed "Thank you" before heading to her car with Gil right behind.

As they pulled away, Conyers walked to the counter and stared at the still scowling Soseby. "Mr. Soseby, I'd suggest you revise your business plan. You can begin by taking down that sign because you no longer have the right to refuse service to anyone. Your gas station is a public accommodation, and if someone walks through that door, black or white, you must serve them. You may not like it, but that's the law."

Soseby reacted with as much contempt as he could muster. "Well, we'll see about that. Sheriff McSwain's a family friend. I think we'll not be changing a thing."

Conyers sighed deeply and began looking around the dim interior of the station. A few more "Pike for Governor" signs were scattered about amid the Penzoil and Pabst Blue Ribbon advertisements. A large rebel flag was nailed to the wall near some small tables and a vending machine.

"Mr. Soseby, I'm curious about something. Did you see or hear anything suspicious on the night Jarvis Pendry was murdered not two miles from here? That was on July second. Anything at all? Hear a shotgun blast maybe?"

Soseby was quick to answer no. Conyers thought it curious that Soseby had no questions about the crime.

"Well, I'm sure you'll let your good friend Sheriff McSwain know if you remember anything or hear anything."

Conyers turned to leave. As he opened the screen door, he looked back at Soseby. "Oh, one more thing. You're going to be seeing a lot of investigators and reporters in this area over the next few weeks. I'd suggest you give that some thought before you start chasing people away. Folks may think you have something to hide."

As Soseby watched Conyers guide his Fairlane onto the blacktop, his son Caleb emerged from a back room.

"Damn, Dad...do you think they know anything?"

Soseby slowly shook his head. "No. We covered our tracks. They can't tie us to anything. Just be sure you keep your mouth shut, and we'll be fine."

"That GBI agent makes me nervous. Have you talked to the sheriff?"

The elder Soseby nodded. "Lucas came by yesterday for a Coke and a Moon Pie. Told me about the missing black and asked if I'd seen anything or heard any talk. Of course, I said no. But now that they've found him there'll be a lot of heat. We've just got to lay low."

Soseby turned on his radio to catch the news at the top of the hour, national news followed by local items. The announcer's voice rose over a slight field of static. "The top national story: a murder mystery in the South with racial overtones. A Baltimore businessman—a Negro war veteran—has been murdered on a rural Georgia highway..."

As the newscast continued, Soseby reflected on the fact that the story he was hearing had moments ago been dictated from this very spot. He felt a sense of excitement that his deed was being proclaimed to the world, but there was also regret that he would never receive the credit he deserved. He would have to be silently content with the knowledge that his bold and violent action had sent a message the world could not ignore.

SEVENTEEN

DEADLINE

GIL ARRIVED AT the station at four fifteen, well past the normal deadline for getting film in the processor for the six o'clock news. He immediately ran the film magazine to the lab chief, who had been alerted and understood the urgency of developing the film as quickly as possible.

Gil jogged down the long hallway back to the newsroom, aware that he reeked of perspiration after his hike through the brambles of Peavine Creek. He made a half-hearted attempt to pick off the beggar lice clinging to his blue jeans as he approached the news director's office.

Tom Burke was going over some copy with a young reporter but brushed him aside when he saw Gil.

"Hey, Gil. You're a mess, but it sounds like you got really good stuff. The story's been on the wire for an hour. Unbelievable! It's a clean exclusive for TV, so nice going. Did Mindy tip you off?"

Gil swiped his dripping forehead with his shirtsleeve. "Yeah, Mindy has a good source with the GBI. She wanted me to go with her. I don't blame her. Pickett's a pretty rough place."

"Okay. The film should be out in thirty minutes. We'll open with shots of the car coming out of the creek. We've got a family photo of the victim and some biographical info. We've been getting a lot of stuff from a station in Baltimore. Here's what we have."

Burke handed Gil a folder containing some wire copy and information from Baltimore about Jarvis Pendry.

"Go write the story. Take as much time as you need, but with so little film and information we're guessing three minutes max. We've got an interview with the state GBI chief that will be about forty-five seconds. Carney is taking care of that, but he'll want to coordinate with you.

The network will be taking your story as a feed for their six thirty news, but"—he added with a slight grin—"don't let that make you nervous."

Gil turned to look for a vacant typewriter. It was ten after five. Fifty minutes before air. He inserted a five-copy carbon script pack into the Royal typewriter, swiveled the roller to engage it, and began pounding out his story. The clattering of keys from his typewriter and others around the newsroom, the constant metallic jangle from the row of wire copy machines, the cross talk and yelling of information and instructions as the deadline tightened all created a cacophony that would make concentration impossible for most. But for Gil and the other reporters writing their stories, it was a brassy symphony. They had learned to thrive on the high-decibel chaos of an active newsroom, and they had no problem shutting everything out and putting their immediate task in sharp focus. The tighter the deadline, the more intense the concentration. The more stress, the better the final product.

Anchor Grayson Kincaid walked over and placed his hand lightly on Gil's back. "Sorry. Know you're busy. Let me know when you've got a script I can time."

Gil barely acknowledged the anchorman and kept his head bent forward as he typed sentence after sentence, always thinking of the film he would use with his copy, the special language melding words and pictures. Kincaid understood and moved on to another desk, another reporter. It was his pre-newscast ritual—talking to reporters and learning their stories so he would be knowledgeable when he read them on the air. Some anchors were simply readers, but not Kincaid. And for that he was a respected figure in the newsroom and the community.

A staffer came running into the newsroom with a reel of the processed film in hand just as Gil seized the last page of his script and ripped it from the typewriter. Kincaid, who'd been hovering, quickly timed the script, and Gil ran to the editing room to cut the film. It was five forty. Twenty minutes to air.

The film danced between the editing reels as Gil selected his shots then cut and spliced the film. His images looked fine. The shots were crisp and colorful. The viewers would get a good feeling for what it was like to be on that creek bank when the murdered man's car was pulled from the stream. Only the pungent smell and the mosquito bites would be missing.

He quickly selected a sound bite from Sheriff McSwain, which wasn't difficult because his answers were so terse. The interview segment he chose showed McSwain looking at the ground, obviously ill at ease and sharing as little as he could.

"We don't have any suspects. We'll let you know when we come up with something."

Gil spliced the sound bite into the story, rewound the film onto a reel, and quickly headed for the projection room. It was five fifty-six. Four minutes to air.

Kincaid was already at the anchor desk and gave a slight nod when he was told that his lead story was edited and ready. He had little doubt Gil would come through. He always did.

The anchorman finished off his pre-newscast routine, shuffling through his stack of scripts and then straightening the pile by constantly tapping the papers on the desk to align the edges. From the corner of his eye he could see the closing credits of *Mr. Ed*, the talking horse lead-in show, rolling in the studio monitor as the familiar theme played.

For a split second the screen faded to black before springing back to life with a burst of edited scenes of the city accompanied by the upbeat musical theme of the six o'clock news. Then came the announcer's voice as the music reached a crescendo.

"Now live from Atlanta, Georgia, WDX-TV's News at Six."

Viewers then saw scenes of Jarvis Pendry's car being dragged from Peavine Creek and heard Kincaid's voice, grim and authoritative.

"Sudden death on a country road…" His narration continued as the scene unfolded, giving the audience the details of the grisly murder. "A shotgun blast claimed the life of Jarvis Pendry, a Baltimore businessman and Army veteran on his way home from reserve duty at Fort Benning. This is exclusive film from the scene of the murder."

At this point a photo of Pendry in his Army uniform filled the screen. "Pendry was a World War Two combat veteran," Kincaid continued. "He leaves behind a wife and two children."

The photo of Pendry slowly dissolved into the face of Kincaid, looking slightly off screen and then turning his gaze to face his viewers.

"Good evening. I'm Grayson Kincaid."

His brow furrowed, his eyes intense, his tone somber, the anchor continued reporting on the murder, introducing filmed interview segments with Sheriff McSwain and GBI Chief Barney Peters, who vowed the killers would be tracked down and punished, though his slow drawl and deadpan expression drained any sense of urgency from his promise. Kincaid then told viewers that his news team would continue to cover the story over the days and weeks to come.

There were rare times when Kincaid, though isolated in the studio, could sense his unseen audience responding to a story on his newscast. He could feel that vibration tonight. He knew the coverage of the Pendry murder was having an impact. Some would react with horror, others with outrage, and some with disdain, accusing the station of sensationalizing the story. But there was little doubt that the murder of Jarvis Pendry would dominate the news over the summer and beyond. Kincaid was sure the coverage would depict Georgia as the heart of darkness, a place where black people faced death simply by driving state roads after sundown, and Pendry would be portrayed as another martyr in the long and bloody battle for equality.

Gil's film would lead the network news in a matter of moments. Scenes of the grim discovery on Peavine Creek and the photograph of the handsome, smiling face of the victim in his uniform would be seen in living rooms around the nation. The crime would bring scores of national and international reporters over the coming days. The unremitting onslaught would sweep state leaders, law enforcement, and reporters into the maelstrom created by the murder of Jarvis Pendry, with an outcome no one could foresee.

EIGHTEEN

HAPPY HOUR

AS TWILIGHT FADED into darkness, the blue neon sign over the door of Marty's Tavern flickered to life, beckoning regulars and visitors alike to come in and enjoy a brew. A local newspaper columnist had made owner Marty Mason a local hero with frequent columns about the colorful characters and political goings-on at his watering hole. Marty's was a popular hangout for politicians, media figures, and the assortment of lesser knowns who wanted to be around them. Framed autographed photos of celebrities gripping and grinning with the legendary bar owner covered the walls. It was a place where political opinions were discussed and debated with good-natured passion. Most views were tolerated, but the prevailing opinions resided on the moderate to liberal end of the spectrum.

Political debate wasn't on Gil's mind when he stopped off at Marty's on his way home. He just needed a drink after a long day. He also thought he might have a chance to mingle with the network guys in town for coverage of the Jarvis Pendry killing.

As he made his way to the bar, he heard a familiar voice call his name from a nearby booth. It was Mindy.

"Hi, Gil. Like to join us?"

Gil saw that Mindy was with a couple of men he didn't know. Both were sitting across the table from Mindy, so Gil slid into the seat next to her. He was thankful he'd freshened up at the station and put on the clean shirt he kept there for situations like this.

He was amazed at the way Mindy had transformed herself after a day of tramping through the woods at Peavine Creek. She was wearing blue jeans and a pink blouse and looked refreshed, relaxed, and lovely.

Her hair, released from its ponytail, fell to the top of her shoulders, and a hint of her perfume softened the coarser scents of the bar environment.

"Gil, I want you to meet a couple of colleagues with AP. Bill Hirsh and Jerry McDonald. Bill covers the race beat for AP, and Jerry is in our Baltimore bureau. Gentlemen, meet Gil Matthews of WDX, one of the best photogs around."

As they shook hands across the table, Hirsh congratulated Gil on his exploits covering the violence at Southside Stadium, and McDonald chimed in as well. Gil was flattered that they knew his name and what he'd done. For once he'd escaped the anonymity that was the norm for most photographers.

Hirsh had an angular face that was darkened by his eight o'clock shadow. He was in his early forties, but his deep-set eyes and creased forehead made him appear older. He was also going bald, and the thin strands brushed across the top of his head only emphasized that fact.

They were all drinking beer from large frosty mugs, so Gil waved to a waiter and ordered one for himself.

Hirsh took a sip of his beer. "I watched your station's newscast tonight. Very nice job on the car and body recovery. I'm sure your competitors were eating their hearts out." Then, grinning ever so slightly, he added, "I hear you might have had a little assist with the story."

Gil smiled, looked down at the mug he was cradling with both hands on the table, and then nodded in Mindy's direction. "I have very good sources."

Mindy smiled too and said, "We work as a team. I get the tip and Gil drives me to the story."

Gil gave a brief chuckle. "This was Mindy's story from the get-go. She knew about it before anyone else and was kind enough to pass the tip on to me. There'll be a day when I'll repay the favor. You scratch my back...well you know..."

"How well I do know," said Hirsh. "Where would we be in the news business without our sources? Mindy, I guess if you tell us who tipped you off you'd have to kill us."

They all laughed at that and ordered another round of beers.

Hirsh raised his mug and tipped it toward Mindy. "How about a poem for the occasion from our in-house bard?"

Mindy looked toward the ceiling and stroked her chin. "Let's see, let's see. How about this little ditty courtesy of A. E. Housman? I think it works for this distinguished occasion.

"Malt does more than Milton can
to justify God's ways to man
Ale Man, ale's the stuff to drink
For fellows whom it hurts to think.
Look into the pewter pot to
See the world as the world's not."

"Perfect," Hirsh said, laughing. "If we drink enough, maybe we'll forget the stuff we have to cover. That may explain why I'm a borderline alcoholic."

After more laughter and small talk, McDonald asked about what he was likely to discover when he traveled to Pickett County tomorrow. It was obvious he had not covered the South before, and he was apprehensive about what might happen.

Hirsh, a veteran wire service reporter who'd been on the race beat in the South since the late '50s, couldn't give much reassurance.

"It's a rough place. I've never been there, but I know what kind of place it is because they're all over the South. Ignorant white folks, intimidated black folks, and a high sheriff whose word is law. You will not receive a warm welcome. Oh, the black folks will be glad you're there, but they can't express that. Most white folks will resent your presence and some of them could be dangerous. Our safety will be in numbers, and I'm happy to say there will be a shitload of media in Pickett County tomorrow. And if we're lucky, we'll have some state lawmen who will buffer us from the local deputies and let us do our jobs. But I wouldn't count on it. Just stick with me, Jerry. You'll be fine."

Gil chimed in. "Not a bad appraisal for a guy who's never been there. The sheriff is a bully, but he's not dumb. He seems to understand that offering too much resistance will only increase his problems. I don't think he wants to be another Bull Connor."

Hirsh shook his head. "I think you're giving him too much credit. These Southern sheriffs are all the same. Just like their constituents—stupid and mean."

Hirsh's supercilious attitude was rubbing Gil the wrong way. And the beer was having a quick effect because he hadn't eaten since lunch. "Bill, I'm curious. Where did you grow up? Where'd you go to school?"

Hirsh picked a couple of beer nuts and popped them into his mouth. "I'm from New York. Grew up in the Albany area. Got my journalism degree from Columbia, got a job with AP, covered local governments for a while, then moved up to congressional reporter in the mid-fifties."

Gil took a sip of beer and nodded. "And how long have you been in the South?"

"Since '59. God, I can't believe it. Six years on the race beat. It's been an ordeal, but I guess in our business you go where the news is."

"You're making the South sound like a third world country. Anything you like about it?" Gil's once congenial tone had taken a sharper edge.

Hirsh stroked his chin with his fingers and looked around the room as if searching his brain for something good to say about the South.

"Well…the women are good-looking." He smiled and winked at Mindy, who barely acknowledged the remark. "You've got some good college football here, and once you develop a tolerance for grease, the food is tasty."

Gil fought the impulse to call Hirsh on his condescension and instead responded calmly but firmly. "But what about the people of the region? What do you tell your readers around the world about our people?"

98

Hirsh could see that he had offended Gil. "You're a born and bred Southerner, right?"

"That's correct. Born and bred. A native. And I probably don't fit your template of a white Southerner. I'm not ignorant, I'm not mean, I don't hate, and on occasion I can even speak in grammatically correct English."

Hirsh pushed his palms toward Gil, trying to calm him. "Hey—no offense meant. Sorry."

But Gil ignored that remark and kept on pressing. "In fact, Bill, there are a lot of Southerners like me. People of good will who understand the plight of black people, who want to do the right thing, who recognize that racial segregation is against everything America should stand for. But I'm pretty sure that a sizable segment of white Southerners has not been represented very well by your reporting or, for that matter, the reporting of any national news organization. What we see are the stereotypes in town after town, county after county. They are irresistible for the media, but there's a deeper story about what's happening in the South, and that's just not being told."

Hirsh seemed taken aback by Gil's deeply felt remarks. "Where are those decent Southerners you refer to? I'll grant you they do exist, but for the most part they are drowned out by the loudest voices who embody the worst of the South—the worst of humanity. You have a few enlightened leaders—your mayor for example—who get plenty of coverage. But they are the exceptions, not the rule. The rule is Southern bigotry and all that goes with it—racial insults, racial violence, and a 'forgit hell' attitude that drowns out everything else. I do agree with some of what you say, Gil, but do you think you might be letting your roots in the South influence your objectivity?"

Gil expected the question and was quick with an answer. "I would acknowledge that possibility if you acknowledge that your roots in the great, white North influence your reporting. You came of age in an affluent area with hardly any black folks around. We, on the other hand, black and white, know each other for better or worse. We engage,

we talk, we banter, and to a great extent we understand each other because we are thrust together in this region. Our dialogue is often tense
and sometimes messy, but we know who we are. I do believe that ultimately the fact that we have a multiracial society in the South will bring
about change more quickly than you might imagine. But I will grant
you we are just beginning that journey."

Gil put a few dollars on the table and prepared to leave, but Mindy
grabbed his arm, and Hirsh pushed the money back across the table.

"Well said, Gil. I know you're a talented photographer, but you
should probably be doing commentaries for NBC. I do appreciate your
point of view and—touché—you're right about me. As reporters we
sometimes do fall into patterns—use templates as you say—to bolster
stereotypes that fit the expectation of our audiences. Thanks for reminding us of that. I'll remember it tomorrow when we go to Pickett
County."

Jerry McDonald, who'd been sitting back in his rumpled suit listening, finally spoke. "I appreciate this dialogue. It's helpful to this
Yankee who's seldom been south of the Mason-Dixon line...and I
wouldn't be here now if it weren't for the murder of one of our Baltimore citizens. I must say I find the South a very complicated place.
Thanks for helping me understand better. I have to tell you we certainly
have our own racial problems in Baltimore, and our time in the ring is
probably coming."

Jerry was interrupted by raucous laughter across the room. Marty
Mason was working the room, shaking hands, slapping backs, and
sharing stories with the network correspondents who often came to
visit when their assignments brought them to town.

Mindy, who'd not said a word for some time, swiveled in her seat
and faced Gil. "Methinks thou doth protest too much, Gil. I appreciate
how you feel about the South. I'm a local too, and it sometimes pains
me to have to report on the nastiness of this racial revolution we've
been covering for so long. But when you talk about the good white
Southerner, I have to ask why don't we hear from them? Dr. King has

been very outspoken on this point. What was it he said in his letter from the Birmingham jail? Can't remember the exact quote, but the essence of it is those who ignore evil—who fail to speak up, who do nothing about discrimination—they are just as guilty as those who actually cause the evil."

Gil gave a vigorous nod. "Mindy, it's true. Too many people of good will don't have the guts to speak out. There's too much to lose. They'd get the cold shoulder from neighbors, might put their job in jeopardy, might subject their husbands, wives, or children to some abuse. It's just too easy to do nothing. It takes courage to stand up for what's right, and white courage in the South is in short supply these days."

Hirsh jumped in. "Exactly. But the great irony is that while racism seems to always be center stage, ultimately all the attention is counter-productive. The more extreme the racists get, the more coverage they get, and the more they hurt their own cause. They are hastening their own demise. And they just don't get it. I guarantee black protesters would much prefer to deal with a bunch of violent rednecks than a bunch of so-called moderate white folks. With the rednecks they'll get coverage, which is what they need to stir the nation and pressure Congress to reach their ultimate goal."

Hirsh raised his mug. "Lady and gentlemen, a toast. Here's to all the rednecks. Where would we be without 'em?"

And with that everyone laughed, clinked their mugs, drank deeply, and ordered a full pitcher for the table. After about half an hour, Hirsh and McDonald headed for their hotel. Gil and Mindy walked toward the rear exit and the lot where they'd parked their cars. Mindy seemed unsteady, and Gil linked his arm with hers to give her some support as they walked into the dark lot.

"You okay?" Gil asked.

"I'm fine," Mindy responded. "Just sitting too long and maybe a beer too far."

"I'm happy to drive you home."

Mindy laughed. "Now that I see you drive a VW Beetle, I don't think so. Where's that air-conditioned news cruiser?"

"Sitting at the station waiting for the drive to Pickett County tomorrow. And you are most welcome to join me then."

"That's an offer a girl can't refuse. Thank you, Gil. And let me just add that you really impressed me tonight. It's not easy to defend the South these days, but you were thoughtful and eloquent. Even if you do drive a Bug."

"Why, thank you. Hanging around you gives me poetic inspiration. Are you sure you're okay to drive?"

Mindy pulled her keys from her purse and bent slightly to unlock her car, a bright red Karmann Ghia convertible.

"I'm absolutely okay. I live close by. And yes, I confess, I drive a VW too, though it's a lot sportier than your Bug."

Gil laughed and opened her door. "Thanks for not saying classier, even if it is true."

As she slipped into her car, she grabbed Gil's hand and gave it a squeeze. "See you tomorrow, partner. Pickett County awaits. Only an hour's drive but a whole world away."

NINETEEN

REWARD

IN A CITY of ornate churches with towering spires and beautifully landscaped grounds, Mount Gilead AME was among the least of these. It was nestled on the eastern edge of the city in a black neighborhood of small ranch-style homes, duplexes, and a few rundown apartment buildings. The more well-to-do occupied the single-family homes, most of them well maintained and surrounded by small but nicely manicured yards. The neighborhood had once been populated entirely by lower middle-class whites who made their livings in the General Motors assembly plant or other nearby factories, but once blacks began looking at homes in the area the exodus began. The white stampede cratered property values, making houses affordable to those who once only dreamed of having their own home. These new homeowners occupied a lower middle-class beachhead within sight of several decaying apartment low rises, shabby rental homes, and abandoned houses. Mount Gilead AME was the focal point of this community, bridging the gap between the poor and those working to rise economically despite the odds. All were welcome no matter their circumstances.

The church, at the geographical midpoint of the neighborhood, was a white brick and cinder-block two-story with a columned façade. The worn wooden floor of the small sanctuary sloped down toward the pulpit and lectern on opposite sides of a raised chancel. A multitiered choir loft rose behind the chancel. Sunlight entered the dim interior through cathedral windows of stained glass faded by age and lacking the biblical figures that adorned church windows in more prosperous white churches, where an anglicized Jesus looked down on his homogeneous colorless flock.

The modesty of the building belied its important place in the life of the city's black community. Reverend Elijah Timmons had transformed Mount Gilead AME into a landmark of the local movement. And while the sanctuary could only hold about three hundred worshippers, Timmons's following had grown to the point that he performed two services on Sunday mornings as well as evening services on Sundays and Wednesdays. His booming animated sermons had the power to move not only those within the sanctuary but also a larger audience beyond the church walls who listened on one of the city's black-oriented radio stations. The humbleness of his surroundings only added to his charismatic performances. His sermons shunned fire and brimstone in favor of hope, redemption, and delivery to the Promised Land.

But on this morning Timmons was worried about more temporal matters. He was concerned that his aging little church might not be able to handle the crowd of news people arriving for the news conference he'd scheduled. Normally he handled interviews in his office or in one of the conference rooms behind the sanctuary, but today he had little choice but to direct the camera crews into the sanctuary itself because it was the only space big enough to accommodate TV teams from the three major networks, three local stations, and two stations from Baltimore, not to mention the radio, wire service, and newspaper reporters who'd shown up.

His major fear was that Mount Gilead's aged electrical system couldn't handle the lights that the TV crews were placing around the chancel. And, sure enough, as the lights were turned on the fuses tripped and the sanctuary darkened. Some of the network technicians cursed, apparently oblivious to the fact that they were on holy ground. They conferred and agreed to reduce the number of lights and hope for the best. The fuses were reset, and miraculously the lights stayed on, bathing the empty chancel with a pallid glow. The cameramen, also grousing about the low light levels, made their aperture adjustments and prepared to film the event about to take place. The print reporters took their seats in the front pew while the television reporters stood by their photographers and tripoded cameras to be sure they rolled at the right times.

Emanuel Slocum, who'd been assigned the thankless job of placating the media, stuck his head through the door of Timmons's office. Both Timmons and Evelyn were standing, poised for their moment.

"They're all set, boss. Waiting for you and Mrs. Pendry to take the stage."

"Are you ready, Evelyn?" Timmons asked.

"I am," she responded. "Let's go."

As they began walking toward the sanctuary, Timmons silently thanked God for leading Evelyn to him. He viewed her as a providential gift, allowing him to be the heroic instrument of justice for this fine woman and her murdered husband. At the same time, he would forcefully counter the leadership challenge from Marcus Turner and his followers. They would not dare call him Uncle Tom Timmons now.

Timmons broke from his reverie as he entered the sanctuary, leading Evelyn up the three side steps onto the center of the chancel. A table normally used for communion had been placed there, and Timmons gestured for Evelyn to take a seat behind a row of microphones. He then sat down beside her and squinted into the bank of lights before them.

"On behalf of Mount Gilead AME Church and the Christian Action Council, let me welcome you all. And I'd also like to welcome Mrs. Evelyn Pendry, who has shown great courage and fortitude to come here today to tell her story. Her husband, Colonel Jarvis Pendry, was gunned down by night riders on a highway not far from here in Pickett County, a place where racism rules, a place where no black person is safe, a place where the light of justice has yet to shine. But all that is about to change because a brave and innocent man has died a senseless death, and we will not rest until his killers are found and called before the bar of justice. Mrs. Pendry, please tell us about your husband and why you are here today."

Evelyn was a beautiful and imposing woman, petite and slim with her dark hair pulled tightly around her head into a bun that emphasized the delicate features of her face. She was dressed in a skirt and jacket of matching beige and a white blouse. Every camera in the room began a slow zoom to a tight shot of her face as she studied the many microphones on the table in front of her. She paused for several seconds, looked into the glare, and spoke with a strength and firmness no one expected.

"Our family has suffered an irreplaceable loss. I have lost my husband. My two boys have lost their father. Our community has lost a strong and committed leader. Now we must ask 'why.'

"Jarvis was a good man. A wonderful husband, a devoted father, a patriot who fought for this country, a man who had given so much and who had so much more to give. But now he has been taken from us— taken from us in an alien land, taken from us in a place where black people die simply because of the color of their skin.

"My husband was murdered. We do not know who pulled the trigger, but we do know that the racism that runs rampant in the South is as much to blame as the killers themselves.

"I am hurting today. Lord, I am hurting so bad. But I know I must be here to tell you that I will not rest until the people who did this to my husband are brought to justice. I call upon the governor, the GBI, the FBI, and people of good will in this state and Pickett County to work together to arrest the murderers, bring them to trial, and make them pay for what they have done. To that end, I today am offering a ten-thousand-dollar reward for information leading to the arrest and conviction of my husband's murderer or murderers. There is someone out there who knows what happened but may be afraid to come forward. I am hoping this reward will encourage that person to summon up their courage and do the right thing. Thank you."

As she finished, her voice trembled but did not break. She dabbed at her left eye briefly with a tissue she had clutched throughout her remarks and then stared straight ahead with complete composure. Reverend Timmons gently patted her on the shoulder and offered her another tissue, which she declined with a slight shake of her head.

"There is very little I can add to Mrs. Pendry's powerful words, except to say that the CAC will keep the pressure on the governor and state law enforcement to root out the evil that resides in Pickett County. Thank you all for being here."

And with that, Timmons ended the news conference, ushering Evelyn down from the chancel and through a rear door.

The print reporters headed for the front door to file their stories, while the television reporters positioned themselves to film their stand-ups that would introduce their reports.

They all knew that Evelyn's moving performance had propelled the story into a new dimension. Who, whether black or white, could not identify with her grief and her desire for justice? The grieving widow from Baltimore had the power to stir consciences, perhaps even in Pickett County where racism was as embedded and pervasive as the red clay and kudzu that covered it.

TWENTY

WALLS OF JERICHO

WALKING BACKWARDS IN front of the oncoming marchers, his right eye smothered by the rubber viewfinder and his left eye closed, Gil could only see where he had been, not where he was going. He prayed he wouldn't back into a curbstone and go sprawling on the pavement. He had to trust Carney Roberts to keep that from happening. Roberts, the reporter assigned to cover the march with him, walked sideways behind him, watching for obstacles. Roberts's open hand was planted firmly in the small of Gil's back, ready to support him should he trip. His other hand clutched a microphone, which he waved in the general direction of the chanting marchers. The mike was plugged into an amplifier that swung from a strap around Roberts's neck. An audio cord linked the amplifier to Gil's shoulder-mounted camera, making them a single, clumsy organism. If Gil fell, Roberts would go down with him.

The students were walking quickly, waving their placards and their fists as they chanted.

"Justice for Jarvis! Justice for Jarvis!"

About thirty marchers had departed Morehouse College half an hour ago. Gil and Roberts had decided to intercept the group as it reached the main boulevard leading to Atlanta City Hall about two miles from the campus. Gil could see the building looming in the distance, its cream-colored terra-cotta tiles sharply contrasting with the cold, gray granite of the state capitol building just across the street.

The arching, twisting, and running with the heavy camera atop his shoulder shot pains through Gil's lower back. Sweat oozed from his forehead and pooled in the small gap between his eye and the viewfinder, blurring his vision. He tilted his head and quickly wiped the sweat away from his eyes with the sleeve of his shirt.

"How're you making it?" Roberts asked.

Gil responded sarcastically. "I don't guess these guys are planning any rest stops. I'll make it. Not too much further."

He noticed pockets of white spectators gathered on the sidewalk, mostly teenagers and young men. They began paralleling the marchers, their numbers growing as they merged with other clusters of bystanders. The marchers ignored them, but the onlookers were getting increasingly vocal, hooting and yelling racial slurs.

As Gil swiveled his camera toward the sidewalk group, he caught a movement out of the corner of his eye just before he heard a shattering sound. A bottle hit the street about five yards from Gil, spraying shards of glass in the path of the protesters. The marchers reflexively drew into a tighter group, but they kept moving, carefully walking around the glass. The cameramen converged, pointing their lenses down at the point of impact and then panning up to the whites milling on the sidewalk. Another bottle flew from the crowd, striking a network cameraman on the shoulder.

Everyone, marchers and news crews alike, began quick-timing to city hall, where police were waiting. Gil wasn't sure how much protection they would provide, but he felt sure they wouldn't allow the young toughs to continue attacking them. Another bottle shattered on the asphalt and small rocks began pelting the marchers and news crews.

The police massed before city hall made no move to stop the whites' shelling, but the proximity of the police cordons brought an abrupt ceasefire. A stern, beefy police captain in a riot helmet raised a bullhorn to his lips. His face was crimson and huge veins crisscrossed his nose. His jowls shook as he spoke.

"This is an unlawful march. You have no demonstration permit. Turn around and go back or we will have to make arrests."

Behind him about fifty officers waited, billy clubs in hand, all wearing riot gear. The marchers stopped, clumped together in the middle of the street about fifty yards short of the city hall steps. The camera crews hustled up to the police captain and began filming him and his phalanx of officers. The policemen gazed straight ahead impassively. The whites on the sidewalk had stopped throwing things and now just hurled jeers and catcalls at the marchers.

No one seemed sure what to do next. Finally, one of the march leaders came forward, turned his back on police, and raised his arms to address his followers. The camera crews surged forward to capture his remarks. Some kneeled, some stood, forming a tight semicircle in front of Marcus Turner as he began his tirade.

"Do you see, my brothers and sisters, what we face? The might of the white racist police state is here. Why? To protect us from these ignorant redneck racists who would kill us if they had the chance? No, these cops are here to protect the entrenched white politicians and white bureaucrats whose sole purpose is to keep us in our place and preserve the status quo. They are the ones who allow black brothers like Jarvis Pendry to be murdered while driving down the road in that po-dunk Pickett County. Brother Pendry deserves justice. We all deserve to see those who shot him down prosecuted to the full extent of the law and executed. And that is what we demand today."

Marcus did not have a powerful voice. It was several octaves too high to sound authoritative, and laziness in his diction and his rapid-fire speech sometimes caused his words to run together. But his anger and emotion, punctuated by dramatic gesticulations, overcame those flaws.

He looked directly into the mass of cameras and reporters that now virtually surrounded him. It did not escape his notice that two of the camera teams were network.

"We are the Student Coordinating League. We follow in the footsteps of those who have put their lives on the line for freedom. We demand justice for Jarvis. We are taking to the streets and, like the walls of Jericho, the racist system which has oppressed us for so long will come tumbling down."

The bullhorn blared, "Disperse or we will begin making arrests."

Marcus looked back at the police force preparing for contact. He alone held the power to decide what would happen next. The forces were arrayed, the reporters and cameras were in place, the moral position had been established, and now it was just a matter of how he wanted this confrontation to end. If police moved in for mass arrests, if there was violence, he was sure he'd make the network news. If he walked away, the play would be all local. The choice wasn't difficult.

"My brothers and sisters. We cannot allow this racist system to turn us around. We must continue."

And with that, Marcus wheeled and began walking toward the police lines, his followers moving up abreast of him. When they reached the captain with the bullhorn they stopped.

"Captain. Let us pass," Marcus said with all the dramatic emphasis he could muster.

The camera crews were falling over themselves to get in position for whatever might follow.

The captain had not expected this but did not let it fluster him. "This is my final order. Disperse or we will begin making arrests."

Marcus pointed toward city hall. "We have demands," he said with a rising voice. "We have a constitutional right to march and voice those demands in front of city hall. Let us pass."

With that, the captain raised his arm and brought it forward. His baritone voice had a trace of resignation as he ordered the arrests to begin.

"All right, boys. Round 'em up."

The police lines surged forward, merging with and absorbing the group of marchers. Some of the students fell to the street, forcing the officers to drag them to nearby paddy wagons. Others stood firm and had to be subdued. Gil's camera captured one resisting marcher being hit across the mouth with a billy club. Blood dripped from his lower lip.

The whites across the street whooped and laughed as the arrests continued, but they made no effort to get involved. Cameramen were everywhere, running amid the melee, generally ignored by the police. Gil was filming an officer manhandling a marcher when he felt Roberts grab him on the shoulder.

"Quick. Over there."

Roberts began running, and Gil, attached to him by the audio cable, had no choice but to follow. Then he saw what Roberts had seen. Marcus struggled in the grasp of three policemen as they hustled him to one of the wagons. When he spotted the camera and microphone, Marcus began shouting.

"Do you see this, America? Do you see? This is what it means to be black in America. This is the system that killed Jarvis Pendry."

Marcus tried to raise his fist, but an officer pinned his arms to his body. Another had an arm around his neck, choking Marcus so he could barely be heard. Another tried to grab his feet, but Marcus kicked for all he was worth. The officer clubbed him hard on the kneecap, and Marcus screamed in pain.

As they dragged him away, the scream lingered. It would be heard again and again that night on the evening news.

TWENTY-ONE

PRESSING FLESH

SOME CANDIDATES LOVE the art of campaigning, the glad-handing, the small talk, the baby kissing, the constant smile plastered on their faces like a mask. Harrison Parker was not among them. But here he was, striding with all the enthusiasm he could muster down the main street of Marble Valley, practically chasing people down to grab a hand and clutch it until he could deliver his spiel. His aide Billy Watson shadowed him every step of the way, handing out campaign brochures and echoing the candidate's message.

It was high noon by the clock on the courthouse spire, but you didn't need a clock to know the most intense heat of the day was at hand, drawing sweat from the body and energy from the soul. Parker had shed his sport coat half an hour ago, stripping it off and tossing it to Billy, who clumsily stuck it under his arm and tried not to drop the stack of flyers he was distributing as he ran to keep pace with his candidate.

Politicians were expected to visit communities and press the flesh, but Parker didn't enjoy it and wasn't sure it was worth the effort. He clung to the hope that the fleeting person-to-person contacts in Marble Valley and countless other towns might mean the difference on election day.

The Magnolia Café on the town square was packed with a lunchtime crowd as Parker and Billy plunged through the door and began working the tables. Parker hated brashly interrupting people eating their meals, but usually diners reacted with the restrained courtesy expected from those steeped in generations of Southern hospitality. Every now and then a supporter from previous campaigns would return his enthusiastic handshake and offer words of support and encouragement. But there were also those who passed up the handshake, met his eyes only briefly, and returned to their chicken pot pie and sweet iced tea without saying a word. That was a blunt reminder that he was treading on Roscoe Pike's turf.

Parker noticed a young woman smiling and waving at him from a booth by the window. She was sitting with three other women who weren't quite as enthusiastic. Parker motioned to Billy to follow him as he approached.

"And how are you ladies doin' today? How's that fried chicken?" Parker was buoyed by their cordial welcome.

"Why hello, Harrison." The slim brunette who'd waved spoke right up. "Remember me? I worked in your campaign for attorney general. We're all pulling for you."

"Well of course I do," he lied. "How you doing? How's the family?"

"We're just great. The name is Molly Burton in case you don't remember. This here's Betsy Barron, Anne Thacker, and Sally Jones. We all work in the courthouse."

Parker smiled and gave a half bow. "Ladies, a pleasure. I hope you're all doing what you can to help me in Marble Valley."

"Well, we have to be careful these days, you know." Molly lowered her voice. "Feelings are running pretty high. Lots of Pike supporters here. We think he's an embarrassment. That's why we're voting for you. You're more the image we think is best for Georgia."

"Thank you, Molly. Mighty good to hear that. Wish I could hear that from all the other tables in the Magnolia Café."

Molly's three companions were reticent, and one even seemed embarrassed by Parker hovering over their table. After a slight but awkward silence, Parker was about to move to the next table when one of the women spoke up.

"What do you think about the murder of that nigra in Pickett County? What do you think should be done about that?"

Before Parker could respond, a bearded man in dungarees snarled from the adjoining booth. "Hell, what do you mean what should be done? That man was an agitator from up north and he had no business down here. I'm not saying he asked for it, but I've got a feeling he pushed things a little too far and paid the price. What should be done, you say? Nothin' should be done. Let the sheriff in Pickett County handle this and keep the news people and the feds out of it. And while we're at it, we should elect Roscoe Pike governor and forget about this guy." He thrust a thumb in Parker's general direction. "Pike is the only one who will keep the coloreds in their place. Okay...that's it."

He dismissively turned his reddened face away and took a long swig of his iced tea as his table companions snickered.

Parker wasn't sure how to respond, but he knew he had to say something. Before he could speak Molly pointed to the man who had spoken and said, "*You* are the problem, Brad. It's attitudes like yours that will keep us in the dark ages forever. Jarvis Pendry was a black man, yes, but he was a human being, and what happened to him was terrible and wrong. Did you see his widow on TV last night? Broke my heart. You should be ashamed."

Brad looked down at his tea and muttered a racial slur aimed at Molly. The clinking of silverware and lunchtime conversations ceased as all eyes looked toward Parker. After years in elected office Parker prided himself on his ability to think on his feet, but his glibness had deserted him.

"Now folks, let's all calm down. I think part of what Brad here says is correct. The Pendry murder is a local matter for the Pickett County authorities to resolve, and they should do so without outside interference. Now if the GBI can be helpful that's fine, but we don't need the FBI."

Brad shifted in his seat to face Parker, the veins in his forehead pulsing, his jaw muscles clenching. "You goddamn right about that. The whole thing is a waste of time. For a goddamn coon."

It was at that instant that Parker's carefully plotted campaign of moral ambivalence collapsed. He and Mary had watched Evelyn Pendry on the evening news, and they both had been deeply affected by her heartfelt plea. He couldn't let Brad's comment go unanswered.

"Sir, those are hateful remarks. Colonel Pendry was a citizen of our country, a man who served heroically in the war, and the fact that he fell to a cowardly killer in our state is a stain on all of us. You should be ashamed, and anyone who agrees with you should be ashamed as well."

Parker scanned the faces looking at him as stunned silence in the room gave way to murmurs. Two men sitting at Brad's table held his arms as he shook his head and muttered unintelligibly.

Billy grabbed Parker by his elbow and urgently whispered, "Let's go."

Without saying another word, Parker nodded to the women in the booth who were staring blankly at him, backed away, turned, and walked with Billy out into the stultifying heat.

"Politically speaking, that was not your finest hour." Billy was guiding Parker to a shady spot under the awning of a five and dime to regroup. "But I'm still proud of you. And I've got some bad news. A reporter for the Marble Valley Courier was standing in the corner. He had to see it all."

Parker shook his head in disbelief. "Okay. I'll deal with it. And we're still doing the interview with the editor, right?"

"Oh yeah. In fifteen minutes. And I think you're going to have to do some explaining about what you said back there. You just insulted half the people in Marble Valley."

"Find me a telephone," Parker snapped. "I've got to make a call before the interview."

Billy pointed to a phone booth across the street on the square's southeast corner. "That's our best bet. Let's go."

Parker entered the booth through its bi-fold door, lifted the receiver, placed coins in the slot, and was rewarded by a dial tone. As he began dialing, Billy stood outside the phone booth, ready to intercept the Courier reporter quickly approaching, notepad in hand.

On the fourth ring, Devereaux Inman answered his private line. "Hello?"

"Mr. Inman…Harrison Parker. You told me to call if I needed advice, and I could use some right now. I'm in Marble Valley, and questions are being raised about the Pendry murder in Pickett County. I've got a newspaper interview in a few minutes, and I just wanted to get your perspective on this."

There was a long pause before Inman responded.

"Harrison…good to hear from you and thanks for calling. What newspaper? The local rag?"

"Yes sir. Marble Valley Chronicle—uh, Courier, I think is the name. A weekly."

"Okay. That's good. Minimal impact. But you never know when the wire services might pick something up and spread it everywhere. Be careful."

The heat in the confines of the phone booth was suffocating, but Parker couldn't open the door for fresh air with a reporter not twenty feet away.

"Mr. Inman, there's something you should know. I lost my cool in a crowd of people when a redneck started spouting racist opinions about Pendry and the murder. I couldn't let it go. I told him his views were shameful. A local reporter was there and heard everything."

Inman paused and then responded with slow and deliberate tones. "The Pendry case is a huge problem for us. Normally this sort of thing is a local county issue, but this murder is drawing national attention. It's a ready-made issue for Pike, and I expect him to exploit it. You've got to be very careful how you handle your public comments on this."

Parker was nodding at the phone as he replied. "Well, I wasn't careful. This guy was your worst nightmare. A Pike fanatic. I had to say something, and I feel like I did the right thing. Maybe not the right political move, but it was the right thing for me and my conscience."

"I understand. Your emotions got the better of you. But Harrison, in politics you can't let your conscience be your guide. You must acknowledge that this was a terrible crime, and the killer must be arrested and punished. But don't go overboard. Keep it restrained. No criticism of local law enforcement, no pressure on the sheriff. Certainly no insults for the local miscreants. Keep it a law-and-order issue. Stay away as best you can from the racial angle."

"Well, how in hell am I going to do that?" Parker sputtered. "The racial angle is what makes it a big deal!"

Parker was aware that Billy and the reporter were observing his agitated state, even though the phone booth kept his voice muffled to the outside world.

Inman lowered his voice to a calm monotone. "Calm down. Of course you can't avoid race. But downplay it as best you can. I'm worried about where this will all go. That march by young black power upstarts from Morehouse is what I'm talking about. It was just twenty kids but look at the news it made."

"And you know Pike will take full advantage," Parker said. "I'm not sure how to react when he does."

"Your challenge will be to not take the bait. Keep calm and be the voice of reason without giving those on the fence any reason to tilt toward Pike. God help us if that happens."

Parker put the receiver back in its cradle and exited the phone booth, dripping with sweat. The Courier reporter, a pudgy young man wearing khakis and a short-sleeved shirt, approached.

"Mr. Parker, any comment on what happened just now in the Magnolia Café?"

Parker brushed by him, striding toward the newspaper office just off the square. "Let's go to your offices to talk about it. I think your readers will be interested in what I have to say."

TWENTY-TWO

PIKE COUNTRY

ROSCOE PIKE HAD reluctantly accepted the inevitability of change in the South, though he would never admit it even to his closest friends. Signs of old guard retreat were everywhere, from so-called New South politicians to liberal newspaper columnists to business leaders who protected their profits over their heritage. Pike saw himself as the leader of a valiant rear-guard action who would continue fighting on the hilltop while blacks and their white supporters moved steadily upward to destroy him. When that day finally came, Pike sometimes imagined being celebrated as a martyr to the lost cause, but he saw little glory in that. In his view martyrs were losers, and Pike planned to win. A victory in the governor's race would delay the inevitable, and that would be a grand accomplishment.

To achieve that victory, Pike would rely on the support of diehard segregationists who were solidly behind him, but their votes alone would not be enough. Vital to Pike's chances was the ocean of less outspoken voters, mostly in rural areas, filled with dread of looming racial apocalypse. His strategy was to seize on the fear and resentment in the hearts of these voters and stoke their feelings relentlessly.

This strategy appeared to be working as he shook hands with people on the main street of Buxton, a small farming community in southwest Georgia. It was just one stop on a barnstorming tour of a cluster of rural counties that most campaigns usually overlooked. These were poor counties with dead or dying businesses, shoddy schools, and an aging and declining white population. The whites who remained were worried about their futures, terrified of a rising black majority, and desperate to hold on to a way of life they felt they were entitled to because of their race. That's why many of them viewed Pike as a savior, a man who would make things right and put the blacks, liberals, and bureaucrats in their place.

As he strolled down Main Street, he heard their cries of support:

"Go get 'em, Roscoe."

"Tell it true, Roscoe."

"We're with you all the way, Roscoe."

Pike would wave at passersby, sometimes engaging them in conversation while his aide passed out his campaign buttons and pocket brochures. The brochure's first page was a photo of Pike making a speech against a background of a huge Confederate battle flag. He appeared angry and his right arm was fully extended with a clenched fist. Below the photo was printed, "Pike. He's one of us."

Pike's unannounced visit to Buxton was attracting much attention. Women who'd come into town to visit the Stop-and-Shop grocery just off Main Street gathered to see the candidate who gave voice to their fears, who assured them that all was not lost and promised to save them from the unthinkable.

Pike stationed himself in the grocery parking lot and greeted the women as they entered and emerged. He was a natural campaigner and genuinely enjoyed his exchanges with the people. He had been raised in a community like this and felt right at home with the plainspoken and unpretentious, those who had limited education but unlimited ability to work hard and deal with privation. They were his people—at least the white ones. Blacks also came to the Stop-and-Shop, but they kept their distance. Pike acted as if they were not even there.

Pike was telling racially tinged jokes to a group of about twenty, mostly women, when a white station wagon pulled into the parking lot. Pike glanced over his shoulder and saw three men get out of the vehicle, one wearing a sport coat and the others in short-sleeve work shirts and blue jeans. It was a network TV crew.

As they opened the station wagon tailgate and began assembling their camera gear, Pike turned back to his audience.

"Ladies, I'm sorry but the network TV boys are here, and I can't finish that joke. When they leave I'll give you the punch line. Wouldn't be wise for me to be telling jigaboo jokes on national TV, now would it?"

The women and a few men laughed, nodded, and watched the camera crew and reporter walk briskly toward Pike as he turned to greet them.

The correspondent, who appeared to be in his mid-to-late thirties, held out his hand and introduced himself. "Mr. Pike, I'm Tim Cosgrove, NBC News. Good to meet you."

Pike appraised Cosgrove, who was of average height and build though his rumpled clothing made him appear pudgy. He had a handsome face and a full head of brown hair that was beginning to flatten as the midday sun coaxed sweat from every pore.

Pike was thinking Cosgrove had the look of an aspiring anchorman as he accepted the correspondent's moist right hand, gripped it hard, and shook it a single time.

"Mr. Cosgrove. Congratulations on catching up with me. I thought you boys never set foot outside the big city."

Cosgrove showed a glimmer of a smile. "Oh no. We go wherever the story is. Your headquarters said you'd be working in this area today. We just didn't know exactly where. This is the third town we've been to looking for you. Some of these places aren't even on the map."

"Well, welcome to Buxton. Not too many folks here like the network news boys. But don't worry. They're good people, and you're a lot safer here than you'd be in New York. I assume you want an interview?"

"That would be great. Thanks."

Pike's image was that of an angry, aggressive rabble-rouser, but in person he could be charming and articulate. Reporters loved to cover him because his stump rhetoric sold well in every media market. Evening news viewers in Manhattan or San Francisco could be properly appalled while many viewers in the vastness of rural America that extended far beyond the Mason-Dixon Line could shout agreement at their television screens. When Pike was off the stage, he was a different man. His message didn't change—just the tone.

Cosgrove aimed his stick microphone with the NBC logo at Pike's chin and turned his head briefly to nod to his team, a cameraman with his camera mounted on a shoulder pod and a soundman connected to him by an amplifier cord.

"Ready Bob?"

"I'm rolling."

Pike stood stoically, preparing himself for what he called "the interrogation." He knew what to expect.

"Mr. Pike, your critics say you are a race-baiting, rabble-rousing racist. How do you answer that?"

Pike looked sternly at Cosgrove and then chuckled. It was his standard reaction to questions from reporters who thought they could get a rise out of him.

"People who say that don't know anything about me. Racists hate black people, but I don't hate anybody. Now I will tell you I am a segregationist. I believe God put us on earth as separate races, and I believe he would not want to see us mixing the races. So I believe in keeping the races separate. Separate but equal of course."

Cosgrove thought he detected a slight wink but chose not to make an issue of it as Pike continued.

"I condemn the government, the liberals, Washington bureaucrats, news people, and so called civil rights leaders who would force us to mix races in our schools, our restaurants, and eventually our families. But that's not racist. That's Christian. That's American."

Cosgrove was trying not to show his excitement at getting an answer like this on film. It was really all he needed for his report, but he plowed on, hoping for more. "Some would say your rhetoric creates a climate for racial violence. For example, the murder of Jarvis Pendry, which was obviously a crime of racial hatred."

"Mr. Cosgrove, you don't know why that boy got killed. You don't know who did it or what the circumstances were. You liberal news boys jump to conclusions about those of us here in the South. You're the ones creating a violent atmosphere. You're the ones stirring things up. If you'd just leave us alone and mind your own business, we'd do just fine. Don't you have enough crime of your own to deal with in New York? How safe do you feel walking the streets up there where you're from?"

"Mr. Pike, we're talking about Georgia. We're talking about what's happening in the South. How do you feel about the way the Pendry case is being handled?"

"I know Sheriff McSwain up there in Pickett County. He's a good man. He's doing a fine job, and he'll get to the bottom of it if the GBI and FBI give him a chance."

"Do you think the Klan was involved?"

"You people are always blaming the Klan. It could have been anybody. Could have been another black. We just don't know, but you shouldn't be jumping to conclusions. You news people all think alike."

"Your main opponent, Attorney General Parker, has been quoted as saying Pendry was the innocent victim of a racist killer, that his murder stains the people of this state and the South, and it's time for us to reject hate and those who preach it. Was he talking about you?"

"Well, sounds like my opponent has chosen the side he's on, and it's not the side of our people. You can't blame them or the way they think for the unfortunate thing that happened in Pickett County. Looks like Mr. Parker is taking his marching orders from our liberal governor and the silk-stocking crowd in those big-city skyscrapers. They do not speak for the people of this state—but I do. I am not a tool of the establishment. I am my own man, and the people know where I stand. That's why you and your liberal friends better get used to calling me Governor Pike."

The group of spectators gathered behind Pike started clapping and hooting, and Pike turned to them with his thumbs up. Before Cosgrove could ask another question, someone called out.

"Why don't you take that camera and get out of our county. Your kind isn't welcome here."

There was a murmur of approval, and Cosgrove began to look uncomfortable.

Pike turned briefly to the crowd. "Easy, folks. These boys are just here to do a job. They are not on our side, but they'll put that film on the national news tonight, and everybody in the country will hear me speaking for you."

The crowd erupted in applause and yells of support.

"And when I'm governor they'll have to listen to me every day standing up for you."

Pike raised his fist high overhead and shook it back and forth.

Cosgrove and his camera team backed away as the photographer widened his shot to include the boisterous and growing crowd closing in behind Pike, slapping him on the back and pumping his hand.

Pike accepted the congratulations enthusiastically as the crew filmed the scene.

"You boys got what you came for, right? Tell it true now. Tell 'em what you saw here today. Tell 'em the people stand with Roscoe Pike. Now get on back to Atlanta. You're a long way from the interstate."

Cosgrove didn't hear that. He was too busy filming his closing stand-up with Pike and his crowd in the background. "This is Pike Country—the rural South where Pike's racial rhetoric is welcomed and applauded. But is his appeal in places like this enough to win the governor's race? Only time will tell. Tim Cosgrove, NBC News, Buxton, Georgia."

The crew then quickly loaded up their gear and peeled out of the parking lot, heading to Atlanta. Cosgrove hunched in the front seat scribbling his story on a notepad while the cameraman drove, speeding along the two-lane highway toward the interstate miles away. With luck they would have the story ready to feed to New York by the afternoon deadline for the evening news, and Roscoe Pike would have his Southern Gothic moment on the national stage. And no doubt the morning shows would clamor for the opportunity to run it again tomorrow.

TWENTY-THREE

FEDS

PICKETT COUNTY'S BEST days were long gone. Founded shortly after the Civil War, it bore the name of the Confederate general whose men charged up Cemetery Hill at Gettysburg into a vortex of steel and fire that shredded both gray-clad bodies and any hope they ever had of winning the war. The people of Pickett County clung to the view that their county's namesake was a valiant figure of the Lost Cause whose reputation was unjustly tarnished by superior officers who sent him on a suicidal mission. A large statue of General Pickett presided over the courthouse square in the county seat Armistead, named for a brigade commander mortally wounded leading the charge. In chiseled grandeur atop a granite pedestal, Pickett sat on his steed with saber raised and pointing forward. On the pedestal was this inscription:

GENERAL GEORGE EDWARD PICKETT
CONFEDERATE HERO
THE PRINCIPLES FOR WHICH HE
FOUGHT CAN NEVER DIE

Pickett County was in northeast Georgia, an area out of the path of Sherman's ruinous march from Atlanta to the sea. Even though the region was spared the physical destruction of war, scores of families were left to grieve for the young men who never returned and to care for those who did come back with mangled bodies and minds. The decades following the war were grueling for Pickett County, but after the turn of the century the farm economy began to improve, more people moved in, and Armistead grew into a bustling community. The

Great Depression wiped out most of those gains, and then came World War Two and the exodus of strong young men, many of whom never returned.

The picture was now bleak for Pickett County. Interstate 85, which would have provided economic salvation, was being constructed several counties away. Travelers passing through the state would never see Pickett County, would never spend their money in local businesses. Young people coming of age left the county at a steady rate, leaving behind those who were too poor, too old, or too sick to pull up stakes and move.

A couple of sizable farming operations helped keep Pickett afloat, but for the most part it was a wasteland of kudzu-covered buildings, tattered roadside billboards, and people who struggled to try to look beyond the gloomy pall of reality.

Sheriff Lucas McSwain observed this world daily as he prowled the blacktops and dirt roads of his domain, musing about the way his jurisdiction was changing. Up until now it had been a relatively quiet, orderly county, a good place for a lawman with little ambition. But all that changed when Jarvis Pendry ventured into Pickett County in the dark of night to visit his uncle Willie and got himself killed. Now Pickett was the latest dateline in the civil rights movement, and Sheriff McSwain was not handling the glare of publicity very well.

Reporters and cameramen were everywhere it seemed, interviewing people on the town square, doing stand-ups at the murder scene, borrowing telephones at local businesses to make their calls, and hounding the sheriff about when a suspect would be arrested. The stories that appeared in the newspapers or on television did not show Pickett County or McSwain in a favorable light, and that had a corrosive effect on the sheriff's attitude.

Slumped behind the wheel, McSwain guided his cruiser into his personal parking spot behind the Sheriff's Department just off the square. His blood pressure began to rise when he saw a WDX-TV news car parked in the area reserved for deputies. As he strode through the back door and into the central office area, he attempted to stifle the anger he felt at having his territory invaded by media interlopers.

Gil Matthews and a reporter McSwain hadn't seen before were standing by the water cooler chatting with one of his more affable deputies, Bobby Suddeth. McSwain ignored them, walked into his office, and started looking through the papers on his desk.

Though his eyes were not on the door, he could sense that the newsmen were moving toward his office. He looked up to face them with a scowl and an unfriendly nod.

"Good morning, Sheriff. Gil Matthews. I'm the cameraman. We met before. This is Carney Roberts, my reporter."

Roberts held out his hand, smiled, nodded, and said, "Sheriff, nice to meet you."

McSwain slowly reached across his desk to give the offered hand a reluctant shake but said nothing. He then folded his arms and leaned back in his swivel chair, eyeing his visitors with a blank expression.

"How's the investigation coming? Any suspects yet?" Roberts tried to keep his tone upbeat despite the sheriff's coolness.

McSwain looked at Roberts impassively and responded after a long pause. "We're making some progress. Can't talk about it yet. Hard to get anything done with all you news people around. Now y'all run along. I'm pretty busy."

Roberts and Gil didn't budge.

"Sheriff, we'd like to interview you," Roberts persisted. "We understand the GBI is developing some leads. What do you know about that?"

McSwain's veins were pounding, and he hoped the crimson color that surely was engulfing his face wasn't too obvious. What the hell were they talking about? What leads? And what were the damned state agents doing behind his back?

"I really can't comment on anything regarding the Pendry investigation, boys. Maybe later. Not today. Now you need to get your car out of my deputy lot. You're not supposed to park back there. You damn news people think you own the world."

Gil and Roberts backed out of the office and ambled through the back door and into the parking lot. McSwain watched them from his window as they walked toward their car. Then he saw a Ford Fairlane pull into the lot.

Agent Bill Conyers emerged from the car and walked over to the newsmen, shook their hands, and appeared to be answering their questions.

"What the hell is he telling them?" McSwain wondered aloud. "What does he know that I don't?"

Conyers again shook hands with the newsmen and walked toward the sheriff's office. As soon as he entered, McSwain accosted him in a voice shaking with rage. "What the hell is going on? What are you telling those reporters? Who's running this investigation, bureaucrats like you or the duly elected sheriff of this county? Answer me that, Agent Conyers!"

Conyers seemed initially stunned but quickly recovered. "And good morning to you, Sheriff."

Conyers walked to the window that looked out to the grassy glade of the courthouse lawn across the street, hoping a momentary pause would calm the sheriff before he cut to the heart of the matter.

"You're supposed to be running this investigation," he said quietly, "but the reality is you've done almost nothing. Sheriff, this isn't just any black man's murder. This is a case of national significance, and you can't just write it off because your white constituents don't care."

McSwain seemed deflated. He collapsed into his desk chair and rubbed his temples. "Is that what you told those news boys? That I don't care about this case?"

"Absolutely not. But I did tell them we're making some progress, even though that's a bald-faced lie. Somebody's got to talk to them. The public is engaged in this case, and we can't stonewall it, even if we have to fudge a bit to make them believe we're not stuck in the mud."

McSwain raised a fist and brought it down hard on his desk.

"Look, I'll find out who did this, and I'll take him to trial. But I can't be rushed. Sooner or later, someone will talk, and we'll find our guy. But I can't do it overnight no matter how many reporters they send here."

Conyers began slowly pacing from the window to the desk and back, hands behind his back, head down.

"Sheriff, there are a lot of people around the country who think you're a racist redneck who'd like to sweep this crime under the rug. How many creeks and ponds have you dragged for the murder weapon, how many people have you interviewed, how much help have you requested from us? A big fat zero. And the eyes of the nation are on you and Pickett County and Georgia. You'd better get a move on because if you aren't willing to do what's necessary, we are."

Conyers stopped pacing and stood in front of the desk to look down on the seated sheriff. "And, he added, "there's a new development, and that's the real reason I'm here. J. Edgar Hoover has sent in the FBI and the governor fully supports that move. Some agents are already here and a lot more are on the way. They may give you a courtesy call, but I thought you should have a heads-up from me."

McSwain slumped in his chair, sagging as though he'd absorbed a physical blow, the rancor and combativeness so much a part of his demeanor melting away. "It's bad enough that you guys and reporters are breathing down my neck. But the feds? Why?"

"The governor needs to show that the state is willing to do whatever it takes to solve this case. It's a big blemish on the 'New South' image he's been projecting. But frankly, it's more than that. It's the feeling that you will not conduct a proper investigation—that your history would indicate a less than enthusiastic approach to solving the murder of a black man, even a black man as prominent as Jarvis Pendry."

McSwain ran his stubby fingers through his thinning, short-cropped hair. "Bill, I'm sure you know what I'm up against. You know there are elements in the county who will crucify me if I push too hard.

You and I know there are Klansmen here who might know something about what happened, but if I start bringing them in for questioning all hell will break loose."

Conyers nodded slowly. "The way I see it, you've got two choices. You can offer full cooperation with state and federal investigators, or you can sit back and let them solve this case without your help. I'm betting an FBI agent will be dropping by shortly to see where you stand."

Conyers turned to leave, stopping when he got to the office door for a last parting shot. "If I were you, I'd offer full cooperation."

McSwain remained at his desk for a long time, staring into space and silently cursing Jarvis Pendry and the night he'd altered McSwain's universe. The all-powerful sheriff had been rendered virtually impotent by forces far beyond his control. He didn't want to yield to state and federal investigators, but he knew their resources and expertise would solve the case far sooner than he could. He realized he had little choice but to work with the feds while acting out the fiction that he was still in charge. When it was over, they would leave and he would remain, taking credit for the outcome if it suited him to do so. He knew the white people of Pickett County would understand and reelect him as they had always done.

McSwain settled back in his chair, interlocked his fingers behind his neck, closed his eyes, and longed for the time when his word was law, and no one dared question it.

TWENTY-FOUR

FISH ON

A WELCOME BREEZE stirred small ripples on the pond, refracting rays of the relentless afternoon sun into a blinding shimmer. As that slight disturbance on the surface subsided, the triple-hooked lure created another larger one as it splashed and sank into the depths.

Caleb Soseby began to reel the lure slowly through the water, praying the flashing spinner would be noticed by a hungry bass lying low on the cool bottom of the pond. He moved the rod from side to side, putting more movement on the lure. Suddenly the clicking of the reel's slow retrieve stopped as he felt the line jerk and tighten. He raised the rod and began to reel furiously, but the fish was a fighter and demanded more line as it dove for the shelter of tree stumps on the bottom.

"Fish on," Caleb yelled. "Feels like a hog."

He repeatedly lowered the rod, reeled in the slack, then raised it, careful not to put too much pressure on the line as the fish fought and shook. At one point the huge bass exploded from the pond, twisting and turning before splashing back. Caleb let out a squeal of joy at the sight and began reeling fast, sensing the fish was tiring and about to surrender. His companion, Rufus McLeod, shouted encouragement and ran to the edge of the pond to help retrieve the bass as it was inexorably pulled to shore. It was a five-pound beauty, and both men admired it as Caleb held up the glistening trophy dangling from the hook, its gills struggling in the alien environment.

"Damn, what a beauty. Nice going, Caleb."

Rufus seemed genuinely happy for his friend, despite his own lack of success at the pond. Caleb threw the bass into a bucket, pulled another beer from the ice chest, sat down on the grass, and took a long drink. He wiped his mouth with the back of his hand and looked up at his friend.

"Well, like I always say. Fishin' is fun, but catchin' is better."

Both men laughed as Rufus opened a beer and sat beside Caleb. The two had been friends all their lives, growing up in the same neighborhood in Armistead, playing high school sports together, and occasionally getting into trouble. They'd been part of a group of teens who vandalized Pickett County's black elementary school, breaking windows, strewing trash in the classrooms, and spray-painting racial slurs on the school's brick walls. Sheriff McSwain had been lenient, dropping the charges after the boys cleaned up the mess and their parents paid a small fine.

After that, Rufus's parents had tried to cool off his friendship with Caleb. It was apparent to Caleb that they considered him a bad influence on Rufus. They remained friends, but the bond was never the same. Caleb's father said the McLeods considered themselves too good for the Sosebys.

Now that they were twenty-two, Caleb and Rufus had gone their separate ways. Caleb was tied down most of the time helping his father run the family gas station. Rufus worked with his dad as well at the auto repair shop his family owned.

They'd both managed to get some time off on a Saturday, and Caleb had suggested fishing at a stocked pond on the property of a mutual friend. It had been an enjoyable afternoon, attested to by the fish in their pail and the empty Pabst Blue Ribbon cans scattered around the ice chest they'd brought. The heat and the alcohol made for rambling and disjointed conversation about sports, girls, and eventually the topic of the day in Pickett County, a topic Caleb wanted to avoid.

"Hell of a thing about that Pendry murder," said Rufus. "FBI agents all over the damn place. You hear anything about it lately? Any idea who might have done that?"

The questions hung in the heavy air unanswered. Caleb and Rufus lay on the grass, the bills of their baseball hats pulled down to shield their eyes from the afternoon sun.

"I just wonder why anyone would do something like that," Rufus continued. "Whoever it was, I bet they never thought it would get the President involved. Biggest thing ever to happen in Pickett County."

Rufus was about to doze off when suddenly Caleb sat up, spat on the ground, and gave a growl of frustration and anger. "It's all crazy, blown way out of proportion. Who would think so much fuss would be made about a black man?"

Caleb was slurring his words, running them together incoherently, and something in his inebriated mind told him to shut up. But for some reason he couldn't.

"Damn Colonel Sambo comes into our gas station that night. Starts acting all uppity and important. Really pissed us off. I mean he was just arrogant. He was asking for it. And he got it. We gave it to him."

The mind fog Rufus had been drifting in suddenly lifted. He rolled over to face Caleb, raising his upper body to rest on his elbow. "What? What are you saying? You actually saw him that night?"

"Uh-huh. Sure as hell did. We're the last people he saw."

"Caleb, you're drunk. You don't know what you're saying."

Caleb gave Rufus a glassy-eyed stare, and a realization seemed to dawn on him. He pushed himself to a standing position and began walking drunkenly in circles. "Uh, yeah. I'm drunk. I don't know what I'm saying. Forget everything I said. Okay? Let's say this never happened. Okay? Okay?"

Rufus was shaken and suddenly cold sober. "Sure, Caleb. Never happened. Let's go home now and sleep this off."

The two young men began picking up the empty beer cans and tossing them into the cooler. They said nothing as they loaded the cooler and fishing gear into the back of Rufus's pickup and pulled away from the pond along the grassy access road, through the wooden gate, and onto the road heading back toward town. Dark cumulus clouds were rising in the distance, thick and purple, laden with moisture, waiting to release it in torrents on the parched land below.

When they approached Soseby's gas station, Rufus slowed and pulled his truck up to the pumps. Caleb got out, retrieved his fishing gear and bucket of bass, and then walked to the driver's side window where Rufus was staring straight ahead.

"That was all bullshit, Rufus. All bullshit. It cannot be repeated. Do you understand? Do you?"

Rufus continued to look through his dirt-streaked windshield. Thunder rumbled. The storm was about to break. "Yes, I do," he said. "All bullshit. See you later."

The truck slowly pulled away, leaving spirals of dust drifting as Caleb watched it fade into the distance. A sense of dread welled up within him as a silent voice kept repeating, "What have I done? What have I done?"

The first drops of rain began to spatter on the dirt and gravel turn-around, leaving hundreds of tiny craters. The tentative sprinkles increased in speed and power until the rain fell in pulsating sheets, puddling around the pumps and sending rivulets of muddy wash in all directions.

Caleb slowly walked toward the screen door of the gas station, his drenched clothing clinging to his skin. He pushed the door open and disappeared into the interior darkness, pursued by rumbles of thunder that would continue ominously until darkness fell.

TWENTY-FIVE

THE NOTE

GRAYSON KINCAID ROSE from his seat at the head table and walked to the lectern, leaving his plate of sliced chicken, dressing, and green beans almost untouched. It was his habit to eat sparingly before he made a speech to avoid food particles in his teeth and reflux in his esophagus. He could flash his famous smile and speak in his familiar basso profundo without worrying about having to stifle an untimely burp.

He looked out over his politely applauding audience composed mostly of businessmen who were members of the Downtown Kiwanis Club. A few women were also in attendance, most of them wives or guests of members. He could sense the warmth toward him in the room, something to which he was accustomed. After a decade in the anchor chair at WDX, Kincaid was a widely respected and admired figure in the community. He'd earned his reputation by demonstrating intelligence, poise, and journalistic integrity night after night, newscast after newscast, year after year.

Kincaid was in his mid-forties but looked younger. He had the build of an aging athlete, with broad shoulders and a torso that was only beginning to show signs of thickening. He worked to stay in shape, running every other day and playing tennis in the mornings before he went to the newsroom for his evening and late-night newscasts. He was fortunate to have the anchor's prerequisite full head of black hair, but he worried about the strands he observed in his comb every morning and constantly examined his hairline for signs of recession.

As the applause died, Kincaid launched into his opening remarks, thanking the club for the invitation, pointing out some of the club members he knew, and telling a joke or two guaranteed to generate laughter and relax everyone, including himself. Kincaid's tone was easygoing and conversational, not the dramatic projection he used when anchoring the news. Being with his audience face to face called for a more personal style. He had mastered the art of speaking extemporaneously, though he hardly needed notes for the stock repertoire of speeches he'd been giving for years.

Today, for the Downtown Kiwanis, Kincaid was going with his "Principles of Broadcast Journalism" remarks. His method was to acknowledge the public's deep distrust of the news media while reassuring his audience that he and the people with whom he worked were honorable, intelligent, objective, and dedicated to telling it like it was for better or worse. It usually worked like a charm.

He looked around the room, locking eyes with individual after individual, as he made his points. "Viewers say they want us to be objective, and that is always our goal. But none of us is totally objective. We are all influenced by our upbringing, our environment, our heritage, our preconceived ideas, notions, and prejudices. No one in this room is totally objective, including me. But we as journalists must try hard to rise above our preconceptions, our prejudices, telling all sides of a story no matter how difficult that can be. When you think we are not being fair, not representing all sides of the issues, then we lose you because our credibility is gone. And once credibility crumbles, it is very difficult if not impossible to get it back. I only ask you to judge us with the same sense of fairness you expect of us."

Kincaid continued, talking about the need for accuracy, perspective, and balance in the news. He knew his remarks would last about twenty minutes, followed by five minutes for questions. The club's program chairman had made it clear that finishing on time was much more important to him than what Kincaid had to say. These were, after all, business people who had to get back to work.

After answering a few friendly questions, Kincaid thanked the audience as they applauded politely. He accepted a Kiwanis Club paperweight to add to his unwanted but growing collection of civic club handouts, shook a few hands, and headed back to the station.

He ambled into the newsroom with his coat slung over his shoulder, nodding to colleagues as he made his way to his desk inside a small cubicle across from the editing rooms. He hung his jacket on the coat rack and turned his attention to the pile of mail on his desk.

He sat down and began flipping through the envelopes, setting aside the ones obviously containing press releases or speaking invitations. He was looking for handwritten viewer mail, messages from his audience that sometimes contained compliments but more often criticism or condemnation. He had learned over the years that viewers who were angry about something were far likelier to take the trouble to write a letter than those whose feathers had not been ruffled.

He pulled out one letter that immediately caught his attention. The address was printed in big block letters, and his name had been misspelled—Grayson Kincade. He opened the envelope with his Rotary Club letter opener, another gift for making a civic club speech, slipped out the almost wadded piece of lined notebook paper, and unfolded it.

The text was written in the same block lettering as the address, almost as though the author was a child. But it quickly became apparent to Kincaid that no child would have written this.

"Mr. Kincade. I know who killed Pendry. Soseby and his boy. KKK."

There was no signature or any indication of where the letter came from except for a postmark from the Armistead post office dated two days ago.

Kincaid carefully picked up the letter and the envelope and hurried toward News Director Tom Burke's office no more than thirty steps away. Burke was chatting with Gil Matthews when Kincaid walked in and laid the letter on Burke's cluttered desk.

"Probably better if you don't touch it, Tom. I've already got my fingerprints on it, but no sense making it any worse for the crime lab boys if this thing pans out."

Burke studied the paper as Gil moved behind him to take a look.

"Damn. Interesting. Wonder if it's for real. KKK certainly makes sense, but Soseby? Wonder who that is?"

"I think I know," said Gil. "I've already had a run-in with him, if he's same guy."

Burke swiveled in his chair and looked up at Gil. "What do you know about him?"

"He's got a run-down gas station just down the road from the murder scene. I wouldn't call him a model citizen. It doesn't take too much imagination to picture him all decked out in Klan gear."

"Okay. Let's get this to the law pronto. Could be nothing, but then again you never know. And let's keep this quiet. Hopefully they'll let us be in on the arrest if anything comes of this."

Kincaid stepped back and closed the office door, even though there was no indication that anyone in the newsroom was paying attention. Still, Kincaid lowered his voice. "Gil, who's your best contact in the Pendry case?"

"Bill Conyers. GBI agent. He knows Soseby too. I could get Bill here, and maybe we can work out a deal for exclusive coverage. But let's not get ahead of ourselves. So far all we know is that this letter is just a piece of potential evidence. No way can we give anything away by running up to Soseby's gas station and sticking a camera in his face."

Burke nodded. "Absolutely. We've got to be careful. Gil, call Conyers and get him over here. We'll show this letter to him and see what happens. God, I do hope it leads to something."

Kincaid headed back to his office to prepare for the evening newscast, while Gil used the telephone on Burke's desk to alert Conyers about the possible lead.

Burke made a beeline down the long corridor to the office of his general manager to share the news that a break in the Pendry case might be at hand thanks to Grayson Kincaid and WDX. If all the pieces fell into place, it would be a real coup for the station. Burke was not a religious man, but he prayed it would be so.

TWENTY-SIX

OLD TIMES' SAKE

HIRAM SOSEBY HADN'T attended a Klan rally in several years. When he was younger the doctrine and regalia had appeal for him, and he was an eager disciple. He felt inspired by the nighttime rallies where robed and hooded Klansmen stood in a semicircle before a huge burning cross, their arms raised in a Nazi-like salute. The bond of brotherhood at those moments was powerful, and he always left the rallies with a sense of righteous mission to preserve and protect the white race from threat of black incursion.

Soseby still believed in that mission, but he no longer went to rallies, wore his robes, or distributed Klan literature. There was social stigma against being a Klan member, even in Pickett County. Soseby blamed the news and movies for that. They always portrayed Klansmen as ignorant, stupid, clownish louts, and that constant portrayal had diminished the Klan, pushing the remaining members even further underground. Soseby's robes, his hood, and other trappings of the White Knights had been boxed up in his attic for years. He'd probably have to destroy them one day.

The Klan presence in Pickett County still remained an ominous undercurrent. People were aware the Klan existed but seldom if ever mentioned it. Their attitudes may have been in sympathy with what the Klan stood for, but few viewed it as anything more than a dark anachronism of the post-Civil War era when nightriders wreaked vengeance on blacks they considered "uppity."

After the murder of Jarvis Pendry, the Klan was on everyone's mind. Who else would be patrolling the highways late at night and taking aim at a black man with a Maryland license tag? The violence was so random, so spontaneous, it had to be an act not of premeditation but of raw, unreasoning racial hatred.

The enormous attention focused on the Pendry murder made Hiram Soseby very nervous. A number of people in the county knew of his ties to the Klan. Even Sheriff McSwain was aware, though he had never seriously probed Klan activities. If anything, Soseby viewed McSwain as a fellow traveler who would look the other way if they had some vigilante matters to take care of.

McSwain stopped by from time to time, and it was not surprising when the sheriff pulled into the gas station driveway shortly after sunset. Soseby became more concerned when McSwain drove his car around to the rear of the building where it couldn't be seen from the highway.

Caleb emerged from the rear room of the station. "Dad. The sheriff is here. What's this about?"

Before his father could respond the sheriff appeared, following Caleb into the main area where Hiram sat on his stool behind the counter. McSwain paused at the rack of candies and chips and pulled off a pack of Cheetos.

"Hello, Hiram, Caleb. Got a beer?"

"Why sure, Sheriff." Soseby opened the cooler by the cash register, pulled out a Miller High Life, popped the can open, and set it on the counter.

McSwain took a deep swig, put a couple of Cheetos in his mouth, then took another swig. "Thanks. How y'all doin'?"

Soseby tried to sound as calm as possible. Caleb stayed in the background leaning against the wall just below the Confederate flag.

"We're good, Sheriff. Just closing out the register. Don't think we'll get much more traffic tonight."

McSwain set his beer down and looked around the room. "You had any GBI or FBI agents coming around lately asking questions?"

Soseby felt his throat tighten. "A GBI agent came by a week ago but he just wanted some gas. A real smart-ass. It was the day they pulled that car out of the river. Did you say FBI?"

"Hiram, I have to tell you the feds have been asking questions about you and some of the other boys you know or used to run with back in the day. Why do you think that is?"

"Well, Sheriff, I don't know why they'd be doing that. I'm just a small businessman trying to make a living. I can't help it if a crime happened near my place. I certainly had nothing to do with it."

McSwain nodded and looked over his shoulder at Caleb, who was cowering in the shadows. "What about you, Caleb? You hear anything from your friends about lawmen asking questions about y'all?"

Caleb responded almost too quickly. "No sir. I ain't heard nothing."

The sheriff lifted his can for another long swig.

Caleb was nervously trying to decide what to do with his hands, finally shoving them into the pockets of his ragged, grease-stained jeans.

Sheriff McSwain kept his eyes on Caleb for a long moment, seemingly amused by his discomfort, before turning back to the elder Soseby. "These outsiders, the feds and the state boys, they aren't talking much to me, but something's up. You boys better watch yourselves, you hear? You might want to be ready if someone comes knocking. Wouldn't want them to find anything—um—incriminating now, would we?"

"Sheriff, we've got nothing to hide," Hiram said. "But you're making me real nervous."

McSwain popped a Cheeto into his mouth, chewing noisily. "Well, I'm not trying to scare you, but these boys need to make an arrest as soon as they can. Your, um, background, Hiram, along with some other boys you run with puts you in a special category, if you get my drift. I'm just giving you a courtesy call for old times' sake. Watch yourself. And keep me posted on anything you think I should know about."

McSwain left the beer can and crumpled wrapper on the counter and turned to leave. "Thanks for the beer and chips."

"Any time, Sheriff. Thanks to you."

Caleb watched McSwain's car pull back on the highway, then turned to his father with a frantic look on his face. "Daddy, he knows! He knows!"

"Relax, boy. He may suspect, but he doesn't know anything. And even if he does know, he's giving us a break. No one else knows, right? Only you, me, and Randall. You haven't mentioned this to anyone right, boy? Right?"

"Oh no, Daddy. I would never do that. I don't know about Randall."

"I need to find him to make sure he keeps his mouth shut. He worries me 'cause he's stupid and drinks too much."

Soseby ran over the mental checklist of steps he'd taken since the Pendry murder. The weapons were hidden and his alibi was set. But there was at least one thing he had yet to do.

"Caleb, mind the store. I've got to run home and take care of something."

Soseby strode to his pickup in the rear, cranked the engine, and fishtailed from the gravel to the asphalt heading for home. The time had come to haul down that cardboard box in his attic and burn it and everything in it to ashes.

TWENTY-SEVEN

A DRIVE IN THE COUNTRY

BILL CONYERS TRIED to enjoy the last few moments of relative cool as he walked, briefcase in hand, from his motel room across a cracking asphalt parking lot to his sedan. The rising sun would soon begin heating the dark pavement to baking temperature, challenging even the sprigs of crabgrass that had found purchase in the tiny fissures and somehow managed to survive.

The Monarch Courts Motel was fortunately located just off the I-85 exit ramp near Suwanee, a ramp motorists had no choice but to use. The paved interstate ended there, but beyond the barricades construction of the remaining seventy-mile stretch to the South Carolina border was nearing completion. The Monarch Courts was a stopover point for highway construction workers, traveling salesmen, and couples seeking a spot for amorous liaisons, but for the past ten days—ever since the discovery of Jarvis Pendry's body—it had been home for Conyers. The rooms were basic but reasonably clean and comfortable, far better than any accommodation in Pickett County thirty miles away. Several other GBI agents were staying at Monarch Courts along with some out-of-state newsmen, but not the FBI. The feds worked out of their Atlanta office, making the daily one-hour commute to Armistead before morning traffic and returning after dark. If they needed to stay overnight for any reason, the Monarch Courts would be happy to oblige so long as the agent wasn't black. The motel wasn't exactly embracing the new civil rights law, and the feds weren't interested in testing it yet, even though everyone knew that day would come.

Conyers drove east, squinting into the rising sun as he tried to adjust his car's visor and dial up a radio newscast. After about twenty-five minutes, he crossed the Pickett County line and pulled into a small strip shopping area, the only one for miles. He spotted the man he was to meet, sitting in a beige Chevy sedan parked near the Chubby Boy drive-through restaurant sipping a coffee and reading the morning newspaper. Robert Smithers looked up without expression as Conyers pulled in alongside him.

Smithers was the lead FBI agent on the Pendry case. He had picked his vehicle from the government carpool for its innocuousness. Most government cars were white or blue Fords and easy to identify. For today's mission, Smithers needed a vehicle that blended in, one that would not be a dead giveaway for any reporter who might spot them.

Both men got out of their cars and shook hands. Then Conyers grabbed his briefcase, locked his vehicle, and got in Smithers's car. They were on their way to Shiloh Crossroads to visit Hiram Soseby, even though no invitation had been issued.

Conyers had seen the anonymous note delivered to Grayson Kincaid, and he had immediately shared it with fellow state and FBI investigators. They'd had a number of anonymous tips about the Pendry case, but this was the first time a name had surfaced, the name of a suspected Klansman. Conyers and Smithers agreed to team up for a surprise interview. They decided not to share their plan with Sheriff McSwain.

Smithers guided the car along the undulating highway toward Armistead. He planned to cut off on side roads before reaching the county seat to minimize their chances of being spotted.

The roadway had once been a major artery, but the almost completed interstate to the west had made the old highway irrelevant to all except those living in the area. On this sultry morning, the two lawmen had the highway to themselves aside from the occasional pickup truck that slowed them to a crawl until they had enough straightaway to pass.

Conyers had been raised in the country, and a drive along a rural road like this was an evocative experience. He much preferred vistas of pastureland, crops, and livestock to the commercial clutter that multiplied at every freeway intersection. As he gazed at the passing countryside, he reflected on the childhood trips to visit relatives in North Carolina, driving on this very road, playing cow poker with his younger brothers—one point for every cow, two for every horse.

Smithers broke into his reverie. "The land that time forgot."

Conyers chuckled and nodded. "Probably not where you thought you'd be when you graduated from Quantico."

"No, that's right. Thought I'd be in some white-collar job in DC or maybe Chicago. Instead, I get posted to the South. Been down here three years, and it's been tough. At least I get to live in Atlanta, but I spend most of my time out in the boondocks running down the KKK."

With his narrow, vacant face, slim body, and crew cut, Smithers looked like an FBI agent prototype. He was in his early forties and radiated competence and experience. Conyers didn't want to miss this opportunity to learn from him.

"Do you think Pendry's killers are Klan?"

Smithers shifted slightly in his seat and began to slow down as the car approached a tractor creeping along the highway ahead of them.

"Not much question in my mind. It has all the earmarks of a targeted Klan execution. Pendry was in the wrong place at the wrong time. He probably encountered some Klansmen who were liquored up, and they killed him, pure and simple."

Smithers suddenly pulled to the left and accelerated around the barely moving tractor.

"It might or might not be actual Klansmen. They might not wear white robes and hoods and gather around burning crosses, but in counties like this you will often see groups of white men with shotguns or pistols, roaming the back roads or even the sidewalks of the county seat. They may not be 'official' Klan, but their actions are the same. You see it in rural areas all across the state. They are allowed to intimidate. No one will stop them. Certainly not the sheriff. Certainly not here in Pickett County. My God, he grew up with them here and is probably in complete sympathy with their beliefs and actions."

"So it's up to us," Conyers said.

"Exactly. It's up to us. And we've got a brand-new law that should help us make a case even if McSwain won't push for murder charges once we find some suspects. We can go with civil rights violations. These local yahoos have Uncle Sam to reckon with now. It's a new day in the South, and it's about time."

Smithers turned onto a narrow county road that would bypass Armistead and take them to Shiloh Crossroads.

"So what do you know about Hiram Soseby?"

Smithers slowed to cross an ancient one-lane bridge over a small creek, which was so clogged with brush and debris that you couldn't see the almost stagnant water below. "No criminal record. Lived in Pickett County all his life. Served in the Pacific with the Navy on a supply ship. Never saw combat. He's got a twenty-year-old son named Caleb. Owns and operates a service station. We believe Soseby is connected to a loose group of die-hards who could be Klan. We're not sure. It's just damn hard to get good information from these people. You can't even pay them to talk. That's why that tip you got is important. At least we'll see if it leads anywhere."

Some state agents resented the FBI and its air of superiority, but not Conyers. He hoped one day he might become a federal agent and enjoy the pay, benefits, and prestige that went with the job, not to mention the full backing of the United States Government.

"Can you tell me how you're approaching this case? Where you're putting your resources?"

Smithers kept his eyes on the road, nodding at Conyers's inquiry. "We've got twenty agents assigned. We're running down every lead that comes our way, but we're obviously paying special attention to suspected Klansmen. We follow them around, ask a lot of questions in their neighborhoods, and lately we've been canvassing gun stores within a fifty-mile radius for information on rifle and shotgun purchases. You really have to look at everything. Most of it yields nothing.

But all it takes is one hit, one clue, one piece of information that leads to another piece of information that ultimately leads to the person or persons behind the crime. It's very painstaking work. But it's what we do, and in almost every case we solve the crime. And we will solve this one."

Smithers and Conyers passed through the tiny Shiloh Crossroads community and turned right onto the main highway, which immediately began descending toward the bridge where Jarvis Pendry's life had been taken. The vehicle slowed as it crossed the bridge so the two lawmen could once again see the cratered concrete left by the deadly shotgun blasts.

They continued on for two miles until they spotted Soseby's service station, a dirty cinder-block building sitting back from the road just far enough for cars to access the pumps. Smithers slowly pulled up to the pumps, cut the engine, and waited.

After about a minute, a skinny young man in a t-shirt and stained blue jeans came through the screen door and sauntered to the driver's side window. He pulled the gas hose from the pump and held it, waiting for Smithers to give him some instruction.

"How much y'all need?" the attendant drawled, hitching up his loosely fitting jeans with his free hand.

Smithers looked him up and down for about ten long seconds before answering. "Give me ten dollars' worth."

The young man appeared nervous after Smithers's appraisal. He stooped slightly to look into the car and recoiled when he recognized Conyers.

Caleb was obviously addled as he walked to the rear of the car and began putting fuel in the tank. As he stood there pumping, Smithers and Conyers got out of the car and walked toward him. He watched them approach, hoping the gas hose trigger he was holding masked his trembling hand.

"What's your name, boy?" Smithers knew Caleb would take the term of address as an insult. It was intentional.

"Caleb Soseby. What is it y'all want?"

"Ten dollars' worth of regular, but I see you've already put in thirteen dollars' worth."

Caleb took his hand off the hose trigger and yanked the nozzle out, still dripping. "Damn!" he muttered.

Smithers chuckled without smiling. "Your daddy inside?"

Without waiting for an answer, Smithers and Conyers headed for the screen door.

Once inside, it took a moment for their eyes to adjust to the room's relative darkness. Then they saw Hiram Soseby sitting on his stool behind the counter. When he recognized Conyers from their previous encounter, he slipped off the stool to stand and face them, his arms folded over his ample belly.

Conyers spoke first. "Hello, Mr. Soseby. Remember me? Agent Bill Conyers. This is Agent Robert Smithers with the FBI."

Smithers pulled out his wallet to show Soseby his credentials. Soseby ignored the gesture.

"Mr. Soseby, Agent Conyers and I wanted to ask you a few questions about the murder of Jarvis Pendry."

Soseby scowled. "Don't know nothin' about that. The sheriff has already interviewed me. I can't tell you anything about what happened 'cause I don't know."

Unfazed, Smithers continued. "You were open that night, right? Are you sure Colonel Pendry didn't stop here for some gas or a snack? Were you here all evening?"

"Me and my boy. We was here. We didn't see nobody. You go and talk to Sheriff McSwain. I already told him everything I know, which ain't much."

"We'll do that, Mr. Soseby. Even though the sheriff hasn't been very helpful to us so far." Soseby did not respond, but Conyers could tell he was nervous at the line of questioning.

"Mr. Soseby," Smithers continued, "you have connections with the Ku Klux Klan, do you not?"

"Now that's a damn lie. I don't know what you're talking about. But what if I did? Last time I checked it's a free country—or at least it used to be."

"Quite right, Mr. Soseby. Quite right. A free country. Even for a black man like Jarvis Pendry. Thanks for your time."

Smithers put thirteen dollars on the counter and headed for the screen door followed by Conyers.

Caleb was still outside standing in a shady spot just beyond the door. He'd obviously heard everything.

Conyers stopped in front of him. "How about you, Caleb? What do you know that you're not telling us?"

Caleb didn't answer. He grabbed the screen door handle and quickly went inside.

Smithers and Conyers got back in their car and pulled onto the highway.

"That should give them food for thought," Smithers said.

"We need to keep a close eye on them," Conyers responded. "Think we could get a search warrant?"

"Not yet. We got nothing on him so far, aside from the fact that he's a Dixie Neanderthal. I guarantee if he didn't kill Pendry, he's got blood on his hands from other racial crimes. And I'm pretty sure he knows a lot more than he's telling."

"No doubt," Conyers mused. "Think we should brief the sheriff?"

"I don't think that would be a good idea. He'll find out we were here. I just don't trust him. What we have to do is find out who wrote that note to Kincaid. We just have to hope he makes contact again."

As the two agents reached the Chubby Boy drive-through where they'd left Conyers's car, Smithers's pager beeped. He looked at the telephone number displayed and told Conyers it was the FBI's regional office. He got out of the car and headed for a telephone booth across from the parking lot to call in.

Conyers ordered a chocolate milkshake and waited in the air-conditioned burger joint for Smithers to return. When he walked in, he was smiling broadly.

"First time I've seen you smile today. Good news?"

"Oh yes," Smithers said. "Very interesting news. Our check of gun stores in the area turned up the fact that Hiram Soseby purchased a double-barreled twelve-gauge shotgun in April along with ten boxes of shells."

"No kidding," Conyers responded. "Like you just said, every now and then you get a hit that can lead to something."

"Yes indeed. Now we've got to find that weapon and tie it to the murder. I think this may give us enough probable cause to get a search warrant. I'll set the wheels in motion, but first I've got to have one of those chocolate shakes."

TWENTY-EIGHT

AMEN, BROTHER

WHEN ELIJAH TIMMONS was growing up in South Georgia, he always looked forward to trips to town with his father. William Timmons worked the land as a sharecropper on a small farm about ten miles from Wortham, the small county's only town. Occasionally he made a few extra dollars by doing odd jobs for white farmers in the area, and when he'd saved up enough, he'd drive his ramshackle black pickup to town to pick up food and other essentials at the grocery just off the town square.

Little Elijah could always sense his daddy's unease with so many white folks also walking about. His father kept a strong grip on his tiny hand as they strolled along Wortham's main street. Sometimes they'd step off the sidewalk into the street to wait for white pedestrians to pass. Some nodded to his father in a cordial way, but most seemed oblivious to the deference they'd been shown.

Elijah particularly enjoyed looking through the drugstore window where white children sat on red-cushioned stools at the soda fountain and enjoyed their ice cream cones and milkshakes. He could hear their squeals of laughter as they spun themselves around in circles on the swiveled seats, their parents hovering nearby prepared to catch them should they fall. The children were having so much fun that they never noticed the little black boy in ragged coveralls standing on the sidewalk watching them through the window.

One day Elijah asked his father if he would take him to that soda fountain, buy him an ice cream, and let him spin him around on the stools. William Timmons knelt and reached out his arms to hold Elijah by his shoulders, gently caressing them with his calloused fingers as he looked into his son's eyes. Elijah would never forget what he said and the sadness with which he said it.

"Son, that would be a wonderful thing, and I know you would love to do that and so would I. But we can't go in that place unless we're buying some medicine. We can't go to the soda fountain. But maybe someday we will, and I'll spin you around so much you'll laugh and get dizzy. But not today, son. Not today."

Elijah was only five, but he knew he couldn't sit at the soda fountain because he was black. He didn't understand it, but he knew. That night he prayed for change, and as he grew older, he prayed for the Lord to make him an instrument of that change.

Timmons was musing about that experience just before his Sunday morning service at Mount Gilead AME. The Lord had answered his prayer by making him an instrument of change, but he knew if he took his children to that soda fountain today, they would suffer humiliation or worse. Change came slowly and at a great price. Timmons understood that if change was to come in Pickett County, he had to be the instrument of it, not the apostate Marcus Turner and his ragtag street rebellion.

Looking out over the expectant faces of his flock, Timmons launched the sermon that would make this clear.

"We all lost a brother when Jarvis Pendry was taken away from us, taken away from his wife Evelyn, from his boys, from his community by unreasoning hatred on a Pickett County highway in the dark of night."

With every sentence the congregation murmured in a chorus of agreement.

"Tell it true," someone yelled, and Timmons gave a nod of acknowledgement.

"Who knows what good works he might have performed, what contributions he might have made, what happiness he could have had. All that was taken from him—and from us—by a cowardly assassin's shotgun blast. And in a larger sense he was taken from us by a system that devalues the lives of all blacks, and while times are slowly changing in the South, there is no change in rural backwaters like Pickett County where there is no law but the white man's law, and black people are gunned down while their killers remain free."

A chorus of "Amens" rose from the packed sanctuary.

"Sometimes I watch the news on TV like you do. This morning I saw a candidate for governor on NBC, Roscoe Pike, raising questions about whether the murder of Brother Pendry was a racist act. He even implied another black man might be the killer. And this is the man who could become our next governor—an unapologetic racist demagogue."

Timmons looked out on a sea of shaking heads and heard the collective moaning from his audience. He pulled a local newspaper from a shelf in his pulpit and raised it to show the congregation.

"It's not all bad news. One of the candidates, our Attorney General Harrison Parker, apparently has a conscience. The paper here quotes him as saying the Pendry murder was a racist act that shames the entire white community. For once I can actually agree with a southern white politician."

The congregants reacted with laughter and applause as Timmons held the newspaper aloft and pointed to the article.

"Now we don't do political endorsements in this church, right?" Timmons smiled and tilted his head as he gave an exaggerated wink. His audience laughed and nodded as one.

"But I do believe Brother Parker is on the right track. We'll be keeping an eye on him."

Timmons waited for the congregation's reaction to subside before delivering the crux of his sermon.

"The wheels of justice grind slowly, my friends. As Dr. King recently said, 'The arc of the moral universe is long, but it bends towards justice.' But we cannot sit back and wait. We must bend that arc toward the justice we all seek and deserve. We must take action to keep the nation focused on justice for Jarvis Pendry. I call on people of good will from every corner of our land to join us next Saturday as we march in Pickett County. It is a march for the rule of law. It is a march for justice. It is a march for the moral core of our state and of our nation. Will you join me, my friends? Will you join me? Praise God. Hallelujah. Hallelujah. His truth is marching on!"

The congregation rose to its feet, chanting, applauding, swaying, and screaming "Amen." They did not notice the beam of light that moved across them, a light almost invisible because of the sunlight streaming through the sanctuary's high stained-glass windows. The light came from a camera positioned on a tripod in the balcony, a camera Gil Matthews aimed at the sanctuary below. Timmons had alerted the station that he would have an important announcement at this morning's service, and Gil was there to cover it.

Timmons launched into "We Shall Overcome," and the people of the congregation joined hands, singing and swaying as the hymn resonated throughout the sanctuary.

We are not afraid; we are not afraid today...
Oh, deep in my heart, I do believe,
That we shall overcome some day.

Tears mingled with the sweat on the glistening faces of the worshippers as the strains of the anthem faded in the sweltering old sanctuary. Timmons was genuinely moved by the loyal and emotional response of his flock, and he knew the images would be compelling on the evening news. Though the planned march would be controversial and even dangerous, his people would follow him wherever he led them, even into the godless Gomorrah that was Pickett County.

TWENTY-NINE

BY ANY MEANS NECESSARY

MARCUS TURNER CROUCHED over the basketball and slowly dribbled in place, eyeing his younger brother Tyrone who faced him in defensive posture, arms raised, knees bent, eyes intensely focused on Marcus waiting for his move. It came suddenly as Marcus feinted left and darted to his right. Using his body to protect the ball, he continued to dribble with his right hand, edging toward the netless hoop nailed to his parents' garage since he was seven years old. Tyrone moved with him, swiping his hand in hopes of knocking the ball away, until Marcus stopped, pivoted, and launched the ball toward the goal. The arc of the shot was high and slightly offline, but the sagging hoop had lost its rigidity over time and cushioned the bounce just enough to allow the ball to rattle through.

"Aw man, you gotta be kiddin' me. No way that ball goes in. Damn!"

Tyrone grabbed the ball, dribbled out a few feet, and lofted a hook shot that caromed off the backboard, clanged against the outside lip of the rim, and bounced through. "That's my Bill Russell shot. You just can't stop it."

Marcus laughed as he stooped to rub his still swollen knee. "Oh, I could stop it—even with my bum knee."

"That's what you get messing with those honky police." Tyrone snickered as he draped his arm around Marcus and pulled him toward the house where Sunday supper was waiting.

Andrew and Luvetta Turner looked forward to these Sunday evenings when Marcus could join them for a home-cooked meal. Such occasions were relatively rare because Marcus was so involved with his studies and civil rights protests.

His parents were determined to keep the conversation away from Marcus's firebrand ideas. It was hard to restrain their son from his pontifications no matter the circumstances, but all hope of a quiet evening was lost when he walked through the back door and saw Reverend Elijah Timmons holding forth from his pulpit on the evening news.

Marcus walked up to the television set as Timmons was shouting, "I call on people of good will from every corner of our land to join us next Saturday as we march in Pickett County."

As the flickering black and white images of the congregation swaying and singing the civil rights anthem played on the screen, Marcus turned around and saw his parents and little brother watching him.

"Well, it looks like Uncle Tom Timmons is getting ambitious. I wonder if he can pull this off. I wonder if he might need a little help."

Andrew Turner spoke in a stern voice that Marcus knew well and respected. "Reverend Timmons is a fine man, a leader you should respect. When you try to do things your way you end up injured or in jail with nothing to show for it. I understand you want to be involved, but I beg you to do so with Timmons as your leader."

The four Turners moved to the dining room table and its sumptuous spread of roasted chicken, dressing, squash, green beans, and hot cornbread. After grace, they began passing the food around the table as Luvetta tried to lighten the mood with small talk.

Marcus ignored her banter, looking down at his plate, obviously brooding over Timmons's march and the reproach of his father. Finally, he spoke.

"Dad, Mom, you know I love you and respect you, but you're too patient. You can afford to wait for incremental change because you have a good job, a nice house, and standing in the community. But my generation is not patient. We want change now—by any means necessary. That's why I've got to go to Pickett County. And if there's a price to be paid—and there always is—so be it."

Andrew shoved his plate aside and crossed his arms on the table, looking at his oldest son with deep-set, furrowed eyes.

"Marcus, you have no concept of what we've been through, of what life used to be like in the South for black folk. Things are so much better now, and they'll be better tomorrow because of all Dr. King, Reverend Timmons, and so many other leaders are doing to bring about change. Even our president, who used to be a segregationist, is now leading the charge for civil rights laws that will change everything. It is happening. This is not the time to break away from our nonviolent way. Conflict within the movement can only weaken us and embolden our enemies."

Marcus laughed, looked down at the table, and shook his head.

"Dad, I hear you and I do not wish to disrespect you, but I disagree. We will be kept down until the white man realizes the price of keeping us down is just too high. Nothing will happen unless we raise the stakes, openly challenge power, and, yes, fight back. It must be done. It will be done. I will do it."

Marcus leveled a stare at his father, then his mother, and then young Tyrone, who seemed bewildered about what was happening.

His mother was on the verge of tears, her voice trembling. "Marcus, please don't go to Pickett County."

"Mom, I have to go. I can't let Timmons grandstand like this. The Student Coordinating Council must have a presence, and I can assure you we won't be singing Kumbaya. In fact, I need to get back to campus and start putting our plan together."

Marcus rose from the table and walked into the kitchen, heading for the back door. He spotted the blackberry cobbler his mother had prepared for dessert. "Mom, okay if I grab a piece of cobbler?"

His parents had joined him in the kitchen. His mother embraced him while his father stoically looked on. Then she quickly cut a piece of cobbler and wrapped it in wax paper. "Take it, Marcus. Take it and enjoy it, and when you eat it think of your parents and your brother. Godspeed, my son. Please be safe."

As Marcus walked to his car in the driveway, Andrew called out to him. "Remember, son. Nonviolence is the only way. Violence begets violence and will set our cause back. We will be sick with worry for you."

Marcus paused before closing his car door. "Don't worry, Dad. I'll be fine. Thanks for dinner. I'll be in touch."

He tapped the accelerator, and the rust-flecked Chevy lurched in reverse toward the street. Luvetta and Tyrone joined Andrew in the driveway to watch Marcus rumble away, heading to a future they could not predict or alter. It was as though he was going off to war.

THIRTY

NO TURNING BACK

IT WAS NOT yet seven a.m., but downtown traffic was already beginning to build. Early-rising commuters trickled into the city, trying to beat the vehicular flood that would follow. Devereaux Inman's driver, Clarence Fortson, shook his head as he braked for a motorist who had ignored a caution light and was blocking the intersection for his left-hand turn. Fortson resisted the impulse to blow his horn. Mr. Inman wouldn't approve of that.

"Guess we'll have to start leaving the house a little earlier," Inman groused from the rear seat. "Too much damn traffic. Getting worse by the day."

"Yes sir. That sure is right. Good thing we're almost to the office."

Inman gave lip service to the universal traffic lament, but secretly he rejoiced. Traffic was the lubricant of commerce, the literal wheels of progress. While others might complain of the inconvenience of occasional gridlock, Inman knew it was a welcome symptom of good times to come. The four-lane expressway through the heart of Atlanta was still incomplete, forcing motorists to exit at barricades onto the city's crowded surface streets and follow the detour signs until they could reconnect with the interstate to continue their journeys north or south. When the uncompleted section of the so-called Downtown Connector was finally finished next year, traffic could flow unimpeded through town, bypassing the hodgepodge street grid that had evolved from foot trails and cart paths of the last century. Inman knew that as more people arrived traffic would increase and new roads would be built, maybe even rapid rail transit one day in the future. Atlanta was growing, the future was bright, and he would protect that future with everything he had.

Fortson pulled the black Lincoln Town Car into a narrow one-way canyon between two towering buildings and then made a sharp right turn into an underground garage beneath the Southland Capital Bank Tower, the city's tallest structure. He guided the car into the parking spot near the elevator, coming to a stop just below the sign that read "Reserved for Devereaux Inman, President & CEO, Southland Capital Bank."

Fortson had been Inman's driver for the past ten years. When he wasn't driving, he made himself available for whatever assignment his boss gave him. The hours could be long and sometimes boring, but Fortson never complained because Inman treated him with respect and paid him well.

Fortson hopped out of the vehicle, quickly straightened his tie and buttoned his coat, and then opened the rear door for Inman.

"Thank you, Clarence," Inman said as he grabbed his morning paper from the back seat and headed for the private elevator that would whisk him to the thirtieth floor. Suddenly Inman stopped in his tracks and turned to look at his driver.

"Clarence, have you heard about the march Reverend Timmons is planning this weekend in Pickett County?"

Fortson seemed surprised, but it was typical of Inman to use him as a sounding board for what the black community was thinking. "Yes sir. I heard about it."

"Well, what do you think about it? What are your people thinking?"

"Mr. Inman, I'm not sure what to think. You know I do respect Reverend Timmons. He's done a lot to help our community. I guess I think he's doing a courageous thing, going into Pickett County. Sort of like Daniel going into the lion's den, you might say. But I'm worried about something bad happening."

Inman pursed his lips and slowly shook his head. "So am I, Clarence. So am I."

Moments later Inman walked into his corner office atop the

Southland Capital building and surveyed the scene beneath him through walls of thick but absolutely clear glass. His vista spread out to the north from the core of downtown with its high-rise office buildings, apartment towers, construction cranes, and narrow congested streets to the green canopy of the in-town residential areas to the hazy view of the far suburbs with their scattered pockets of commercial development. On clear days he could see Kennesaw Mountain, where Confederate and Union troops shed their blood a century ago as a prelude to the historic Battle of Atlanta.

This was his city, and Inman never tired of watching it grow. He felt like a parent guiding the development of a restless teen, keeping her out of harm's way as best he could, giving her the love and resources to keep her on the straight and narrow. When a threat arose, he would do everything in his power to thwart it.

His secretary entered the office with a steaming cup of black coffee. "Good morning, Mr. Inman. Will there be anything else?"

"Yes. Good morning, Millie. Could you get Reverend Timmons on the phone for me please?"

Moments later Inman heard Timmons's groggy voice on the line. "Hello? This is Elijah Timmons."

"Reverend, it's Devereaux Inman. Sorry to be calling so early, but I thought you'd be up planning your march."

"We were doing that until two o'clock this morning, Mr. Inman."

Inman dispensed with further pleasantries and got right to the point. "Reverend, what the hell are you thinking? Trying to march in Pickett County. Don't you realize you could get people killed?"

"Mr. Inman, I am quite aware of the risks. But we must put pressure on the reactionary forces running Pickett County. It is time that arrests were made in Brother Pendry's murder. We will keep pushing until that happens."

Inman was exasperated and angry. Timmons was an old adversary, always pushing the city leadership for racial concessions. Inman stayed behind the scenes in those negotiations but played an influential role.

When Timmons and the CAC had recently demanded black officers on the police force, Inman had convinced the mayor that a handful of Negro cops would be acceptable so long as they couldn't arrest whites. It was a small price to pay, he argued, to keep protesters off the streets and out of the news. Inman considered that a victory, but with Timmons there was always another battle looming.

"Reverend, when people think of Birmingham they think of police dogs, cattle prods, and fire hoses washing black protesters down the street. When they think of Atlanta, they imagine a progressive community that looks to the future, a city where black people have a voice, a city where we can reason together for the benefit of all races. A blowup in Pickett County could jeopardize all that we've accomplished. I realize Pickett County is not Atlanta, but if there's violence there, people around the world will say 'That's Georgia, that's the South,' and our city will be tarred with the same brush. I urge you to hold off until they can make an arrest. The FBI has to be close. If you march, you're just going to make everything more difficult."

Timmons responded calmly, but it was clear to Inman he was suppressing his anger.

"If we stopped every time a white man put up his hand, we would still be sitting in the back of the bus and drinking out of water fountains labeled 'colored.' Come to think of it, you can still find those 'colored' rest rooms and water fountains in Pickett County. You can't turn us around, Mr. Inman. It's too late."

Inman paused for a moment to collect himself.

"Look, Reverend. I realize you are under pressure to assert your leadership in the black community given the student uprising that's challenging you. Those young hooligans are clouding your judgement. If you march in Pickett County and all hell breaks loose, your irresponsible actions could hand the governor's race to Roscoe Pike. You need to look at the big picture, Reverend. You will be hurting your movement if you go through with the march."

"You think you pull all the strings, don't you, Mr. Inman? You try to choreograph the way everyone should act to fit your own notions of what is best for our city. This is not altruistic on your part. You act out of self-interest—enlightened self-interest to be sure—but self-interest, nonetheless. It's time you realize you do not call the shots for us. We will be marching this Saturday. And we will send an unmistakable message. Good day, Mr. Inman."

Timmons was tempted to slam the phone down but resisted the impulse and gently lowered the receiver into its cradle as he abruptly ended the call. He visualized Inman in his downtown aerie overlooking his domain, sputtering in frustration over the insolence he'd suffered from Timmons and the realization that his vast power extended only so far.

Mattie, sitting next to her husband on their den sofa, slid closer and kissed Timmons on his cheek as she began to rub his back and neck, kneading the tension from his body.

"I'm proud of you," she said. "You stood up to the bully."

"Thank you, hon. It was not an easy call. But I can't help but wonder if Inman might be right."

"Well, he may be. You know how worried I am about this march, but I also know that you have a calling and there is no turning you around. Pointless to try."

Timmons placed his arm around Mattie and drew her close. "You know how much I want you there with me on Saturday. You are my strength. But I think it's best you stay here with the boys."

Mattie put her head on his chest. "I understand and won't complain, even though I know Evelyn will be there with you, as she must be. I will be so worried about you both. I know God will look after you and bring you home to me."

"Yes, Mattie, I believe He will. Though I walk through the valley of the shadow of death, I will fear no evil for He is with me."

Mattie responded in a barely audible whisper that failed to disguise her doubt and her fear. "Lord's will be done. Amen."

THIRTY-ONE

THE RIGHT THING

"THAT'S THE NEWS on this Tuesday evening. I'm Grayson Kincaid. Thanks for being with us. Stay tuned for Chet Huntley and David Brinkley. And we'll see you back here at eleven."

The camera pulled back for a wide shot of the studio as Kincaid shuffled and stacked the pages of his script and waited for a quick credit roll and fade to black.

He rose from his chair, stretched, and called out, "Nice job, everybody. Good show."

As Kincaid walked toward the studio exit, he saw Gil approaching.

"There's someone here to see you," Gil said, almost in a whisper.

"Who?"

"A woman and her son. Showed up just after six. They're from Pickett County, and they only want to talk to you."

Kincaid paused in the now darkened studio. "I wonder if…" He didn't complete the thought. "Let's go. Where are they?" He began striding toward the exit with Gil rushing just ahead to push open the heavy studio door.

"They're in the conference room. They are very nervous. Burke's in there with them, but they aren't very good at small talk."

Kincaid and Gil hurried down the long hallway to the wide curving stairway that descended to the station's ornate entry hall. The board conference room was across the lobby from General Manager Ron Hill's office, but Hill, his secretary, and the receptionist had left for the day.

Kincaid stopped at the closed conference room door, tapped it lightly, then opened it and entered the room followed by Gil. He saw a plump middle-aged woman, a young man in his twenties, and a very relieved-looking Tom Burke seated at the long mahogany table.

Burke pushed his chair back and stood up to greet him. "Grayson, this is Ella McLeod and her son Rufus. They say they've got something to tell you about the Pendry murder."

Kincaid walked over to the visitors and offered his hand to Ella and then Rufus. They both appeared in awe of meeting the man they'd watched on television for years, but Kincaid was used to this reaction and skillfully tried to put them at ease.

"It's so good to meet you both. Thanks for coming to the station. What can we do for you?"

He rolled one of the executive chairs back, sat down, put his arms on the table, and looked at the McLeods with an expectant smile.

Ella glanced at Rufus then turned to Kincaid. "Grayson, if I may call you that..."

Kincaid nodded vigorously. "Of course...please."

"Grayson, we have prayed about this, and we feel we have to share something with you about the murder of Jarvis Pendry in our county. Caleb Soseby told Rufus here that the Sosebys—Caleb and his daddy Hiram—were the ones who killed Pendry. Rufus kept it quiet for a while, but he just couldn't live with it, so he came to me and my husband Tom and told us what he'd heard. As I said, we have prayed over this. We didn't feel like we could go to Sheriff McSwain because he has connections with that crowd. We had to find someone we trusted—someone outside the county—someone like you. So, now you know. I hope we are doing the right thing."

Kincaid, Burke, and Gil sat in stunned silence.

"Of course you are." Kincaid in a soft, reassuring voice. "Rufus, can you tell me how you learned about this?"

Rufus, obviously uncomfortable, looked down and spoke in a laconic, barely audible mumble. "We was out fishing. Drinking. He was drunk and just said it. Out of the blue. He said a black man came into his gas station smartin' off, and they killed him. Plain as that. He told me not to say nothin', but I can't live with this. Had to tell my parents."

Ella was fighting hard to stifle her emotions. She reached out to pat Rufus's trembling hand. "You did the right thing, son. You did the courageous thing."

She turned to look at Kincaid. "My husband did not want us to tell anyone about this. We have lived in Pickett County our whole lives. We have a business there. This could ruin us. But what happened to that man is wrong. It's a horrible crime. And there are good people in Pickett County who want the killers brought to justice, but they're afraid to speak out. Bad things could happen. But the Lord told me we had to tell this story, so here we are, and I hope to God we won't regret it."

Kincaid reached out to take Ella's hand. "Mrs. McLeod, were you the ones who sent the letter to me naming the Sosebys?"

"Yes. I told Rufus to write it, but we weren't sure you'd get it or understand it. That's why we decided to come see you in person."

Kincaid patted her hand and then released it. "What you are doing is very brave. And it *is* the right thing to do. We turned your note over to the GBI. I can assure you they are already looking at the Sosebys, but what you have told us will give them what they need to start making a case. Would you be willing to talk with investigators?"

"Yes, we will," said Ella. "But not Sheriff McSwain. We don't want anyone in Pickett County to know what we've done. If it gets out, we could be ruined—lose our business, have to move away, or worse. Can you guarantee we'll be protected?"

Kincaid nodded and then lied. "Yes. I think so. It will be up to law enforcement, but you will be protected, I'm sure."

Ella looked unconvinced but smiled nervously. Her voice quavered. "We heard there might be a reward."

Her question disappointed Kincaid, but he was not surprised by it.

"The victim's widow has offered a reward leading to the arrest and conviction of her husband's killers. Beyond that I don't know much. Once the guilty party is behind bars and convicted, I guess they'll work that out."

Gil and Burke sat silently watching this exchange, realizing that any comment from them would break the connection Kincaid had so expertly established with the McLeods.

"Could we call the agent we've been working with?" Kincaid asked. "Bill Conyers? He's a Georgia boy, and he will deal straight with you. We could probably get him here in half an hour."

Ella looked at Rufus, who continued to slump in his chair and stare down at the table.

"Yes," she said. "I think so. We do trust you, Grayson. Thank you for listening."

Gil rose from the table and backed away toward the door. "I'll call Conyers right now. Hopefully he'll be here soon to get your statements."

As Gil left the room, an awkward silence set in. Kincaid and Burke exchanged glances that conveyed an understanding of the momentous revelation they'd just received. Had the McLeods not been present they would be shaking hands, even hugging, to celebrate the achievement. But the circumstances dictated a solemn demeanor, an acknowledgement of the dangerous path the McLeods had taken. Rufus had betrayed a friend, and his mother had put her family at risk. They had every reason to be afraid of what the future might hold.

Kincaid rose and smiled in an attempt to lift the pall that filled the boardroom. "Would you two like a station tour?"

Ella brightened immediately. Rufus barely acknowledged the offer.

"Why, that would be wonderful. We'd love to see the station."

Kincaid ushered them from the boardroom, up the staircase, and down the hall to the newsroom where the night shift was busily preparing for the eleven o'clock news. He thought of the irony that Ella and Rufus had handed him the biggest exclusive of his career, but he couldn't say a word until what they told him resulted in arrests and charges. He felt confident that would happen very soon. He was much less confident about what lay ahead for the McLeods.

THIRTY-TWO

MIDNIGHT VISIT

LUCAS MCSWAIN WAS having difficulty sleeping, as was often the case these days. He was slumped in his recliner watching the closing moments of *The Tonight Show* and waiting for Johnny Carson's sign-off, which would be followed by scenes of tanks, fighter planes, military parades, and the American flag as the National Anthem played and the station went off the air for the night. He reached for his almost empty beer can and lifted it to his lips. Some liquid spilled on his sleeveless undershirt. He still wore the rumpled pants of his uniform, covered in crumbs from the chips he'd been eating all evening.

The phone on a table across the room began ringing, and McSwain, with a curse, laboriously rose from his chair and shuffled over in his stocking feet, hoping the ringing wouldn't awaken his wife. She'd been asleep for an hour.

"Yes? Hello? This is Sheriff McSwain."

"Sheriff, it's Hiram. You'd better get over to my house. Right now. The feds are here, and they've got a search warrant. They want to take me and Caleb in for questioning."

McSwain crushed the beer can in his hand and let it fall to the floor. "Shit. I'll be right there. Don't say anything until I get there. You understand?"

"Okay. But hurry. They're going through our closets. My wife is hysterical. What's this all about?"

"Hang on. I'm coming."

McSwain retrieved his uniform shirt from the sofa and hurriedly put it on, cramming the shirttail into his wrinkled, stained pants. He was aware he'd be only marginally presentable, but he needed to get to

Soseby's as soon as possible. He strapped on his pistol belt as he rushed out the door.

The sheriff had known something was up. He knew the FBI had been following suspected Klan members around the county and asking a lot of questions, but he'd been kept out of the loop. That made him furious, and he often publicly berated the "outsiders" who were making it more difficult for him to solve the case, even though he had done virtually nothing to find Pendry's killers. He could not, however, stand by and let the state and feds make him appear impotent in his own domain.

Soseby's house was seven minutes away, and the sheriff floored the accelerator, swerving along the narrow residential streets. He knew there would be no pedestrians. Folks went to bed early in Pickett County.

As he rounded the last corner, he saw the flashing red lights outside Soseby's ranch-style home. He pulled to the curb, lumbered out, and climbed the sloping driveway. He saw a figure approach from the shadows and recognized Bill Conyers. McSwain was out of breath and sputtering.

"What the hell is going on here? Why wasn't I informed? This is outrageous."

"Now Sheriff," Conyers tried a soothing tone, but it had little effect. "Things were moving quickly, and it was late. We were going to call you but had to move when we got the federal search warrant. We have reason to believe Soseby and his son know more than they're telling about the Pendry murder."

As they stood in the driveway, McSwain could see the light show of flashlight beams as agents walked around the yard. Through a picture window he saw others going through drawers and a bookcase in the living room.

"Agent Conyers, I am the sheriff of Pickett County. This is my jurisdiction. You have no right to do what you're doing without my involvement." McSwain suppressed a burp. He regretted drinking that last beer, but the circumstances of the past half hour had sobered him.

FBI Agent Robert Smithers, having heard the confrontation, walked over and stood at Conyers's side.

"Sheriff, I'm Robert Smithers, FBI, agent in charge. Agent Conyers and I have coordinated on this, and I apologize for not letting you know sooner. We want to give you a full briefing. And we would appreciate your cooperation in letting us take Mr. Soseby and his son to your headquarters in Armistead so we can question them."

McSwain, struggling to control his temper, said nothing. He suddenly brushed by both men, walked up the brick steps, and headed through the open door of the house. Smithers and Conyers followed closely behind him.

Hiram Soseby sat on the sofa in the living room, comforting his weeping wife as agents moved around the house. His son Caleb sulked in the corner with a bewildered, frightened look on his face. When he saw McSwain enter the room, the elder Soseby rose to greet him.

"Lucas, what's this all about? They say they're taking us in for questioning about the murder. Can you help us?"

"Hiram, I'm as surprised by this as you are. They kept it from me. The feds are stripping every aspect of local control out of our county. But I'm here now, so I won't let them get away with anything. Tell Sadie not to worry. It's all a big mistake."

McSwain strode back to the edge of the room near the front door where Smithers and Conyers waited for the confrontation to continue.

"Let's step back outside," Conyers said. "We can fill you in on the situation."

"A little late on the professional courtesy," McSwain snarled.

When they were back on the front lawn, Conyers began to explain. "We have someone who says Caleb Soseby told him he and his father murdered Jarvis Pendry. We've long suspected the murder was Klan-related, and as you well know Soseby has been involved in the Klan for some time. We are still trying to pin down elements of the story, but considering the reliability of the source and the urgency to make an arrest, we felt like we had to act quickly. We again apologize for leaving you out of the loop."

McSwain hitched up his pants and spat. "Shee-it! Are you telling me you're acting on hearsay? I think you just had to do something because of this march coming up Saturday. I think you boys jumped the gun on this. No way I can cooperate if this is the way you're going to act."

Smithers stepped toward McSwain. He spoke in low tones edged with anger. "Sheriff, you have not cooperated at all throughout this investigation. In fact, you have made it very difficult for us. That's why we're moving ahead with or without you. I think it would be in your best interest to stop the bullshit and work with us for a change."

As Smithers was talking, a harsh glare bathed McSwain's face. The beam came from Gil Matthews's light atop his camera as he moved toward the sheriff, focusing as he approached. Mindy was right beside him with the mike. She had awakened Gil two hours earlier after Conyers tipped her off about the search warrant. It took him some time to assemble the gear, pick up Mindy, and make the trip to Armistead.

McSwain raised his arm to shield his face from the beam of light. He was furious that reporters, obviously tipped off, were now involved. He was painfully aware that the only possible outcome would make him look very bad.

"What the hell are you doing here? Who told you about this?"

The light was blinding, but McSwain could make out the silhouette of the television camera and the small frame of a woman. When she spoke, McSwain recognized Mindy's voice.

"Sheriff, what can you tell us about what's going on here?"

Smithers and Conyers, wanting no part in the coverage, had stepped back into the shadows, leaving a confused McSwain to face the music. McSwain quickly realized he was in a no-win position, being questioned about an operation he'd had no part in and knew almost nothing about. He felt his only choice was to bluff his way through the interview and at least give the impression that he was running the show.

"Well, we're here on a warrant to search this home and take the residents in for questioning. The FBI and GBI are assisting me in this, but that's about all I can say right now. I'm going to ask you to step back and not interfere with this operation."

Gil spoke out from behind his camera, his right eye against the viewfinder as he kept filming. "Sheriff, is Hiram Soseby a suspect in the Pendry murder?"

McSwain began walking back toward the house, speaking over his shoulder as he moved. "I can't really comment on that at this time. We may want to take Hiram in for some questions, but I doubt it will amount to much."

"What about his son Caleb?" Gil was slightly out of breath as he sidestepped to keep pace with McSwain, the camera on his shoulder mount recording everything. Mindy moved with him, holding a hand mike connected to the camera.

"Look, now. Caleb is a fine young man. Known him for years. We just need to talk to him and his dad. It's all routine."

As McSwain quickly retreated into the house, Gil pivoted with his camera and light to show Smithers and Conyers, who'd been standing in the shadows. "What can you tell us about what's happening here tonight. Agent Smithers?"

"We're executing a federal search warrant here at the home of Hiram Soseby. We are hoping Mr. Soseby and his son might have information that would be helpful to us in the Jarvis Pendry murder investigation."

Smithers nodded toward Conyers. "This is a joint operation involving the FBI, the state, and, of course, Pickett County authorities are assisting."

Mindy spoke up, giving her normally soft southern drawl an insistent edge. "Why a federal warrant?"

Smithers hesitated for a second before responding. "This is a murder case, but we believe it's also a civil rights case, and that gives us federal jurisdiction. We needed to act quickly to get this warrant, and the most expeditious path was through a federal judge. The murder of Jarvis Pendry was the ultimate violation of his civil rights. We hope to act in concert with the state and Sheriff McSwain to bring about justice in this case. That's really all I can say at this point. Now if you'll will just step back onto the lawn and stay out of our way. Thank you."

Smithers and Conyers turned and walked back toward the house, Conyers looking over his shoulder to make eye contact with Mindy and give her a barely perceptible wink and nod. Gil noticed the silent exchange through the lens of his camera, and once the two lawmen were inside, he turned to Mindy.

"What's going on with you two?"

Mindy ignored the question, and Gil did not pursue it. Not the time or place, he thought.

For the next hour Gil and Mindy stood on the home's front lawn, watching the searchers move in and out of the house carrying bags of presumed evidence. Gil shot some film of the activity, even though he already had more visuals than he could use.

Shortly after one a.m., Mindy nudged Gil and pointed to the front porch. Hiram Soseby and his son Caleb were being escorted from the home to a government car in the driveway. Gil quickly hefted the camera and ran toward the front walk, Mindy alongside him holding the mike. He moved in front of the agents and the two subjects and backpedaled as they strode down the concrete walkway toward the vehicle. Both Sosebys, now bathed in the camera's light, turned their heads away and raised their hands to their faces as if to ward off the penetrating glare.

"Mr. Soseby," Gil called out. "Are you now a suspect in the murder of Jarvis Pendry?"

The Sosebys did not acknowledge the question as the agents surrounding them hustled them into the rear seat and closed the doors. Gil stepped into the driveway to film the car backing into the street and pulling away.

He spotted Sheriff McSwain walking down the sloping lawn to

his car parked along the curb.

"Where are they taking them, Sheriff?" Gil yelled.

"Armistead," McSwain mumbled as he opened his car door and slipped behind the steering wheel. "But you've got all you're gonna get tonight," he barked as he slammed the car door and pulled away.

Gil and Mindy rushed to their car. Gil opened the station wagon's tailgate, dumped his camera gear inside, and they sped toward Armistead. Mindy sat beside him, furiously scribbling in her notepad the story she would dictate to her wire service once she found a telephone.

As they drove, Gil could hold his thoughts no longer. "Okay. I need to know what's between you and Conyers. My station supplied the break on the Sosebys. You know as well as I that Conyers owed me and the station—so why are you the favored one? Is there something going on here I should know about?"

Mindy put her notebook aside, sighed deeply, and looked straight ahead as the taillights of the sheriff's car led them down the narrow road toward Armistead's town square. "It's really none of your business. He's been a great source, and your station has reaped the benefits because I've shared every tip with you. Just let it go, Gil. It's been a long night, and it's not over yet. We don't need this distraction. Not now."

Gil did not reply. He should have felt the surge of energy a big story brings along with the unadulterated joy of owning it. Instead, he felt, perhaps unfairly, that Mindy was depriving him of that. He tried to shake it off, to concentrate on the mission at hand, but he couldn't push from his mind the silent connection he had witnessed between Mindy and Conyers. Try as he might, he couldn't let it go.

THIRTY-THREE

THE ACCUSED

HIRAM SOSEBY SAT on a metal folding chair barely substantial enough to hold his obese body. His ample thighs and buttocks spilled over the small unpadded seat, so much so that even a slight shifting of position was difficult.

He was sequestered in a windowless, stuffy room just down the hall from the sheriff's office. The florescent light fixture overhead bathed the room in a pallid institutional glow. It was three o'clock in the morning, and he was tired, sweaty, and slightly nauseous. He yearned for a glass of water and a fan to stir the air as he waited nervously for whatever came next.

He could hear murmurs as lawmen conferred in the hallway. He couldn't make out what they were saying but recognized the voices of agents Smithers, Conyers, and Sheriff McSwain. Finally, the two agents came into the room followed by the sheriff. Conyers and McSwain stood against the wall while Smithers pulled over another metal folding chair, opened it, and sat down facing Soseby, so close their knees almost touched.

Soseby was the first to speak. "Where's Caleb? What have you done with my boy?"

Smithers gave him slight reassurance. "Caleb's fine. He's right down the hall with one of our men. We just talked to him."

At that moment, another man entered the room holding a notepad. He opened a third folding chair and sat down with the pad in his lap, his pen poised to take notes on the interview.

Soseby tried to hide his apprehension with the bravado he had cultivated throughout his life. It was an innate part of his rural Southernness, to project a rough nonchalance that reflected pride in ignorance and contempt for authority. He folded his short arms across his chest and curled his lip in a sneer.

"You boys trying to scare me? Not gonna work. I ain't done nothing. I want my lawyer."

Smithers moved ahead impassively. "Hiram, we just have a few questions. If you want a lawyer, you can get one later. Just tell us what we want to know. No bullshit."

Soseby glanced over to Sheriff McSwain standing against the wall, arms folded, hoping to detect a glimmer of support in his eyes, but the sheriff just stared blankly at the floor.

"Let's start with the night Jarvis Pendry was murdered. Did you see him that night?" Smithers's tone was mild, almost conversational.

"No."

"He didn't stop by your filling station asking for directions?"

"No."

"You didn't follow him up the road?"

"No! I done told you that over and over. I did not see that darkie, and neither did my boy. Now let me go home."

Smithers nodded slowly before asking his next question, this time with more urgency. "Hiram, if Pendry had come to your place, you would have served him, right? Let him buy a snack or use your restroom as the law requires?"

"Hell no! That law is unconstitutional. It violates my private property rights. Coloreds can buy gas from me, but they ain't using my restrooms. And I don't particularly want them in my store. But it never happened, so it's silly to even talk about it."

"Are you a member of the Ku Klux Klan?"

Soseby shifted position slightly, his chair creaking under the strain. "No."

"Have you ever been a member of the Ku Klux Klan?"

"No."

"Hiram, we have reason to believe otherwise. We know about your

Klan history."

"Well, I used to run with some of those boys. Old friends I grew up with. We ain't done nothing wrong, you know. Play cards, drink beer—that sort of thing."

Smithers glanced over at the agent with the notepad, giving him time to finish writing down Soseby's latest response.

"Hiram, do you own any shotguns?"

"I used to, but not anymore. I quit huntin' so I don't need a shotgun."

"What would you say if I told you we know you purchased a double-barreled twelve-gauge shotgun on April fifteenth at Shot Shack Gun Store in Cherokee? Along with ten boxes of shells? You are apparently a regular customer there. But we couldn't find that shotgun at your home. What happened to it?"

Soseby's belligerence was being eroded by growing confusion and dread. "I, um, I gave it away. It was a gift."

"Who did you give it to?"

"That's my business. This is crazy. I'm not answering any more questions. Let me out of here."

"We found that shotgun in a burlap bag under a shed behind your house. We believe it's just like the weapon that killed Jarvis Pendry. How did it get there? Did you remove it from your house after the murder to avoid detection?"

Soseby rose from his chair. Smithers also stood and inched back as Conyers stepped forward with his hand on the pistol in his shoulder holster. McSwain still leaned against the wall as if he was an impartial bystander.

Soseby quickly realized he had no options and sat down. Conyers moved his hand away from his weapon and stepped back against the wall.

"I ain't answering any more questions. Now let me see my boy. And my attorney."

Smithers remained standing. "In good time. But the fact of the matter, Hiram, is that we have reason to believe you and Caleb murdered Jarvis Pendry and violated his civil rights. We are placing you both under arrest. If you know a lawyer, you can call him tonight. But you won't be going home. You're both heading to the county jail, but you and Caleb won't be together. Seems like he has a story too, but it doesn't agree with what you're telling us. No point in letting you two get on the same page."

Soseby practically spat his reply. "You don't have nothin' on us. No evidence. You're bluffing. And you know there ain't a white person in this county who will vote to convict a white man for killin' a black."

Conyers stepped forward and put cuffs on Soseby's chubby wrists, grabbed his elbow, and pushed him roughly toward the door. As they marched him into the main office area, Soseby saw Caleb also in cuffs, tears streaking his young, fearful face.

Agents and deputies shepherded the suspects into the parking lot as two government cars pulled around to pick them up for the trip to the county jail about a mile away on the outskirts of Armistead.

Gil and Mindy were waiting in the lot, having been denied entrance to the sheriff's department. They immediately realized that the Sosebys were under arrest. Gil aimed his light and camera at the group of lawmen as they pushed the handcuffed suspects into separate cars.

"Sheriff, Agent Smithers—tell us what's going on," Gil yelled.

Smithers walked into the circle of light as Conyers and McSwain stood silently behind him. "We have arrested Hiram Soseby and his son Caleb Soseby on federal civil rights charges related to the murder of Colonel Jarvis Pendry. We are hopeful state murder charges will also be forthcoming. The suspects will be held in the Pickett County jail until further notice. That's all we have to say at this time."

Gil stopped his camera, shut off his light, and began loading his equipment into his station wagon while Mindy ran to a phone booth on the street corner nearby to dictate her story. When she finished, Gil called to tell the station's overnight desk to prepare the film processor for an early run for the morning news. Then he and Mindy began the forty-five-minute drive back to the city.

There was no conversation. Mindy worked on updating and refining her hastily written initial version while Gil mentally composed the story he would write once he arrived at the station. Mindy's story would be on the wires and thus radio newscasts, but it wouldn't make the deadline for the morning newspaper. Gil's filmed story would lead the morning newscast, a major TV exclusive.

It was almost four o'clock in the morning, and the full moon cast a dull glow over the countryside and the road ahead. Mindy set her notebook aside and looked to the western sky as small clouds scuttled across the lunar reflection.

"A ghostly galleon," she thought, "tossed upon cloudy seas."

It was one of her favorite poetic images, but she chose not to share it with Gil.

THIRTY-FOUR

MR. SOLICITOR

SHERIFF LUCAS MCSWAIN had not often experienced the sting of complete humiliation, but on the morning after the arrests of the Sosebys he felt humbled, embarrassed, and angry. It was bad enough that the feds had come into his county and wrested control of the murder investigation from him, but to arrest two of his constituents on federal civil rights charges was outrageous.

When they had arrived at the sheriff's office with the Sosebys the night before, he had demanded that Smithers and Conyers give him a complete briefing on their case. With some reluctance they had agreed. Whether they could trust the sheriff or not, they understood he had an important role to play in the prosecution of the case. In short, they needed him, but he also needed them to help him save face.

The case they outlined to him was, in his view, flimsy—a hearsay statement from someone who said Caleb admitted that he and his father murdered Jarvis Pendry, a hidden shotgun similar to the murder weapon that had been purchased by Hiram Soseby and stashed under a shed in his backyard, and Soseby's known history with the Klan in Pickett County. Smithers acknowledged they needed more evidence, but he was optimistic that news of the arrests would generate more leads to bolster their case. He also admitted the civil rights march two days away put extra pressure on them to act quickly, even if it meant making arrests before the case was airtight.

Now, as news of the arrests and federal charges broke, McSwain knew he had to find a way to regain control. That's why he had driven to the town of Troy in neighboring Whitney County, where the office of the solicitor general was located.

Solicitor General Carson Baker was the chief prosecutor for the Lanier Judicial Circuit that included Pickett County. If murder charges against the Sosebys were to be pursued, Baker would present the case to the grand jury for indictment.

McSwain entered the courthouse rotunda and climbed the marble stairs to the second floor, nodding to courthouse staff and citizens who seemed to recognize him along the way. The Whitney County Courthouse was a much more substantial structure than its counterpart in Pickett County. Troy was the largest town in the judicial circuit and enjoyed relative prosperity of which the people of Armistead were quite envious. The pride of the town was Whitney College, a small liberal arts school of about a thousand students. The presence of Whitney's administration, faculty, and students moderated the county's basic conservatism, giving the community a veneer of educated civility that was totally absent in adjoining Pickett County. This moderating influence tempered the political climate and helped Carson Baker hold the solicitor general's post for decades.

Baker enjoyed the luxury of being a veteran incumbent in a race so far down the ballot that voters often didn't even vote for the office. And even if they did, it really didn't matter because Baker seldom had any opposition. In his early campaigns he had recited the segregationist mantra as approving audiences cheered him on, but over the years his views had softened. He knew that if all men were, indeed, created equal, the system of Southern apartheid was doomed. He had long ago determined that he would not be an activist in the system's downfall but rather do all he could to be a fair and impartial administrator of the law, with the understanding that fair and impartial were relative terms when it came to racial justice in the South.

One of the crosses he had to bear was working with a man like Sheriff Lucas McSwain, whom he viewed as a petty potentate who made little secret of his racist views and used the law to suit his own prejudices. But, despite his disapproval of McSwain, he felt an obligation to deal with him as a fellow elected legal professional, and that's the way he welcomed him when he came through the office door.

"Morning, Lucas," Baker said with a welcoming smile. "Good to see you. You had quite a night, didn't you?"

Baker was sixty-two years old, but his slim frame, ruddy complexion, and bright, curious eyes made him appear much younger. He had a full head of wavy, silvering hair, a shock of which was constantly flopping onto his forehead, necessitating a quick sweep of his hand to put it back in its proper place.

"Good to see you, Carson. Yes, quite a night. I didn't get much sleep, so I hope I make sense."

McSwain was nervous. He was out of his domain and facing a man who always made him feel somehow inferior. Baker seemed to realize this but chose not to stoop to compensate.

"I know why you're here, Lucas. But why don't you fill me in?" Baker pointed to a padded leather chair, and McSwain settled into it with a deep sigh.

"As you know, the feds arrested Hiram and Caleb Soseby on civil rights charges. I think they jumped the gun because of that protest march Saturday, but I'm feeling great pressure to charge them with murder. That, of course, will depend on you and what you can sell to a grand jury to get an indictment."

Baker walked around his desk and sat down in his chair, leaning back. "How strong is the case?"

"Not very," McSwain replied. "In fact, it's weak. They've got a friend of Caleb's who says Caleb confessed to him, but Caleb denies that. They've got a shotgun that belongs to Hiram Soseby that theoretically could have been the murder weapon. And of course, there's the Klan connection. They may have more, but they're not sharing everything with me. We may have to file murder charges to get this case back in our jurisdiction. What do you think?"

Baker rocked back and forth in his executive chair and stroked his chin.

'You'll need more for a murder indictment. I'll need more

evidence to make a case. Do you think the Sosebys killed Jarvis Pendry?"

"I've known them for a long time," McSwain said. "Hiram's a rough guy. He's run with the Klan. Hates blacks. I wouldn't put it past him to try to take one out if maybe he'd been drinking or got riled up."

"I've heard of him," Baker responded. "We've looked into Klan activity over the years. I remember the name, but I have to have more evidence to get an indictment."

McSwain hunched forward, his forearms resting on his thick thighs. "We need to work on Caleb. He's scared to death and pretty stupid. I don't think he'll turn on his father, but we might be able to get more out of him. Like I say, he's a dimwit. I've got a hunch someone else might have been in the car—probably the driver. So we'll keep working on Caleb. The problem is we don't have much time."

Baker leaned forward too, placing his elbows on his desk. "Lucas, I need to be real honest with you. When you have suspects who are charged, I will be ready to prosecute them. The murder of Jarvis Pendry is a crime that demands punishment. I will mount a vigorous prosecution. While some may think white people will not vote to convict a white man of killing a black man, I strongly disagree. But that's beside the point. I believe in the law. And I am ready to prosecute to the full extent of the law if you will bring me a case. We do not excuse the murder of a black man in this jurisdiction, even in your county where standards may be a bit more—shall we say—lenient."

Baker's shock of unruly hair had slipped down his forehead as he spoke, and he swept it back with his hand. "Bring me a case. I'll take it from there."

McSwain gripped his chair's armrests and pushed himself laboriously to a standing position. "Mr. Solicitor, I appreciate your time. I will bring you a case. Hopefully soon. Thank you."

McSwain turned to leave, but when he reached the office door Baker offered a parting question. "Lucas, before you go, you were with Patton in Europe, right?"

McSwain turned to eye Baker with a skeptical look. "Yes, I was. Twenty-sixth Infantry. Metz to the Rhine. Why?

"Then you were at Bastogne."

"Proud to say I was. Why?"

"Did you know Jarvis Pendry was at Bastogne? I read about it after his murder. His platoon took out a machine gun nest."

McSwain tried but failed to hide his surprise. "I knew he was a war vet. I just assumed he was in the rear like most blacks over there."

Baker leaned back in his chair and looked up at the ceiling fan slowly revolving overhead. He spoke pensively. "It's interesting to think that Patton's rescue of the troops at Bastogne—which involved your outfit—might have saved Pendry's life. And who knows? By taking out that machine gun, he might have saved yours."

McSwain nodded dismissively and turned to go. "Well, Carson, that's pretty far-fetched. The war is over, and I try not to think about it. Now if you'll excuse me, I've got things to do. I'll be in touch."

The sheriff walked into the hallway and down the marble stairs to the rotunda lobby below. He resented Baker's condescension, his imperious lecturing, and his inane musings about the war. Baker had no right to question him about the personal nightmare that was Bastogne. That bitter experience had changed him forever. And as much as he resisted the thought, he couldn't help but wonder if the same had been true for Jarvis Pendry.

THIRTY-FIVE

MARCH EVE

FULLY EIGHT MINUTES of Friday's six p.m. news was devoted to the arrests of the Sosebys and the reaction to the break in the Pendry case. Gil and other reporters and photographers had been in Armistead most of the day interviewing officials and people on the street about what had happened early that morning.

Gil's brain felt numb after only three hours of sleep, but the excitement of a big story kept him going. Now he sat in the newsroom, sweaty, disheveled, and unshaven, sipping lukewarm coffee from a vending machine cup, watching a monitor on the newsroom wall as a cool and professional Grayson Kincaid delivered the news they had gathered.

"Federal agents came to the Soseby home armed with a search warrant signed by a federal judge," Kincaid read as scenes of the previous night played on the screen. "Pickett County Sheriff Lucas McSwain arrived as the search was already underway."

The scenes Gil had filmed of the agents with flashlights faded into a sound bite with Sheriff McSwain, looking rumpled, tired, and out of sorts. "Well, we're here on a warrant to search this home and take the residents in for questioning. The FBI and GBI are assisting me in this, but that's about all I can say right now."

Kincaid picked up the narration over scenes of the sheriff holding up his hands and walking away apparently in anger. "FBI and state agents were there to coordinate the search, and they were the ones who took the Sosebys in for questioning."

At this point viewers saw Hiram and Caleb Soseby being walked from their home to the government car in the driveway. It would have seemed obvious to most viewers that Sheriff McSwain, despite his comment, was definitely not in charge of the operation.

As exterior scenes of the Pickett County Sheriff's Department filled the screen, Kincaid continued. "The suspects were taken to the Pickett County Sheriff's Department in Armistead where they were questioned. Our Gil Matthews, the only television newsman on the scene, was not allowed to enter the building and had to wait outside. After about two hours, the Sosebys were escorted out of the sheriff's office in handcuffs, loaded into separate cars, and taken to the Pickett County Jail. They have been charged with conspiracy to violate the civil rights of Jarvis Pendry. Today we asked Sheriff McSwain if state murder charges will be filed against the Sosebys."

McSwain reappeared on screen, looking much more professional than the night before. He was clean-shaven and his uniform had been pressed, but the puffiness around his eyes and his drawn expression showed the strain of a sleepless night.

"We do anticipate filing murder charges against Hiram and Caleb Soseby. I talked with Solicitor General Carson Baker this morning, and we hope to take the case to a grand jury soon. We do appreciate the assistance of the FBI in the case, but I'd like to assure you that the people of Pickett County are fully prepared to handle this terrible episode in our proud history without undue outside help. In the meantime, we welcome any further evidence that anyone might have to aid in the prosecution of this case."

A wide shot showed several cameras and reporters clustered around the sheriff. A network reporter spoke up.

"Sheriff, can you detail the evidence against the Sosebys? Is there a Klan connection?"

"Well, you boys know I can't go into evidence," McSwain responded. "Let's just say we have a good case."

Kincaid resumed his narration. "This morning's arrests come just before a civil rights protest march in Pickett County tomorrow. Local civil rights leader Elijah Timmons is leading what he is calling a March for Justice and in this interview says the arrests will not change his plans."

"We will continue our March for Justice," Timmons said, "because the light of truth needs to shine on Pickett County. This is a county permeated by racism and dominated by the disgusting philosophy of the Ku Klux Klan. We will be out in force, joined by the widow of Jarvis Pendry and people of good will from all over. Let freedom ring."

The solemn visage of Grayson Kincaid appeared on the screen. "We will have full coverage of tomorrow's march and, of course, any updates on developments in the arrests of suspects in Pickett County and the continuing investigation. Now we pause for a brief commercial break. Please stay with us."

Gil slowly rose from his chair. The fatigue that had been accumulating for the past thirty-six hours began hitting him full force. He had to shake off a brief dizzy spell, but a few sips of his now cold coffee revived him.

Tom Burke came out of his office and slapped him on the back. "Helluva a job today. Helluva job. You must be exhausted."

"Pretty tired. Think I'll head home. I'm not sure I can sit through Weather and Sports."

Burke laughed. He was in the best of moods. "Well, I'm sure Grayson would like to congratulate you too, but I guess he can wait. You've got a big day tomorrow. Carney and a couple of photogs will be there to back you up. Think that's enough manpower?"

"I think so. Mindy will probably ride up with me. She'll be an extra reporter for us even though her first obligation is the AP. Maybe you ought to think about hiring her."

"Not a bad idea. Sooner or later, we'll have to have a female reporter, I guess. Couldn't do much better than Mindy. She's really cute...and smart," Burke quickly added. "Plus, she's got great sources. Any idea where she gets these tips?"

"Well, I'm pretty sure it's Bill Conyers. She won't talk about it.

Something's going on with them, and I'm not sure what."

"Hmmm." Burke gave a sly smile. "Who wouldn't want a cute brunette as a"—he raised his hands and air-quoted—"confidant." He was surprised when Gil turned away with a somber expression and headed for the door.

"Gil," Burke said, lowering his voice an octave as he always did when he was trying to sound sincere. "Please be careful. We don't know what could happen tomorrow, but I'm worried. Just watch yourself. No story is worth getting hurt."

"Goodnight, Tom," Gil said as he ambled toward the rear door of the newsroom. "We who are about to die salute you."

"Not funny," Burke said to his departing cameraman-reporter. "Not funny at all."

THIRTY-SIX

VALLEY OF THE SHADOW

A thin layer of overcast kept the rays of the rising sun at bay over Pickett County, but it would be a brief reprieve. Soon enough the sun's heat would begin burning off the clouds, allowing beams to diffuse through the foliage of oak, pine, and poplar. And once that barrier had been cleared, the sun would have free rein to bathe the earth in scorching heat that would grow in intensity by the minute as its arc rose ever higher.

Three buses full of marchers lumbered around a curve and pulled single file off the highway onto a field on the outskirts of Armistead. TV camera teams jostled into position to film the first marchers to descend from the lead bus. Gil had to elbow a network soundman to have a clear shot at the bus door.

First to get off was Reverend Timmons, smiling broadly, obviously pleased by the number of news teams gathered to cover his march. Wearing khakis, a short-sleeve plaid sports shirt, and brogans, he looked very out of place to those who knew his usual formality.

When he stepped to the ground, Timmons immediately turned and extended his hand upwards to Evelyn Pendry. She took his hand as she carefully descended the steps, releasing it once she stood on the ground by Timmons's side. She wore tan slacks, a yellow blouse, and white tennis shoes.

Timmons gestured for her to walk with him a few steps beyond the bus as the other marchers clambered out and began to gather behind the reverend and the widow. Timmons didn't wait for all three buses to empty before he pivoted to face the sun and began his statement.

"Thank you all for being here to cover this historic occasion—our March for Freedom in Pickett County. We are truly honored today by the presence of Mrs. Evelyn Pendry whose husband Colonel Jarvis Pendry was senselessly gunned down not far from here. This assassination was carried out by cowardly night riders, no doubt members of the Ku Klux Klan, who somehow viewed Jarvis Pendry as some kind of threat—Jarvis Pendry, a war hero, a prominent businessman, a beloved husband and father."

"We are pleased," Timmons continued, "that arrests have been made and more may come, but that does not address the core problem here in Pickett County, and that is the problem of racism and hate. We march today to say to the world that Pickett County must change— that black people can find a new day of freedom in a place where they still exist in a form of slavery—because fear is a form of slavery—and we march to hasten the day when we and all of God's people are free."

Satisfied that his preamble had properly set the stage, Timmons turned to Evelyn.

"Evelyn, I know you want to say a few words before we begin."

"I am here today," she said in an unwavering voice, "because my husband would want me to be here. We are not from the South and never imagined Jarvis would become a victim of the violent racism that you all have had to deal with for so, so long. There is a time for every purpose under heaven, and this is the time for change in Pickett County. That is why I join Reverend Timmons and all of you. The scriptures say God will be with us as we walk through the valley of the shadow of death. He will protect us today so have no fear."

Evelyn looked up at Timmons and then back at the bank of cameras focused on her. It was a look so full of strength and resolve that the normally inquisitive and sometimes rude reporters kept silent.

"All right," Timmons shouted. "It's time to march. We will go up this road to the main highway and follow it for two miles into Armistead. Once we get there, we'll have a rally on the courthouse lawn. Follow me."

And with that Timmons stepped off toward the roadway, Evelyn by his side, his aide Emanuel Slocum following behind and checking his clipboard as he walked. The other marchers filed in—about a hundred of them—a mixture of young and middle-aged blacks with a few young whites sprinkled among them, mostly college students who wanted to show their support.

The television news crews followed along, stopping periodically to film wide shots of the group and doing walking interviews with the marchers. Mindy and other print reporters mingled with the marchers, talking with them and taking notes.

Timmons turned and walked backwards to survey the scene. He began to sing in a strong baritone, belting out an old spiritual and gesturing with his arms for all to join in.

"Ain't gonna let nobody turn me 'round
Gonna keep on a walkin', keep on a-talkin'
Marchin' to that freedom land."

The marchers sang heartily as the ragged line spilled onto the roadway and headed for the main highway half a mile away. If all went well, they would be in Armistead by noon.

Timmons could barely suppress his euphoria as his flock followed in his footsteps. He felt that his day had finally arrived, and his reputation would only grow with all the news coverage he'd attracted.

He had failed, however, to notice a rusting red '57 Chevrolet sedan pulling onto the field when he was making his pre-march statement. Nor did he notice the six young men emerging from the car, all wearing black T-shirts with red lightning bolts on the back. Each of them pulled on small backpacks covering up the lightning bolts. They carried four-foot wooden poles as walking staffs and worked their way into the ranks of the marchers, with their leader Marcus Turner setting the pace.

The interlopers all knew the words of the spirituals Timmons was leading, songs they had grown up singing, songs of overcoming hardships, trusting in the Lord, having faith that better times would come.

They knew the lyrics, but they refused to sing. The hymns no longer applied to the world they had experienced nor the new world they wanted to see. They were ready to make that point in dramatic fashion very soon.

SHERIFF MCSWAIN SAT in his idling car as the marchers approached the highway. He was still fuming over having to deal with this protest despite the arrests of the Sosebys. Solicitor General Carson Baker had persuaded him to accommodate the marchers within reason. With the eyes of the nation on Pickett County, Baker had counseled polite firmness to make the best of the situation, and the sheriff grudgingly agreed.

The focus of McSwain's resentment was Reverend Timmons, who was practically prancing as he led his disciples toward the intersection, waving his arms and singing.

"Damn showboat," McSwain muttered.

Evelyn Pendry was at Timmons's side, a diminutive figure whose natural elegance was only slightly diminished by the tennis shoes and baseball cap she wore. She was not singing but rather looking straight ahead with stoic determination, much as she had the day they first met when she glared down at him from Willie Brooks's porch. Although she was still fifty yards away, McSwain felt like she was staring right through him.

The sheriff slid out of his cruiser and shuffled toward the intersection, hitching up his pants as he walked. He stepped into the middle of the road as the march leaders approached, spreading his legs slightly and tucking his thumbs under his pistol belt. He sucked in his gut as best he could as camera teams and reporters occupied their positions on either side to get unobstructed views of the confrontation.

Timmons stopped singing as he walked right up to the sheriff, swiveled to face his followers, and raised his hands to halt them. He paused briefly to give the camera crews time to settle, thrust their microphones toward him, and begin filming. He then turned to McSwain with a glimmer of a smile on his face.

"Good morning, Sheriff McSwain," Timmons said in a booming, confident voice. "Thank you for being here to assist us today."

McSwain chose to ignore Timmons's patronizing tone.

"Reverend, Mrs. Pendry, this is a law-abiding county, and we don't want any trouble. If that happens things could get—well—difficult."

Murmurs of disapproval worked their way through the marchers. Timmons turned toward his followers and silently raised his hand, and the murmuring ceased. Then he turned to back to McSwain. "Sheriff, if this were a law-abiding county we wouldn't be here, and Mrs. Pendry's husband would still be alive."

McSwain pointed to his wristwatch. "We expect you to be out of Armistead by two p.m. Your buses will be waiting for you off the square." He stepped back two paces and pointed north. "Armistead is two miles thataway. Keep your people under control, and we won't have any problems."

Timmons nodded, turned toward the marchers, and signaled for their trek to resume. As he passed McSwain, he had one last thing to say. "Sheriff, if there are problems today we won't be the ones causing them."

The column began moving onto the highway, clinging to the left shoulder. A deputy's cruiser drove slowly ahead, red lights flashing. Another cruiser pulled in behind the marchers to bring up the rear.

McSwain watched them pass and then looked at his watch. They should be approaching the town square in an hour. He went back to his car and slowly pulled away, paralleling the march briefly before moving on toward Armistead, where preparations for the arrival were still underway. He passed a couple of state patrol cars parked along the highway, and he knew more would be waiting in Armistead. The governor sent the troopers without even asking, but McSwain swallowed the insult. He knew he might need the help.

Shortly before he reached the city limits, he passed Milltown

Bottoms, a hodgepodge of small homes and house trailers occupied by poor whites. When the mill had operated at full capacity the neighborhood had thrived, but the textile depression in the South was beginning to take its toll with layoffs and rumors of closing. Now many of the people in Milltown Bottoms were unemployed, uneducated, and sometimes troublesome. As he drove through the community, he saw a few people in their yards, some children playing, but nothing that warned him of impending trouble.

The Armistead city limits sign was less than a hundred yards from Milltown Bottoms. McSwain drove slowly up the hill leading to the town square, passing small shops, a service station, and Sally's Diner where he often stopped in for coffee and pie. The businesses were just opening, but he imagined most of their customers would stay home today because of the march. He noticed a Confederate battle flag filling the large picture window at Sally's. There were also small rebel flags stuck in the ground along the roadway.

As he approached the town square, he was comforted by the presence of deputies and state troopers on the courthouse steps, waiting to intercept the marchers and keep them contained to a roped-off area under a massive oak tree, not far from General Pickett's granite gaze. The marble steps leading up to the century-old courthouse were blocked by sawhorses and yellow crime scene tape. The building was closed for the day, and the huge doors were bolted.

McSwain felt ready. He glanced at his watch yet again. Three more hours and it's over, he thought. Everything's under control.

THE BODY OF the march had elongated over the past hour with younger marchers moving closer to the front of the column and others falling farther behind. About a hundred yards now separated the patrol cars at the head and rear of the march. As the heat intensified, some of the young volunteers from Mount Gilead AME roamed through the ranks and handed out cups of water from canteens hanging from their belts. There was no shade along this stretch of road, only pastures where grazing cows stared indifferently at the passing crowd.

Gil moved among the marchers with the camera on his shoulder mount, looking through his viewfinder for interesting faces. Every now and then he did a brief interview with a marcher.

"Excuse me, ma'am. Why are you marching today?" he asked an overweight middle-aged woman who was having difficulty keeping the pace.

"We marchin' for our rights. For our freedom. Praise the Lord."

Gil kept an eye out for Carney Roberts, who'd been paired with him to cover the march. Roberts was circulating through the crowd, periodically grabbing Gil and his camera for quick interviews. Gil also kept track of Mindy as she moved among the marchers, interviewing and occasionally photographing them, a tough professional disguised as a lovely sprite deftly doing her job. Gil shot some film of her. She'll get a kick out of seeing it later, he thought.

Gil noticed a group of young men near the front of the column. Their Afros and black T-shirts jogged a memory. Then he recognized Marcus Turner.

Gil worked his way forward until he was just behind the group. Quickly, he stepped in front of Marcus and focused the camera on him.

Marcus was startled and raised his hand to block the camera. "Goddamn it, get out of my face, honky!"

Gil stepped back out of arm's reach, keeping his camera rolling and firing a question. "What are you all doing here?"

Marcus and his companions tried to move away, weaving through the other marchers toward the head of the column. Gil chose not to follow them, but their presence made him uneasy. Mindy saw the exchange and hurried over.

"What happened?" she asked. "What was that all about?"

"Looks like the Student Coordinating League has infiltrated the march. Remember Marcus Turner? He's right up there. He wouldn't let me interview him. He cussed me out and ran away. Not sure what they're planning to do, but there's bound to be trouble. Think we should tell Timmons?"

"Definitely," Mindy responded. "This thing could get nasty fast." Then, under her breath she muttered, "Black flak and the nightmare fighters."

Gil looked briefly at her with a puzzled expression. "You can explain that comment later. I'm moving up to warn Timmons."

Gil reached the lead element of the column as it rounded a curve and entered Milltown Bottoms. He noticed about fifteen teenagers and young men ambling into a group on an embankment overlooking the road. As the marchers began to pass by, the whites yelled catcalls, slurs, and curses, but they gave no indication they would do more than taunt the protestors.

Reverend Timmons kept his eyes straight ahead and kept on walking, Evelyn by his side also refusing to acknowledge their harassers. Suddenly Timmons turned to look at his marchers, began walking backward, and launched into another civil rights anthem.

"I'm on my way to Freedom Land…
I'm on my way, Good God, I'm on my way."

His voice boomed over the racist insults that continued to rain down from the top of the embankment. Slowly the marchers, looking nervously at their taunters, began tentatively, then enthusiastically, to join in.

"It's a long, long journey to Freedom Land…
But I'm on my way, Good God, I'm on my way."

Gil moved his camera from face to face as they marched and sang. Then he stepped to the side of the road and aimed at the group of hecklers. They began to curse him and the other media. Gil expected them to throw rocks or bottles, but apparently the presence of lawmen was enough to keep them from going that far.

He looked for Marcus and his group, but they had melted into the crowd. Then he spotted them on the left flank, passing the rabble-rousers, giving them cold stares but otherwise not responding, not even giving them the finger. Gil wondered exactly what they had in mind.

He was trying to get to Timmons when it happened.

The marchers were climbing the gradual hill up to the town square. As they passed Sally's Diner, a small group of young toughs emerged from behind the building, heading directly for the marchers. They all wore blue jeans and t-shirts, and each of them carried a baseball bat.

The middle of the column collapsed as the marchers moved to the far side of the road in fear and confusion. Timmons turned to see the mayhem and called to his people to stand firm. He put his arm around Evelyn and moved her away from the roiling crowd, yelling for lawmen to come to their rescue. The deputies were still in their cars at either end of the march and apparently had yet to realize the danger.

Just as the attackers were about to use their bats on the fleeing marchers, Marcus and his five comrades ran between them and the retreating crowd. They raised their heavy walking staffs and started swinging at the young whites. Two of the black students pulled rocks from their backpacks and began throwing hard at close range. The attackers were so surprised they began to back away under the onslaught of crashing poles and painful rock missiles.

Marcus yelled out. "You didn't expect this, did you, honky assholes? We don't lie down and take it. That day is over."

Some of the whites had dropped their bats, raising their arms to defend against the rocks flying toward their heads and torsos. One of them had fallen and was trying to ward off the blows as Marcus pounded him with maniacal fury. Camera crews had rushed up to film the violent encounter, but they, too, tried to stay out of harm's way as the melee intensified. Gil filmed while Roberts used his body as a shield to try to protect his cameraman from flying rocks. Gil heard Mindy call out to him.

"Gil, please be careful. You've got enough. Get out of there."

Two state patrol cars and two deputy's cruisers pulled up with sirens wailing and lights flashing. The officers ran up to the fight with guns drawn. As they approached, they heard gunfire, two shots from a small-caliber handgun. Two state patrolmen went into a crouch to lower their profile but continued toward the center of the conflict. The local deputies, confused about where the shots came from, waved their pistols wildly, mainly toward the scattering marchers.

The state troopers, well-trained veterans of civil rights conflict, moved in to stop the fighting. They grabbed the black students first, cuffing them while several of the white attackers scampered away, leaving their bats behind. One of the attackers still lay on the ground moaning, blood seeping from a head wound. Near him another person lay facedown on the ground, a black student with an Afro.

A burly state patrolman knelt to handcuff him. "All right, boy," he gasped, trying to recover his breath. "You are under arrest."

Getting no response, he grabbed the youth by the shoulders and flipped him over. It was then that he saw the dark stain creeping across the black T-shirt and the unblinking eyes of Marcus Turner staring vacantly at the cloudless sky.

THIRTY-SEVEN

BLOOD ON YOUR HANDS

GIL SURVEYED THE skirmish aftermath through the lens of his shoulder-mounted camera. All but one of the white ambushers had fled, leaving their bloodied companion rolling from side to side in pain. Two black students were also on the ground, one slowly rising to his feet, the other lying motionless with a state trooper kneeling over him. Three others were being handcuffed by Pickett County deputies and roughly pushed up against a fence, where an officer held a gun on them.

The clash had lasted only about three minutes, with Gil's camera rolling throughout. Other camera crews did the same. They all stayed on the edge of the melee, as much out of harm's way as they could be and still get the shots they needed.

The marchers who had dispersed when the attack began were slowly moving back into the roadway to watch as the officers restored order. Gil spotted Timmons still hovering protectively over Evelyn, looking as though he were in a state of shock.

During the chaos, Gil thought he'd heard gunshots, but there was so much yelling and confusion he couldn't be sure. When he focused his camera and zoomed in on the trooper kneeling over the fallen student, he could see the bloodstained T-shirt and lifeless face of Marcus Turner.

The officer, whose uniform name tag identified him as Lieutenant R. Hightower, looked up at his colleagues with a grim expression. "This one's dead. Shot in the chest."

Lieutenant Hightower abruptly rose and walked over to the injured white teen who was now sitting on the ground, moaning and bleeding from a wound across his forehead where Marcus had battered him with his staff. Hightower knelt to examine the teen and was startled to see a small pistol barely visible under his leg. He motioned to other troopers to come over and hold the teen so he could carefully pick up the pistol.

"This your gun?" Hightower asked. "Did you shoot that boy over there?"

The teen choked out a reply, stifling a sob. "He was trying to kill me. I had to shoot him."

At that moment Sheriff McSwain lumbered up. He'd been on the square waiting for the marchers to arrive, and he'd rushed on foot to the scene when he realized what was happening.

"I'm here now," he wheezed, still trying to catch his breath. "Give me a status report."

Gil and the other camera crews moved in behind the sheriff to film his conversation with the trooper in charge. McSwain realized he was once again at risk of humiliation, this time with the nation witnessing it.

"Sheriff, we have a fatality." Trooper Hightower motioned with his head toward Marcus's body. "One of the blacks got shot."

Hightower then nodded toward the white teen, still on the ground but with two troopers guarding him. "This boy says he shot him in self-defense. We've got the weapon."

McSwain knew the white teen. He was Wade Irvin, the eldest child of Ronald and Olivia Irvin of Milltown Bottom. He'd been in trouble before, but nothing like this.

Lieutenant Hightower pointed to the students' backpacks lying on the grass, palm-size rocks spilling out of them.

"These boys had backpacks full of rocks. My guess is they were planning to use them to break windows and cause problems once they got to the square. Looks like they found another use for them when the fighting broke out."

"Thank you, Lieutenant." McSwain had caught his breath but was having trouble giving his voice the tone of authority necessary at such a time. "Looks like these black boys didn't quite get the nonviolent memo. I think we can take it from here. Appreciate your help."

Suddenly Reverend Timmons pushed his way through the camera crews to stand between Sheriff McSwain and Trooper Hightower.

"That's not what happened!" Timmons aimed his remarks more at the cameras than McSwain or Hightower. "These young students did infiltrate our peaceful march, and they no doubt planned some disruption. But make no mistake. We were attacked by a white mob. These students protected us. If they hadn't been here, I shudder to think what would have happened. None of us had firearms. Only the thugs who attacked us. Why were we not better protected? Sheriff, why were you not better prepared? This is another disgrace for Pickett County, and there is once again blood on your hands."

McSwain struggled to suppress the fury rising in him. He could not afford to lose control. Too many cameras. "Reverend, this is all your fault. You came here to stir up trouble, and you have succeeded. Get those buses down here, load 'em up, and get out of here before I start arresting you and your followers. You stay one more minute, and I'll charge you with disturbin' the peace."

Timmons showed his anger as well, mingled with frustration and grief. "We are leaving, but we will return. We will return in even greater numbers. And we will remember this young man's sacrifice in the cause of justice for all God's people. Mark my words. We will be back."

He stormed away to rejoin the marchers who had gathered nearby as the buses pulled in to take them home. They moved slowly like a retreating army, exhausted and despondent, their dreams of triumph over the forces of evil shattered.

McSwain spotted Evelyn standing alone behind the media scrum, staring at him. There was no anger in the way she looked at him, only sadness. McSwain felt ill at ease as she continued to fix her gaze on him. Then she slowly turned away and joined the line of those trudging to the buses.

The sheriff tried to shrug it off. He had work to do.

McSwain ordered his deputies to take the black students to the jail for booking. They'd be charged with assault and battery as well as disorderly conduct. Wade Irvin, who'd fired the fatal bullet, would be driven to the closest hospital in Whitney County for treatment of his injuries, after which he'd be released to the custody of his parents. He, of course, would have to be charged with the homicide, but McSwain viewed that only as a formality. To him it was a clear case of self-defense, a white man protecting himself from a black man's attack. In all likelihood the charges would be dropped, saving the jury the effort of acquittal. And as for the white teens who escaped, McSwain had a good idea of who they were but chose not to try to track them down. He knew their parents would appreciate that and repay the favor in the next election.

THIRTY-EIGHT

AIRTIME

VIEWERS WERE NOT used to seeing Grayson Kincaid on the weekend news, but the events of this Saturday compelled him to be at the anchor desk lending his authority to the coverage of the Pickett County debacle. It was the top story on every newscast in the country, and Kincaid knew his viewers would prefer to hear it from him.

The coverage consumed the first twelve minutes of the newscast. The filmed scenes shifted rapidly—the arrival of the buses, Reverend Timmons's kickoff speech, walking interviews with the marchers, the taunting at Milltown Bottom, and the baseball bat attack. Gil's footage of Marcus and his band blunting the onslaught and then wading into the attackers swinging their walking staff clubs and hurling stones was horrifying. For so long, whites had been comforted by the fact that civil rights protesters never fought back. That was no longer the case, but it came with a price.

Gil had filmed Marcus's body from a distance, knowing that a gruesome tight shot would not be allowed on the early evening news. Still, even at middle distance, the scene was stark, particularly when Lieutenant Hightower looked up and, without a trace of emotion, said, "This one's dead. Shot in the chest at close range."

Kincaid explained to viewers that Marcus Turner had been in the news before when he disrupted a news conference by Reverend Elijah Timmons and later when he was arrested at a protest march melee near city hall. He reported that Turner headed up the Student Coordinating League at Morehouse College and that his five comrades were in the Pickett County jail on assault charges.

As the film showed Wade Irvin sitting on the ground nursing his bleeding head wound, Kincaid reported that Irwin admitted shooting Turner, claiming self-defense. Kincaid added that, according to the sheriff, charges were pending.

The next sequence of edited sound bites revealed Reverend Timmons berating Sheriff McSwain.

"These students protected us. If they hadn't been here, I shudder to think what would have happened. Why were we not better protected? This is another disgrace for Pickett County."

Next, viewers saw Sheriff McSwain angrily waving a finger in Timmons's face.

"Reverend, this is all your fault. You came up here to stir up trouble, and you have succeeded."

Kincaid reported that Timmons vowed to return, then he segued into reaction from the two leading gubernatorial candidates, Roscoe Pike and Harrison Parker, both of whom were interviewed shortly before the newscast.

To no one's surprise, Pike condemned the marchers and the students who had fought violence with violence. He spoke with anger and vindictiveness, staring directly into the camera and raising his fist.

"Today we saw the ultimate outcome of the civil rights movement—violent black men forcing their way into a quiet community of law-abiding folks like you and me. This so-called nonviolence is a big lie disguising a racial power grab that will forever change our way of life. If it can happen in Pickett County today, it could happen to your community tomorrow. As your governor I will stop it in its tracks."

Parker reacted in measured, reasoning tones.

"What happened today in Pickett County was just horrible. A young man lost his life, others were injured, and some are in jail. But positive change cannot be achieved by violence. We all want peaceful, law-abiding communities. We all want our children to be educated. We all want good jobs. And this is possible for all of us if we continue working toward those goals nonviolently. As your governor I will do everything in my power to reach those goals."

Then Grayson Kincaid appeared on screen, standing in the studio, illuminated by multiple lights all focused on him against a background dark as midnight.

"There is much more to this story, and we will be covering it in the hours and days to come. Among the questions still to be answered: Why was Pickett County not better prepared to prevent violence? Why was Reverend Elijah Timmons unaware that his march had been infiltrated by radical elements? What does all this mean for the future of nonviolent civil disobedience in the cause of civil rights? Back in a minute after this break."

The camera slowly faded from Kincaid's stoic, chiseled face to blackness. The director, overlooking the studio from the control booth, mercifully gave the viewers a two-second pause before rolling a commercial featuring a buffoonish announcer practically screaming about the great car deals at Bubba Bailey's Chrysler Plymouth. Grayson Kincaid, awaiting the next block of the newscast, felt embarrassed by the juxtaposition of his weighty, somber coverage and the sideshow theatrics of television salesmanship. But he understood only too well that Bubba Bailey and other sponsors essentially paid his salary, buying pricy ads in his newscasts for the credibility Kincaid implicitly conferred on their products. There was no question that on this day Bubba Bailey had gotten his money's worth.

THIRTY-NINE

FRIENDLY PERSUASION

CLARENCE FORTSON PULLED the Town Car up to the front steps of WDX-TV at ten a.m. sharp. Before he could put the vehicle in park he saw General Manager Ronald Hill, briefcase in hand, emerge from the double front doors of the stately plantation-like edifice and walk briskly toward him.

"Good morning, Clarence," Hill said as he slipped into the back seat. "Nice to see you again. Right on time, as usual."

The morning rush was over, so the only traffic they had to worry about was the backup caused by street repair crews at every other intersection, the city's almost desperate effort to continually patch up an infrastructure unequal to its increasing burden. Fortson knew his way around the construction zones, and they pulled into the underground garage of the Southland Capital Tower at ten twenty. Once the vehicle was berthed in its reserved spot, Hill thanked Fortson and headed for the elevator and his appointment with Devereaux Inman.

Hill and Inman had known each other for a decade, ever since Hill arrived to take the general manager's job at WDX. Inman had always tried to bring media management into his circle, respecting their power to shape image and opinion. Until recently his focus was on the local newspaper, where he'd cultivated relationships with the editor and several key columnists, but Inman realized the ground was shifting. Newspaper columns, no matter how intelligent and perceptive, reached a relative few compared to television's ability to touch a huge cross section of people instantaneously. TV's visceral coverage of the civil rights movement was stoking a societal revolution. Inman had vowed to do everything he could to keep Atlanta on the right side of history and protect it from negative media images that could never be erased.

"Good morning, Ronald." Inman smiled and extended his hand as Hill entered his office. "Good of you to come on such short notice."

"Always a pleasure, Mr. Inman." Hill had never taken the liberty of using Inman's first name. Hill was a respected community leader, but Devereaux Inman was a revered elder, a city legend, and entirely deserving of whatever deference Hill could show him.

Inman did not offer Hill a chair but rather took him by the elbow and walked with him to the wall of windows looking out over Atlanta.

"There it is, Ronald. Our city. A city in a forest. And under those trees, lovely homes. And all around us buildings are going up. And people are coming, and we are on the verge of enormous growth and economic opportunity. Think of it, Ronald. Major league sports teams calling Atlanta home. Flourishing museums, theaters, and symphonies. Expressways from all directions merging here, creating a dynamic, pulsating metropolis that will lead the South and one day the nation— maybe even the world."

Inman had extended his arms as if to embrace the sprawling vista before them.

"But standing in the way of all that is the problem of race relations. We have done pretty well guiding the city through this time of turmoil, but what happened Saturday in Pickett County is the kind of thing that can derail our future. You can say it didn't happen in Atlanta, but people around the country who saw your film of all that violence are thinking 'That's the South.' We're put in the same basket as those rednecks up the road. We are all damaged by the violence and racial mayhem that you so vividly put on the television screen. And I know there is nothing you can do to change that."

"No sir, there's not." Hill turned to look at Inman, who continued to stare through the window. "We can't change what happens. But I share your concerns about what this does to our image, and we do try to provide as much balancing perspective as we can."

Inman nodded and finally looked up at Hill. "Ronald, we need the power of television to help us through this. I can talk to the boys down at the paper and get some strong editorials, but who the hell reads them? I do, and you do, but the ordinary guy on the street, the housewives, black or white, they never see them and don't care. I need to see editorial support from you and your station, because what you say will be heard, people will watch and listen, and it could make a difference."

Hill pondered that for a moment and then responded. "I had been thinking about an editorial on the evening news—maybe tonight. An editorial condemning the violence and urging all sides to come together. It may be a tough sell against the backdrop of the Pendry murder and the turmoil that's resulted, but I agree with you that the media, particularly those of us in television, need to step up and be a voice of reason. But it's a risky area. We don't want to drive away viewers who disagree."

Inman smiled and nodded. "I certainly understand. But whatever risk you take will be worth it in terms of community respect for your courage in speaking out. And there is one more thing I think we need to do."

Hill stepped back slightly, his eyes narrowing as he waited for Inman's next request.

"I think you need to host a gubernatorial debate. Roscoe Pike is a cancer, and his candidacy is a threat to our city and our state. At first, I felt his offensiveness would doom his chances, but after what happened this weekend, I'm not so sure. You know I work behind the scenes, but I'm sure you won't be surprised to hear that I'm supporting Harrison Parker. He has many faults, but he is our last and best hope to continue the progressive solutions we need if we are to advance socially and economically. While there are many risks involved in putting these two men on live television, I must put my faith in my candidate and in the good judgment of the people of our state. What do you say?"

"Again, there are risks," Hill said. "You never know what might happen if we put Pike and Parker on live TV. Let me talk with my staff and come up with a plan."

"I couldn't ask for more, Ronald," Inman replied, escorting Hill toward the office door. "This remains between us. I look forward to seeing all of this come to pass."

They shook hands, and Hill headed for the elevator, descending to the subterranean parking lot where Fortson was waiting to take him back to the station.

As Fortson eased the car into the stream of downtown traffic, Hill settled back and became lost in thought, pondering what he would say to his audience. Finding the right words delivered with the right tone would be one of the biggest challenges of his career.

HOURS LATER, AT ten after six, Hill picked up the script he'd been agonizing over all afternoon and walked to the studio, pulling open the heavy soundproof doors as Grayson Kincaid introduced a commercial break. It was unusual to see Hill in the studio during a live newscast, and the technicians silenced their normal commercial break banter.

Hill carefully stepped over the camera cables crisscrossing the floor as he walked to the news desk to greet his anchor.

"How are you, Grayson?"

"I'm good, Ron. Glad to see we're taking an editorial stand on the recent violence."

"I hope it will have some impact. You never know."

Hill walked to a blue studio wall that would be his backdrop as he delivered the editorial. He was no stranger to broadcasting live. Before he entered the management track years ago, Hill had done radio and television newscasts in much smaller markets in the Midwest. Yet, despite that broadcast experience, Hill felt a hint of nervousness as he prepared to address his audience.

When the last commercial in the break ended, viewers saw a wide shot of the studio from a camera mounted on the ceiling. Kincaid was at his desk, and across the studio Ron Hill stood with script in hand. Then came the booth announcer's voice.

"And now a WDX-TV editorial. Here is Vice President and

General Manager Ronald Hill."

The wide shot dissolved into a head-and-shoulders shot of Hill standing at the blue wall. "Editorial" was superimposed in the top right-hand corner of the screen. Hill appeared at ease and confident, and when he spoke his voice conveyed the persuasive power of a broadcast veteran.

"Good evening. Tonight, I want to talk with you about the violence last weekend in Pickett County, violence that claimed the life of a young Morehouse student named Marcus Turner. There is still much to be learned about how this happened, but one thing is clear: racial hatred was at the center of this violence.

"Our city and our state have faced many challenges during the civil rights movement. We have met most of those challenges by finding ways to span our differences with bridges of reason, finding common ground between those who demand significant change and those who wish to preserve the status quo. It is not easy. It is a struggle. And we have made progress by finding reasonable compromises that all can live with to keep the peace.

"But when there is no reason, there is no peace. Saturday's march in Pickett County was supposed to be a nonviolent protest, and yet the forces of racial animosity broke loose with terrible results.

"Somehow we must find reason amid the chaos. Whether we are black or white, we must find a common ground of our humanity. We must select leaders who have the wisdom and ability to lead us to that common ground even in the darkest of times. We must reject violence in all its forms and continue to work together for the common good. Our future depends on our ability to do this. And I believe we can. Thank you."

The camera faded slowly to black as the announcer said, "This has been an editorial opinion of WDX-TV Vice President and General Manager Ronald Hill. We welcome your opinions."

After a two-second pause the next commercial began to roll. Hill folded his script and began walking toward the studio door, his head slightly bowed.

Across the studio Kincaid called out. "Well said, Ron. Strong. I'm sure we'll get flak, but what the hell? I'm proud of you and the station for taking a stand."

Hill gave a half wave to Kincaid and pushed the heavy door open. Instead of going directly back to his office, he stepped into the newsroom where staffers were deluged with critical phone calls. Tom Burke had warned them that the editorial would incite reaction and made sure plenty of people were available to man the phones.

Hill walked up to Burke, who was sitting on the edge of a desk, telephone to his ear. He was patiently listening to an angry diatribe from an irate viewer.

"Thank you very much. We appreciate your opinion," Burke said before placing the phone back in its cradle.

"Well, boss, looks like you unleashed the whirlwind. I'm proud of you."

Hill looked around the room as staff members took call after call.

"It would be nice if some of those calls were supportive," Hill said with a smile.

Burke chuckled. "Boss, you have to remember that if viewers agree with what you're saying, they don't call to compliment us. It's the viewers who are angered by what they see who are motivated to call. They just need someone to chew out. This in no way reflects how other viewers feel about what you had to say."

"I sure hope you're right about that, Tom."

Hill firmly shook the hand of congratulations Burke offered and moved on down the hallway to the executive offices. He could hear the din of ringing telephones until he reached his darkened office and closed the door. He moved to his desk and sat down heavily in his chair. He knew that the major sponsors and city leaders wouldn't call him until tomorrow. Some would complain, some would approve. He might even lose a sponsor or two. In the grand scheme of things, it didn't really matter. He had taken a stand. And it felt good.

FORTY

THE DRIVER

THE PICKETT COUNTY chapter of the Veterans of Foreign Wars was headquartered in a single-story cinder-block building on a side street behind Sally's Diner. The structure was painted pale green shortly after World War Two ended, but the paint had peeled and faded to the point that the building now appeared anemic white. Vets who showed up there every evening for poker, bingo, and beer didn't seem to care.

A few of them were in their seventies and eighties, fading veterans of the Spanish-American War and World War One, but most were World War Two vets, some of whom also served in Korea. When they gathered, they sometimes shared war stories, but mostly they liked to drink beer, gossip, and talk politics. Pickett was a dry county, but the alcohol laws were ignored when it came to the VFW. In fact, Sheriff McSwain, a combat vet, was known to stop in from time to time for a drink.

Randall Scoggins was one of the regulars. He usually arrived in the late afternoon and left, sometimes with assistance, when the bar closed at eleven. He was wounded in 1944 at Monte Cassino, receiving a Purple Heart, a short hospital stay, and a ticket home. He had arrived in Italy as a raw replacement who often threw up at the thought of combat. So many good men were killed or wounded during that dreadful battle to take the mountaintop monastery that no one investigated the circumstances of Scoggins's injury, a single bullet wound that took off his left little toe. The foot wound kept him out of combat, which was what Scoggins was hoping for when, in the midst of a shelling attack, he clenched his teeth, closed his eyes, and squeezed off a round from his rifle, shattering his boot tip and a single toe. Overburdened medics assumed it was a shrapnel wound, and no one ever questioned that initial judgment.

Scoggins had never married and made a living doing odd jobs around Pickett County. As a wounded war veteran, he was accorded a certain amount of deference from the people in the community, even though they knew he was a ne'er-do-well and a drunk, one of those poor fellows who never quite got over what they'd been through in the war.

When he wasn't drinking beer at the VFW hall, he liked to hang around with fellow veteran Hiram Soseby at his filling station on the outskirts of town, a fact Scoggins never mentioned when the FBI interviewed him along with several other Klan hangers-on early in the Pendry murder investigation. Since the murder, Scoggins had dropped out of sight during the day, surfacing only after dark at the VFW hall for round after round of beer.

The drunker he got the more fearful he became. Usually, the demons of his wartime cowardice came to visit, but over the past few weeks he'd been tortured by memories of the night Jarvis Pendry was murdered. After four or five beers, he began to relive the blurring mental images of Pendry coming into the station asking for help, the confrontation with Hiram and Caleb, his drunken confusion as Hiram pulled him to his feet and into his car to pursue Pendry, and the red dots of taillights that grew larger as he sped toward Pendry's idling car on the side of the road at Peavine Creek.

Scoggins struggled to purge the images from his brain, but they were indelible; Hiram telling him to pull alongside the car, Caleb in the back seat pointing a flashlight out the window to illuminate Pendry's look of surprise and fear, and then the staccato blasts, one after the other, an acrid smell filling the car, and Hiram yelling for him to speed away.

He sat alone at a corner table, draining yet another bottle of Pabst Blue Ribbon. But the anesthetizing effect he sought wouldn't come.

He groggily recalled the drive back to Pendry's blasted car, the blood-ied, faceless body slumped across the front seat, the exuberance of Hiram and Caleb as they appraised their murderous actions. He re-membered listening numbly as his companions came up with a plan to drive Pendry's car down the old path along Peavine Creek and then push it into the water. Caleb was ordered by his father to slide into the driver's seat slicked by blood and brains and do the deed. Hiram walked ahead of the car with the flashlight after ordering Scoggins to stay be-hind as a lookout on the dark highway.

Then, once Pendry's car sank in a torrent of bubbles in the murky water, Scoggins drove the Sosebys back to the gas station and dropped them off. He remembered Caleb complaining loudly about Pendry's blood covering his hands and clothing.

Before he could drive away, Hiram had told him to wash out his car, lay low, keep quiet, and not come around for awhile. Then Scoggins drove to his rented trailer and drank himself into oblivion.

After another PBR, Scoggins felt that the relief he needed was close. His head began to sag, and he lowered it onto the cradle of his forearm on the table. He was slowly drifting away when he sensed someone sitting beside him. Maybe two people.

He lifted his head slightly and struggled to open his eyes. Two men were sitting on either side of him. He was vaguely aware of the other people in the hall standing at a distance, staring at them. Then one of the men at the table spoke, and he recognized the voice. Sheriff Lucas McSwain.

"Hello, Randall. We've been looking for you. This here's agent Bill Conyers of the GBI. Mind if we take you down to the sheriff's office? We've got a few questions to ask you."

Scoggins struggled to comprehend. "Wha...what about? I ain't done nothing."

Conyers put his lips very close to Scoggins's ear. "Caleb Soseby wants to know if you remember the night Jarvis Pendry was killed. You know anything about that, Randall?"

"Uh, no. No I don't. I lost touch with Caleb and Hiram some time ago."

McSwain spoke next. "Well, Randall, we understand you spent a lot of time with them. You just might have been with them the night Pendry was murdered."

Scoggins felt dizzy, his thoughts a blur. "No, I, uh, I don't know what you're talking about, Sheriff. You got me real confused."

Sheriff McSwain moved his hand to Scoggins's armpit and, with Conyers's help, raised him to a standing position. "Randall, we need to take you in for questioning about the murder of Jarvis Pendry. We need to examine your car for evidence. We have reason to believe you're involved. In fact, Randall, you are under arrest for the murder of Jarvis Pendry."

Scoggins tried to collapse into his chair, but McSwain and Conyers yanked his slumping body back to a standing position and hustled him out of the building into their waiting squad car. Other vets in the hall came outside to watch. They could hear Scoggins's drunken screams as the car pulled away.

"It wasn't me who killed him. I was just the driver."

SOLICITOR GENERAL CARSON Baker was doing morning sit-ups on his bedroom floor when he got the call from Sheriff McSwain at six fifteen.

"Sorry to call so early, Mr. Solicitor, but we now have that case you wanted."

McSwain sounded like he'd been up all night, which in fact he had.

"Caleb gave up a third suspect. We had to lean on him pretty hard, but he stumbled into mentioning a name, and we took it from there. It gave us the opening we needed to take a guy named Randall Scoggins into custody last night. And Scoggins confesses to driving the car. We've impounded his car, and if we're lucky we'll find some blood evidence. The state crime lab is helping us with that. Looks like we got what we needed."

"Nice going, Sheriff." Baker was still breathing hard from his sit-up routine. "What else can you tell me about Scoggins?"

"He's one of the town drunks, a wounded war vet, hangs around with Klan members, and we know he's spent a lot of time with the Sosebys. He was three sheets to the wind when we picked him up, so I'm hoping he will still be cooperative when he sobers up. I think we can offer him a deal since he claims he didn't really understand what the Sosebys' intentions were when they took out after Pendry."

"Okay, Sheriff. Sounds like there may be some problems with this witness, but he may be enough. Let's get those charges filed. Hopefully we can get a trial scheduled quickly. I know you want this over with."

"Lord, yes I do," McSwain responded wistfully. "And Carson, we've got another problem. Those four black boys we arrested during the riot last week. Still got 'em locked up on assault charges. Any advice on how to proceed?"

Baker paused slightly before responding. "Sheriff, you didn't arrest any white boys, did you? It's pretty clear they attacked first, and you could argue the blacks were acting in self-defense. After all, the kid who died was black. Bringing these boys up on assault charges will just bring more negative coverage to you and Pickett County, and you've already had more of that than you can handle. You want my advice? I'd quietly drop those charges and let 'em go."

After a long silence the sheriff spoke, a tone of resignation in his voice. "Looks like the tail wags the dog these days. I appreciate your input, Mr. Solicitor. I'll think about it."

After agreeing with Baker to confer later in the day on formal charges for the Sosebys and Scoggins, McSwain hung up the phone, leaned back in his chair, stretched, and sighed heavily. Fatigue and depression were taking their toll, but he knew this day would bring little relief.

He rose from his chair and shuffled to the open door of his office. He spotted his deputy Bobby slumped at his desk across the room, washing down a honeybun with a cup of black coffee.

"Bobby, listen up!"

Bobby immediately sat upright, coffee sloshing from his cup onto his uniform pants. "Damn it." He grabbed a tissue from his desk and attempted to blot the dark stain spreading across his crotch.

McSwain ignored Bobby's gesticulations. "I want you to get those black boys out of their cells, take 'em to the county line, and drop 'em off. You'll need two cars. Be sure their cuffs are on until they're out of the car. Then just leave 'em there. They can get their mamas to come and get 'em."

FORTY-ONE

CARRY ME HOME

MARCUS TURNER'S PARENTS insisted that his funeral be held in their home church, Mount Zion AME, even though the building was much too small to accommodate the mourners who came. Church members were allowed into the sanctuary, but all the others, mainly reporters, cameramen, and students from Morehouse, were told to remain on the grassy area between the parking lot and the sanctuary entrance. Two boxed speakers were placed on chairs on either side of the entrance so they could hear the service.

As Gil filmed outside the church, he noticed some students carrying signs that said "Remember Marcus" and "By Any Means Necessary." Several of them wore the signature black T-shirts of the Student Coordinating League. He approached one of them with his shoulder-mounted camera, thrusting a mike toward him with his free left hand.

"Why are you here today?" he asked the student. "Did you know Marcus?"

The student, tall and thin with sweat droplets glistening in his Afro, sneered at the camera.

"I did not know Marcus well, but he is a hero of our movement. He spoke for us. He showed us the way to free ourselves of the Uncle Toms who kowtow to the white man. He is a martyr for our cause."

Gil heard a rumbling in the crowd of students and looked to his left. Reverend Elijah Timmons was striding toward the church, his assistant Emanuel Slocum following close behind. Students moved in front of him, blocking his way. The students began taunting the minister.

"Uncle Tom Timmons. Uncle Tom Timmons."

"You do not belong here."

"Marcus is dead because of you."

Cameras and reporters moved en masse toward the disturbance, trapping Timmons between them and the students. Scores of microphones waved in the air, picking up the sounds of the clash between the new guard and the representative of the old.

Timmons raised his arms, trying to reason with the students. "Please! Please! I come to honor Marcus for his courage and leadership. We had our differences, but we wanted the same thing. Please, let me pass. Let me pay my respects."

The students only closed in tighter, engulfing Timmons and Slocum, who both showed signs of fearful concern.

Suddenly four of the city police officers assigned to the funeral appeared, shoving through the crowd and clearing a path for the two men. The students grudgingly stepped aside as Timmons and Slocum quickly moved toward the church. An usher held the door for the two men to enter the darkened sanctuary.

As reporters, cameramen, and students settled back into their respective areas, the assistant minister came out and walked toward the media cluster.

"We know you want to photograph the service, but there is no way we can allow all of you into our tiny sanctuary. We can allow one camera and one reporter in if they will share with the rest of you. Pool coverage—is that what you call it?"

The reporters quickly huddled and agreed that Gil would be the cameraman and Mindy the pool reporter. The assistant minister led them into the church, cautioning them to be discreet with their movements so as not to disrupt the service.

Gil stood at the rear of the small sanctuary in the center aisle and began filming. Marcus's open casket was just below the minister's pulpit, and congregants filed past in a long line, rising from their seats row by row to view the body and then returning to their pews. The organist segued from hymn to hymn, filling the church with rich, floral tones, rising and descending as mourners swayed with hands and faces raised in supplication.

When Timmons walked up to the casket, every eye in the church was on him. He stood staring down at Marcus's embalmed mannequin-like face, placed his hand on the casket, and bowed his head in silent prayer. Timmons was a respected figure among the aging Mount Zion AME congregation. They viewed him as a preeminent local civil rights leader, and they had difficulty understanding why the young man they came to mourn held Timmons in such contempt.

Gil carefully moved up the aisle to a point where he could film Timmons at the casket. His camera lens followed Timmons as he left the casket and approached the family sitting with bowed heads on the front row. Timmons knelt before a weeping Luvetta Turner, who slid forward slightly to accept his gentle embrace and then slumped back into the pew. Andrew Turner slowly rose to grip Timmons's extended hand. Timmons leaned over to whisper to him.

"Marcus was a very brave young man. For some reason he abandoned our teaching of nonviolence, and I know that was a challenge for you. Despite the way he treated me, I loved him like a son."

Timmons gripped Andrew's hand more tightly and pulled him into an embrace.

"Thank you, Reverend Timmons. I appreciate what you say. And we are thankful for your leadership. But Marcus was impatient. The young are impatient. And we must listen to what they have to say. That is what Marcus wanted."

Next on the pew was Marcus's brother Tyrone, sitting in a slouch with an expression of pain and contempt. Timmons held out his hand, but Tyrone ignored it, turning his head away. Timmons kept his hand awkwardly suspended for several seconds, then slowly withdrew it and with a sigh of resignation walked to the seat Emanuel was saving for him five pews back.

As the last of the mourners filed past the casket, the organ music faded slowly. The only sounds were the rustling of programs and an occasional cough. Most in the audience fanned themselves vigorously with the church-supplied hand fans adorned with the praying image of an Anglo-Saxon Jesus.

A large woman wearing a deep purple robe stepped from the choir and walked to the center of the chancel. She looked out at the crowd, closed her eyes, and began to sing a cappella, her mellifluous tones enveloping the sanctuary.

"Swing low, sweet chariot
Comin' for to carry me home
Swing low, sweet chariot
Comin' for to carry me home."

The congregation swayed from side to side, mouthing the words of the old spiritual, letting the singer give voice as she picked up the tempo and emotion.

"I looked over Jordan, and what did I see
Comin' for to carry me home
A band of angels comin' after me
Comin' for to carry me home."

The choir began to hum in accompaniment, and some in the audience sang softly along with the soloist. The Turners stared straight ahead, tears streaking their cheeks.

"If you get there before I do
Comin' for to carry me home
Tell all my friends I'm a-comin' too
Comin' for to carry me home."

Gil panned from face to glistening face, zooming in tight to show the tears when he saw them. Not only was he capturing the emotion, but he was also feeling it. It was impossible not to. The open expression of grief and joy, the intensity of feeling evoked by the beautiful music, the genuineness of celebrating faith and belief in the hereafter all underscored for him the enduring customs of the black religious tradition. That faith had always been the tie that bound them together as a people, from the fields and hovels of slavery to the cruel indignities of Jim

Crow, to the campaign for equality in a Southland determined to deny it. How different, though, from his experience in the white establishment church with its worship services that were formal, staid, doctrinaire, and distant.

The funeral service continued at a leisurely pace. A scripture reading, a hymn, another scripture reading, and a choral presentation came before the minister rose to deliver his homily. Reverend Clarence Good had been pastor at Mount Zion AME for twenty-two years. The congregation had aged along with him, while younger members had gone to other more activist churches or dropped religion altogether. The Turners had always been comfortable in a church that stuck to scripture and avoided the controversial issues of the day, but Marcus had turned his back on Mount Zion, along with his brother Tyrone, who had not set foot in the church for years.

So it was that Reverend Good, a slight man with short, graying hair, had trouble capturing the essence of Marcus with his funeral eulogy.

"Marcus was a wonderful young man, a true child of God, destined for greatness as he pursued his studies at Morehouse. Brother Andrew and Sister Luvetta were so proud of their son, so hopeful of a bright future for him."

A muted chorus of "Amens" and "Say it brother" bolstered Good's attempt to portray Marcus, even though virtually everyone realized that Marcus was nothing like the youth he described.

"It is so sad that Marcus died demonstrating for peaceful change. He was committed to improving the lives of his people, but he was cut down in the prime of his young life, much the way our Lord and Savior sacrificed his life for our salvation."

Gil was filming Reverend Good when he noticed a shaft of light as someone opened the sanctuary door and brushed past him, heading up the aisle toward the pulpit. It was one of the students who'd been demonstrating outside, a tall, wiry young man with a large Afro, wearing the black T-shirt with a red lightning bolt emblem on the back. Gil recognized him as part of Marcus's group during Timmons's Pickett County march, one of the students who'd been arrested, charged, and then later released.

"That's enough Reverend," he yelled as he strode up the aisle toward the open casket. When he reached the front of the sanctuary, he spun around to face the congregation, leaving Reverend Good speechless and looking around in confusion as his sermon was hijacked.

"Reverend Good may be a good man, but he don't know nothing about our brother Marcus. You need to know the truth, and I'm going to tell it like it is. Marcus Turner had nothing but respect for Gandhi and King, and he even had a little respect for Uncle Tom Timmons over here. But they have had their time. They brought about change, but it was too slow. Marcus knew the time for patience, the time for accommodation, the time for being satisfied with scraps from the white man's table is over."

Two city policemen began walking up the aisle, each holding a billy club.

"They're coming to get me and take me away, but that's okay. I'm doing this for Marcus, a true hero of our movement, who sacrificed his life to a redneck peckerwood in godforsaken Pickett County because he had the courage to fight back, to take the fight to our oppressors."

The officers rushed to the speaker, grabbing him by the arms and dragging him down the aisle while the audience looked on in shocked silence.

The young man struggled with his captors and continued to yell as he was dragged away.

"What you see is America. What you see is what we have to change. Celebrate our blackness, celebrate our character, our appearance, our history. Stand up to power. Don't be afraid to take your freedom. That's what Marcus would want. That's who Marcus was. And we'll never stop fighting for him and our cause."

Two more officers arrived to help haul the student out of the church and into a squad car that would take him to jail. The students gathered outside the church chanted, "Black power, black power" and "Remember Marcus." More police began arriving, forcing the students to back away from the church as television cameramen circled the crowd to capture the scene.

Inside the church, Reverend Good tried to restore order, apologizing for the rude interruption as an usher comforted the Turners. Tyrone had already left, apparently to join the continuing protest outside in memory of his brother.

Through it all, Marcus lay serenely in his casket, dressed in his best suit, oblivious to the turmoil he had caused by his untimely and violent death. Those who knew him best thought that he would have been very pleased.

FORTY-TWO

JOHN HENRY BLANKENSHIP

ROSCOE PIKE'S MOTORCADE sped up the highway toward Armistead. Pike's light blue sedan led the way, followed by two cars of aides and supporters and four vehicles carrying reporters and cameramen. There had been little advance notice of Pike's trip to Pickett County. In fact, reporters got word before the sheriff, which infuriated Lucas McSwain.

The sheriff was standing outside the county jail when Pike's motorcade pulled into the small parking lot. Pike waited inside his car while the news people piled out and scrambled for position. Once they were set, Pike opened his car door and strode up to McSwain, who stood on the sidewalk with arms crossed, still chafing from Pike's discourtesy.

Pike smiled and reached out to shake McSwain's hand as cameramen and radio reporters with their tape recorders scrambled closer to the two men. McSwain gave a tight grin and played along.

"Welcome, Roscoe. Welcome to Pickett County."

"Thank you, Sheriff. It's always good to be in Pickett County. Sorry we didn't give you more notice, but I'm sure you understand I've got a lot of balls in the air, running for governor and all."

"Of course," McSwain mumbled, struggling to rise above Pike's dismissiveness.

Pike turned and beckoned to a tall, thin man with a goatee wearing a white suit and a Stetson hat who had just emerged from Pike's car.

"Sheriff, this here's John Henry Blankenship. I'm sure you've heard of him. He's one of the best defense lawyers in the South. Done a lot of work for me and my people. I've hired him to defend the

Sosebys on this trumped-up murder charge you've filed. Now, if you please, may we see the prisoners?"

Blankenship was well known as the Klan's go-to lawyer, a man with no compunction about defending Klansmen accused of the most brutal and racist of crimes. Most recently he had won the acquittal of a white farmer accused of chaining a Negro man to his pickup truck and dragging him half a mile down a dirt road. The victim had the temerity to question his sharecropper earnings, which sent the farmer into a rage. The sharecropper, who was in his sixties, almost died. There were several witnesses and enough evidence to seal the case, but the local prosecutor was lackadaisical and inept, and Blankenship easily exploited his weaknesses. He had no problem convincing the jury of white men, mostly farmers, that the Negro had been impudent, disrespectful, and a problem tenant—accusations the jurors were predisposed to quickly accept. They returned the not guilty verdict after deliberating for half an hour.

So it was no surprise that Pike recruited Blankenship to defend Hiram and Caleb Soseby against charges of murdering Jarvis Pendry. It was an easy sell. This trial was made to order for Blankenship, and he loved the idea of being a central figure in a trial of national interest.

The sheriff, resentful at being turned into a bit player on his own stage, glumly turned toward the jail entrance and said, "This way."

Pike, Blankenship, and a couple of Pike aides moved onto the sidewalk in single file following McSwain. Cameramen and other reporters ran along on either side of the procession. Gil had had the foresight to move away from the clutch of newsmen and position himself on a concrete stoop at the jailhouse door so he could film the group as it approached. Pike and his followers climbed the three steps to the entrance of the ancient red brick building and went inside. As the double doors closed, two deputies moved in front of the entrance to bar reporters.

"Sorry, but you boys got to wait right here," the burlier of the two deputies said with a tight smile. "They might have something to say when they come out."

Gil stepped down off the stoop and joined the other cameramen and reporters milling about on the sidewalk. They were all intensely competitive, but whenever they had to kill time as a group, the conversation was friendly and gossipy.

Gil spotted the Atlanta Journal's veteran political reporter Charlie Crown talking with several other print journalists. Newspapermen and television crews seldom had much to do with each other, but Gil walked over and tried to strike up a conversation.

"Hi, Charlie. Nice column on the governor's race yesterday. What's the latest on Harrison Parker? Seems like he's laying low since the violence at the march."

Crown didn't like television news or those who reported it. He thought reporters with cameras were interlopers, unwelcome invaders of a domain he and his print colleagues had always commanded. He resented the fact that candidates preferred giving a twenty-second sound bite to a TV reporter rather than an hour-long in-depth interview that would run in the daily paper. He understood the reality, but that didn't mean he had to willingly accept it. And now this kid with a TV camera on his shoulder was asking him questions about the political landscape. Because he recognized Gil and knew him to be a good photojournalist, Crown accepted the question, answering tersely with only a hint of the condescension he felt most TV types deserved.

"Parker is laying low these days, trying to figure out how to get black votes without openly asking for them, trying to keep moderate white votes by being less Neanderthal than Pike, and hoping the big-money boys will keep the dollars flowing so he can do some advertising and launch a huge get-out-the-vote effort."

Crown turned to resume his conversation with his print brethren, but Gil wasn't finished. "Thanks, Charlie. Appreciate your opinion. Keep your ears open. I hear my station is planning a Pike-Parker debate."

Crown turned to look back at Gil, his left eyebrow slightly arched.

"Really? Well, I might watch that. Even if it is on television." He offered only a hint of a smile.

Gil spotted Ned Brockett, the grizzled network cameraman, sitting in a patch of shade. "How's it going, Ned?"

"You know. Same old same old. Where's Mindy?"

"Beats me," Gil responded. "I offered her a ride but she said she was working on another assignment."

Brockett lifted his camera and gently wiped the lens with a soft cloth. "You know, I saw her yesterday. I was up at the Monarch Courts to touch base with some agents, and there she was. She was in a car with Bill Conyers in the parking lot. Looked to me like they were having quite a conversation. When she saw me, she looked embarrassed and didn't acknowledge my wave. Conyers started the car and they skedaddled. Wonder what was going on."

"I wonder," Gil replied softly as a cold numbness spread through his chest.

Brockett sprang to his feet, hefted his camera atop his shoulder, and began running toward the jail.

"Here they come."

The jail doors opened, and the two deputies emerged, striding down the steps and pushing the media cluster back to create room for Pike, Blankenship, and the sheriff.

Pike and Blankenship stepped forward toward the battery of outstretched microphones, while Sheriff McSwain stayed in the background.

Pike surveyed the pack of reporters in a semicircle before him and the bystanders behind them who had gathered to watch the goings-on.

"Mr. John Henry Blankenship and I have just met with Hiram and Caleb Soseby, and I am happy to tell you that they have accepted my offer to supply them with the exceptional legal services of Mr. Blankenship, one of the finest trial lawyers in the South or anywhere for that matter. It's clear to me that these men are innocent, and that will become apparent once the trial begins. John, do you have anything to add?"

"Well, of course I do, Roscoe." Blankenship smiled broadly as he removed his Stetson with one hand and patted his mussed white hair back into place with the other. "We have yet to see the state's evidence in this case, but I can tell you Hiram and Caleb Soseby are the real victims, unjustly accused of a crime they did not commit. Authorities have charged them and locked them up based on flimsy hearsay evidence and the alleged confession of one Randall Scoggins, a local drunk and ne'er-do-well who can barely remember where he got his last drink, much less what happened on the night that black boy was killed. We will show that Hiram Soseby, a distinguished war veteran, a solid businessman, a lifelong resident of Pickett County, and his son Caleb were convenient targets of J. Edgar Hoover and his FBI minions who desperately had to find someone to arrest for this crime. The Sosebys are in jail because of the intrusion of LBJ and the federal government, and they are the ones behind this prosecution—not Sheriff McSwain and his fine staff of deputies."

Gil pulled his eye away from the camera eyepiece briefly to look for McSwain, but the sheriff had drifted off and was nowhere to be seen.

Blankenship continued, mopping his sweaty brow with a yellow handkerchief he pulled from his coat pocket. "Now boys, I know you have questions, but that's all I have to say for today. Give me a chance to spend some time on how best to defend the Sosebys, and then I'll be happy to talk further with you. Thank you very much. And thank you, Roscoe, for reaching out to me. You're going to make one helluva governor."

There was scattered applause from some of the bystanders on the fringe of the crowd of reporters. Pike slapped Blankenship on the back, then raised both arms to acknowledge his supporters. "Any questions for me, boys? I got time for a few."

Charlie Crown raised his hand and fired a question simultaneously. "Mr. Pike, why are you inserting yourself into this case? Do you see political advantage?"

Pike glared at Crown, an old nemesis, then crinkled his gaunt face into a tight grin. "Charlie, I will always go to battle against sinister forces of the federal government that seek to control our lives. The feds have moved in and, in essence, told the good people of Pickett County that they are not capable of solving this case on their own. I will fight them with everything I've got. If that helps my candidacy—then so be it."

Gil, his camera still rolling, spoke up. "Would you debate Harrison Parker? One on one?"

"You damn right, I would." Pike nodded vigorously. "Anytime, anywhere. But I'm not sure he has the guts to face me, to show the people where he truly stands."

Pike looked at the watch sliding up and down along his slender, sweaty wrist. "Boys, I'd love to keep talking, but I've got a rally to attend in Sizemore County and I need to get moving. We'll see you all later. Thank you for being here today."

Pike, Blankenship, and their entourage began moving down the sidewalk toward their waiting motorcade. Gil, Brockett, and another cameraman followed them, continuing to film as they entered their vehicles and pulled away.

Sheriff McSwain watched the motorcade depart as he stood alone on the stoop at the jail's entrance. He had stepped away from the news conference because he felt discouraged and diminished. Once again outsiders had come into his county to work their will on him—first the FBI, now Pike and Blankenship. McSwain had deeply resented the pressures by the FBI to charge the Sosebys, but he was now convinced they were guilty. He realized that working with Carson Baker to convict them might be the only way to regain his self-respect, but against Blankenship and Pike that would be a long, hard hill to climb.

FORTY-THREE

A PROPOSAL

REVEREND ELIJAH TIMMONS was lost. He had allowed extra time
to locate the address he'd been given, but he was navigating terra in-
cognita—the winding lanes of Buckhead in the city's most exclusive
residential enclave. A full moon bathed the majestic mansions in a pale
luminescence but offered little light for Timmons to read his street
map. He pulled his car to the curb, turned on the interior lights, and
scanned the map with his index finger, looking for Forrest Trace amid
the other crisscrossing lines on the crumpled paper. He cursed silently,
careful not to take his Lord's name in vain, and slowly pulled away
praying that Providence would lead him to his goal.

As he approached the next intersection, he received resounding
reaffirmation of the power of prayer. The street sign told him he had
found Forrest Trace. The double "r" in Forrest told him the street was
not named for its idyllic setting. It was homage to Nathan Bedford
Forrest, legendary Confederate general and first Grand Wizard of the
Ku Klux Klan. Timmons tried not to think about that as he turned onto
the street and quickly found the address he was seeking.

At the top of the sloping, curvy driveway he pulled his car into the
parking area to the right of the house. As he opened the car door, floodlights over the garage clicked on, and one of the three paneled garage
doors began to open. He saw a man walking toward him, a silhouette
backlit by the harsh beams from the floodlights. But Timmons knew
exactly who it was.

Devereaux Inman extended his hand, a gesture of respect
Timmons had seldom seen from an old adversary. "Reverend
Timmons. Welcome. We've been waiting for you. Hope you didn't

have too much trouble finding the house."

Timmons took Inman's hand loosely for a couple of shakes. "Well, Mr. Inman, I'm not used to driving around this neighborhood at all, much less at ten p.m. I'm happy your neighborhood patrols didn't spot me before I got here."

Inman laughed at the remark but quickly realized Timmons wasn't joking. "Right this way, Reverend. Since we're already here, why don't we just go in through the garage? Quicker that way."

Timmons followed Inman into the garage, past the expensive vehicles parked there, and through the door into the kitchen. Timmons couldn't help but wonder if Inman's other guest had gotten the same back door treatment.

They walked across the marble floor of the open foyer and into the oak-paneled library. Harrison Parker rose from his chair and stepped forward, extending his open hand.

"Reverend Timmons, thank you so much for coming. I have long admired your dedication to nonviolence and your courage. It's a pleasure to shake your hand."

Timmons was somewhat taken aback by Parker's graciousness. "Why, thank you, Mr. Attorney General. I appreciate that."

"Gentlemen, why don't we all sit down and talk about why we are here." Inman gestured to a chair for Timmons and then sat next to Parker on a small sofa facing Timmons. Between them was a glass-topped coffee table adorned with a large photo book titled *Antebellum Southern Plantations*. Three glasses of water sat on the table within easy reach of each man. Timmons noticed that Inman seemed a bit uneasy, as though he had never before had a black man as an invited guest in his home and wasn't sure how to act.

"First of all," Inman began, "we're doing this late at night at my home for a reason. We want it to be confidential. It would be damaging to all three of us if the public found out about this discussion. I hope we can all agree on that."

Inman looked at each man expectantly, waiting for nods of

acknowledgement that he quickly received.

"Reverend, as I'm sure you know, Harrison here has the support of the business community, and we're doing all we can behind the scenes to help him, mainly pumping money into his campaign. We understand—as I'm sure you do—that Roscoe Pike simply cannot be allowed to become our next governor. It would be disastrous not only for your people, Reverend Timmons, but also for the business community and all of those who want this state to progress economically, educationally, and racially. Do I make myself clear?"

"Very clear." Timmons nodded as he spoke. "Very clear. You want Mr. Parker to win this race, and I understand that. I agree he is the best—really the only—choice. But what do you want of me?"

Inman was about to respond, but before he could Parker quickly jumped in. "I appreciate that, Reverend Timmons. The fact is I'm going to need a lot of Negro votes to win this thing. We know Pike's support will be substantial. He is playing on the racial fears of white voters, and frankly the Jarvis Pendry murder and all the fallout from that horrible crime are just fuel for his fire. We know his people will turn out, and they will be enthusiastic. I've positioned myself as the reasonable alternative to Pike, but I have to admit there's an enthusiasm gap that's very difficult to overcome."

Timmons sat back, slowly nodding with each point Parker made.

Inman spoke next. "Here's our problem, Reverend. Harrison has to sound like a conservative without the racist appeals. The aim is to attract white moderates and those conservatives who object to Pike's...um...coarser qualities. But that approach won't appeal to Negro voters. So, Reverend, we need you to help us send a message to the black community that Harrison Parker is worthy of their support."

Timmons looked at Inman, then at Parker, and gave a slight laugh. "And how do you expect me to do that? I can't be out campaigning for you, Mr. Parker, when you are offering nothing to the black community other than the fact that you are not Roscoe Pike. You want black votes? Then you make a speech tomorrow pledging support for integrated schools, endorsing the Civil Rights Act, and starting up jobs programs for the downtrodden people of this state—not all of whom are black, I might add."

"If I do that, Reverend, I lose in a landslide. I'm sorry, but that's just the way it is."

Timmons scratched the back of his head, a quizzical expression on his face. "Then exactly what do you expect me to do, gentlemen?"

Inman leaned forward in his seat, placing his forearms on his knees. "Reverend Timmons, we would like for you to do some radio commercials for Harrison. These commercials would only be heard on black radio stations across the state. If we're lucky, white folk, who certainly don't listen to black radio stations, will never know. We'll run the spots on the day before the election so that even if the word does get out to the wider community, it'll be too late to have much negative impact. By urging your people to vote for Harrison, you could be the difference in denying Roscoe Pike the governor's office. What do you say?"

"Gentlemen, I hate to sound crass," Timmons said, "but what's in this for me? Seems to me I'm the one taking all the risks."

"It's true. You are," Parker responded. "But I can guarantee you that if I can win this race with the help of the Negro vote you generate, then you will be a valued part of my administration, and you can count on that. As governor I can do a lot of things, and I promise you that I will do everything in my power to advance the interests of our Negro citizens. You have to take my word on that because to promise that now in public would doom my election chances. You'll just have to trust me."

Timmons made a half-hearted attempt to suppress a snicker. "My trust is something you have yet to earn. But despite that, I will reluctantly agree to your request. I'll do what I can to get out the vote in the black community—not because I believe in you but because the election of Roscoe Pike would be a tragedy for the people of our state, both black and white."

All three men rose from their seats and Parker reached over to pump Timmons's hand. "Thank you, Reverend. You will never regret this."

Inman also took Timmons's hand and after two shakes held it for his parting words. "Reverend Timmons, this decision is going to pay huge dividends for all of us. We'll start working on those radio spots right away. And you'll have whatever resources you need to get your people to the polls. Just ask, and we'll take care of it."

As Timmons descended the driveway from Inman's hilltop mansion, he felt a great sense of unease. How could he endorse a man who would not publicly be a champion for his cause and his people? And yet how could he not do everything in his power to prevent an archenemy of his race from seizing the pinnacle of power? It was a high-stakes gamble, but as a black man he understood that in the South he often had to choose the lesser evil.

At the end of the driveway, he turned left onto the street named for a man who fought to keep his people enslaved and drove toward home.

FORTY-FOUR

MINDY

GIL WAS NERVOUS as he strolled into the newsroom the morning after the Pike-Blankenship news conference in Armistead. He'd worried overnight about his question to Pike about a debate because he didn't think the invitation had been officially issued. He was concerned he might have overstepped a bit, and he was sure if he had he'd find out about it this morning.

Sure enough, Tom Burke spotted him and waved him into his office, a glass-enclosed space that gave Burke a full view of the newsroom. Burke walked to his desk and sat in his executive rolling chair, motioning Gil to take a seat in one of the cushioned chairs opposite the desk as he swiveled from side to side. Gil was aware that everyone in the newsroom had a full view of what was going on in the office, but at least Burke seemed calm, even chipper.

"You'll be happy to know, Mr. Matthews, that the station sent out the debate invitations this morning. An announcement had been planned for today, but you kind of forced the issue with your question yesterday. And Charlie Crown made mention of it in his article this morning as well. So—thank you very much. Now it's official."

Gil gave a small sigh of relief. "Well…good. Sorry I jumped the gun. I hope the GM wasn't upset."

Burke chuckled. "No, Ron was fine with it. He's just nervous about how we're going to pull this off. It's going to be a half-hour live debate two days before the primary. Just Pike and Parker. The minor candidates will squawk, but screw 'em."

"Okay," Gil responded. "Will it be statewide?"

"Yes. Other stations around the state are planning to carry it live.

This will be a big deal."

Gil rose to leave, but Burke wasn't finished. "There's one more thing I should tell you, even though you may already know. We've hired Mindy Williams. Might as well since she practically works for us anyway with all the tips she's given you."

Gil was stunned but delighted to hear this news. "Great news, Tom. About time you took my advice. When does she start?"

"Right away. She's never done TV, but she'll be a natural. She looks great, and I think viewers will love her. And her great sources now belong to us. We'll have to wring that print tradition out of her and teach her how to do good TV. I know you can help her, so we'll probably let her team with you. You don't have a problem with that, do you?"

Gil ignored Burke's wry grin. "No problem at all. When will she be here?"

"She's here right now. Up in personnel."

Gil left Burke's office and headed up the hallway. He peeked through the open doorway of the personnel office and saw Mindy at a table filling out her various forms for employment. He watched her for a moment, admiring her new hairstyle and makeup touches, not to mention the new blouse and clinging skirt he'd never seen before. She had always been attractive. Now she was beautiful.

As he walked in she looked up and rose to greet him. Gil smiled broadly and opened his arms. Mindy smiled too, but her posture made it clear she was hesitant to accept his full embrace. Gil immediately realized his gesture had been presumptuous and inappropriate, and he dropped his arms with a shrug. But once he'd done that, she reached out and gave him a brief shoulder hug with minimal body contact.

"Mindy, what a surprise. You never told me!"

"I know. I didn't want to jinx anything. But Tom and Ron called me, made an attractive offer, and here I am. And I'm excited—but worried about all I've got to learn. I'll need your help."

"Of course," Gil responded. "We're a team. More now than ever.

Now get those i's dotted and t's crossed. I'll see you back in the newsroom."

Mindy sighed deeply, smiled, and pronounced a poetic benediction. "Behold, the Door of Hope ajar and Freedom freely beckoning."

Gil, smiling and shaking his head, left Mindy to finish her paperwork and returned to the newsroom. The morning meeting was over, and reporters and their cameramen were heading out the door to cover their assigned stories. Those manning the assignment desk looked over wire copy and newspapers from around the state to be sure no story was missed.

Burke was pacing around the newsroom as he did every morning, obsessing over every detail of the day's coverage plan. He looked relieved when he spotted Gil.

"Did you hear the news? Trial date set in Pickett County. Two weeks from today. You'd better get up there now to get the latest from the sheriff and solicitor—and we need to track down Blankenship to see what he has to say. This is moving very, very fast."

"Okay. On my way. Should Mindy join me?"

"Of course. She's covering the trial with you. Nothing like a baptism by fire, eh?"

"Ten-four, boss. On my way."

Gil began collecting his gear as Mindy walked into the newsroom.

"Saddle up, rookie," he said jokingly. "We've got a murder trial to cover. Are you ready?"

"I'm ready," she replied. "Half a league, half a league, half a league onward!"

MORNING TRAFFIC HAD moderated to a steady flow and diminished by the mile as Gil headed outbound on his now familiar route to Pickett County. The sun, dull red through the haze only two hours ago, was now blazing full force on Gil's face as he drove northeast. He flipped the sun visor down to ease the glare, glanced at Mindy, then turned his eyes back on the road. It was time to get some answers.

"I hate to bring this up at this particular time, but now that we're an official team I just need to get some things straight. I need to know about what's going on between you and Conyers. I heard you paid a visit to him at the Monarch Courts two days ago."

Mindy stared straight ahead, frozen in place, as the euphoria of the morning evaporated. "Ned Brockett told you, right?"

"Right. Ned told me he saw you talking to Conyers in his car. I'd just like to know what's up with you two."

Mindy sighed deeply but said nothing as she turned her head away from Gil and stared vacantly at the passing scene. Finally, she spoke, her tone flat. "You don't need to know anything about me that I choose not to share. But since you are obviously not going to let this go, I'll tell you this. Bill and I were once engaged to be married. How's that for breaking news?"

"What?" Gil sputtered. "I can't believe it."

"Hardly anyone knows. I met him in a journalism class at UGA. We dated, hit it off, and one thing led to another. I broke it off when I realized I wasn't ready for marriage. I wanted a journalism career and realized I needed to focus on that above all. I knew I couldn't do that as a cop's wife. So I've moved on. Unfortunately, he hasn't."

Mindy turned to look at Gil, awaiting his response, which came haltingly.

"I never imagined. It was obvious you two had a connection. But I'm stunned to hear this."

"And I know what you're thinking," Mindy said with an air of resignation. "Rest assured the relationship between that lawman and this reporter was completely professional. He helped me and my career, no question, but he neither asked nor expected anything in return."

After a long pause Gill replied, making no effort to disguise his skepticism. "Okay. If you say so."

"You don't believe me?"

"It's pretty obvious he expected something. Feeding you all those tips. He must have felt there was something in it for him."

Mindy shook her head and looked down at her hands clasped in her lap. "If he did, he's disappointed. I've ended my relationship—personal and professional—with Bill. That's what our meeting was about at Monarch Courts. I'll always be grateful to him, but I've got to chart my own course."

Gil said nothing as he exited the interstate and took the two-lane highway toward Armistead.

Mindy broke the silence, her voice rising. "Do you have any idea what it's like to be a woman in this business? I work in a world of men. No matter how good my reporting is, they are always judging me on my body, my personality, and their chances at getting me into bed. I always thought you might be different, Gil, but I guess I was wrong about that."

Gil swerved the car over to the shoulder of the road, the station wagon bouncing to a stop on the rutted, hard-packed clay. He turned to look at Mindy. "You weren't wrong about me. My respect for you and your work is enormous. I admit my comment about you and Bill was unfair. I was just frustrated at being blindsided about your relationship. I do care about you as a friend and colleague. And I have to know you feel the same."

Mindy gave a slight smile. "It's okay, Gil. I get it. We're a team. And it's my first day in TV news, and I need you a lot more than you need me, at least until I learn the ropes. Let's try to get beyond this for both our sakes."

Gil held her gaze for a few seconds before tapping the accelerator and easing back onto the blacktop. "Done," he said, more as a period than a statement of fact.

They drove on in silence, each of them wondering what more they could say to recapture the easy relationship they'd once enjoyed. But the words wouldn't come, and they both feared it would never be the same.

FORTY-FIVE

DO YOUR DUTY

THE TRIAL BEGAN seven weeks after Jarvis Pendry's murder. Solicitor General Carson Baker had assembled his case quickly, and John Henry Blankenship was ready with his defense. Most people in Armistead just wanted it all to be over so the reporters would leave and the normal patterns of life in Pickett County could resume unchanged.

The tension that would normally prevail during such a potentially sensational trial was muted. Spectators hoping for a seat in the courtroom lined up in front of the old courthouse chatting and laughing. Members of the Ladies Auxiliary of the local VFW served up lemonade from a makeshift concession stand on the courthouse lawn. Television cameramen roamed the grounds, getting their scene-setting shots and occasionally interviewing townsfolk about this historic occasion. They had to make use of the opportunity because the judge had already ruled that once the opening gavel came down, no cameras or recording devices would be allowed in the courtroom or anywhere on courthouse property while court was in session.

The heat built inside the courtroom as people filed in. Floor fans brought in for the trial whirred away, stirring the stagnant air but offering little relief. It would be even hotter in the courtroom balcony, where Pickett County's black citizens were relegated.

By eleven o'clock all participants, spectators, and reporters were seated to await the entrance of Judge Obadiah Plunkett. Everyone stood after the "all rise" command as Judge Plunkett appeared through the door outside his chambers and climbed the three steps to his bench. He was a portly, balding man of sixty-two and had been a respected Superior Court Judge for twenty-five years. He was known as a strict disciplinarian who would not tolerate any courtroom shenanigans. If he was apprehensive about presiding over a controversial trial in the national spotlight, he didn't show it as he brought his gavel down.

"Ladies and gentlemen, this court is now in session. Please be seated."

The defendants, Hiram Soseby and his son Caleb, sat at a long table to the judge's left with their attorney John Henry Blankenship. Hiram looked relaxed wearing a short-sleeve shirt and narrow tie. Caleb had similar attire but appeared much more tense, nervously fidgeting, clenching his jaw muscles, and looking around the courtroom with rapidly blinking eyes. Just behind them sat the wife and mother of the accused, Sadie Soseby, who stared out at the courtroom with sunken, dark, and doleful eyes. She was so thin the subdued print dress she wore enveloped her body like a wrinkled shroud.

On the judge's right was another long table where Solicitor General Carson Baker sat with two young associate lawyers on his left who would assist him. All three were dressed in dark suits. Baker wore his trademark red bowtie. On Baker's right sat Jarvis Pendry's widow, Evelyn, dressed in a pastel outfit with her hair pulled back in a tight bun, her face a stoic shield. Behind them was a section reserved for reporters, among them Mindy and Gil, whose camera remained locked in his car because of the judge's prohibition.

Looking over the courtroom from a tiny balcony in the rear were about thirty black spectators who were not allowed to sit with whites in the lower courtroom. Many others had been denied entry altogether when the balcony reached capacity.

The first order of business was jury selection, and it went quickly. Only five blacks were among the fifty potential jurors, and the defense struck them quickly. The final panel consisted of twelve middle-aged white men.

After a brief recess the opening statements began, prosecution first. Carson Baker rose and walked to the front of the jury box, slowly looking at each of the twelve men who were also sternly eyeing him.

The only sounds were the humming of the floor fans and the fluttering of the hand fans passed out to spectators by a local funeral home as they filed into the courtroom.

"Gentlemen of the jury, I'm Solicitor General Carson Baker, and it's my job to prosecute this case and convince you that these two men, Hiram and Caleb Soseby, are the cold-blooded killers who took the life of Jarvis Pendry.

"We will prove that Hiram Soseby killed Jarvis Pendry, a war hero and upstanding citizen, by ambushing him at the Peavine Creek Bridge with a double-barrel, sawed-off shotgun. We will also prove that Hiram's son Caleb Soseby aided and abetted this heinous crime by shining the light that illuminated their target so his father couldn't miss. As far as the law is concerned, that is tantamount to pulling the trigger himself.

"You will hear from a man named Randall Scoggins who confesses to driving the vehicle from which the fatal shots were fired. He is not on trial with these men because he has confessed, has pleaded guilty, and will be sentenced for his part in this crime. You will also hear from a witness who will tell you Caleb Soseby confessed to the crime during a fishing outing. We will support that testimony with other evidence that will prove beyond the shadow of a doubt that these two men are guilty of the vicious crime with which they are charged.

"This crime has received an awful lot of attention here and around the country. Do not let outside factors sway you as you discharge the heavy responsibility now on your shoulders. Please just focus on the facts of this case, listen to our witnesses, and remember always that a great injustice was done here in Pickett County, and it is up to you to make it clear to the world that the good people of this county will not let that stand. We owe that to Jarvis Pendry's widow Evelyn, who's sitting right over there. We owe it to our fellow citizens, white and black. And we owe it to the cause of justice and righteousness."

Baker paused and once again looked each juror in the eyes.

"I know you will do your duty. Thank you."

As Baker walked toward his table to take his seat, Blankenship rose and quickly walked to the jury box. He pulled the lapel of his white suit coat aside, exposing a red suspender. He hooked his right thumb in the suspender and began walking back and forth before the jury.

"Good mornin', gentlemen of the jury. I am John Henry Blankenship, and I will be offering a defense for these two men, Hiram and Caleb Soseby. They are unjustly accused of a horrible crime, and I will show you beyond any reasonable doubt that they are not guilty.

"Hiram Soseby is a prominent businessman, a pillar of this community, a man who gave his country distinguished service in the Pacific Theater of World War Two. Caleb is a good son who works with his father and hopes to inherit the family business one day. He's got big ambitions and a lifetime of promise. He does not deserve to be branded a murderer. He and his father are not guilty, and we will show you that.

"And what about poor Sadie Soseby—a faithful, loving wife who must endure agony because of the trumped-up charges against her husband and her son? This is an outrage, gentlemen of the jury, an outrage.

"Now we will hear what the prosecution's witnesses have to say. We will see if the testimony from a man who is obviously troubled, who is known to be a chronic alcoholic, who no doubt sold his soul to the devil to escape significant jail time—we'll see if he can be believed. I think not.

"As for any other witnesses, I say bring 'em on. We have nothing to fear because the truth is on our side. And the truth will set Hiram and Caleb free.

"Thank you very much for listening."

Blankenship returned to his table and slumped a bit in his chair, mopping the perspiration from his forehead and then drinking from a glass of tepid water.

Judge Plunkett looked toward the prosecution table. "Counselor, are you ready to call your first witness?"

Baker stood and addressed the judge. "We are, Your Honor. The people call Mr. Randall Scoggins."

A side door in the front of the courtroom opened and through it walked Scoggins, escorted by two uniformed Pickett County deputies. A low murmur rose from the spectator area, but the judge quickly hushed it with one bang of his gavel and a warning.

"Silence please. We will not tolerate any outbursts in this courtroom."

Scoggins wore khaki slacks and an unbuttoned blue sport coat that appeared to be a size too small. The fabric was taut across his back, and the sleeves strained to cover his bulging arms. He walked in an unsteady shuffle, as though he still wore the shackles that had been removed for his testimony. He looked around the room with no expression before turning his eyes straight ahead and plodding to the witness stand, the deputies helping him up the two steps and into the chair.

After Scoggins took the oath, Carson Baker rose and approached his star witness. Scoggins seemed to be in a fog and looked at Baker as though he had no idea who he was, even though they had rehearsed this testimony many times over the past week. Baker assumed the extreme stress of testifying coupled with the fact that Scoggins hadn't had a drink for weeks were taking their toll. He silently prayed Scoggins would snap out of it.

"Good morning, Mr. Scoggins." Baker spoke in an abnormally loud voice, which seemed to startle Scoggins into a state of awareness. He looked at the solicitor and nodded, and Baker felt a wave of relief.

"Now, Randall, please tell the jury about the first time you ever saw Jarvis Pendry."

Scoggins's eyes darted briefly to the table where Hiram and Caleb Soseby sat watching him intently, then focused his gaze on Baker.

"It was July second, I believe. About eleven p.m. That's when this black guy came into Soseby's gas station asking for directions. That's the first time I saw him."

"Did you know who this man was? Did you know he was Colonel Jarvis Pendry on his way home from Army duty at Fort Benning?"

"No. I didn't know who he was until later. Until after he got killed."

"What happened when Colonel Pendry entered the gas station to ask for directions? Who else was there?"

"Well, I was sitting down having a beer with Caleb. Caleb Soseby. His dad Hiram was closing up the cash register for the night—"

Baker interrupted. "Do you see Hiram and Caleb Soseby in this courtroom? Could you point them out?"

Scoggins pointed toward the defense table, trying to avoid the withering stares from the defendants.

"Continue, please."

"Well, this nigra—"

"You mean Colonel Pendry," Baker interjected.

"Yes. Colonel Pendry came in and asked for directions to his uncle's house. Said he was lost."

"And what happened then?"

"Well, Hiram and Caleb started mouthing off at him, asking about where he was from, if he was one of them agitators sent down here to test out the new civil rights law."

"At any time did Colonel Pendry object or argue? Was he aggressive in any way?"

"Not that I can remember. He just figured he was not welcome I guess and left."

"And then what happened, Randall?"

"Well, Hiram grabbed his shotgun from under the counter and says, 'Let's go get us a nigger.'"

Baker turned away from Scoggins and faced the judge.

"Your Honor, I apologize for the use of this vile term in your courtroom. It is an offensive term that dehumanizes our fellow Americans and should never be used. But it was the contemptuous term applied by the defendants to Jarvis Pendry before they murdered him, and it is important the jury knows that."

"Duly noted, Solicitor Baker," Judge Plunkett responded. "Let's continue."

"Okay, Randall. What happened next?"

"Hiram ordered me to drive my car with him in the front seat and Caleb in the back. He kept yelling at me to step on it. Said we had to catch him and teach him a lesson. So I floored it and pretty soon we seen his taillights. He was parked by the bridge."

"You mean the Highway 21 bridge over Peavine Creek."

"Yes sir, Peavine Creek."

"What happened next?"

"Hiram told me to slow down and pull alongside his car. He propped his shotgun in the open window, and Caleb shined a light at the man. That's when Hiram opened fire. Two shots one right after the other."

"Randall, did you know at that moment that Jarvis Pendry had been fatally wounded?"

"No sir. Remember I was just the driver, and I really couldn't see much. All's I know is that Hiram was shouting he'd killed him. He was real excited."

"After the shots were fired, what happened next?"

"Well, Hiram told me to get out of there, so I floored it again, and we sped away across the bridge and up the hill. Before we got to the top, Hiram told me to pull to the side so we could look back at the bridge to see if anything was going on. It was real quiet, and there wasn't any traffic at that hour, so we turned around and went back to the bridge and the car."

"And when you got to the car, what did you see?"

"Well, it was a mess. The nigra—"

"Colonel Pendry," Baker corrected, a harsh edge to his voice.

"Yes, Colonel Pendry was blown across the front seat. His head was pretty well gone. Blood and brains everywhere. I had to puke. Didn't seem to bother Hiram and Caleb. They were kind of celebrating."

"What happened next?"

"Well, Hiram said we had to hide the car and the body. He forced

Caleb to get in the bloody car and drive it down the old overgrown path running alongside the creek. I stayed back on the highway, so I didn't see what happened, but they said they rolled the car into the creek, and it sank. They were really happy about that."

"Then what happened?"

"I drove Hiram and Caleb back to the gas station and dropped them off. They told me I had to clean up the blood in my car as soon as I could. Then I went home and had a few drinks. Hiram made me promise never to mention what had happened to a living soul."

Baker looked at Scoggins and gave a nod and a wink that only the witness could see.

"No further questions, Your Honor." He turned toward the defense table. "Mr. Blankenship, your witness."

Blankenship rose from his chair and walked around the defense table, slowly nearing Scoggins, who nervously awaited cross-examination.

"That's quite a story, Randall. Quite an unbelievable story. What did Mr. Baker offer you to get you to make up these lies about your friends Hiram and Caleb?"

Baker shot to his feet. "Objection, Your Honor!"

"Sustained," Judge Plunkett said without hesitation. "Mr. Blankenship, you need to rephrase that prejudicial question."

"Of course, Your Honor. My apologies. Randall, why did you decide to plead guilty in this case, and what were you promised by the state to testify?"

"I'm pleading guilty because I am truly sorry for the role I played in the murder of Colonel Pendry. And it is my hope I will get favorable treatment when my sentence is announced, but I have no guarantees."

Blankenship shook his head dismissively and chuckled. "Oh, I'm sure the state is going to take care of its star witness. You know what quid pro quo is, don't you Randall? Well, maybe not. You dropped out of school before you could learn much Latin. It means something for something. You scratch my back, and I'll scratch yours. You give me what I want, and I'll take it easy on you. Well, Randall, I believe you were involved in that crime, and they had you dead to rights. You had to offer up some sacrificial lambs to reduce your sentence, and you turned on your friends, the Sosebys, who had nothing to do with the murder…"

"Objection, Your Honor!" Baker interrupted. "Mr. Blankenship is badgering the witness."

"Sustained," Judge Plunkett intoned. "Watch it, Mr. Blankenship."

"Sorry, Your Honor. Now Randall, let's talk about your drinking. On the night you were arrested, were you drunk?"

"Objection!"

"Overruled."

"Randall, before I was so rudely interrupted, I was asking if you were drunk on the night you were arrested."

"Well, I'd had a few drinks. Don't think I was drunk, though."

"You, in fact, confessed to being a part of the murder. If you'd had an attorney, do you think he would have let you talk to police in your condition? Did you even know what you were talking about? Were you just shooting off your mouth because you were drunk, or were you just sober enough to want to claim to be some kind of big shot because you are such a loser in this community?"

Baker practically leapt over the table before him. "Objection! Objection! Your Honor, this is getting out of hand."

Blankenship calmly turned his back on Scoggins and said, "No problem, Counselor. I withdraw the question. And I have no more questions for this stellar witness. He's said more than enough."

Judge Plunkett called a five-minute recess for both sides to collect themselves. The Sosebys and Blankenship huddled at their table, Hiram patting Blankenship on the back. Baker conferred with Evelyn, who was sitting next to him with a look of concern.

"Should we be worried?" she asked. "That was pretty rough."

"We knew all along Scoggins's credibility would be a problem," Baker answered. "But I think his direct testimony was strong and convincing. More than enough to make our case. From this point on we'll build on that. We both know this is not going to be easy, but if I do my job right, we will get justice for you and your husband."

Evelyn closed her eyes briefly as if to shut out the hostile world surrounding them. "Solicitor Baker, I trust you completely, but I am not so naïve as to have much faith in Southern justice. I can pray and I can hope, but I fear it will be a while before my soul is finally rested."

"Evelyn, I understand. And I too pray and hope that the time for justice is now. The only thing I can promise is that I will do my best to make it so."

Baker started to reach out to her delicate hand resting on the table to cover it with his own but instinctively stopped short. This gesture of comfort would have to wait for a more private setting.

FORTY-SIX

GOLDEN GOPHERS

THE STIFLING COURTROOM began to take a toll on the spectators and reporters crammed shoulder to shoulder in every available seat. Gil decided to shed his sport coat, twisting in his seat and unintentionally elbowing Mindy, who was sitting next to him on a long bench full of reporters.

"Watch it," she said in a harsh whisper.

"Sorry," he replied, extracting his right arm from a damp sleeve and draping the coat across his lap.

Gil was the only cameraman credentialed to be in the courtroom for the trial because he'd been so involved in coverage of the murder from the beginning. Most of the other cameramen waited in a park across the street from the courthouse, being very careful not to set foot on courthouse property. Several Pickett County deputies were posted around the courthouse with specific orders from Judge Plunkett to arrest anyone who ventured onto the grounds with a camera or tape recorder while court was in session.

Gil and Mindy sat two rows behind the prosecution table, watching Carson Baker as he attempted to bolster the keynote confession of Randall Scoggins. The jury was shown photos of the Peavine Creek bridge, the bridge abutment where stray buckshot chipped the concrete, the grass-matted depressions of tire tracks along the overgrown road next to the creek, Jarvis Pendry's car being hauled out of the water, and, finally, carefully chosen shots of the victim's body lying in mud and blood in the car's front seat.

Baker had selected those photographs with extra care. He wanted them to shock the jury, but he thought close-ups of Pendry's broken, faceless, partially decayed body would be too much. He also had to consider the impact on Evelyn, who had never seen the photographs. Strategically, a tearful reaction from Evelyn might have been useful to his case, but Baker simply could not put her through it. Even with the milder though still grotesque photographs, Evelyn turned her eyes away, clutching a tissue but not shedding a tear.

Next came the displays of the shotgun and the records proving that Hiram Soseby had purchased it. Then came a risky but in Baker's eyes essential move—calling FBI agent Robert Smithers to the stand. Most people in Pickett County resented the FBI's presence as another federal incursion on their turf, but Smithers had testimony Baker could not do without.

"Agent Smithers, is Hiram Soseby now, or has he ever been, a member of the Ku Klux Klan?"

"Well, Solicitor Baker, from our investigation we believe Hiram Soseby has been an active Klan member for some time. He has many friends and associates who are Klan sympathizers."

"And how do you come by this information, since we all know the Klan doesn't share its membership rosters with law enforcement?"

"During the course of our investigation in Pickett County after the murder of Colonel Pendry, we concentrated on the theory that the Klan was involved in the crime. We talked with several witnesses who confidentially told us about Soseby's Klan activities. While his activity may have diminished in recent years, we have evidence that indicates he is a true disciple of the Klan's doctrine of white supremacy."

John Henry Blankenship, who'd been doodling on a note pad, suddenly bolted upright. "Objection, Your Honor! Objection! This is complete hearsay and has no supporting witnesses. I move that this testimony be struck from the record."

Judge Plunkett quickly responded. "Mr. Blankenship, I'm going to sustain the objection and instruct the jury to ignore that last remark from the witness. Next question, Solicitor Baker."

"Very well, Your Honor. Agent Smithers, you have been

investigating the KKK in the South for years. What have you learned about the Klan in that time?"

Smithers took a handkerchief out of the pocket of his dark suit jacket and blotted his forehead just below the widow's peak of his crew cut.

"It's called the Invisible Empire for a reason. It's a shadowy group that primarily intimidates Negroes and their sympathizers. The Klan's mission is to protect the white race from Negro advancement. They use Christianity to justify what they do, which often includes violence."

Blankenship shot to his feet again. "Objection! This is all very interesting, but it has nothing to do with my clients. Judge, this is really taking liberties, and I object strenuously."

"I'm afraid I concur," Judge Plunkett responded. "You've not shown any direct link between the defendant and the Klan, and once again I will rule in favor of the defense."

Baker had anticipated difficulties with Smithers's testimony, but he felt his purpose had been served.

"No further questions, Your Honor. Your witness, Mr. Blankenship."

Blankenship sauntered up to the witness stand and paused a moment, giving Smithers the once-over.

"Mr. Smithers, what part of the country are you from?"

"Minnesota. Born and grew up there. Edina, Minnesota."

"I see. Minn-e-so-ta. Isn't that where Hubert Horatio Humphrey is from? Our liberal Vice President?"

"Yes. He was mayor of Minneapolis and a longtime senator."

"Uh-huh. And agent Smithers, I'm curious. How many black people did you know in Minn-e-so-ta?"

"There are very few Negroes in Minnesota, so I didn't have much opportunity."

"So I guess it's fair to say the civil rights laws you come down south to enforce really wouldn't have much impact in Minn-e-so-ta, would they?"

"Probably not, Mr. Blankenship. We don't discriminate against Negroes in Minnesota."

"If you can even find one, you mean." Blankenship spat out the remark and looked at the jury with a leering smile before continuing. "Agent Smithers, how long have you been working for the federal guv'ment in the South?"

"About three years."

"You ever eat grits, Agent Smithers?"

"On occasion."

"You like grits, Agent Smithers?"

"It's okay. Not a big fan."

"How about our Bulldogs? You pull for our football team?"

"Sure, I like the Bulldogs. But I grew up following the Big Ten and the Golden Gophers."

Chuckles could be heard around the courtroom. Judge Plunkett gave a light tap with his gavel.

"Oh, I see," Blankenship responded with a mocking tone. "The Golden Gophers? Pray tell, who are the Golden Gophers?"

"That's what we call the Minnesota football team. The Golden Gophers."

"Objection." Baker stood and raised his hand. "Your Honor, what in the world does any of this have to do with this trial?"

"Mr. Blankenship," Judge Plunkett said, looking at the defense attorney who now had a wide smile on his narrow face. "Your response?"

"Your Honor, I'm just trying to establish the credentials of this witness. And I think I have done so. No further questions."

Blankenship walked back to the defense table to be welcomed by the smirking defendants, who both reached out to shake his hand.

Baker remained standing and asked the judge, "Your Honor, redirect?"

The judge nodded and Baker began trying to undo some of the damage.

"Agent Smithers, have you ever been wounded in the line of duty?"

"Yes sir."

"And what were the circumstances?"

"It was a standoff outside a bank during a robbery. There were hostages inside. I was hit in the arm when the gunman came out shooting, just before I was able to take him out."

"Agent Smithers, have you been cited for bravery in the line of duty?"

"Yes, I have."

"And what were the circumstances of your heroism?"

"I got a citation for my actions during that bank robbery and also a commendation for some undercover work exposing terroristic activity in Mississippi involving the Ku Klux Klan."

"And Agent Smithers, how do you feel about the South?"

"I love the South. I've been down here for three years, and I've developed a deep affection for the region."

"One final question, Agent Smithers. How'd the Golden Gophers do last season?"

The courtroom erupted with laughter. Judge Plunkett banged the gavel several times, even though he, too, seemed amused.

Agent Smithers kept his most stoic FBI countenance and, as the laughter subsided, said, "I'll have to take the Fifth Amendment on that one, sir."

Baker felt he had partially salvaged Smithers's testimony on redirect, and he quickly moved to restore the serious tone more appropriate for this murder trial.

"Thank you, Agent Smithers. Thank you for your service to your country and your courage in doing your duty. No further questions. You may step down."

Baker had one more witness to call, and he worried about how Rufus McLeod would perform. From the beginning McLeod had been a reluctant witness. Despite being prodded by his mother to do the right thing, Rufus had been less than forthcoming about the "confession" he'd heard from Caleb Soseby. But because this event was so key in unraveling the mystery, Baker felt he had to put Rufus on the stand.

It was clear to all that Rufus did not want to be a prosecution witness from the moment he slouched his way to the stand and slumped down in the chair. He barely lifted his hand to be sworn in, and when Baker approached him, his puffy eyes burned with hostility and apprehension.

"Rufus, how long have you known Caleb Soseby?"

Rufus stared down at his shoes and spoke in a laconic mumble that was barely audible. "All my life. We grew up together."

"Are you good friends?"

"Well, we were good friends. Until recently."

"What was it that changed your relationship?"

Rufus shifted in the witness chair and for the first time looked up at Baker. "It was that damn murder. That changed everything."

"How do you mean?" Baker's voice was gently probing.

"Well...I mean...you know...it was when Caleb told me he and his daddy had done it."

Baker let the remark hang for about five seconds before following up. "Caleb told you he and his father, Hiram Soseby, murdered Colonel Jarvis Pendry? Just out of the blue?"

"We was fishing down at old man Miller's pond. We started talking about the murder, and that's when he just up and said he and his daddy killed him after he came to their gas station looking for directions."

"Did he tell you anything else?"

"Yeah, later he told me he was just kidding. That it wasn't true. Then he told me never to tell anyone."

"Rufus, do you believe Caleb was 'just kidding'?"

"Hell, I don't know."

"But you did mention it to your parents, right?"

"I did."

"And they urged you to come forward with the information, right?"

"Yes, we took the story to that TV guy…Grayson Kincaid…and I think he contacted the law. I'm really not sure."

"Rufus, you've shown courage to tell this story. Thanks to you and your parents for coming forward. Your witness."

Blankenship rose from his seat and meandered toward Rufus. "Now Rufus, you say you heard this story when you boys was fishing at the pond, right?"

"Un-huh."

"Pardon me?"

"Un-huh…. That means yes."

"Was it hot out there by the pond?"

"Yeah."

"Did you boys have some beer while you sat on the grass and fished?"

"We had a little—a few beers."

"In fact, you had quite a few beers, didn't you? You were raging drunk, weren't you?"

"No sir! I wasn't drunk if that's what you're trying to say."

"Oh no, Rufus. I'd never accuse you of being drunk—lying out there by that pond with a full cooler of beer in the hot summer sun. I won't accuse you of being drunk. Let's just say you had a buzz on—feeling no pain—three sheets to the wind."

Baker rose and shouted, "Objection, Your Honor! Badgering the witness."

Without waiting for Judge Plunkett to speak, Blankenship jerked his head toward the bench and said, "Judge, my clients are on trial for a murder they did not commit and this…this…kid, this Judas…is helping the prosecution frame my clients. I have every right to probe his story in every detail—including the very relevant factor of whether or not he was drunk."

"All right, all right," Judge Plunkett responded. "I will overrule the objection. Please continue."

"Thank you, Your Honor. Now Rufus, you say you're Caleb's good friend, but isn't it true your parents tried to bust up that friendship? Isn't it true they didn't like Caleb very much and worked pretty hard to keep you two apart? They're the ones pushing you to testify, right? You don't really believe any of this, do you?"

Rufus sat a little straighter in the witness chair. "It's true that I didn't really want to testify, but my mom made it clear I didn't have much of a choice. So here I am. But I'm telling the truth."

"Rufus, did your mother ever mention the reward money—ten thousand dollars? Did she ever say she wanted that money for helping solve this case?"

"She might have mentioned it, but we ain't seen no reward money."

Blankenship turned his back on Rufus and began walking back to the defense table, muttering just loud enough for the jury to hear. "What some will do for thirty pieces of silver. No more questions."

IT WAS JUST after three o'clock when the prosecution rested. Judge Plunkett adjourned the trial for the day with instructions to be back at nine the following morning when the defense would begin presenting its case.

The spectators quickly left the courtroom, yearning for some open air after five hours in the oven-like atmosphere. Reporters scurried out of the building and across the courthouse lawn to begin preparing their reports. Wire service and newspaper reporters would write and dictate their stories by telephone back to their home offices, but television teams had a more complicated task. They had to get their film shot and back to the city to be processed under a tight deadline. The scenes Gil had filmed earlier in the day—crowds around the courthouse and a few man-on-the-street interviews—had already been couriered to the station an hour away. That film was now developed and ready for editing. Gil and Mindy hoped to grab a quick interview with Solicitor General Baker, film a closing stand-up, and get that film back to the station in time for the six o'clock news.

They spotted Baker walking their way as he had earlier agreed to do after court adjourned. He stopped on the sidewalk, and a swarm of media enveloped him, microphones waving at him from all directions.

Mindy spoke up first. "Solicitor Baker, how do you feel about your case today?"

"Well, I think we have a very strong case, and you saw it presented today, I think very effectively. Between the testimony of Randall Scoggins and Rufus McLeod, I believe we have compelling evidence of the guilt of the accused."

Another television reporter just behind Mindy shouted out. "What do you expect tomorrow when Blankenship begins his defense? Any surprises?"

Baker gave a tight smile. "Mr. Blankenship is known for his skillful defense, and I would not be surprised if it takes some unconventional turns. We'll just have to wait and see. Thank you very much, but I really have to go."

Gil kept the camera rolling as Baker walked down the sidewalk toward one of the network crews for a prearranged interview. Mindy scribbled notes for her stand-up in her notepad.

"You ready for your stand-up close?" Gil asked. "Stand over here where I can get the courthouse in the background. Or would you prefer General Pickett?"

"Not sure I want to share my shot with such a loser." She laughed as she positioned herself, checked her hair in the mirror-like reflection in the camera lens, and signaled Gil to start rolling.

"Solicitor General Carson Baker seemed confident that he'd presented a strong case to the jury. But tomorrow John Henry Blankenship will have his turn for the defense, and some surprises could be in store. This is Mindy Williams, WDX-TV News, at the Pickett County Courthouse in Armistead."

Gil cut the camera, but he kept looking at Mindy through his viewfinder, zooming in on her face and following her with his lens as she picked up her notepad and moved toward him. She is a natural, he thought. Only one week in TV news and she is totally confident on camera, poised, relaxed, and real.

"Good job," Gil said as he lowered the camera to see her face to face. "A star is born."

She looked at him, expecting to see a cynical smirk, but his gaze was steady and sincere.

"Really? You're serious? Well, thank you, Gil. Flattery will get you everywhere. I'm as green as they come, and I've got a long road ahead. But at least I'm on that road. We're on it together, despite everything. And I'm very happy about that."

"Me too. Stick with me on your journey to stardom. After all, I am the guy with the camera. Now let's head for home."

The tension that had hovered between them ever since Mindy's revelation about Conyers had evaporated. They hustled to their car, loaded their equipment, and drove south toward Atlanta.

"Quite a day," Gil mused as their vehicle passed Armistead's city limits sign and picked up speed.

Mindy dropped her notepad in her lap, closed her eyes, and relished the currents of cooled air rushing from the AC vents.

"Baker was very good. Scoggins was not the ideal witness, but I think he was convincing enough. I believed him. McLeod was problematic but helped Baker's case. The question is how will Blankenship respond tomorrow?"

"Well, we know one thing," Gil said. "With Blankenship it's not so much guilt versus innocence. It's black versus white. And you know how that usually plays out. I just wonder who'll testify."

Mindy flipped her notepad open and began reviewing her notes. "I'm thinking we'll see the defendants take the stand."

"No way." Gil chuckled as he shook his head. "He'll never let Baker cross-examine them."

"He won't have to," Mindy said. "I'm pretty sure he'll use a defense attorney's special weapon. And there's nothing Baker can do about it."

FORTY-SEVEN

UNSWORN

ON THE MORNING of the trial's second day, Carson Baker checked his watch as he waited on the sidewalk in front of the courthouse for Evelyn's arrival. A driver supplied by the FBI was assigned to bring the victim's widow to the courthouse each morning from her Atlanta hotel.

The vehicle pulled to the curb just before nine with Evelyn in the back seat and an armed FBI agent sitting next to the driver. Baker stooped slightly to open the rear door and help the widow out. Townspeople stood off to the side and silently watched her emerge, blinking as the sun beamed onto her olive-brown face. The agent in the passenger seat also got out, stood tall, and eyed the bystanders with a cold hard stare.

Baker ushered Evelyn toward the courthouse, the bodyguard striding just ahead of them. Before they could reach the steps, Mindy moved toward them, holding a microphone with Gil shoulder-podding his camera. The bodyguard recognized them and allowed them to approach.

"Solicitor General Baker, word is the defendants will make unsworn statements today," Mindy called out. "Your reaction?"

Baker waved them off and kept walking. "No comment on that. We'll see what happens. Now if you'll excuse us...."

Baker, guiding Evelyn by holding her arm, moved past the camera team and followed the agent up the courthouse steps. Sheriff's deputies moved to block Gil and Mindy at the door, warning them that the judge's no-camera ban was about to take effect for the day.

Once inside the building, Baker hustled Evelyn down a long corridor, their footsteps echoing off the marble floor. Their destination was a small conference room reserved for the prosecution team. A deputy standing guard at the door watched as they entered. Two of Baker's young assistants sat around a table drinking coffee from paper cups and reviewing the morning paper and their trial notes for the day. They stood as Baker and Evelyn entered, and one of them pulled a chair over and helped Evelyn into her seat. She accepted the cup of coffee handed to her, took a quick sip, and gave Baker a concerned look.

"What was all that about an unsworn statement? What was that reporter talking about?"

Baker looked over his shoulder as he poured his own coffee. "Welcome to Georgia, Mrs. Pendry. We're the only state in the country that allows defendants in a capital case—one involving the death penalty—to take the stand and say just about anything they want. They are not under oath, and neither the prosecution nor defense can question them."

Evelyn sputtered in disbelief. "Wait a minute! Soseby can stand up before the court and deny he's guilty, and you can't even cross-examine him? That's crazy!"

Baker nodded as he sat down at the table across from her. "Yes, I know. Crazy and unconstitutional in my view. I'm confident one day it will be overturned, but that doesn't help us now, does it? The judge will point out to the jury that the statement is not under oath, but still you always wonder how much it affects the jury—which, let us not forget, is a jury of the Sosebys' peers—rural white male segregationists. We've always known this is an uphill climb. This is just another hurdle for us."

There was a knock on the door just before Sheriff McSwain opened it slightly, looked inside, then walked into the room.

"Mornin', Mrs. Pendry, Solicitor. Just checking to be sure all is in order. I'll continue to post three deputies on either side of your table for your security. Anything else I can do for you?"

"Just keep watching our backs, Sheriff," Baker responded. "It's not exactly friendly territory for us. We appreciate your help."

"Just doing my job. Everything seems to be going well."

McSwain had originally objected to Evelyn sitting at the prosecution table. Normally the only black people on the courtroom's main floor were defendants. Negro spectators were confined to the balcony. McSwain, however, made it clear that his reservation was not racial. After the recent violence in his county, he was concerned about Evelyn's safety. But Baker insisted the victim's widow deserved a place at the prosecution table, and Judge Plunkett, after a bit of reflection, reluctantly agreed. The victim's uncle, Willie Brooks, would still have to sit in the balcony with the other blacks.

As the sheriff turned to go, Evelyn rose and approached him. She lowered her voice so that only he would hear her.

"Sheriff, I know we have had our moments, but I do want to thank you for helping arrest those men and bringing them to trial. I realize this is not easy for you because you are a lifelong member of this community, and I know many here are unwilling to accept the seriousness of this horrible crime or your efforts to solve it. But Sheriff, I hope you are beginning to see that you do not have to be a prisoner of your past. You can break free. I pray for you, Sheriff."

McSwain, deeply embarrassed, mumbled unintelligibly, reached for the door, and hustled out into the hallway. From the day they'd first met at Uncle Willie's house, Evelyn had always seemed to take his measure. He felt she could see into his soul.

Baker, too, had realized early on that Evelyn was a powerful presence. He hoped the quiet, strong dignity of this grieving widow would transcend racial stereotypes and make the jury think hard about granting her the justice she sought. But as they walked to the courtroom Baker had to remind himself that this was, after all, Pickett County.

No sooner had people in the courtroom taken their seats after the judge's arrival than John Henry Blankenship did what everyone had predicted.

"Your Honor, my client Hiram Soseby wishes to make an unsworn statement to the jury. Mr. Soseby, please rise, take the stand, and listen to the judge who will instruct you."

Soseby stood and walked stiffly to the witness stand, looking nervously at Blankenship, who simply smiled with a trace of impatience and jerked his head toward Judge Plunkett.

"Mr. Soseby, your defense attorney states your desire to make an unsworn statement, which is legal in this state in a capital case. You won't have to take an oath, and you will not be cross-examined. Neither can your attorney, Mr. Blankenship, offer any comments. Your statement will stand on its own. Do you understand?"

"Yes. I understand, Your Honor."

"Then you may begin."

Soseby raised the yellow legal pad he carried and began reading in an unsteady voice. His index finger traced an invisible line under the hand-printed block letters as Soseby read aloud the words they formed.

"My name is Hiram James Soseby. I was born in Pickett County and have always lived here, except for the time I was serving my country in the Navy in World War Two. I own a gas station just outside of town."

Soseby nervously cleared his throat and wiped his forehead with a handkerchief he pulled from his coat pocket.

"I want you all to know that I am innocent of this crime. I have never met—never even seen—Jarvis Pendry. I did not kill him. I have been unjustly accused by the federal government and in turn by local prosecutors for a crime I had nothing to do with. And I will tell you that my son, Caleb, is innocent and falsely accused too. He wanted me to tell you that, so he won't have to get up here and do it. Thank you."

Soseby rose and shuffled back to the defense table, looking relieved. Blankenship shook his hand, and Caleb gave him a half hug before he was able to sit down.

Then, as the courtroom prepared for the next defense witness, Blankenship stunned everyone.

"Your Honor, the defense rests."

There was a stirring in the room, a low humming sound of people reacting with surprise to the defense decision to call only one defendant for an unsworn statement.

Judge Plunkett brought his gavel down twice, and the hubbub subsided.

"We'll adjourn for three hours. Without objection, closing arguments will begin when court resumes at two p.m."

Baker leaned toward Evelyn and cupped his hand to his mouth to whisper to her. "John Henry must feel pretty good about this one. But don't worry. So do I."

Evelyn, recognizing his bravado for what it was, whispered back. "I've never expected justice from a Dixieland jury, and frankly, I don't expect it now. I know you'll make your best case in closing. Let's fight the good fight. At this point, it's all we can do."

FORTY-EIGHT

APERTURE

WHEN CARSON BAKER was a college student, a group of his drunken fraternity brothers decided to go find a black man and rough him up. Baker's normally sound judgment was clouded by group pressure and the six-pack of beer he'd consumed, so he went along with them.

It was well after midnight when they spotted a vagrant black man sitting on the sidewalk drinking from a bottle of cheap wine. Five of the students walked up to the man, knocked the bottle out of his hand, and began pummeling him with their fists and kicking at him as he lay moaning in the street.

Three students stood by and watched, among them a suddenly sober Carson Baker. He was sickened and appalled by what he was witnessing, but he did nothing to stop it.

To the best of his knowledge the victim never reported the crime, and the assailants resumed their classes the next day without any concern that they might one day be held accountable. Now, thirty-four years later, Baker still felt shame and remorse for standing aside and doing nothing while the old man was beaten and degraded. The profound memory of that incident had stayed with him through law school and his years of legal practice, and it would be with him today as he delivered his closing arguments in the Jarvis Pendry murder trial.

When Baker was a young lawyer on the way up, desire for political success had tempered any notion of speaking out for racial justice. That would have been political suicide. He had found ways to justify his many compromised principles over the course of his career, but he knew that if there were any hope of expiation for his sins of the past, it would be realized on this day in a Pickett County courtroom.

The courtroom was packed with spectators well before the session began. There was a low murmur of anticipation as Judge Plunkett entered, settled himself, brought his gavel down, and called for closing arguments.

Baker rose from the prosecution table and slowly walked around it to the front of the jury box, where he stood with slightly slumping shoulders and an unruly shock of graying hair poised to fall over his forehead.

"Gentlemen of the jury, thank you for your attentiveness during this trial. You have listened carefully, and you know the evidence. You know that Randall Scoggins, flawed though he may be, was an eyewitness to the murder of Jarvis Pendry. He was there! You heard him describe how Hiram Soseby fired the fatal shots while his son Caleb spotlighted the hapless victim, Jarvis Pendry, with a flashlight. Scoggins heard the blasts from Soseby's double-barreled shotgun. He saw the body of Colonel Pendry. He watched Hiram and Caleb Soseby celebrating their heinous act. His remorse led him to plead guilty and help us present the truth of what happened that night. He will be punished for what he did. But put all that aside and recognize that there can be no doubt that he is telling the truth, that Hiram and Caleb Soseby, in a frenzy of racial hatred, chased Jarvis Pendry down and murdered him at the Peavine Creek bridge in the dead of night. They then dumped his car and body into the creek to hide the crime.

"Then you heard Rufus McLeod describe Caleb's confession to him that Caleb and his father murdered Jarvis Pendry because he was a so-called 'uppity' Negro. You've seen the shotgun, you've heard about the Sosebys' Klan activity, and you've seen those horrible crime scene photos. You know the facts of this case, and it should make your decision clear—guilty as charged!"

As if to emphasize the point, Baker swept his lock of wayward hair back into place with his right hand. He then turned his back on the jury and walked a couple of steps toward the center of the courtroom,

quickly glancing at Evelyn, who watched him intently from the prosecution table. He then swiveled and walked directly toward the jury box,
coming to a full stop at the edge of the barrier. The courtroom was
absolutely quiet save for the humming fans and an occasional spectator
cough.

"We are all natives of the South, a region that has been through
so much. We are the only Americans whose ancestors lost a war, who
had enemy troops occupy our land. We have suffered as a people. Our
scars are still visible a hundred years later. And because of our privations
through history, I believe we are a stronger, better people. We care
about and help each other. Southern hospitality is no myth. It is our
way of life. And yet when it comes to racial justice, too often we turn a
blind eye and a deaf ear.

"Today I am asking you to open your eyes, to see the world not as
it is but rather as it should be. I ask you to punish the injustice that's
been done to Jarvis Pendry, his widow Evelyn sitting right over there,
and his two little boys who are too young to be in this courtroom. Those
little boys will grow up without a father. Evelyn Pendry must deal with
the loss of a loving husband. Our nation suffers the loss of a patriot, a
war hero, a successful businessman, a respected citizen. Jarvis Pendry
lived a life that offered so much to so many. Jarvis Pendry—who just
happened to be a black man traveling through Georgia, through Pickett
County, and that is what cost him his life. Just think about that.

"There are those who say a Southern jury will never convict a white
man for killing a Negro. I do not believe that for a second. This is your
opportunity to prove to those who look down on us that we understand
justice is colorblind. This is your chance to demonstrate to the nation
and the world that we Southerners know the meaning of God's com-
mandment, 'Thou shalt not kill,' and are willing to punish those who
violate it no matter their color or station in life.

"So often we see through a glass darkly, but as the illumination
increases we see more clearly. Our mind is like the lens of a camera.
We cannot fully understand what we're looking at until we open the

aperture of our mind to fully illuminate our view. And when we do that, we see the truth.

"The moment of truth is here, gentlemen of the jury. The eyes of the nation are upon you. Do the right thing. Do your duty. Show the world that justice can prevail in Pickett County by pronouncing these two men guilty of murder."

Baker swayed slightly, took two steps back, then slowly turned and walked to his table, slumping into his chair next to the victim's widow. She turned her head to him and gave a tight nod of gratitude.

Judge Plunkett broke the silence. "Thank you, Solicitor Baker. Mr. Blankenship?"

John Henry Blankenship stood up and addressed the judge. "Your Honor, before I begin my closing arguments, I ask the court's permission to allow a special guest of the defense to enter the courtroom and sit with the Soseby family. Mr. Roscoe Pike. He arrived late from a campaign appearance and couldn't be here before we began."

Judge Plunkett tapped his gavel to silence the murmurs as Baker leapt to his feet to object. "Your Honor, this is highly unusual and an attempt by the defense to add a political advantage. I object in the strongest terms. If Mr. Pike wanted to be here, he could have come in like any other spectator before the opening gavel."

Judge Plunkett looked down at his trial notes, appearing confused and hesitant about what to do next. Finally, he looked up and spoke. "I'm going to allow Mr. Pike to join the proceedings as a spectator. He can sit with the defendants' family. He's as entitled to be here as anyone, and I might add his political opponents would be welcome if they showed up as well."

The judge nodded at Blankenship, and Roscoe Pike entered through the main courtroom door, smiling and nodding to people in the crowd before slipping into a place on the family bench next to Sadie Soseby, who seemed surprised and embarrassed. As the courtroom settled down, Blankenship approached the jury box.

"Thank you, Your Honor, and welcome, Mr. Pike. Thank you for taking time out of your busy campaign schedule to lend your support to these falsely accused gentlemen."

Baker appeared to be in a state of disbelief, pinching the bridge of his nose and slowly shaking his bowed head. Evelyn looked on in silent fury as Blankenship began his final defense of her husband's murderers.

"First of all, gentlemen of the jury, let's dispense with the obvious. The state ain't proved nothin'. They ain't laid a glove on these boys—Hiram and Caleb. We should all be insulted that the prosecution trotted out the town drunk who cut a sweet deal to lighten his sentence and a mealy-mouthed turncoat of a friend who can only offer the weakest of hearsay testimony. Why, these defendants should not even be here. They should be home with their families enjoying life like the innocent people they are. Instead, they sit before you charged with murder. I tell you, gentlemen of the jury, the real victims here are Hiram and Caleb Soseby.

"They are the victims of the all-powerful federal government. LBJ, J. Edgar Hoover, and all those bureaucrats who sent the FBI down here to little Pickett County like we was some kind of danger to the civilized world. They just about took over down here. And when you put in that kind of effort—well—you got to get results, right? You got to arrest somebody. You got to find some white suspects, frame them, come up with concocted evidence, bring in a liberal solicitor general, and back him up with all the FBI has to offer. With those odds, what chance do these boys—Hiram and Caleb—have? They might as well just roll over and ask for a seat in the electric chair."

Blankenship was sweating heavily, and damp spots were spreading across the back of his coat and under his arms. Suddenly he whipped off the coat and flung it into a nearby chair. Then he put his hands on the paneled partition of the jury box and bent over so that his glistening face was mere inches from a juror on the front row.

"But there's one thing LBJ and J. Edgar Hoover and the FBI and all those liberal bureaucrats and congressmen and senators didn't figure on," he practically snarled. "They didn't figure on these boys putting up a good fight. But they have fought back. That's why I'm here. That's why Roscoe Pike is here. And that's why just about everybody in this courtroom is here—to support Hiram and Caleb and protect them from the godless power of the federal government."

Blankenship stepped back, pulled a red handkerchief from his rear pocket, and mopped his brow.

"As Anglo-Saxons we have a long judicial tradition involving judges, prosecutors, and defense attorneys. But the key part of our legal heritage, the most important part, is the jury. No matter how powerful the prosecutors are, they must convince a jury of peers that there is guilt beyond a reasonable doubt. They don't make that decision. You do. You hold the power. You hold the ability to tell all-powerful LBJ, and J. Edgar Hoover, and the FBI, tell all of them that the only power that matters is what you hold in your hands and in your heart. The power of the jury! And I know that you will use that power today to end this case against two of your fellow citizens—to find them not guilty and to let them walk free back to the righteous lives they have always led. And in so doing you uphold our great heritage and tradition. Gentlemen of the jury, you have kept the faith. Go now and do your duty as God calls upon you to do that duty. Return a verdict of 'not guilty'!"

Blankenship practically staggered back to his seat. The Sosebys shook his hand and Roscoe Pike leaned over to pat him on his sodden back. Sadie Soseby dabbed at her eyes with a lacy handkerchief.

Judge Plunkett read a brief charge to the jury, and then the twelve men who would decide the fate of Hiram and Caleb Soseby rose and filed out to the jury room to begin their deliberations.

Sitting three rows back from the prosecution table, Mindy and Gil planned their next move.

"Better get our gear ready," Mindy muttered. "I don't think this is going to take very long."

FORTY-NINE

VERDICT

THE JURORS SHUFFLED single file into the jury box and took their seats, their solemn faces masking any sign that they felt the tension hovering in the courtroom. They were all natives of Pickett County—two farmers, two mechanics, a grocery cashier, a drug store clerk, a teacher, a school bus driver, two retirees, and two unemployed. They wore the clothes they normally saved for church—short-sleeved shirts, gray slacks or khakis, brown lace-up shoes. None of them would have chosen to sit in judgment on Hiram and Caleb Soseby, but they had soberly accepted their duty, reached a verdict, and now waited for their foreman, a brawny mechanic named Wilson Cantrell, to reveal it.

Defendants Hiram and Caleb Soseby sat at the defense table, flitting nervous glances around the room and then back to the jury. John Henry Blankenship sat with them, occasionally looking over his shoulder to exchange comments with Roscoe Pike and Riley Swint, who had joined Pike in Armistead for the verdict. Sadie Soseby clutched a handkerchief to her face, her eyes closed, her lips moving silently in prayer. At the prosecution table, Carson Baker and Evelyn Pendry sat side by side, staring blankly at the jurors without a glimmer of expectation as they awaited the trial's denouement.

Despite the slight cooling of the day's gloaming, the crowd jamming the courtroom radiated heat to midday levels, and spectators put their funeral parlor fans to vigorous but futile use. All motion and murmurs ceased as Judge Plunkett entered the courtroom and rose to the bench. He examined the crowd and then looked to his left at foreman Cantrell, who stood awkwardly in the corner of the jury box.

"Gentlemen of the jury, have you reached a verdict?"

Cantrell ducked his head slightly before addressing the judge. "Yes sir, Your Honor, we have."

Judge Plunkett turned his eyes to the overflowing courtroom. "We will have no outbursts once the verdict is announced. Sheriff, be prepared to make arrests if my order is violated."

The judge looked down as though reading from a script. "And, jury foreman, what is your verdict?"

Cantrell ducked his head again and then looked down at the piece of paper in his hand. "We find the defendants not guilty of all charges."

Judge Plunkett banged his gavel three times, even though the courtroom was silent except for the sobs of Sadie Soseby and the slapping sound of Pike's open hand pounding Blankenship's sweaty back.

"Hiram Soseby. Caleb Soseby. You have been found not guilty. You are now free men. Thank you, jurors, for your diligent service. This court is now adjourned."

The crowd in the courtroom rose as one, and, amid the turmoil, reporters struggled to push and shove their way through the mass of bodies to file their stories. The former defendants, looking bewildered, accepted congratulations from family and friends. But at the prosecution table, Baker and Evelyn still sat, Baker silently gathering his papers and Evelyn watching the celebration in the courtroom with a resigned stoicism that masked her bitter disappointment.

FBI agent Robert Smithers walked over and sat down between them. "Carson, you did the best a man could do under these circumstances. You deserved better. And Mrs. Pendry, I am so sorry. I know you realized a guilty verdict was a long shot, but still I know it hurts you, and I am ashamed of what's happened here. But this is not the end. We will move on those federal civil rights charges immediately, and with a federal jury I feel certain we will get a conviction. It won't be what those lowlifes deserve—the death penalty—but we can send them away for a number of years. Your husband's murder will not go unpunished."

At that moment someone in the roiling crowd yelled.

"Go home to Baltimore, you black bitch. See what happens when you come down South? So high and mighty, thinking you're better than us. Time for you to get out of our town and back to Yankeeland."

Sheriff McSwain, who was on his way to the prosecution table, immediately rushed toward the woman, put her in handcuffs, and placed her under arrest. She screamed and struggled as a deputy dragged her away.

"What's wrong with you? Y'all become nigger lovers too? You'll regret this, Sheriff."

Evelyn watched the outburst and then turned to Smithers as though nothing out of the ordinary had happened. "Thank you, Agent Smithers. I am very disappointed but not surprised. And I hope these men who murdered my husband will see justice fulfilled in whatever form that may take."

"Count on it," Smithers responded, his jaw clenching with determination.

Baker leaned in to comment. "We will, Robert. Thank you, and let me know if there is anything I can do. Now Evelyn, we'll let the Sosebys and Blankenship have their day outside with reporters. Then, when they're finished crowing, I'll go out and have my say. Will you join me?"

"I will, Carson. I will."

MINDY RAN ACROSS the courthouse lawn toward the phone booth on the corner of the town square, the only public phone in Armistead. Out of the corner of her eye she saw another reporter matching her stride for stride as he raced her to this link to the world beyond. Mindy knew he could outrun her, but she also knew Gil had paid a local teenager to stay in the phone booth and hold it until Mindy got there. She was fifty feet away now, close enough to see that the booth was empty. The kid must have taken the money and left.

She looked to her right to check on her competitor, and that's when she tripped, sprawling on the grass, her notes scattering. She quickly grabbed her notepads and continued moving with a slight limp toward the phone booth, but the other reporter was already there, ready to seize the phone and delay her live report until he'd finished.

She couldn't see very well in the growing darkness, but someone was blocking the reporter from the phone booth. She heard the winded man practically screaming. "Let me in. Baltimore Evening Sun. Need to call this in immediately."

Then she heard the voice of Bill Conyers. "I'm sorry. I'm with the GBI, and this phone is reserved for official use. Miss Williams has reserved the line, and here she is. Step this way, ma'am."

Conyers pushed against the bi-fold door, opening the way for a still frazzled Mindy while the Sun reporter loudly objected. With Conyers standing guard, Mindy closed the door, dropped her coins in the slot, and dialed the station's hotline. Grayson Kincaid answered on the first ring. "Mindy! I can't believe it! We're hearing it's 'not guilty.'"

"Afraid so. Are you ready?"

"Yes. Hold on. We're breaking into programming."

Mindy, panting heavily after her run from the courthouse, tried to compose herself. She heard Kincaid use his urgent broadcast voice.

"And now a special report. A verdict in the Jarvis Pendry murder trial. Good evening, I'm Grayson Kincaid. We interrupt your program to report on a verdict in Pickett County. Hiram and Caleb Soseby have been found not guilty of the murder of Colonel Jarvis Pendry. Our Mindy Williams was in the courtroom when the verdict came down, and she joins us live over the phone. Mindy?"

Mindy took a deep breath and began her ad lib report.

"A twelve-man jury found Hiram Soseby and his son Caleb Soseby not guilty of the murder of Colonel Jarvis Pendry. The verdict came down in a crowded courtroom ten minutes ago. The jury was out only two hours. The Sosebys celebrated, but prosecutor Carson Baker and the victim's widow who sat by his side throughout the trial showed no emotion when the verdict was read. The Sosebys now walk free, but there is some question about whether they will face federal civil rights charges, which are still pending. Civil rights charges would be tried by a federal jury, and that would be quite different from a local Pickett County jury. We are now going to get interviews with the acquitted men and also the prosecution team. We'll have the latest tonight at 11. This is Mindy Williams, WDX-TV News."

Mindy slowly placed the phone back in its cradle, slumped against the side of the booth, and expelled a deep sigh of relief. She pulled the door open and stumbled into the thick night air as the Baltimore newspaperman angrily clambered into the booth and began placing his call.

"You okay?" Conyers asked with an expectant smile.

"I think so," Mindy responded as she straightened her blouse and skirt, which had grass stains along her hip. "Bill, I don't know what to say. Thank you."

"No problem. I was here and thought you could use an extra hand. Gil can't be everywhere, right?"

"No, he can't. But I really need to go find him now. We've got to get verdict reaction."

"Sure. I understand. Great seeing you, Mindy. Glad I could help."

Mindy took three steps toward the courthouse, then paused and looked back at Conyers.

"Good luck, Bill. See you around?"

Conyers shook his head. "Probably not. I'm going to work for the FBI. Leaving for Quantico next week."

"Bill, that's wonderful. I'm so happy for you."

"And I'm happy for you. I wish things could have been different, but in the final analysis you got what you wanted, and I'm heading for a new life without you. Somehow it will all work out. Goodbye, Mindy."

He turned and walked away. Mindy briefly watched him go, but there was no time for reflection. She began hustling back across the darkening courthouse lawn, through clumps of people milling about, until she spotted Gil under his shoulder-mounted camera.

"Everything go well? Did the kid do what we paid him for?"

"Everything went fine. Now let's wrap this up, partner."

The Sosebys and Blankenship were just coming down the steps to meet the media horde forming a semicircle, facing them with microphones extended. Mindy quickly pointed the mike toward the acquitted men and their attorney, asking her first question as she did so.

"Mr. Blankenship, were you surprised by the verdict and how quickly it came?"

Blankenship was bathed in the harsh beams of portable television lights. Their glare made it impossible to see the faces of those questioning him. He was flanked on either side by Hiram and Caleb Soseby, both of whom seemed nervous and confused by the media onslaught and content to let Blankenship do the talking.

"Of course I was not surprised by the not guilty verdict or the rapidity with which it was returned. The state had no case. Testimony from a drunken vagrant and a turncoat friend urged on by his mama who wanted a reward was beneath the dignity of this prosecutor and certainly did not even come close to convincing this good jury to convict. I commend the jury for rendering the correct decision so that Hiram and Caleb can resume their lives as upstanding members of this community."

Another question was shouted from the media crowd.

"What's your reaction to reports that federal civil rights charges may now be officially pursued against your clients?"

Blankenship gave a brief chuckle and shook his head. "Hiram and Caleb have been found not guilty by a jury of their peers. If the almighty federal government cannot accept the judgment of our people, then we will be ready to meet them again on the field of legal battle. And once again we will prevail."

Whoops and cheers erupted from the crowd of supporters that had gathered behind Blankenship on the courthouse steps. Pike was among them, alternately applauding and shaking his fist in the air.

Another question came from the faceless mass behind the bank of lights.

"What about you, Hiram? What are your thoughts on the trial, the verdict, and the possibility you may face federal charges?"

Hiram Soseby shaded his eyes and squinted into the glare, but the lights were too bright for him to identify the questioner.

"I'm, um…I'm just happy to walk out of here a free man. Me and Caleb, we didn't kill nobody. The state didn't prove nothin'. I hope this is the end of it, but if the feds won't let it be, then we'll keep fightin'. That's it. I got no more to say."

Blankenship quickly stepped in. "That's going to do it for now. If you'll please excuse us, we have a victory party to attend down at Sally's Diner. We'll even let you news boys in if you behave yourselves."

Blankenship grabbed the Sosebys by their elbows and began ushering them through the crowd, the lights and cameras following their progress. Several Pickett County deputies stepped in to help clear the way as Blankenship and his entourage headed toward Sally's a block off the square. Bystanders offered scattered applause and yelled congratulations as the group passed them.

Once the courthouse steps were relatively clear, Carson Baker emerged arm in arm with Evelyn. The reporters quickly reassembled as the pair descended the steps, stopping at the bottom to face the questions, but Baker immediately launched into his statement.

"We felt we proved beyond the shadow of a doubt that Hiram and Caleb Soseby were the nightriders who took Jarvis Pendry's life. The verdict is disappointing but, I am sad to say, not surprising. We have seen this type of verdict before as Southern juries disregard the clearest of evidence to excuse acts of racial hatred and injustice. I am sad for this community, and I am sad for our state and our South."

Baker held up his hand as if to ward off any questions. "Hold on a minute. Mrs. Pendry wants to offer her thoughts."

Evelyn stepped forward slightly, looking pale and fragile under the searing lights. She spoke in a quiet voice devoid of emotion.

"I'd like to thank Solicitor General Baker for his heroic efforts. It took courage to fight for justice for my husband's murder in this…this…environment. Carson, thank you for your sacrifice and for helping me believe that people of good will and principle—whether they be black or white—will ultimately prevail in our search for racial justice in the South.

"My husband was shot down on the highway not two miles away from here. Tonight, his killers walk free. Tonight, I struggle with my emotions as I think of men filled with murderous hate and violence celebrating their acquittal. I am comforted by my faith that justice will ultimately prevail. I do not know when, I do not know how, but I know we are well on the way to a day of reckoning. May our Lord hasten that day. Thank you."

Baker took Evelyn's arm and began to move away. "I'm sorry, but that's all we're going to say. Thank you and good night."

At least one reporter ignored Baker's wishes. "What about the possibility of federal charges?"

Baker tossed an answer over his shoulder as he and Evelyn moved through the crowd. "That's up to federal authorities. But I would welcome it."

Gil held the shot of the departing solicitor and widow and then lowered his camera. Mindy watched them go, muttering to herself.

"Things fall apart, the center will not hold."

"That's one way to put it," Gil said. "Enough reflection. Time to head back. It'll be tight but we should make the lead at eleven."

Gil and Mindy hurriedly packed their gear into the station wagon and pulled away from the town square. As they left town, they passed Sally's Diner, where crowds of boisterous Soseby supporters were jamming the restaurant and surrounding yard as the victory party continued to build. They saw one old, bearded man in coveralls waving a large rebel flag as partygoers drunkenly screamed their anthem. The familiar refrain faded as the news crew left Armistead to its night of celebration.

"Look away, look away, look away, Dixieland."

FIFTY

SMARTY-PANTS LIBERAL

ON THE MORNING after the verdict the first rays of sunlight filtered through the huge white oak in Carson Baker's front yard, dappling the porch, its swing, and the weary face of the man who sat there. When he got home the night before, Baker had reached the point of exhaustion, but sleep would not come. He tossed until four o'clock and then rose to rock in his swing, sip his coffee, and muse about the events of the past week.

Blinking under the growing glare of sunrise, Baker realized he should already be at his office closing up the Pendry murder file, but he simply did not have the will or the energy to make the effort. Over and over, he replayed each step of the trial, and although he might have done some things differently, he was confident he had done his best.

That's what Evelyn had told him before she left Armistead with her FBI escort. She called him a hero for undertaking the case, for risking his reputation to get justice for her husband, and she absolved him of any responsibility for not getting a conviction. He would always remember her serenity, her faith, and her determination to continue to seek justice in the federal courts. And while some questioned her sitting by him at the prosecution table, he was at peace with that decision. The quiet power of her presence and the graceful way she carried her grief had to have made a dramatic impression in the courtroom, even if it did not sway a jury that was predisposed to acquit.

The crunching of gravel in the driveway broke his reverie. The Pickett County sheriff's car pulled up, and Lucas McSwain eased out of the vehicle, hitching up his pants and adjusting his pistol belt. He sauntered up the flagstone walkway and climbed the three wooden steps to the porch. He slipped off his Stetson and gestured to a rocking chair next to the swing.

"May I?" he said as he lowered himself into the chair.

"Of course. Good morning, Lucas. What brings you here?"

"I was just hoping to talk for a bit in the calm of the day after. I went by your office, but they said you hadn't come in yet. Figured you might be sleeping in."

Baker smiled and rubbed the stubble on his chin. "I didn't sleep a wink. Just been sitting here watching the sun come up and drinking my coffee. Haven't even seen the morning paper. Not sure I want to."

McSwain nodded and rocked a bit while the old wooden chair squeaked in protest. "I saw the early TV news and the morning paper. You got treated real well. Like a man who gave all he had for a worthy cause—an impossible cause. And I just wanted to tell you I admire the way you did your duty."

Baker was startled by McSwain's remark. He never would have expected even slight praise from the formidable high sheriff of Pickett County. "Why, thank you, Lucas. That's very nice and I appreciate it. And I appreciate the job you did keeping things under control in very difficult circumstances."

"That's my job," McSwain responded. "People think I'm a dumb redneck, but I can rise to the occasion."

Baker quickly answered. "Well, people think I'm an intellectual smarty-pants liberal, and I've realized there's not much I can do to change that impression."

McSwain seemed amused by that comment. "I can't imagine why. Maybe their apertures aren't open wide enough. Hell, Counselor, I had to look that up."

"Sometimes I just can't help myself," Baker admitted.

Both men laughed, and the tension that had always existed between them dissolved in an instant.

"You know, Carson, those men are guilty as hell. They did kill Jarvis Pendry. Anybody can see that. We proved it. But we were playing with a stacked deck."

"Oh yes. We were. But we still had to do our best—and I think we did. No apologies. I just wish we could have done better for Evelyn."

McSwain watched a ruby-throated hummingbird flitting from flower to flower in a porch planter, finally dipping its beak into the welcoming blooms of a cluster of red impatiens.

"This may sound strange coming from me," McSwain said, "but she made quite an impression on me. I've never met anyone like her before. She was certainly not like any black woman I've ever known. It took me a while to realize that she had my number. She was not intimidated by me, and I'm not used to that. She seemed fearless—totally confident even though most women in her circumstances would have come unraveled. It's kind of messed me up, if you understand what I mean."

"I do understand," Baker said. "She had much the same effect on me, but you and I, we come from different backgrounds. You've always seen black people as inferior stereotypes. You probably never took the time to look at your Negro constituents as real people with hopes and dreams just like you. But Evelyn defied that stereotype. She opened your eyes—and mine. I think she changed both of us."

Sheriff McSwain sat quietly, absorbing what Baker had just told him.

"You really are a smarty-pants liberal," McSwain said with a chuckle. Then he turned somber. "Just before we went into the courtroom on the final day, she told me I am not a prisoner of my environment. That I can break free. That flustered me. It sticks with me. I can't get it out of my mind."

"Evelyn was right, Lucas. We white Southerners are myth-clingers. Prisoners in a way. It's hard to look to the future when you're bound by the past. Take your monument to General Pickett on the town square. Confederate hero? Hardly. He finished last in his class at West Point and is forever remembered for one of the most disastrous episodes of the Civil War. And yet the county bears his name, and we venerate him with a statue that says the principles he fought for can never die. Well, those principles are dying, yet we stubbornly cling to the myth, which is another word for a lie. One of these days we'll come to see that. Maybe you already have. That's what Evelyn was telling you, Lucas."

"Yeah," the sheriff said wistfully. "I'm pretty confused. That woman I arrested in the courtroom last night…well, you heard what she called me. Makes me wonder if I should just turn in my badge."

"Don't do that, Sheriff. I think this whole sordid experience has given you a new perspective on this county and its people, black and white. It would be a shame if you were to walk away after what we've both been through."

"Hell, you may be right. I'll probably get opposition in the next election, and the people can make their choice. We might even have a few black folks who might vote for me. Wouldn't that be something?"

"Yes, indeed. It would be something," Baker said. "But the times they are a'changing, and sooner rather than later Negroes are going to have impact at the ballot box. It's inevitable. A voting rights act is on the horizon, and it will change everything we've come to accept about how candidates run for office."

Sheriff McSwain slowly rose from his rocker and extended his hand to his host. Baker stood as well and accepted the handshake.

"I'll be seeing you around, Mr. Solicitor General. I think we'll enjoy watching Blankenship and the Sosebys try to fight those federal charges. You take care."

McSwain ambled down the porch steps to his car, but before he got in he turned to look back at Baker. "Oh, I meant to tell you. Somebody burned a cross in the McLeods' front yard late last night. They're pretty shook up. They may decide to pack up and leave town. Not sure I could blame 'em. See you later, Carson."

Baker watched the sheriff slowly pull away. He then stretched, rubbed his stubbly face, and went inside to shower, shave, and get ready for work. The staff would welcome him, applaud him, and praise his courtroom performance. But the killers remained free, the victim's widow was still seeking justice, and the family of a key witness was terrorized by a burning cross. He pondered the depressing thought that despite everything that had happened, nothing had really changed at all.

FIFTY-ONE

STUDIO TIME

HARRISON PARKER SAT on the edge of an executive desk, his arms folded, looking into the studio camera with all the earnestness he could muster. In the background on either side of the desk, flags hung limply from vertical poles, the US flag and the Georgia state flag with its design featuring the St. Andrews cross—better known as the Confederate battle emblem. The rebel symbolism was added to the flag in 1956 as a sign of defiance of the US Supreme Court ruling declaring segregated schools unconstitutional. Parker had carefully arranged the folds of the state flag to obscure as much of the rebel portion as possible.

Technicians moved about in the background, adjusting the lights hanging from metal grids suspended over the cavernous studio. A makeup girl darted onto the lighted set to dab powder on Parker's glistening forehead.

"You want to run through this again?" the studio floor director asked.

"Yes. Please," Parker responded. "One more time."

The floor director held poster boards with Parker's lines printed in large black letters. The cue cards were placed just below the lens to make it appear that Parker wasn't reading but rather speaking from the heart directly into the camera.

"Give me just a moment," Parker muttered. He was still distracted by the conversation he'd had with Devereaux Inman shortly after sunrise. Inman had called to discuss the acquittals in the Pendry murder trial and how Parker should publicly react.

He told Parker that if the shock and resentment over the killers walking free was as widespread as he suspected, then there might be a backlash against Roscoe Pike. He urged Parker to be cautious in his comments about the trial. He should under no circumstances criticize the jury, but he had to somehow deliver the subliminal message that he felt an injustice had been done.

Parker tried to clear his mind for the job at hand, recording a series of television ads for the final weeks of the campaign.

"Okay. I'm ready for the run-through."

The cue card man hoisted the first poster, and Parker began to read.

"Hello, I am Harrison Parker, and I'm running to be your next governor."

The first cue card dropped to the floor, revealing the next.

"I was born and raised in this state I love. I have been your attorney general for the past four years, but now I want to lead Georgia into the future.

"We live in troubled times, and you need a governor who can provide the type of leadership that will move us forward. I will expand and improve our education system for all, I will bring development and jobs to our state, I will work tirelessly to be sure all of our people will be safe in their homes and on our streets.

"And I will be a governor you can be proud of—a governor who exemplifies the values we all share, a governor who will lead the way to a brighter future for all of us.

"Please vote for me in the Democratic Primary. I thank you for your support."

"Sounded real good, Harrison. I think we can roll tape when you're ready."

The woman's voice came from somewhere in the darkness that surrounded the illuminated desk and candidate. It was the voice of Jan Proctor, a local advertising wunderkind hired to assist with the campaign. She emerged from the darkness, a slim attractive blonde of about thirty-five, wearing a lime green pantsuit and brimming with enthusiasm. She had run many successful commercial ad campaigns, but she loved the art of political advertising. Because of her reputation, Inman had quietly signed her up to work her magic for Harrison Parker. He'd also infused hundreds of thousands of dollars into the campaign for a massive ad buy in cities throughout the state.

"One thing, Harrison. You need to try to be a bit more personal—approachable—do you know what I mean? You want people to like you, relate to you."

Proctor bounced on the balls of her feet, raising her arms as if to levitate her client up the enthusiasm scale. "The trick is being warm and friendly while still maintaining a sense of authority. It's a complicated formula, but I think you can do it. Just relax and be yourself. By the time we get out of here you'll have five good spots in the can. We've made a buy that will put you on TV all over Georgia. You're going to be a household name."

"If you say so," Parker replied. "This doesn't come naturally to me, but the more I go over it the better I feel. And I think I'm ready. So let's roll it."

"All right," Proctor chirped. "We've got an hour left in our recording session, so let's get to it. Good luck."

Over the course of the next hour Parker breezed through his recording session with relative ease. He read flawlessly from the cue cards, and Proctor felt he had performed about as well as could be expected. As he shook hands with the studio crew, his aide Billy Watson stepped up to warn him that Mindy Williams was just outside, hoping for an interview. Parker knew her questions would concern the verdict in the Pendry murder trial.

He pushed open the heavy studio door, walked down a short hallway to another heavy door, and then entered a longer hallway leading to dressing rooms, prop rooms, and offices. Mindy and Gil were waiting in that hallway.

"Mr. Parker, could we ask you a few questions?" Mindy thrust the microphone into his face before he could answer. "What's your reaction to the verdict in the Jarvis Pendry murder trial?"

"Well, I've never been one to second-guess juries. The jury system is a cornerstone of our judicial system. The jurors heard the evidence and the testimony and decided they could not convict."

Mindy quickly jumped in with her next point. "There are those who say the trial was unfair—that the jury was handpicked by the defense, that using unsworn testimony gave an unfair advantage to the defendants, and that allowing Roscoe Pike to inject himself into the proceedings tipped the scales against the prosecution."

"Now, Mindy, that is just speculation on your part. I would agree that allowing my opponent to grandstand at the trial was not a wise judicial decision and may have been unfair, but the unsworn statement is a legitimate though controversial part of our system, and the prosecution had jury strikes they could have used to better balance the jury. From all accounts, Solicitor General Baker did a magnificent job under very tough conditions, but the verdict is final, and I will not question it."

"Attorney General Parker, there are those who say a Southern jury will never convict a white man of murdering a Negro. Some say the Pendry trial proves that. What do you think?"

"I disagree. I believe in the judicial process. I believe in the ability of jurors to rise above whatever preconceived ideas or prejudices they might have to render a fair judgment for a defendant black or white. We may or may not agree with the judgment of the jury in Pickett County, but under our system we have no choice but to accept it."

It was obvious Mindy was growing frustrated by Parker's detached and clinical responses.

"Mr. Parker," she pressed, "what would you say to the Negro voters in our state who feel a grave injustice was done by the jury in the Pendry trial? These jurors ignored eyewitness testimony and overwhelming evidence of the Sosebys' guilt to allow those men to walk free. What do you say?"

"I would say that I understand that frustration. It is always frustrating when things don't go the way you think they should. I would say don't give up on the system. You may feel that the system isn't working for you, and that may be true. But I will work to be sure the system is fair. I urge you to work within our system for positive change. Vote for me, and I will work for fairness for everyone. And I hope everyone will watch our debate in two weeks. I think you'll see clear differences between me and my opponent, and I'm looking forward to it. Now if you'll excuse me, I've got some campaigning to do."

Parker, followed by Watson and Proctor, headed for the stairs that would take them to the WDX lobby and the front door exit.

"You did a really nice job in that interview," Proctor said as they strode toward their car. "But in the debate feel free to let your emotions show. Pike will come after you. Don't be afraid to take him on."

"Don't worry," Parker replied as he opened the car door. "I know it will be total war. And I'll be ready."

FIFTY-TWO

BETTER ANGELS

HARRISON PARKER AND Roscoe Pike met for the first time when they entered the television studio for their live statewide debate. Pike came in first followed by Riley Swint and one of his campaign aides. Immediately afterwards, Parker, his aide Billy Watson, and Jan Proctor, wearing a bright orange pantsuit, came through the same door. Both men paused on the shadowy fringe just outside the arc of the beautifully illuminated setting that would host them. The awkward silence was finally broken by Parker, who aggressively thrust his hand toward his opponent.

"Roscoe. Good to finally meet you."

Pike was taller and even thinner than Parker had imagined, and the dark jacket of his suit was a size too large, making him appear almost malnourished. Pike slowly accepted Parker's handshake.

"Harrison. Likewise. Good luck—but not too good."

Both men manufactured brief, mirthless chuckles and proceeded to their respective lecterns. Moderator Grayson Kincaid, who'd been hovering in the shadows, approached and shook hands with each candidate.

"Gentlemen, welcome. We appreciate your being here. Do you have any questions about the rules and the format?"

Pike spoke up quickly. "I think I understand how this thing will run, but I just want to be sure you're fair. You news boys haven't exactly been gracious in the way you've covered me, and I expect equal treatment. Understand?"

Kincaid, trying to control his irritation, gave Pike a cold stare. "Mr. Pike, I assure you we will be fair to you both. If there are no more questions, it's five minutes until airtime."

Kincaid went to his lectern and turned to the panel of reporters seated at the long table to his right. Mindy occupied the first seat. To her right was veteran newspaper reporter Vernon Cartwright, and at the end of the table sat Bill O'Malley, who became Associated Press political reporter when Mindy took her television job.

"Panel, any questions before we begin?"

The reporters all shook their heads and continued reviewing their lists of prepared questions for the candidates.

Kincaid shaded his eyes with his hand as he attempted to pierce the darkness beyond the studio lights where the few spectators with studio access sat, but all he could see was a void.

"To all of you here in support of your candidate, let me caution you that there must be no applause or any other audible sign of approval or disapproval. If there is we will be forced to ask you to join those watching the telecast elsewhere in the building. Thank you."

Skip, the floor director, moved front and center. "Gentlemen, I'll keep time on your answers and will count you down when you have ten seconds left. We are on in exactly one minute."

Kincaid thanked Skip, wished the candidates good luck, then waited for the seconds to tick down to airtime. In the silence of that minute, Parker focused on the advice he'd received from Devereaux Inman several hours earlier.

"You must target your remarks to the middle," Inman had told him. "Speak to those who are wavering between the choice of unrepentant racism and the small voice of conscience that tugs them away from extremism. You must be the 'better angels' candidate."

"Thirty seconds," Skip called out.

Pike seemed very relaxed in those final few seconds before air, like a man who knew there was little his opponent could do to cause his die-hard supporters to waver even slightly.

"Fifteen seconds."

Skip, standing next to the lens of a studio camera, raised his hand as the seconds ticked down to seven o'clock, and then he silently but forcefully brought his hand down, pointing at Kincaid. On the air at last, Kincaid leveled his trademark anchorman's stare into the lens of the camera and began the debate broadcast with all the gravitas he could muster.

"Good evening. Welcome to our gubernatorial debate between Harrison Parker and Roscoe Pike, both men hoping to win their party's nomination in the Democratic Primary on Tuesday. We will begin with opening statements from each candidate. Mr. Pike?"

"Thank you, Grayson. My name is Roscoe Pike, and I am running for governor to represent you, the good people of Georgia. You know me. I am one of you. And you know I will fight with the last breath in my body to ensure we can live as God intended us to live—free and without interference from the federal government.

"My opponent will not stand up for you. In fact, he will cave in to federal demands that will ultimately be catastrophic for our schools, our neighborhoods, our economy, and our individual families. Don't let that happen in our great state. Vote for Roscoe Pike, and the future will belong to us."

"Thank you, Mr. Pike," Kincaid said. "Your turn for an opening statement, Mr. Parker."

Parker paused briefly before beginning, changing his expression from serious to amiable as his gaze locked onto the camera.

"Thank you, Grayson. I am Harrison Parker, your attorney general, and I am running for governor on a platform of progress—progress in education, in jobs, in economic development, and in how we deal with one another.

"My opponent has painted a picture of me that is a lie. I don't want federal involvement in our local affairs. We can handle our future on our own. The best way to keep the feds out of our business is positive leadership, and that is what I will provide. If Roscoe Pike is elected governor, that will invite more aggressive federal intervention, and the result will be very bad for Georgia.

"During the course of this debate I invite you to examine our differences, and as you do so think about who can provide the positive leadership to take Georgia into the future with prosperity for all. I hope you'll vote for me, Harrison Parker, on Tuesday."

Kincaid next introduced the panel of reporters, briefly explained the basic rules, and allowed Mindy to ask the first question.

She looked up from her notes, and, with a slight quiver of nervousness in her voice, addressed Roscoe Pike.

"Mr. Pike, race relations in our state are at a low point. Civil rights protests are almost a daily occurrence, white resistance to civil rights laws and school desegregation continues to be strong, and just two weeks ago two white men were found not guilty of murdering a prominent Negro, Colonel Jarvis Pendry, despite what many considered to be overwhelming evidence that they committed the crime. What would you do as governor to heal the wounds and bring us together?"

Pike hunched forward slightly, attaching his bony hands to the sides of his lectern and stiffening his arms as if to withstand gale-force winds. He glared at Mindy, making no attempt to hide his contempt.

"I knew by coming here that I would be the big target of the liberal news people, and here you are, right out of the gate, Miss Williams, stoking up controversy. Well, let me just oblige you. I have no interest in bringing the people of this state together unless they all want to obey our laws, let private enterprise operate without government interference, and respect our sovereignty as a state. And when I say obey our laws, I am not referring to the unconstitutional so-called civil rights laws crammed down our throats by the federal government. Those laws violate our rights and must be overturned. And as governor, I will not enforce them. Nor will I allow lawless protests by blacks and those carpetbaggers who support them. They will be in jail before they know what hit 'em.

"As for the murder trial, a jury of peers has spoken, and that's all there is to it. I am proud of the people of Pickett County. And if federal charges are filed—and I expect that will happen—that will be a travesty of justice, and I will have nothing to do with it as your governor."

Four enthusiastic claps came from the darkness behind the cameras. Kincaid had no doubt they came from Riley Swint.

"Please let me warn those in the studio audience—no clapping, no cheering. We went over this earlier and I expect you to obey the rules."

Kincaid turned to the candidates and noticed Pike sagging slightly after his bravura performance. Parker, however, was bouncing on the balls of his feet, obviously eager to respond.

Kincaid nodded his way. "Mr. Parker, any response?"

"Grayson, I do have a response. I am appalled by my opponent's comments that we all just heard. I am the attorney general of this state, and it is my job to uphold the law for all our citizens. To hear a candidate for governor threaten to pick and choose what laws he will enforce is a very frightening thing. Like many of you watching tonight, I am concerned about the encroachment of the federal government on our lives. But there are ways we can deal with federal mandates, and physical resistance should not be one of them. That would be a one-way ticket to economic ruin.

"We need to acknowledge that, like it or not, change is coming. It is already here. We need a governor who will provide the leadership we need to deal with these changes in the best way for all our people. It will not be easy, and I would expect significant headwinds from many competing points of view. But we will all get there with the leadership I will provide and, in the process, make Georgia the leader of the South."

Pike immediately jumped in without being called on.

"See there? See what my opponent believes? He's a lily-livered accommodationist. He'll do whatever LBJ, Earl Warren, and J. Edgar Hoover tell him to do. Your kids will have to go to school with 'em, we'll have to eat with 'em at restaurants, go to church with 'em, give up our jobs to 'em, and before you know it our daughters will be marrying one of 'em. So your choice is simple. Do you want me standing between your family and these people who want to take our rights away, or do you want someone like my opponent who will surrender all we hold dear without even putting up a fight?"

Pike had been aiming his message directly at the studio camera, but he suddenly paused and fixed Parker in his hard, cold glare. "You know, Parker, we have a name for someone like you. I won't use it on TV, but you know what it is. You want those black votes so much—"

Kincaid interrupted. "Mr Pike, your time is up. Let Mr. Parker respond, please."

Parker's face had turned crimson, and he was obviously struggling to control his anger. He felt his chest tightening, and he had to take several quick breaths before firing back at Pike.

"What would that name be, Pike? Let's have full disclosure. What do you want to call me?"

Pike seemed startled by the directness of Parker's question. He never anticipated that his opponent might fight back.

"You know what it is. Everyone knows what it is. I'll be a little discrete for our TV audience. Let's just say you love black folk."

Kincaid quickly intervened. He sensed that the debate was sliding beyond his control. He faced the decision of whether to corral the candidates or let them go at each other. A verbal melee would be entertaining for the viewers, but his instincts told him to err on the side of caution.

"I've got to stop you right there, Mr. Pike. This is not appropriate."

Pike laughed and pointed at Kincaid. "You see? Didn't I tell you the media's against me? There's nothing wrong with what I said. My opponent loves blacks. Would you deny that, Mr. Parker?"

Kincaid had expected Pike to bait him, but reining him in was a struggle. "Please, Mr. Pike. Let's stop this kind of personal attack."

Parker raised his hand to be recognized. Although Kincaid appreciated his show of civility, he thought it was a bit ridiculous in the middle of a verbal mud fight.

"Mr. Parker, you certainly have the right to respond to this if you want."

"It's all right, Grayson. It's good your viewers see the kind of person Mr. Pike is. And, Roscoe, I will not deny that I love all our citizens be they black or white. I want them all to have access to good schools, safe neighborhoods, and good jobs. I love them all, and I resent your crude attempt to insult me. I am sure those watching will be appalled and will understand why you are not fit to lead this great state."

Pike folded his arms across his chest, shaking his head from side to side and smiling with a hint of malevolence. "We'll let the voters make that decision, Harrison. They know who I am, and now they know what you are. Every time you open your mouth you make it clear. You are..."

Kincaid raised his voice, cutting off Pike's remark and reasserting his control. "That's enough, Mr. Pike. We need to move on. We have a lot of ground to cover and many issues to discuss. Next question is from Vernon Cartwright."

Cartwright's question concerned education and how to improve the state's abysmal national ranking, giving both candidates a chance to cool down and deal with substantive issues. Questions that followed dealt with other issues, such as crime, transportation, and economic development.

Kincaid knew these issues were important to voters, but he also knew that nothing the candidates said concerning them would eclipse the racially charged confrontation that began the debate. The news was made in the first ten minutes. Now it was just an exercise in filling the remaining time until closing statements.

Finally, Skip gave Kincaid the cue he'd been hoping for. It was time for the candidates 'closing statements. Parker began.

"My friends, you have just seen two starkly different versions of what our state could become, depending on whom you elect as your governor. Under my opponent, Georgia would regress to a dark age of ignorance and intolerance, and all of us would pay the price.

"I want to be governor for all our citizens. My opponent chooses to divide us and makes it clear he will be governor only for those who agree with him. We have so much going for us—our climate, our bountiful farms and thriving businesses, and most of all our people with their dreams for a bright future full of hope. But to realize that future, we must have the right leader. Not a leader who capitalizes on fear and resentment but rather a leader who believes in the better angels of our nature, as Abraham Lincoln once said. Working together, we can achieve great things. I want to be your governor and lead you into a bright and promising future. I hope you will vote for me, Harrison Parker, on Tuesday."

The camera focused on a frowning Roscoe Pike, who began his statement with Skip's crisp hand cue.

"Well, I never thought I'd see the day I'd be running against a man who likes to quote Abraham Lincoln. My choice would be Robert E. Lee, but I'll set that aside for now.

"I agree with my opponent. We have starkly different views, and I make no apology for what I believe. This election is a choice between protecting our freedoms for the majority or surrendering those freedoms to the minority. It's a choice between defending the high ground, as Robert E. Lee so successfully did in battle after battle, or turning tail and running away from the fight like the Yankees did at Bull Run. I say stand and fight. Fight against the federal attempts to control our schools, our businesses, our social contacts, our very lives.

"My opponent says the future will be bright if we just lay down and let the feds trample all over us. I say that is the way to ruin. I couldn't care less about the investment money New York millionaires want to dangle over our heads if we just play ball. They are like the money changers in the temple, and we would be no better than Judas Iscariot if we take their thirty pieces of silver to betray our Lord and Savior Jesus Christ.

"There are a lot of people willing to betray us, including so-called civil rights leaders, bankers, and other fat cats, and there are liberals among us who think they're so much smarter than we are. And of course my opponent, who may be the ultimate sellout. You know who I am and what I stand for. Make your voice heard on Tuesday. Vote for Roscoe Pike for your governor."

Kincaid thanked the candidates, the panel, and the viewers and signed off with a reminder to vote on Tuesday. Then, as the credits rolled on the screen and the music played, the candidates left their lecterns, bypassing the traditional handshake. Parker did shake hands with Kincaid and the three reporters as Pike walked toward the studio exit with Riley Swint enthusiastically slapping him on the back.

Jan Proctor ran up to Parker and gave him a hug.

"Harrison, you were great...aside from quoting Lincoln," she deadpanned. Then she added, in a mock serious whisper, "You did remember where you're running for governor, didn't you?"

Parker managed a tight smile. "Maybe I'd do better in Illinois."

Proctor grabbed him by the arm and led him from the studio. Mary and the children were waiting for him in a special viewing room, and at least he knew their reviews of his performance would be kind. He wasn't sure that would be the case when he heard from Devereaux Inman.

FIFTY-THREE

THE BLACK SPOT

WEEKDAYS FOR CLARENCE Fortson always began well before sunrise. He had to get up at five to drive his beat-up '57 Ford to the Southland Capital building, where he would park in a remote corner of the underground garage and spend the day driving Devereaux Inman's sleek black Lincoln, taking Inman and his friends wherever they needed to go and running other errands.

Fortson lived just west of downtown in a neighborhood of modest but well-kept ranch-style homes. It was one of the city's more desirable black residential areas, where middle-class aspirants could live in relative security and comfort, well buffered from the slum tenements and shabby commercial areas that blighted much of the west side. Fortson, a high school dropout, was always grateful that Inman had made it possible for him and his family to own their home in a good neighborhood. He took a lot of good-natured ribbing from his friends about driving for "the man," but it was a small price to pay for the benefits he received.

The lights of the city's office towers beckoned as he guided his Ford through the dark streets. He tuned his car radio to his favorite station and was startled by what he heard.

"This is Reverend Elijah Timmons, and I am calling on you all to go to the polls tomorrow and cast your ballot for Harrison Parker for governor. Harrison Parker is the best man for this job, and we need a big turnout to elect him. If you need a ride to the polls call Mount Gilead AME Church, and we'll get you there. This is Reverend Elijah Timmons urging you to vote for Harrison Parker for governor. Our future depends on it."

Fortson could hardly believe his ears, and he quickly tuned his radio dial to the city's other black-oriented station. Within a few moments he heard the same message from Timmons. He heard it five more times before he entered Southland Capital's underground lot and lost the signal.

He quickly parked, walked to Inman's Lincoln, and began the drive to Inman's Buckhead home, pondering the role his boss might have played in Timmons's endorsement of Parker. As the Town Car reached the top of the long driveway, Fortson was surprised to see Inman already striding toward him, obviously eager to get to his office.

"Good morning, Clarence. How are you?"

"Very fine, Mr. Inman. Hope you're good."

Inman settled into the back seat, upbeat and animated. "Did you see that debate last night, Clarence?"

"Yes sir, I did."

"And what do you think? Who won?"

"Well, I thought Mr. Parker did pretty well."

"I did too. That Pike is a rough customer. I agree that Parker held his own."

They drove on in silence for a few minutes before Inman spoke again. "I'm curious, Clarence. Did you listen to any of your radio stations on the way in this morning?"

"Yes sir. I normally do."

"And did you happen to hear Reverend Timmons? Endorsing Harrison Parker?"

"Yes sir, I did. I was very surprised."

"Clarence, I'm going to confide in you because I know I can trust you. I talked Timmons into making that radio spot. We simply cannot have a man like Roscoe Pike running our state. We have to have a big black turnout to ensure that doesn't happen. I'm financing a huge get-out-the-vote campaign in the black communities around the state. I'm telling you because every vote counts, and I hope you will see fit to vote tomorrow for Parker. Take whatever time you need tomorrow morning to cast your ballot. You can pick me up at home when you finish."

Fortson resented Inman's assumption that he would vote for Parker, but realistically what choice did he have? He knew that many of his friends had talked of sitting the election out because of dissatisfaction with both candidates, but every black person who didn't vote increased the chances that Pike would be elected. The fact that a respected figure such as Elijah Timmons was campaigning for Parker would definitely increase black turnout.

As they neared Southland Capital, Inman began to muse aloud about the debate as though Fortson wasn't there.

"Yes, Parker did okay last night. Pike overplayed his hand. He went too far. But he knows his base will be there for him tomorrow no matter what. Parker may have overstepped a bit too. Quoting Abraham Lincoln of all things. I gave him the 'better angels' line, but I didn't imagine he'd take it so literally as to attribute it to the man who freed the slaves. But I guess when it's all-or-nothing time, we have to give it everything we've got and let the chips fall where they may. Right Clarence?"

Fortson nodded and with a barely audible voice responded, "Yes sir."

Inman sensed he might have offended his driver but chose to say nothing more for the rest of the drive into downtown. Surely Clarence wouldn't object to his attempt to manipulate the black vote; surely he understood it was for the good of the state. The uncomfortable realization dawned that he wanted Clarence's approval, but he could not ask for it. One day Clarence will thank me, he thought. One day he will understand my role in advancing his people.

Fortson gripped the steering wheel tightly and stared straight ahead as he struggled with the thought that he, Timmons, and all his black brothers and sisters were just pawns in Devereaux Inman's unrelenting game. And they had no choice but to play by his rules.

FIFTY-FOUR

FATHER FORGIVE THEM

Riley Swint's four o'clock call came amid the newsroom's deadline rush for the election eve newscast, but Tom Burke didn't hesitate to take it. Swint was one of the legislature's most colorful and controversial figures, a master of the short and punchy one-liners that made him a familiar face on television newscasts. Despite Swint's racist views, reporters found him friendly and engaging off camera. But on this day the anger in Swint's voice made it clear this was not a friendly call.

"Tom, we've gotten word that preacher Timmons is doing radio commercials for Harrison Parker. Lots of folks been calling us today saying they heard about the spots on black radio stations around the state. We think that a civil rights leader singing the praises of Parker is a big story you need to be covering."

"Well, I agree that's a story," Burke responded. "This is the first I've heard of it, but we'll check it out."

"You need to get on this quick, Tom. Somebody paid for those spots and obviously hoped to spring them on us so late in the game that we couldn't respond. Roscoe is going to hold a news conference in a few hours. People need to know what's going on here."

Burke hung up and quickly walked out of his office and into the newsroom. He spotted Mindy and Gil by the wire machines and called them over.

"What's up, Tom?" Gil asked.

"I just talked with Riley Swint. He says Reverend Timmons is doing radio spots for Harrison Parker. They're apparently airing on Negro radio stations around the state. You two head over to Mount Gilead and track down Timmons. I'll check with the radio stations to see what else we can learn."

TWENTY MINUTES LATER as Gil and Mindy pulled up to Mount
Gilead AME Church, they saw five buses lined up in the church lot.
Emanuel Slocum was moving from bus to bus with a clipboard in his
hands, obviously organizing transportation for voters the next day.

Mindy ran up to Slocum while Gil followed, camera on his shoulder. "Emanuel, what's going on here? Where's Reverend Timmons?"

Slocum was surprised by their arrival and seemed confused about
how to answer. "Why, um, I really don't have any comment. You'll
need to talk to Reverend Timmons, and he's not here."

"Well, where is he?" Mindy demanded.

"I really don't know. Now if you'll excuse me..." Slocum turned
around and began walking briskly toward the last bus in the line.

As Gil filmed him walking away Mindy tapped him on the shoulder. "Quick. There's Timmons. Let's go."

She had spotted the Reverend walking from his car to the church
office.

"Reverend Timmons. Reverend Timmons. Can we have a word?"

Timmons shook his head and kept walking toward the church. Gil
and Mindy stepped into his path with the camera rolling, Mindy firing
questions. "Reverend Timmons, is it true you are doing radio ads endorsing Harrison Parker for governor?"

Timmons pushed by the camera team. "I have no comment. I'm
asking you to leave church property."

"But Reverend, if you're endorsing Parker on black radio stations,
why not now for our news?"

"I told you I have no comment."

"What about all those buses? Part of an effort to get out the vote
for Harrison Parker?"

"Excuse me. No comment."

Timmons stepped around the crew and quickly entered the
church. Gil followed him with his camera until Timmons slammed the

door in his face.

"I think we've got a good story here," Mindy said.

"A 'no comment' from Timmons is news in and of itself," Gil noted with a chuckle. "Let's head for the station. Hopefully somebody got tape of the ad."

They piled into their station wagon, and Mindy immediately radioed the assignment desk. "This is Mindy and Gil. We found Timmons, but he wouldn't talk about the ad. Hoping you got the tapes of the radio spot. We're heading back. Over."

"Hold it. Don't leave." The transmission from the station faded in and out but was understandable. "Roscoe Pike is heading your way. He's making a statement outside Mount Gilead in about fifteen minutes."

"Ten-four," Mindy responded.

Gil got out of the car and opened the tailgate to retrieve his camera. As he adjusted his shoulder pod, he saw a caravan of cars rounding the corner. It had to be Roscoe Pike and his media entourage.

The first car pulled in front of the church and Pike stepped out, carefully surveying his alien surroundings as reporters and cameramen piled out of their vehicles to cover what he had to say. He strode to a spot on the walkway leading to the sanctuary, pausing at a point where the "Mount Gilead AME Church" sign over the door was visible in the background.

"All right, boys. Gather 'round. I've got a few things to say."

A semicircle of television cameras faced Pike, reporters extending their microphones crouched under the camera lenses. Onlookers began gathering on the fringe of the news conference, a group composed mostly of children, but some adults were there as well with more heading over to see what the excitement was all about. Pike eyed them nervously and then turned to the cameras and began talking.

"This morning I learned that Reverend Elijah Timmons—pastor of this church and one of the leading leftist agitators in the South—has endorsed my opponent. I have said all along that Harrison Parker is a lackey for the likes of Reverend Timmons. He is the perfect candidate for the Communist-inspired protesters who want to take our rights away from us. And now Timmons has proved my point. He's encouraging black folks to come out to the polls tomorrow and vote for my opponent. Well, let the black folks come out and vote. I'm not worried at all. The only thing that concerns me is that most of them aren't qualified to vote. So we've put the word out to our people statewide to keep a close eye on the polling places to be sure everyone who votes knows what they're supposed to know about our state and our country and all those things a good citizen is supposed to know to be able to vote. I just want all you Parker supporters to know that. We will be watching."

A burst of simultaneous questions came from the crouching reporters, but Mindy's voice prevailed.

"Mr. Pike, it sounds like you're trying to intimidate black voters."

"Well, Miss Williams, we just need to be sure every voter is qualified before they punch their ballot. Surely even you would agree with that."

The crowd of black spectators had grown, and they didn't like what they'd heard from Pike. Someone in the group yelled out.

"Go back where you came from, you redneck cracker."

Others hooted, jeered, and raised their fists. They could see Pike's ebbing bravado and increasing nervousness. He began walking toward his car as his aides moved in to protect him. The cameras swung around to capture the angry crowd. Several dozen black men moved into Pike's path, blocking his retreat. Mindy moved with Gil and his camera to a point behind Pike, facing the human barricade.

"This isn't good. Watch yourself," she whispered harshly.

Suddenly a voice boomed out behind them, the deep and resonant voice of Reverend Elijah Timmons.

"All right. That's enough. All are welcome here in the house of the Lord—even a virulent racist like Roscoe Pike. And they are also welcome to leave. Move aside and let him pass."

Hearing their beloved pastor, the crowd quieted and stepped away. Pike and his men quickly ducked into their vehicles and gunned their engines, peeling rubber as they careened away from the church.

The cameras turned to Timmons, who was watching the motorcade disappear into the neighborhood.

"Father forgive them, for they know not what they do," Timmons muttered with a slight shake of his head. Then he snapped to attention and addressed the cameras.

"Now if you are still wondering why I have endorsed Harrison Parker, I offer you the hateful statements of Roscoe Pike just now. We cannot allow a man like this to become our governor. Harrison Parker is the man we must elevate to that position. And I call on all voters, black and white, to cast their ballots for him tomorrow. That is all I have to say on the matter. Good evening."

Timmons turned and walked back to his office as the crews scrambled to pack up their cameras and meet their deadlines.

As soon as Mindy and Gil were in their car, Mindy radioed the station. "We are on the way back with one hell of a story. Pike got upstaged by the Reverend."

Mindy signed off and looked at Gil with an impish smile. "You might say Pike was hoist by his own petard."

The Timmons endorsement story led all three of the city's television newscasts that evening. Grayson Kincaid called it "an eleventh-hour bombshell" before playing the audio of Timmons's radio spot followed by film of the Pike condemnation and his confrontation with Timmons outside Mount Gilead AME. On each of the stations the dramatic coverage was followed by anchors on-camera reporting that Harrison Parker was nowhere to be found and, so far, had no comment on the election eve revelations.

WDX General Manager Ron Hill watched Mindy's report with a sense of dread. He had heard about the developing story in the late afternoon and chosen to pass up an evening cocktail reception to remain in his office to watch the newscast. When his private line began ringing, he was pretty sure who the caller would be. He answered anyway.

"Hello?"

"Ron, it's Devereaux."

Instead of waiting for a polite acknowledgement, Inman plunged on, urgency in his voice. "This Timmons thing is a real crisis. This was never supposed to get out. I guess we were naïve to think we could keep it under radar. But what's done is done. The question is how we control it for the next eighteen hours."

Hill paused before responding with more than a hint of skepticism. "We? I was not involved, but I'm guessing this was your idea. Frankly I feel blindsided."

"Harrison and I talked him into the endorsement," Inman confirmed, "along with promising a pile of money for buses to the polls and of course some walking-around cash to pay off local operators in the ghettos to get the vote out for Harrison."

"I see," Hill said. "And now the story's out. I'm guessing no one knows you're behind this. That would only make things worse for Parker. It's hard to say what the impact of all this will be. Probably a net negative for Parker, certainly among those white voters who might have been leaning his way. But most people have already made up their minds, and it's very late to bring about a sizable voting shift."

"Listen, Ron," Inman began, sounding desperate. "I know you're with us, and I need for you to help us out here. I need you to play down the story on future newscasts. Every time it runs it's like saying Harrison is the black people's candidate. We just can't have that. Polls open in twelve hours, and we have to minimize the damage."

Hill met this request with another uncomfortable pause. "Mr. Inman, you know I can't kill the story. It's out there, and you can't put the genie back in the bottle. I will in no way interfere with our news team's reporting so long as it is responsible and accurate. And I have no concerns about that."

Inman gave an audible sigh. "I respect you and your principles. But there are times when we must bend the rules for the greater good, and this is one of those times. It all boils down to black turnout. Can I at least count on you to have your reporters in the field tomorrow checking on voter intimidation? It's going to be a real threat, particularly in the rural areas, thanks to Pike."

"I share your concern about that, Mr. Inman. We will be out covering whatever happens. And for now, I'll keep your name out of this."

The call ended at last, and Hill walked down the hall to the newsroom where Tom Burke huddled with Mindy, Gil, and several others about updating the Timmons story for the news at eleven. They all looked up as Hill approached.

"Great work on the Timmons story," he said. "But let's talk about tomorrow. What's the plan?"

"We'll be at the polling places when voting begins," Burke responded, "specifically checking on black precincts to gauge the impact of Timmons's endorsement. If he can swell the black turnout, we may have a real race after all."

"What about the possibility of harassment of Negro voters?" Hill wondered. "You heard what Pike said. It's a brazen invitation to intimidate them."

"We'll be looking for any signs of intimidation. We'll be in Pickett County tomorrow to see what happens in that garden of equality."

"Okay," Hill said. "Let's do all we can to be sure black voters get a fair shake. I've got a bad feeling about what might be waiting for them when they try to cast their ballots."

"We'll be out there," Burke assured him. "We'll be watching."

FIFTY-FIVE

OUR RIGHT TO VOTE

REVEREND TIMMONS STOOD at the edge of the church parking lot and watched with a growing sense of satisfaction. The buses he'd rented wheezed and rumbled as they shuttled load after load of black voters to their precincts. It was apparent that his radio campaign for Harrison Parker had brought the voters out, not only here but also around the state. Reports from towns and cities and even some rural areas indicated a higher than usual black turnout. But despite the encouraging signs, he worried that news reports about his endorsement of Parker would generate a higher white turnout as well.

He noticed several news crews pulling into the parking lot and decided he'd slip back into the church to avoid being photographed. The last thing he needed today was more television exposure. He would wait until the polls closed to issue any further comment.

FIFTY MILES TO the north in Pickett County, voters were also lining up to cast ballots. Assigned to cover the primary in Pickett, Mindy and Gil had been cruising around the precincts since they opened at seven a.m. It was obvious this was Pike country. His signs were everywhere, particularly along the roadsides and in yard after yard. Even at the county's largest polling place, Longstreet Elementary, hundreds of Pike signs cluttered the area just beyond the legally mandated non-partisan buffer zone. A few Parker signs could be found, but most of them had been ripped up or defaced.

Mindy and Gil pulled into the school parking lot and set out to film the voting and get some interviews. They ignored the hard stares and occasional mumbled slurs. They knew reporters were not welcome here.

They noticed a small group of black voters on the edge of the parking lot, hanging back presumably until their numbers grew sufficiently to enter the school and vote. Apparently, the presence of reporters raised their comfort level enough to allow them to advance. Gil recognized one of them as Willie Brooks, the uncle Jarvis Pendry was trying to locate when he was gunned down at Peavine Creek.

As the camera team got closer, Brooks looked away, refusing to engage. Gil and Mindy understood. Uncle Willie wanted no attention. He just wanted to cast his vote without fanfare.

A table was set up just outside the entrance to the school. Two local election officials sat there briefing voters on procedures and checking their names on the registration list. White voters were quickly checked so they could enter the building and cast their ballot. But when Brooks and his group walked up, they were referred to a third official sitting at another table.

From a hundred feet away, Mindy saw what was happening and told Gil to put his camera down. "Something's going on. I'm not sure the elections people know we're here yet. I'm going to see what's happening. I'll let you know when to join me."

Mindy walked down the grassy slope to the table but hung back at the rear of the group to listen. The black voters had gathered in front of the table, obviously curious about why they had been shunted aside.

"Y'all need to form a line. Don't be crowding me."

The crew-cut man, who wore dungarees and a short-sleeve sports shirt, spoke in a thick Southern accent.

"That's better. Okay, let's be sure y'all are registered and everything is okay. What's your name, boy?"

Willie Brooks was first in line. "I'm William H. Brooks."

"Address?"

"34 Gardenia Drive, Shiloh Crossroads."

"Okay, Willie. Your name is on my list. Did you vote in the last election?"

"Yes, I vote in every election."

The man, who wore no name tag, looked down at his papers. "Well, that's funny. I don't see any record of you voting in the last six years. You sure about that, Willie?"

"Yes I am. I vote in every election."

"You ever been arrested, Willie?"

"No."

"Ever been in trouble with the law?"

"Just a speeding ticket. That was five years ago."

"Well, we'll see about that. So you have a criminal record?"

"No I do not. A speeding ticket. That's all."

"Now, Willie. Don't you get smart with me."

That remark brought an end Brooks's patience. "Excuse me, sir, but I see white voters passing right by this table and going in to vote. Why are you making this so difficult? We only want our right to vote!"

Mindy gestured for Gil to join her with his camera, and he hustled down the slope, focusing on the man at the table as he moved into position.

"Who the hell are you? Damn reporters! Somebody call the sheriff."

Mindy thrust the microphone toward him. "Why are you making it so difficult for these people to vote? Is it because they are black?"

The man at the table was sputtering with rage. "We got to know they're qualified. Who are you? Do you have permission to be here?"

He looked around frantically, finally spotting some help. "Hey, Gabe, you and Randy get over here and handle these news people."

Mindy moved the mike closer. "What is your name? What is your position? Why aren't whites being asked the same questions you asked Mr. Brooks?"

The man stood and backed away from the table. He was much shorter than Mindy had imagined, with skinny, bowed legs that seemed unequal to the tast of supporting his pot-bellied frame. His two henchmen moved toward Gil, attempting to block his camera.

"Don't touch me or my camera," Gil warned. "We have a perfect right to be here."

They closed in on him, one grabbing the lens of the camera and forcing it down. The other tried to put Gil in a headlock. Gil kept the camera rolling.

He was ducking his head and trying to stay on his feet when he heard a familiar voice.

"All right, boys. That's enough."

Sheriff Lucas McSwain grabbed each assailant by their shirt collars and yanked them back. "What's going on here? Don't you boys know that no good ever comes of attacking reporters?"

Then he turned to the crew. "Gil, you okay? Mindy, nice to see you again."

Gil's camera had been pulled off his shoulder, but he shrugged it back in position and straightened his shirt that had been partially ripped in the encounter.

"Thanks, Sheriff. We were just covering the voting when this fellow called his guys on us." Gil cocked his head toward the election official, who stood with his back to a wall, his mouth agape with confusion.

Mindy picked up the story. "We witnessed this man trying to deny Willie Brooks his right to vote. Asked him all sorts of bogus questions about a criminal record and the like. We were just questioning him about it when these guys started attacking Gil."

"Bobby, is that right?"

Bobby began sputtering. "Sheriff, we was just doing our job. Making sure these coloreds are who they say they are. Just routine questions. Same as always. Then Willie started mouthing off, and these TV people showed up and started being pushy. We had to put a stop to that, but they wouldn't take no for an answer. So we had to take action."

McSwain looked over at Willie Brooks, who had stepped back to watch from the sidelines.

"Willie, you okay?"

Brooks was a shy, retiring man, but he spoke with firmness and resolve. "I'll be fine, Sheriff, once me and my friends cast our votes."

McSwain nodded and looked at Bobby and the other poll workers who were staring at him with quizzical expressions. "If these folks are on the registration list, then you let them cast their ballots same as everybody else. Are we clear on that?"

McSwain glanced over at Gil to see if his camera was running. And for the first time in his long career, he was at ease about being recorded.

The sheriff watched as voter lines began to reform and move as whites and blacks resumed the time-honored process. As he turned to go, Gil and Mindy approached.

"Sheriff, can we have a quick interview?" Mindy asked.

McSwain shook his head and said, "I think what I just said should about cover it, don't you?"

And with that he lumbered up the slope, got into his car, and headed to the next precinct.

"I'm not sure I believe what I just saw," Mindy said as the sheriff pulled away.

"He's changed," Gil said as he hoisted his camera back onto his shoulder. "Who would have imagined Sheriff Lucas McSwain as a protector of black voters in Pickett County? Not to mention scurrilous reporters."

"I'd like to think black voters are getting the same break all over the state," Mindy responded. "But we both know that's not going to happen."

"Sadly, I agree," Gil responded. "We're done here. Let's head back and get this on the air. Then we'll wait for the returns. I've got a feeling it's going to be a long night."

FIFTY-SIX

THE COUNT

FOR MOST CANDIDATES, election night headquarters was a place of excitement and anticipation, where colorful bunting adorned virtually every vertical surface and clusters of red, white, and blue balloons bobbed on their tethers. The crowd would wax or wane, depending on what the returns were showing, as the evening wore on. The vote leader could count on a ballroom full of wildly cheering supporters, fueled by campaign fervor and frequent visits to the cash bar. The laggards, if they chose to show their faces at all, would preside over a skeleton crew of diehards lamely applauding the bromides of defeat. But at the beginning of the evening all things were possible, and hope sprang eternal.

For Harrison Parker, election night headquarters at the Heart of Downtown Hotel felt more like a bunker. Ever since Timmons's radio endorsement had been exposed the day before, Parker had kept out of sight. He felt that facing reporters would only amplify the damaging story. He really had no adequate way to explain his alliance with Timmons without confirming the perception of many that he was a scheming, manipulative, hypocritical hack. So, with advice from Devereaux Inman, he chose to lay low and fervently hope that the eleventh-hour revelation would not pierce the collective consciousness of the electorate before the polls closed.

While supporters began to gather in the hotel ballroom, Parker paced the living area in his third-floor suite, checking with operatives around the state to get a feel for how the vote was going. The gross totals posted on the TV screens were meaningless at this early hour. He needed to know where those votes were being cast and the size of the turnout in key precincts.

News for the most part was good. Turnout in urban black precincts was strong, and voters in long lines when the polls closed at seven p.m. were still casting their ballots. It was harder to get a handle on the voting in rural areas, but there was no question Pike voters had turned out in force as well. The race promised to be close throughout the evening, and Parker felt sure it wouldn't be decided until well after midnight.

"Hey, boss," Billy called from across the room, a telephone receiver cradled between his chin and shoulder. "We're getting reports of Negro voters being turned away from the polls in Johnson and Shiver counties. Can you believe those redneck poll workers are asking them to name the Supreme Court justices before they can vote?"

"I'm pretty sure it's the tip of the iceberg," Parker grumbled. "Call the elections supervisors in those counties, and at least let them know we are onto them. Tell them we just might refer it to the Justice Department. I wonder how much of this is going on around the state."

"Too much," Billy responded. "Those are your votes that never get counted. I just hope that mythical white moderate vote is making up for it. Suburban turnout is good, but who knows how many of them are for you?"

Parker shrugged and collapsed onto a loveseat to check the latest results on WDX. It was only eight p.m. and full coverage had not yet begun, but Grayson Kincaid was giving three-minute updates every half hour. He could see Kincaid on the screen but couldn't hear him.

"Billy. Give me some volume."

Billy trotted across the room to the set and turned the volume knob, then joined Parker on the loveseat to watch the coverage.

"It's very early, but here are the latest returns from around the state." Kincaid paused briefly until the governor's race returns came on the screen. "As you can see, with only five percent of the precincts reporting Roscoe Pike has a sizable lead over Harrison Parker. Pike leads Parker by thirty thousand votes. The other three candidates are far behind and not a factor in this race. We can't tell you what parts of the state these votes are coming from, and we caution that it's far too early to read any significance into them as far as a trend is concerned. My guess is that these are votes from rural areas. When the urban and sub-urban votes are counted, you can expect this race to get much closer."

"God, Grayson, I hope you're right," Parker muttered under his breath.

ON THE OTHER side of town, Roscoe Pike's supporters were jubilant. Applause and rebel yells echoed through the ballroom when Kincaid's report appeared on the television monitors rolled in for the crowd.

"We gonna kick some ass tonight," slurred a beefy man in coveralls holding a can of Schlitz Malt Liquor. Then he staggered to one of the several barrels of iced beer placed around the ballroom and waited his turn to grab another.

The crowd had been building since seven, and by nine the ballroom at the Riviera Motel on the south side of town was packed with boisterous Pike supporters chanting and cheering with each update of the returns showing their candidate in the lead.

Unlike Parker, Pike was happy to mingle with his people and made several appearances early in the evening, strolling through the crowd shaking hands and slapping backs. At his nine fifteen appearance he jumped on the stage and moved to the podium microphone. He raised his arms to quiet the throngs, but their chant of "Pike, Pike, Pike" would not subside until he started to speak.

"Thank y'all for being here tonight to celebrate what we hope will be a great victory. It's early, but things are looking good so far."

The crowd erupted for another round of Pike chants.

"We are the underdogs in this election. My opponent has conspired with the liberal big-city power brokers with all their money, and he's in an unholy alliance with the blacks. Putting all those ads on TV and radio, getting that black agitator to endorse my opponent and hoping none of us white folks would catch on—well, we caught 'em red-handed. And tonight, they are going to pay."

Pike raised a clenched fist and shook it in the air as the crowd went wild.

"Pike, Pike, Pike!"

The candidate curled his lips into a sneering smile and waved as he walked off stage.

"I'll be back later," he yelled over the euphoric uproar. "We'll have even better news."

Behind the stage Pike staff workers were breaking the taped seals on two large cardboard boxes filled with items to hand out to the crowd later when the moment of triumph arrived. The boxes contained hundreds of small Confederate battle flags to be waved in unison so that Pike could look out upon a swirling sea of stars and bars as he proclaimed his victory.

The back-stage activity escaped the notice of several television crews in the ballroom, Mindy and Gil among them. Gil had filmed Pike's remarks and was now getting some cover shots of supporters filling the room. It was an interesting mix of mostly middle-aged and older white men. The suburbanites, wearing their sport coats and ties, occupied the center of the ballroom, most of them sipping mixed drinks. Those who appeared to be from the country roamed around the room wearing blue jeans or khakis, guzzling beer and talking boisterously. Some of the women wore red dresses covered with small rebel flags and Pike stickers.

Mindy, who'd been in the back of the room getting some information from Riley Swint, found Gil and tapped him on the shoulder. "Let's head for the station. Swint says Pike probably won't come back down until much later. We need to get our film processed and cut in time for ten p.m. coverage."

"Okay. I've got all we need."

As they left the ballroom, they heard someone yell.

"Y'all come back now, you heah? Come back for the victory celebration. Pike, Pike, Pike..."

IN THE WDX studio Kincaid was trying to analyze the vote totals, which were picking up dramatically. A local pollster, Clancy Durrell, had been hired to help decipher the votes and trends, and as they looked at the latest totals Durrell shared his thoughts with viewers.

"You know, Grayson, Parker's numbers are looking better as the black and suburban precincts are counted. He has a lot of ground to make up, but it's tightening. The rural turnout is heavy for Pike. It's going to be tough to overcome, but it's a long way from being over."

Durrell was something of a local character, an expert in the art of polling but also quite skilled in his colorful turns of phrases. "Yes, Grayson, it's the tortoise and the hare. The question is can Aesop's fable pan out for Harrison Parker, who is definitely the one wearing the carapace tonight."

Kincaid gave an obligatory chuckle. "We shall see. We've got sixty percent of the precincts reporting, and Pike still leads by twenty thousand. Traditionally the inner-city precincts are the last to report. You have to assume that vote will go to Parker by default, but did Reverend Timmons's involvement help get more Negroes to the polls?"

Durrell nodded vigorously. "Grayson, absolutely. But there's more involved. There's some big money at play here. We know about the buses that carried black voters to the polls in big numbers, but my sources tell me paid workers were out in the neighborhoods button-holing people to be sure they voted. From all appearances, the Parker campaign pumped a lot of money into getting Negroes to the polls, but they sure didn't want white voters around the state to know that."

"That's very interesting, Clancy. So, is the key really what happens with the white vote? Will that be the difference? "

"Yes, I think it will. Assuming the black vote goes to Parker and the rural vote to Pike, we have to look at the suburban white vote to decide this race. We know Pike has suburban support, but the Parker campaign has tried to pursue a more moderate path. Generally, in this state you do not want to be perceived as a moderate, but the divisive nature of Pike's campaign may have driven some whites to support

Parker. The question is, will there be enough of them to give Parker the victory?"

ELIJAH AND MATTIE Timmons were in their family room, nervously watching this coverage. The past twenty-four hours had been nightmarish for the reverend. He knew it would be a risk to endorse Parker, but he had hoped against hope that his actions wouldn't be widely known until after the election. Now he realized how short-sighted he'd been.

Mattie, as she usually did in times of trial, had given him a new perspective, convincing him he had done the right thing. It wasn't so much about endorsing a white man who'd committed virtually nothing to the black community; it was a case of stopping a virulent racist from seizing the governor's office. Supporting the lesser evil was commendable, she said. And if he could lay claim to putting Parker over the top, good things would be in store. Timmons would be on the inside for the first time in his life. But it was all dependent on Parker keeping his word, and for Timmons that was a very big gamble.

The phone on the side table rang, and Timmons quickly picked up the receiver. "Hello? Reverend Timmons here."

"Reverend. Good evening. It's Devereaux Inman. What do you think so far?"

"Well, Mr. Inman, I'm very worried. What do you think?"

"I'm nervous, too. But no matter what happens I just want to thank you for what you did to help us. If Harrison wins, you will be a big part of the victory, and I guarantee you will be a part of the new administration. Maybe not at first, but as Harrison grows into the job, he'll hopefully broaden his support enough for you to become a more visible part."

Timmons felt his temper rising. "So you're telling me I put my prestige on the line for you, and yet I still have to wait in the back of the bus until you feel comfortable enough to put me on display?"

"No, no, no! You will be an important part of the team. We just have to be careful how we do this. Surely you understand."

"Oh, I do understand. You white folks have been using us for centuries, and this is just another example. We'll wait to see what happens tonight. Then, if Parker wins, I'll wait to see if he fulfills his promises. I won't hold my breath. In the meantime, I'm quite happy to apply whatever pressure I can as an outsider. That's where I'm more comfortable anyway."

Timmons forcefully put the receiver back in its cradle and looked at Mattie, who was watching him with concern. He spoke through clenched teeth. "I ain't gonna be nobody's house nigga, even if he is governor!"

Mattie glanced at the television set and pointed. "Elijah—look!"

Grayson Kincaid was displaying and analyzing the latest returns, which showed the governor's race tightening.

"It looks like Harrison Parker is making a run at Roscoe Pike," Kincaid reported. "Pike's margin, which was thirty thousand votes early in the evening, has closed to five thousand votes. This is with eighty-seven percent of the precincts reporting. Clancy, looks like we have a horserace."

"Yes, Grayson. What we have is urban and suburban precincts finally reporting. Pickett and a few other rural counties are still out, and they will no doubt heavily support Pike. But if Parker can win the majority of the outstanding votes in the suburbs, he's got a shot. But it's going to be close. Pike has a lot of support in the suburbs."

PARKER RESTLESSLY STALKED around his hotel suite, exulting with every update on the returns. When Clancy Durrell had said he was narrowly winning the suburbs, he grabbed Mary and spun her around while his children, nine and seven years old, jumped up and down, clapped, and sang.

"Daddy. You're going to win!"

"I hope so, kids, but it's too early. A lot of votes are yet to be counted, so let's not get too excited. We are going in the right direction, though, and I've got a feeling ole Roscoe is starting to sweat."

Billy entered the room with an update on the crowd gathering downstairs. "You've got a ballroom full of very excited people. Don't you think you should get down there and say a few words?"

"Yes. Absolutely right. How do I look?"

He pulled on his suit jacket, ran a comb through his hair, and allowed Mary to hold him by his shoulders to examine his appearance.

"You look like a winner," she cooed, and he gave her a kiss.

"Okay, then. Let's go."

IT WAS JUST before eleven p.m. when Mindy and Gil entered the ballroom, Gil with his shoulder-mounted camera and Mindy keeping pace with the microphone in her hand. As they walked in, a local state senator was finishing his too lengthy introduction of the man of the hour.

"Ladies and gentlemen, let's welcome our next governor, Harrison Parker."

The ballroom exploded in a cacophony of cheers, applause, and chants as the candidate entered through a side door, hopped up on the stage, and quickly walked to the podium, extending his arms toward the adoring crowd as if to embrace it. As he did so, the large television monitor on the edge of the stage showed new vote totals: ninety-five percent of the precincts reporting with Parker closing the gap to only fifteen hundred votes.

Parker beamed and pointed to the monitor.

"It's happening. We're closing the gap. Only fifteen hundred votes to go. It's not over yet, but we are showing a lot of kick in the closing lap. The finish line is within sight. Pike is flagging. I'm sprinting. Keep the faith, my friends. We can do this! I'll be back. Stick with me now."

As Parker left the stage waving to the cheering throng, Gil panned away to show the crowd, a mixture of young and middle-aged supporters, all white. They appeared well heeled compared to the Pike crowd.

Gil imagined most of them were graduates of top-flight segregated private and public schools in the city. Their paths into professions and businesses were probably paved for them by their well-to-do families. They were embarrassed by Roscoe Pike and his rhetoric and had gravitated to Parker as the only alternative. They were a bit more reserved than the Pike crowd, but they were doing their best to muster up all the enthusiasm their studied erudition would allow.

Someone ran to the TV set and turned up the volume as Parker's supporters gathered around to watch the quivering black and white images of Grayson Kincaid talking with Clancy Durrell.

"We are seeing something extraordinary, don't you think, Clancy?"

"Without exception, Grayson, this is a remarkable race. It appears Parker is doing much better than we thought with white voters. The polls we've done throughout the campaign have never picked up this level of support for Parker. Of course, it's possible those we surveyed just weren't being honest with us, but you can't argue with what we are seeing tonight..."

Kincaid interrupted. "Excuse me, Clancy. We've got new totals. Parker has cut the gap to nine hundred with only a few more precincts to go."

Whatever dialogue followed that comment was drowned out by an increasingly raucous crowd, jumping up and down and applauding as though they were on the sidelines of a football game.

Across town, Roscoe Pike huddled nervously with Riley Swint and several other advisors. He had seen his lead dwindle throughout the evening, and he was looking for some assurances that the hemorrhaging could be stopped.

"We just need to hold our own in these last precincts. They're probably suburban districts, and I should do really well there, right, Riley?"

Swint was very worried too, but he didn't want to show it. "You're going to be fine, Roscoe. If we can get fifty percent of the remaining vote we should win. I'm not saying it won't be close, but I think we're looking good."

Pike was incredulous. "Who the hell are these white people voting for my opponent? Why would any white person vote for a guy who's going to take their freedoms away? It makes no sense."

Pike glanced at the television set in his suite. New numbers showed the gap had narrowed to four hundred votes.

"Goddammit. What's happening here? I thought we had a lock on the suburbs. Hell, they moved out there to get away from blacks. It should be a clean sweep for me!"

"Take it easy, Roscoe," Swint pleaded. "It is not over. We're going to pull it out. You'll see."

"I'm going down to talk to the crowd. I need to let them know we're still in this thing. There must be some irregularities. Something's fishy."

"That could be," Swint assured him. "But the only irregularities I've heard about were aimed at black folk. There must be something going on, and we'll get to the bottom of it."

Pike swept into the ballroom, where the crowd had been subdued by the steady erosion of their candidate's big lead throughout the evening. When they saw Pike, they began cheering and waving Pike posters. But it was obvious to Pike that the enthusiasm that had lifted him like a thermal earlier in the evening had evaporated.

The numbers on the television screen began turning again, and this time they showed Parker inching even closer, with only two percent of the precincts yet to report.

Pike yelled at the crowd. "Don't believe those numbers. Something's wrong, and all my votes are not being counted. You'll see."

The crowd had dwindled in the past hour, but the faithful remained. They massed by the stage, looking up at their leader speaking from the podium. He didn't look as commanding or forceful as he had in the past. Perspiration glistened on his forehead and soaked the collar of his shirt. His eyes showed something his supporters had never seen in their smugly self-assured candidate—fear.

Suddenly he stopped talking as he saw his audience turn toward the television set once again. The cheering stopped as everyone paused to listen to Grayson Kincaid as though he were an oracle.

"We're looking at the new vote totals, and it appears the momentum Parker has been building all evening has slowed. Pike remains in the lead by a razor-thin margin—two hundred fifty votes. Clancy, what's going on?"

"Well, Grayson, the votes yet to be counted are in the suburbs and a few rural counties. Parker has an edge in the suburbs, but the good news for Pike is that some rural counties—including Pickett County— are still out. If Pike can carry those counties by wide margins—eighty percent—he should win. And that could well happen."

Pike's voice boomed through the microphone. "You see? You see? We are on the road to victory. Keep the faith. As God is my witness, we will prevail."

AT THE HEART of Downtown, Parker was on his knees mere inches from the television screen, silently imploring Grayson Kincaid to deliver the news he so desperately wanted to hear.

"It is neck and neck," Kincaid intoned, rubbing his forehead as the new totals appeared on the screen. "Pike has just increased his lead to four hundred votes with ninety-nine percent of the precincts reporting. About fifteen hundred votes are still out. Too close to call. Clancy? Your take?"

"Well, Grayson, based on my analysis, I just don't see Parker picking up enough votes to overtake Pike. It could happen, but based on past experience, it probably won't."

Parker stared blankly at the images on the screen as Mary knelt behind him and embraced her husband.

"You fought the good fight," she said softly. "I am so proud of you no matter what."

Parker slowly rose to his feet, pulling Mary with him.

"This is not over—not until the last vote is counted. Until then I will not concede."

GIL AND MINDY pushed their way through the crowd in the Pike ballroom. Pike's supporters were at fever pitch, pressing toward the platform as the candidate climbed the steps. Gil focused his lens on Pike as he reached the podium. Sweat streamed down Pike's face, and he looked pale and depleted, but his eyes blazed with maniacal fervor.

Riley Swint stood behind Pike on the platform, tiptoeing to speak into his ear as the crowd noise enveloped the room. Swint seemed concerned and appeared to attempt to restrain Pike as he moved toward the podium. Pike brushed him aside and bent toward the microphone. He raised his arms for quiet, but his devotees continued to roar for their candidate. Pike screamed into the microphone, which distorted his voice into a metallic howl.

"We have won! We have won! Didn't I tell you? Did you see it on TV? We are pulling away. It's over. My liberal opponent won't concede, but he knows the people have spoken. Praise the Lord. Let's celebrate!"

The rebel flags were pulled from their boxes behind the platform and passed out to the crowd. Screams of joy and vindictive curses against the vanquished opponent echoed through the ballroom.

Gil and Mindy were pushed and shoved as the crowd pulsated chaotically. The celebration became a melee. Mindy lost her footing and slid to the floor. Gil reached down to grab her arm and yanked her upright.

Pike looked over the roiling masses, strutting back and forth on the platform, arms folded, eyes glazed.

"It's a new day," he yelled. "The people are back in control. Glory, glory, hallelujah!"

Gil pulled a shaken Mindy to the edge of the crowd, where they paused to survey the spectacle they never could have predicted. Rebel flags waving, particles of red, white, and blue confetti dancing in the air, a country singer belting out "Dixie," and Roscoe Pike basking in the adulation of his followers like a banana republic dictator.

Gil held Mindy protectively. She was still unsteady after her fall and seemed stunned by the scene unfolding before them. As they stared at the raucous celebration, Gil noticed Mindy's lips moving. He bent closer, straining to hear her emotionless monotone.

"The rough beast's hour has come 'round at last."

FIFTY-SEVEN

NASCENCE

INAUGURATION DAY DAWNED sunny but bitterly cold even for early January. Crowds of spectators began gathering on the west side of the state capitol around ten o'clock, yearning for the warming sunshine that would not reach their shadowed position until noon, the hour the governor-elect would take the oath of office.

Mindy, Gil, and a shivering group of media colleagues watched the growing crowd from a camera scaffold, where they had an unencumbered view of the platform erected on the capitol steps for the ceremony. A stiff breeze battered the US and state flags clinging to their flagpoles and penetrated the jackets and overcoats of the reporters and cameramen exposed atop the scaffold. Mindy bounced on the balls of her feet and pulled the drawstrings of her fur-lined parka's hood tighter to repel the wind. Gil moved behind her to shield her from the icy gusts as he prayed in vain for the mercury to start rising.

At eleven o'clock, as WDX-TV began its live telecast, one of the state's premier high school marching bands began to perform a medley of patriotic music from its position at the base of the steps while the crowd continued to file in. With the stirring standards providing audio backdrop, Grayson Kincaid and Clancy Durrell commented from the studio as they watched scenes of the historic event on their monitor, including the arrival of the Governor-elect Harrison Parker.

Parker walked onto the platform with Mary at his side, their two children following, along with the outgoing governor and other state officials. They all took seats looking out at the crowd spilling over the capitol grounds.

"For Harrison Parker, this day marks the end of an incredible political odyssey." Kincaid kept the pace of his commentary slow, following the scenes as they unfolded. "His victory in the Democratic primary wasn't secured until the wee hours of the morning after the vote, even though his opponent, Roscoe Pike, had already claimed victory, prematurely as it turned out. The narrow victory held up despite a court challenge by Pike. Parker then cruised to a lopsided victory over his Republican opponent in November to become governor of Georgia."

"Pike, not surprisingly, is nowhere to be seen today," Clancy Durrell observed. "He is a bitter loser. He never conceded, claiming he'll always be the 'white people's governor.'"

"Clancy, I see Riley Swint is in the crowd with other legislators."

"That's right, Grayson. Swint tried to stop Pike from declaring victory on election night, but Pike wouldn't listen."

"I think Pike was listening to *you*, Clancy," Kincaid responded. "You said it was doubtful Parker could overtake Pike's lead, slim though it was."

"Touche', Grayson. I could see Parker was sweeping an increased Negro vote and narrowly winning the suburban vote, but I didn't see that he was getting more white rural votes than anyone imagined. For example, in Pickett County we thought Parker might get twenty percent of the vote at best. He got almost thirty percent. It was much the same in other rural counties. That extra ten percent was the difference."

"Certainly not a mandate, Clancy, so Governor Parker has a lot of work to do to bring this state together. We'll pause our commentary for a special presentation from the Morehouse College Chorus."

The singers filed onto the capitol steps to the right of the inaugural platform. They were the first all-black group to perform at an official state ceremony. The chorus began by singing "I'll Fly Away," followed by "Swing Low, Sweet Chariot" and "Steal Away." These slave songs had found their way into cultural Americana, and the rich renditions by the young male singers were moving. The chorus usually ended its concerts with "The Battle Hymn of the Republic," but that traditional finale was omitted from the inaugural program.

At two minutes before noon the music ceased. The Georgia Supreme Court Chief Justice rose and walked to the podium, the gusting breeze ruffling his thatch of white hair. He nodded to Parker, who stepped forward in his black overcoat to take the oath of office, right hand raised, left hand on the family Bible held by a beaming Mary. With his promise to uphold the state and US constitutions followed by "So help me God," Harrison Parker became governor. The crowd erupted with cheers of congratulations, well wishes, and hope for the future.

REVEREND ELIJAH TIMMONS chose to watch the inauguration from home. He had received an invitation, but he still wasn't ready to embrace the significant role he'd played in Parker's victory. He would wait to see what kind of governor he'd helped create before taking full credit.

More exciting to him than Parker's election was the fact that the Negro vote, despite many reports of suppression across the state, had been such a powerful force. He felt confident that impact would only grow, and politicians one day soon would have no choice but to court those votes openly without the clandestine maneuverings he'd been reduced to. One day a man such as himself might become an elected leader, perhaps sooner than most believed possible. He said a brief prayer that the Lord would hasten that day.

Prayer, however, had not eased his concerns about the growing strength of the student insurgency directly challenging his leadership. He saw the spray-painted signs everywhere as he drove around town, even on the sidewalk in front of Mount Gilead AME Church. He'd tried his best to have the red paint scrubbed off the pavement. The remaining smudges were indecipherable to all except Elijah Timmons, who could not erase the original message from his mind. He viewed it as an omen.

"Remember Marcus!"

Devereaux Inman also decided to stay away from the capitol. He was gratified that his guidance and financial backing had made Parker's victory possible. Parker had privately expressed his thanks, but Inman shunned all accolades. He preferred to keep a low profile, to remain behind the curtain as the Parker administration took shape. They had agreed to rarely be seen together but would communicate often. Inman would find ways for Parker to repay the enormous debt he owed.

In the meantime, Inman was rewarded in other ways. Already he was getting phone calls from out-of-state business leaders exploring the possibility of moving their companies to the city, something that would never happen if Pike had been elected. There were even rumors of a major league baseball team heading south to a city that was progressive, welcoming, and tolerant. Few would ever understand what he had done to preserve the future of the city he loved. Inman was content to wait for the judgment of history. He was certain it would be kind.

IN ARMISTEAD, SHERIFF Lucas McSwain watched the inaugural on the small television set in his office with mixed feelings. He didn't like Parker, but he hated Pike on a personal level for the divisions he had stoked in the community. Pike and his disciples had made his county a pariah, and it would take years to overcome the negative image that Pickett County was forced to shoulder. McSwain understood that he bore part of the blame, but he looked forward to helping resurrect the county's image over time.

He took small comfort that Hiram and Caleb Soseby were facing a civil rights trial that would probably put them in federal prison for up to a decade, a paltry sentence that could never erase the stain of their acquittals in Pickett County.

McSwain sat back in his desk chair and watched Parker's inaugural speech, which was full of the grandiose promises common to all inaugural addresses. But he sat up when Parker began to talk about race as a defining issue of the campaign.

"My fellow citizens, I need to talk to you about the challenges of the times in which we live. We must bind up our wounds and heal our divisions. We cannot do that so long as we discriminate against each other based on the color of our skin.

"I am going to work hard to find the common ground that we all share as human beings. If we can find a way to walk in the other man's shoes, to see the world as others see it, to open our minds to the possibilities of mutual understanding, if we can try to simply get along with each other, then I think great things are in store for our state, for all of us. May God help us all in achieving that goal."

The muted applause that followed Parker's heartfelt words caused McSwain to wonder if whites and blacks could ever find it within themselves to do what the new governor asked. It was an open question.

"Sheriff, you got some mail. It says 'personal' on the envelope."

The deputy dropped the envelope on McSwain's desk. The sheriff picked it up and immediately noticed a Baltimore postmark. He opened it and began to read.

> Dear Sheriff McSwain,
>
> Willie Brooks told me that you interceded when poll workers tried to keep him and his friends from voting. I feel strange for thanking you for doing a job that should be any sheriff's responsibility, but understanding the circumstances as I do, I feel a note of thanks is justifiable.
>
> It's a hard thing to break free from the past. I will continue to pray for you because I understand the path ahead is a rocky one.
>
> Sincerely,
> Evelyn Pendry

McSwain read the letter several times and then placed it in the center drawer of his desk. He knew he would refer to it often over the course of his law enforcement career and far beyond.

BACK AT THE state capitol, the crowds were departing. The sun had finally reached the building's west side, the breezes had calmed, and the temperature had warmed to a reasonable level for January. Mindy and Gil packed up their gear, threw their heavy coats into the back seat, and headed to the station to write and edit their inauguration package for the evening news.

As they drove away from the capitol, they passed a Pike billboard high on the side of a parking deck. A Pike supporter in the legislature who owned the deck had placed the billboard there early in the campaign. There it defiantly remained after Pike's defeat, the candidate's image battered, torn, and faded by time and weather.

"Look on my works, ye mighty, and despair," Mindy mused as they drove by.

Gil chuckled. "Shelley, right?"

"Very good, Gil," Mindy answered with a tone of exaggerated approval a teacher might use with a student who'd come up with a correct answer.

"It's from 'Ozymandias.' Seeing that ruined image of Pike—his 'shattered visage'—brought that poem to mind."

"Yep," said Gil. "It fits. But let's not forget how close he came to being governor. And his people are still here—angry, intolerant, and looking for the next demagogue."

"So, Gil, to continue the literary analogy, would you say the sands of time are shifting but not enough to bury our racial divide?"

"I couldn't have said it better."

They both laughed.

There was silence between them as they drove toward the station, passing just east of downtown, a route offering the city's most dramatic skyline views. Office towers, high-rise apartment buildings, and gleaming hotels all crisply outlined against the haze-free cerulean winter sky.

"Do you ever think about all we've been through?" Mindy said in a faraway voice. "All we've witnessed in just a few months. Sometimes when you're in the middle of it you miss the big picture. You have to step back to try to figure it all out, how all the pieces connect."

"Yep," Gil replied. "It's a big, crazy mosaic. We just add to it bit by bit. And you know what? It will keep on growing. It will never be finished."

"Yes, the story continues. The next piece of our mosaic will be the federal trial. Surely the Sosebys will get their comeuppance, but in this state you can never be sure."

After a brief pause Mindy added, "I just hope I'll be covering it."

Gil glanced at her. "What do you mean? Of course, you will."

"Gil, I've been meaning to tell you, but I wanted to wait for the right time. I got a call from NBC. They're looking for a female correspondent to join the old boys' club. I got lucky being in the middle of the Pendry case, the governor's race, and all the rest, so I got noticed in New York. I just hope I'm ready."

Gil's chest tightened with the realization that Mindy would soon leave him behind. He knew it was a selfish reaction and struggled to mask it with an overly enthusiastic response.

"I told you I was going to make you a star! Of course you're ready. Don't think twice. It's all right."

Mindy looked at Gil, her face crinkling into a smile. "At last we have a poetic connection! I love that Dylan song. Come to think of it, I *am* going down that long, lonesome road, babe. And where I'm bound, I can't tell."

Without missing a beat Gil chimed in. "Goodbye's too good a word, gal, so I'll just say 'fare thee well.'"

Gil slowed, stopped at a traffic light, and turned to Mindy. "But Mindy, I really don't want to say either one."

Mindy paused and lowered her eyes briefly before returning them to Gil. "Neither do I."

The light turned green, but they didn't notice. The driver behind them tapped his horn, which Gil ignored. When the horn began blaring, Gil broke from Mindy's pensive gaze and slowly accelerated.

"I guess that jerk thought we were wasting his precious time,"

Mindy chortled.

They drove on in silence, mulling their thoughts as Peachtree Street transitioned from the commercial clutter of downtown to the tree-shrouded neighborhoods, parks, and churches of midtown. Before long, white-columned WDX-TV rose into view atop its greensward, a beautiful anachronism in a changing South.

"Hey, when you get to the big time, could you see if there might be an opening for an exceptionally talented photojournalist?"

"Got anyone in mind?" Mindy laughed. "Don't worry, Gil. Your work got noticed by the network too. It's just a matter of time."

Pulling into the parking lot, Gil looked at his watch. "Speaking of time, we've got a deadline."

"Yep," Mindy responded, "I can hear time's winged chariot hurrying near."

"Only you could make crunch time sound so lovely."

As the car settled into its parking space, Gil looked at Mindy with a mock leer. "So, my dear, any 'time' for me after the show?"

"Hmm," came Mindy's playful response. "After we beat the chariot, we'll have all the time we need."

—THE END—

AFTERWORD

In 1964, the year John Pruitt began his career, President Lyndon Johnson fought for and signed the landmark Civil Rights Act into law—and, just a few days later, a decorated war veteran was murdered by Klansmen in Georgia for driving while black. As a freshman reporter, Pruitt covered both those events, and in the decades since, his name has been synonymous with truth and accuracy—a reputation he lives up to even in his powerful, unexpected, and important debut novel.

Pruitt's dramatic narrative is "ripped from the headlines," as they say, but they are the headlines his own coverage helped generate. Like his fictional alter ego, Gil Matthews, Pruitt spent his entire career working in his hometown of Atlanta, Georgia—the place where Dr. Martin Luther King, Jr., still just in his thirties, was leading an impossibly ambitious campaign to "reclaim the soul of America," as he put it. When the young television journalist soon found himself reporting on the Civil Rights movement and all the ugliness that came with that job, he almost did not recognize his own city.

As someone who worked closely with Dr. King and later served Atlanta as a twice-elected mayor, I have always admired John Pruitt's honest, fearless reporting of our struggle and I also believe members of the news media are among the greatest unsung heroes of the Civil Rights movement. Although the characters and events have been altered, *Tell It True* does in fact "tell it true," and in as compelling a way as you're likely to find.

> —ANDREW J. YOUNG, Civil Rights
> leader, former Mayor of Atlanta, U.S.
> Ambassador to the United Nations,
> U.S. Congressman, and co-chairman
> of the Centennial Olympic Games

ACKNOWLEDGMENTS

AS A LIFELONG journalist I always reported just the facts, straightforward and unembellished. Once I retired, I set out to try my hand at fiction with its license to create my own unique world populated with a cast of characters I could endow with traits and quirks of my choosing. I could even create a Georgia governor's race in 1964, a year in which no such election took place.

Even though *Tell It True* is a work of fiction, I have based it on my experiences as a young reporter at a pivotal time in which the landmark civil rights law faced angry—often violent—resistance. The circumstances I describe concerning the murder of Jarvis Pendry are entirely fictional, but there are echoes of an actual event. For those who'd like to learn about the fate of Lemuel Penn, I recommend storied journalist Bill Shipp's excellent account in *Murder at Broad River Bridge*.

I am fortunate to have friends who are accomplished writers, and without their advice and support this effort would probably have fallen by the wayside. Acclaimed novelist Terry Kay prodded me for years to sit down and start writing. Once I took his advice, I sent chapters to him as I wrote them, and he responded with keen criticism, counsel, and solid support until his health failed and he was taken from us. Terry's passing leaves an unfillable void, but his legacy is indelible. I owe you much, my friend.

Another esteemed writer and historian who generously offered his support and critiques is my friend Steve Oney, a Georgian who now resides in Los Angeles. Steve was patient and receptive as I deluged him with draft after draft. He shared his innovative thoughts freely and made my novel stronger. Most of all, Steve was enthusiastic about the project from the beginning and proved to be the cheerleader I needed when frustrations arose.

One of Georgia's most honored writers, Philip Lee Williams, also read my manuscript and offered salient advice about how it could be

better. Prolific author and friend of many deca
weighed in on *Tell It True*, generously sharing hi
on the writing and publication process.

My profound gratitude goes to Andrew Youn
for *Tell It True* is meaningful beyond words. I h
more than half a century in so many roles: couragec
rights struggle, United Nations ambassador, Atlan
and two-term mayor, lynchpin of Atlanta's successful enort to most the
1996 Olympic games, and revered senior statesman. I know of no one
who has done more to make Dr. King's dream of a beloved community
a reality.

I am very aware that many good novels never get published, so I
offer my profound thanks to Mercer University Press for bringing *Tell
It True* to an audience of readers. It's been a pleasure to work with
Director Marc Jolley, Marsha Luttrell, Mary Beth Kosowski, and
copyeditor Kelley Land whose meticulous work made my manuscript
better. Thanks as well to CB Hackworth, Monica Pearson, Maria
Saporta, and Walt Drake for their invaluable support.

Let me also thank my family, all of whom supported this effort
including my two daughters, Lisa and Kristina, and my six grandchil-
dren, Ansley, Mason, Leighton, Ella, Jake, and Sara, who spurred me
on. Thanks as well go to friends I prevailed upon to read my manuscript
and offer honest opinions. Each and every one of you helped me navi-
gate this long, rugged, and ultimately rewarding trek, and I am forever
grateful.

Most of all I give loving thanks to my wife Andrea, who had to
suffer through so many days and weeks with her husband typing away
lost in another world. After more than fifty years of marriage to a newsman, she was more than up to the task. She was a perceptive critic, an
excellent sounding board, and a constant source of love and support.